I0716547

Also by J. A. Collignon

ARROWMOUNT BOOKS SERIES

A Second Story

A LITTLE LUCK

J. A. COLLIGNON

A | ARROWMOUNT PRESS

Book cover art and design by Tessa Brenan, @roguecorner on Twitter.

Interior maps and illustrations by J.A. Collignon

Print ISBN: 978-1-7388682-2-3

Ebook ISBN: 978-1-7388682-3-0

A | ARROWMOUNT PRESS

CONTENTS

Tua Outreach

Antóvers

Dunnaloch Pass

Frelun   ENSGÁRD

Glasrock

Dunvale

Törduun

Ardnablane

Blackshell Reach

Malgard

NERIAN EMPIRE

Falenroch

Northdeep

Underthall

Chârteau

Grenne

ALIEWETH

Deliar

Crestborne

Narveil

Ironcoast   Rossingrove

Claymore

Tage's Reach

BRENEM

Silver Creek

Felgcroan

EMPIRE

Reat

Tanju

Hutton

PRALON

Boarsrest

Notton

Ravenpoke

ARROWMOUNT

Quhar

Caspasian Isles

NARAKAMI

Lilleby

Kenmar

Mosfell

Wolf's Peck

Riefeld

Almsir

Talimar

ZIDIEN

Taimen

Rath

Meadon

Caspasian Sea   RAVÁR

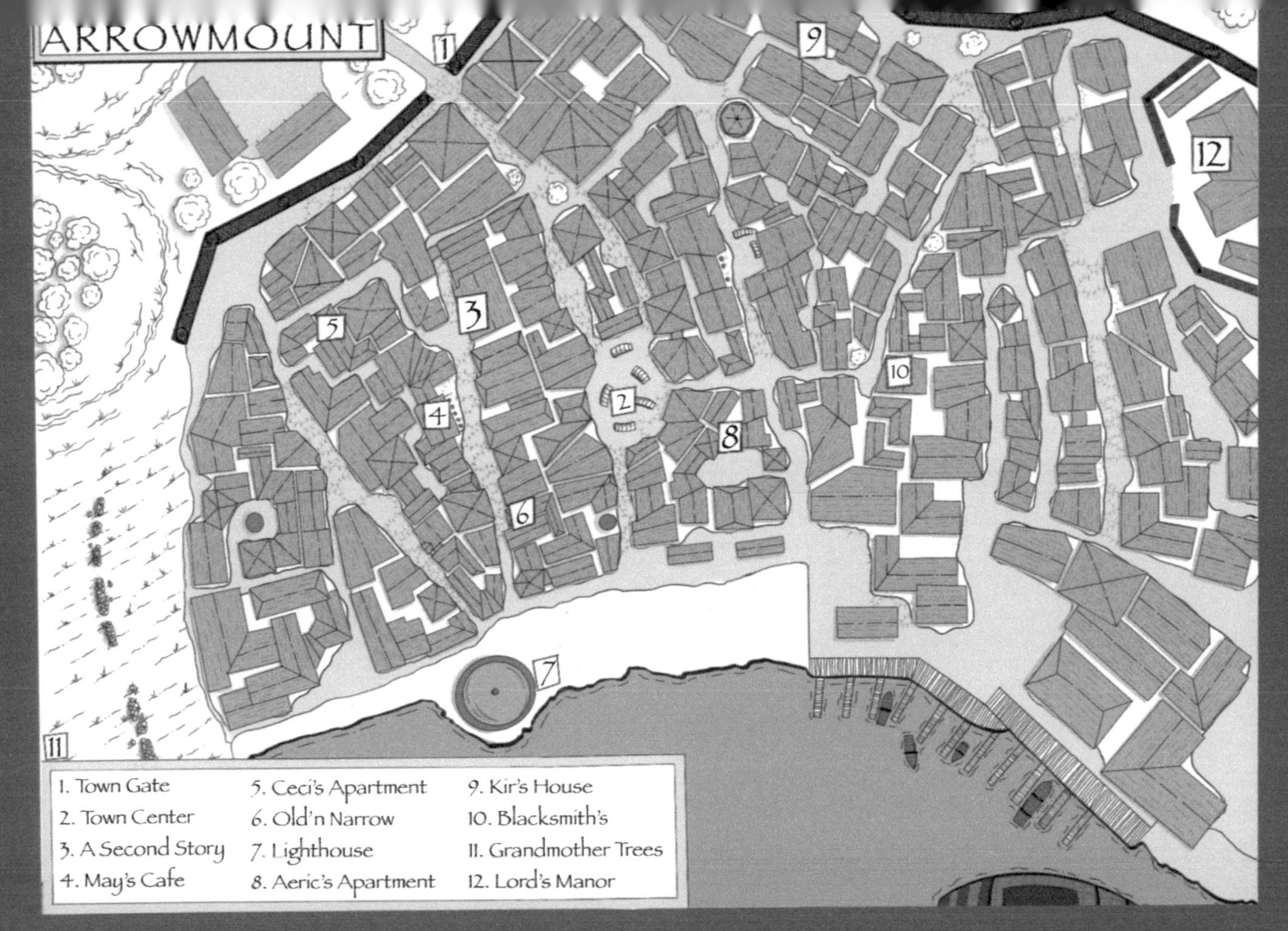

ARROWMOUNT
1. Town Gate
2. Town Center
3. A Second Story
4. May's Cafe
5. Ceci's Apartment
6. Old'n Narrow
7. Lighthouse
8. Aeric's Apartment
9. Kir's House
10. Blacksmith's
11. Grandmother Trees
12. Lord's Manor

PART ONE

A Thief and a Bard

1

NOTHING BUT A THIEF

Lottie – 45 Days Before

L ottie's luck had finally started to turn.

Soft golden light bathed her face as she gazed at the strange, twelve-sided object resting inside the nondescript crate. Light leaked out along cracks on its surface, as though it had been crafted with the purpose to open along joints. Lottie knew next to nothing about this piece, only that this artifact was from the time of the Centurion, back hundreds and hundreds of years ago when gods walked the earth to wage war amongst mortals.

That, and she had been hired by the infamous Guild — one of the most prestigious underground organizations — to steal it.

Lottie wrapped her leather-clad fingers around the dodecahedron. Heat radiated through the material into her hand, comforting and strange all at once. Whatever this artifact was, it oozed magic like a pulse, thrumming against her skin.

She held it up, feeling the power and weight of it. It was small and fit nicely in her hand, but it was heavier than she expected it to be. The dark, tarnished surface was pockmarked and worn with the centuries of life it had lived, immediately pulling on Lottie's curiosity. Warmer tones of bronze showed through in spots, as though it had been brushed by a thumb over and over again.

What can this do? What has it done in all the years of its existence to wind up tucked away in the top of a guard tower?

Before she let herself get too lost, she cleared her throat and slid the artifact into the bag slung across her chest.

"It's here, Seban," she whispered, knowing her accomplice was magically listening, the itch of his presence lurking in the back of her mind. She hated when Seban had to do this, but she couldn't deny it was incredibly handy when they were separated in the middle of jobs. Seban's magical ability to reach Lottie mentally had made him a perfect watchman from afar.

They had always made a great team, even as inexperienced kids on the streets of Pralon.

"*Excellent,*" he hissed back. She could feel the anticipation dripping off his voice as it slid around the inside of her skull.

Lottie didn't have a great understanding of magic, let alone the mental abilities that Seban had, beyond the fact that it was, well. Magic. She'd been around enough magical people in her life to know that with every ability, power showed itself in different ways – but when it came to Seban specifically, something always unsettled her. Maybe it was the fact that he was infiltrating her mind, her thoughts, despite the many times he swore that he never pushed past simple conversations. She couldn't know how far he really went.

Lottie nodded to herself as she turned toward the exit, the only door leading to the top of the tower, a smile spreading across her face. *Easy.* This job was one of the easiest of her career as an artifact finder. Curator of goods? Treasure hunter? She was going to have to keep workshopping her job title.

WAHH WAHH WAHH WAHH —

An awful, grating alarm began to wail through the tower, vibrating into the soles of Lottie's well-worn leather boots.

"Ilmater's disgraced teapot —" Lottie bit her tongue as she spun on her heel, eyes tearing around the room. The ancient artifact had been stored at the top of a guard tower that had nothing in it besides empty crates and layers of dust, making this job all too easy for a thief.

A thief whose time was running short.

"Seban, what's —"

"*It's over, Lottie Luck.*" The gentlest, most disgusting laughter began to ring inside of her head.

"What?" Lottie stood rooted to the spot for a stretch of heartbeats, a sharp bout of dread and panic welling up inside her chest. She searched for a hidden exit, a trap door to an attic, *anything* to get her out of the room.

"*Use that bit of luck you so famously have to try and get out of this one,*" he snarled.

Her eyes snagged on the only window, exactly opposite to the door she'd come through. She hadn't noticed it when she came in, the shutters closed tight. The only light in the room had come from the glowing artifact, leaking through the slats on the crate.

"What did I ever do to you, Seban?" Though he wasn't the best sort of person out there, she had never doubted Seban's loyalty in the fifteen years that they'd known each other. Gods, they'd known each other as *children.* "I got you this job with the Guild, and now you turn on me?"

"*Get fucked, Lottie. This is for Loth.*"

Loth. The name triggered a memory of a night long ago, when everything had truly gone wrong. "Seban, you know your brother's death wasn't —"

The connection between them severed with a snap, leaving Lottie feeling as though the inside of her skull had been scraped clean.

"Godsdamn every single one of the pantheon's shining godly asses," she hissed, taking five steps to the window and throwing her elbow against the shutters. They slammed open, letting in the pale evening light and a strong breeze.

She breathed deep, steadying herself, as the sound of boots crashed up the stairs of the tower. She heaved herself up onto the windowsill and turned, angling her thick, curvy body out of the space to peer down. The ground below swarmed with armored people jostling to get into the open tower door.

She set her jaw. *Up and over it is.* She looked skyward, the movement causing her hood to fully fall away from her face. Two thick braids of summer-green hair tumbled free, flying like whips around her as Lottie balanced herself against the window frame, taking a precious second to adjust her gloves.

Sending a silent blessing to the old man with pure white eyes back in Narveil who had convinced her to spend her entire savings on them, she flexed her fingers before finding the two glyphs stitched into the cuffs. A familiar warmth not unlike the one she felt from the dodecahedron spread through her hands as the magic activated.

The man had given no proper reason, other than he figured one day, they'd come in handy.

They had paid for themselves at least ten times over.

As the sound of boots reached the door inside the room, Lottie pulled herself up and around the windowsill out of sight with the ease of a spider.

A cacophony of frustrated clanks and swears rose with her as the door to the tower burst open. A grim smile broke across her face at the thought of all those heavy armor-clad buffoons, shoved into the small room, clanging around as they realized she wasn't there anymore.

Lottie pulled herself up onto the roof and steadied herself, fingers splayed against the shingles for balance. In the steadily waning light, she tracked the length of the buildings ahead of her, trying to find the easiest escape route.

Three guard towers, separated by stretches of low, thin buildings sat between her and her slim chance of escape. From these buildings, she could reach the part of the guard barracks that exited out to the main thoroughfare of the city. There, she could hopefully blend into the evening crowd milling about and make it through the eastern quadrant of Claymore and out the gates to the stables beyond. It wasn't a perfect option, but if she needed a fast way out, then she was going to have to pay him a visit for the first time in years. She knew a stable hand there who once would lend her a horse for nothing more than a smile and a wink.

If she made it that far. And that was a big *if.*

Her stomach swooped unpleasantly as she moved to stand, sweat immediately breaking out on the back of her neck. She would have to be quiet and fast, which was never a good combination. Especially when balancing on a gable roofline.

Right. Don't look down.

"Just need a little luck," she whispered as she got to her feet, crouching low along the buildings. Lottie took a deep breath, took an extra second to shove it all down — the panic from when the alarm went off, the unease at being up this high, the anger surging at Seban, and the deep seeded worry that all of this had ruined every chance she had with the

Guild — and locked it away.

Lottie adjusted her hood back up onto her head and hoped that the dark brown material would blend in with the roof and the quickly approaching night.

The darkening sky was both a godsend and a curse: she would be less visible, but so would any loose bits that could cause her to slip. Lottie set off across the shingles as fast as she could, keeping her hands down and out by her sides for balance, heartbeat banging in her ears. She passed one unmanned guard tower, sneaking through the shadows around it before shooting off onto the next stretch of roof.

One down.

She slowed her pace approaching the next tower as the flicker of torch-light bouncing off shining plate armor caught her eye. Ever so carefully, she crept along the edge, ducking low under the lip of the lookout, keeping to the darkness.

A shadow cut across the halo of warm, flickering lantern light pouring out of the tower. Lottie froze, listening hard. She tightened her jaw as the guard leaned out over the ledge, plate metal grating against stone.

"Dunno what the commotion is," the guard said, his voice low and gruff.

"If it was important, they'd sound the bells," answered another guard, their voice slightly further back. "Sounds like it was localized to the West Tower."

Lottie let out a long breath as quietly as she could. She crept a few steps further, feeling her way in the shadows.

"Should we —"

Lottie's foot shifted against a loose shingle. She let out the tiniest of shrieks as her body shot out from under her, balance entirely gone down the slope of the roof. With a desperate grab, she slammed her hand down on a nearby shingle and her spider-climb glove held fast, the rest of her body hanging in midair.

The guards stared down in disbelief at the hooded figure in front of them as she made eye contact.

"Shit," said the first guard.

"Shit," echoed Lottie.

"Sound the bells!"

"THIEF!"

Of course.

Lottie tried to think of a succinct curse as she hoisted herself up and ran, but her brain was too preoccupied with not falling off the roof and the new, loudly clanging bells that sounded across the guard barracks.

Arrows whizzed at her from the third guard tower as she ran toward it. She gritted her teeth and made herself as tiny as she could, hoping that their aim stayed off her. But, of course, even if the guards were abysmal archers, on their worst day they wouldn't have any issue hitting a target running straight for them.

Lottie felt the first arrow nick the fabric of her jacket, scraping along the bark of her skin with a sharp, burning kiss. She shrank even further in, eyes skating the roofline for the easiest place to drop off. From this height, a drop could almost guarantee a broken bone.

She swore loudly as the second arrow found purchase in the meat of her upper right arm.

She was going to have to jump. The closer she got, the easier time they were going to have making her a glorified pincushion.

She dropped to her stomach and slid down part of the roof as the next volley of arrows landed right where she had been, missing her by inches. Her gloves stopped her midway, just in time for her heart to lodge itself fully into her throat as her feet dangled from the roof.

She roared in pain as the arrow embedded in her arm lurched with the movement, arrowhead scraping something that felt unpleasantly like bone.

The guard tower nearby echoed with noise as the archers tried to jostle for a better angle. No doubt there would be a battalion of guards rushing to her on this side of the building in a matter of moments, too.

"Come on, Lottie," she hissed under her breath as the world tilted around her. She detached one gloved hand after the other to shift closer to the edge of the roof in a rapid staccato. Soon, she hung over nothing but air.

The tiniest voice inside her head started to scream with terror, but Lottie set her jaw and looked up to the first star that had appeared in the darkening sky.

"A little luck," she breathed, then let go.

2

STAGE LIGHTS AND ANTICIPATION

Kir – 36 Days Before

A stage flickered into view as the arcane lights popped on one by one, casting a circle of soft white light onto the well-worn wooden stage beneath her feet.

The roar of an invisible crowd echoed through Kir's bones, thrumming alongside the anticipatory pulse that she thrived on. Her large, stone-grey hands became illuminated under the lights, the sudden brightness causing spots in her vision. She stood amidst a pool of light and raised her precious lute to its familiar position in her arms.

Her instrument had a gleaming, beautifully curved body made of pale cherry wood. The strings and a stable, stately neck led up to the well-used tuning pegs adorned with wooden details. Touches of that same carved filigree had been carefully added to the base and face of her lute, the edges of the vine-like shapes having been rubbed dull from years of playing.

The crowd quieted, waiting with bated breath as Kir lowered her head, her unbound, unruly black hair cascading over her shoulder, the shadow of it falling across her eyes. There was that tasty, beloved beat of space between breaths and silence as a smile broke across her face.

"Oi," came a voice by Kir's ear as water splashed onto her, yanking her from her fantasy. "Dreaming again?"

Kir grunted, blinking down at the soapy, grungy mess in front of her, feeling distinctly disappointed as the sounds and smells of the Old'n Narrow came back to her. Aeric leaned against the counter next to her, crossing his arms. He was wearing one of his favorite shirts, one that sat open down to his breastbone, showing off his smooth chest. She rolled her eyes at him.

Aeric laughed and flicked his shining black hair over his shoulder, exposing one of his long, pointed jewelry-garnished ears. He sharpened his gaze at her. Kir knew that if she hadn't been one hundred percent *not* into men, that one glance would have melted her into the floor. She'd seen that happen to many folks in this very bar when they didn't know better.

"Tell me you didn't deliberately splash soap on me," she said, lifting the bowl he had tossed in the large sink, frowning at it. "And that you didn't let someone order the day-old stew. This is caked on."

Aeric shrugged. "They were adamant about it, even when I told them the meat was something north of beef." A soft smile crinkled his handsome bravado.

"Are you two complaining about my cooking again?" A voice floated through the sizzling, popping haze that often surrounded Corwek as he cooked. Corwek loomed over, hunched so his head wouldn't hit the low wooden beams along the ceiling, mirroring Kir's own posture. He was one of the few people in Arrowmount that Kir had to look up at, even at her height. He took up so much space in the back of the kitchen that whenever he left to the front, the kitchen felt like it was missing a core piece of its architecture.

Corwek drew a towel over his head, wiping away sweat. His smooth clay-toned face glowed a deep burgundy from the heat of the stove. It always impressed Kir how when Corwek was flushed, his whole head seemed to turn red — from the bald, shining top, down to his ears and his thick neck.

"If your stew is left out longer than a day, it takes on a life of its own," said Aeric with a shrug, turning on his heel to wink back at Kir. "No one should be consuming it."

Corwek made a dismissive sound in the back of his throat and flicked his towel at Aeric. The three of them shook with laughter as Aeric put up his hands in defense and ducked out of the way, heading back toward the front of the bar.

"Busy day," commented Corwek, leaning against the door frame and peering out at the mass of people that had congregated in the main area. "You playing?"

"Later," answered Kir, placing two dripping plates on the drying rack next to her and nodding over her shoulder to where she had her lute case stashed, tucked between the rickety storage unit and the wall.

Corwek nodded in her periphery. "I'll have to make more stew."

Kir snorted and turned back to the dishes in front of her.

The late-day rush came in a flurry of chilled air wrapped around the patrons as they walked in the door, the warmth of the bar comforting as the world outside tipped toward darkness. Kir spent the majority of her day elbow deep in the back basin, scrubbing dishes clean as fast as Aeric could bring them, listening to Corwek hum to himself as the noise of the bar increased.

Once Kir finally dried off her hands hours later, she leaned against the door frame to take in the scene inside of the Old'n Narrow. Like usual, Briar stood behind the bar, ample hips swaying in a swirl of skirts as voluminous as her rich brown hair that she continuously refused to tie back, despite it constantly getting in her way.

Townsfolk gathered along the length of the bar, calling Briar's name for drink and Aeric's for food as he weaved his way around the tables, flirting with the patrons.

The end of summer had come wrapped in misty mornings and the soft change of green into the autumnal blanket of yellows, oranges, and rich shining reds. Weather like tonight's, crisp and sharp and promising a bright morning, brought townsfolk out for warmer food and hearty drinks, and of course, the entertainment Kir provided.

Autumn was Kir's favorite time of year. There was something exceptionally cozy and comforting about the way it would settle into itself after the lasting, heavy heat of the summer. Hearths heated up to keep everyone warm inside even as the sea mist and cool air descended outside. It was also getting closer to the goddess Servune's Harvest Moon, which brought with it the start of the annual Moon Festival. The entire town came out to celebrate the changing seasons with food, drink, games, and enough entertainment to inspire and warm hearts well into the coming colder seasons.

A twinge of pain echoed along Kir's shoulders and into her neck as she stepped away from her basin. She took the time to replace the water and reheat it, prepping for the night's dishes that would be taken care of in turn by Nova, Aeric, and Corwek as she played.

She looked down at her swollen and pruney hands, sighing. It would take at least an hour before they were ready to play.

The back door to the bar opened as though summoned by her thoughts of escape, before it was immediately filled with the presence of boxes.

"Uh —"

"Kir, thank the gods."

She lunged forward as the boxes swayed toward her, cradling them in her much larger arms than the woman now standing in the doorway. Nova, the second owner of the bar and sister to Briar, wiped away a bit of hair plastered to her forehead and shrugged out of her thick woolen coat. Where Briar was curvy, with soft brown features, Nova was wiry from top to bottom and reminded Kir of freshly fallen snow.

"You're a blessing," breathed Nova as Kir brought the burden inside. The two of them began to unload new stock into the tiny backroom. "Can we expect you to play tonight?"

Kir held up her still pruney hands. "Just need a bit more time."

"Whenever you're ready, feel free. It sounds like we've got a positive crowd of folks out there tonight."

Kir smiled as they finished up their job, Nova heading to the front of the bar, and Kir out the back. She groaned as she straightened her spine to stand fully upright for the first time in a number of hours. She stretched her arms overhead and threw her head back, feeling every link in her spine pop and correct itself. Slowly, as she breathed in the cool, salty sea air, she and the knots that had built over the day relaxed.

Kir took her usual trek around the outside of the bar and onto Fetterly Place, massaging feeling back into her pruney fingers. Fetterly Place coursed with folks moving about from shop to shop, carrying their wares home in the fading evening light. A few folks nodded to her as she passed.

A chill wind nipped at her bare neck as she started up the street. Kir smiled faintly as she ducked lower into her collar to cut the breeze, but she didn't really mind. It was refreshing to be outside after working for so long.

She passed May's Cafe, peeking briefly into the windows barely visible beneath the canopy of plant life that draped over the awning protecting the outside eating area. A few patrons were tucked inside, enjoying warm beverages and pastries.

The newly renovated A Second Story a little further up the street was still open, a pool of arcane light leeching out onto the cobblestones through the open double doors. Kir looked in, noting the tall, long eared giantkin Calian hunched among the shelves. The owners of the bookstore, Arileas and Finnean, stood by the front desk, talking to each other.

Kir smiled as Arileas noticed her pass, lifting a hand in greeting. This past summer, she had been hired by him to play a few times outside of the store as they breathed life back into the moldering shop. Though she herself wasn't a huge reader, Kir had spent more time there than she had before, simply because it was a lovely place to be.

Today, though, she continued on her way, walking in a long loop around a few streets to stretch her legs before finding herself back at the bar. By then, she felt ready and fresh for her set, the beginning of anticipation winding itself around her spine. It was delicious, this feeling. Once, it had made her almost sick with nervousness, but now she relished in it.

When she had her lute in hand, everything would melt away.

She continued to massage her hands into playing form as she entered the back, skin thankfully no longer puckered from the hours submerged in water. She took a deep breath in, filling her senses with the spiced soup that Corwek was currently stirring. Noise from the bar leaked into the back, louder now as the hour tipped well into evening.

Kir withdrew her lute case from its hiding spot and walked out into the bar. Nova and Briar had established a small corner stage long ago for performers, just tiny enough that it didn't get in the way of the patrons in the already narrow bar.

Heads turned her way as she passed, knowing smiles from familiar faces winking up at her.

Kir took a seat on the stool waiting for her and began to prepare for her set, lifting her lute into position and plucking at a few strings to make sure it was tuned right. She reached up and let down her hair from her bun, feeling whatever vestiges of tension that remained tumble away with the mass of dark hair that fell around her.

Unlike in her fantasy, Kir didn't have a silent room waiting for her with bated breath. Instead, she felt some folks turn their eyes to her, but conversations continued. That was okay, though. One day, she'd have the rapt attention of a crowd, somewhere beyond Arrowmount. For now, this bar was her home, and it was all she needed.

Kir tapped the edge of her lute twice for good luck, letting her fingers find their spots on the strings, and she began to play.

She chose a crowd favorite to start, a lively song called 'The Witch and the Whale' that began with three distinct sharp chords to pull attention before spinning into a speedy tale of a foolish whale who fell in love with a witch and begged her to turn her into a human.

"The air fell taut and thick one day,
When a grey whale, swam her way
Up toward the bay, to see her love..."

3

POULTICES AND POTIONS

Lottie – 45 Days Before

Thank the gods for bushes. Lottie blinked at her leafy surroundings that had saved her from the fall before lurching over, feeling for her bag on her shoulder, ensuring that the artifact was still inside. Her gloved fingers clasped around its warm shape and she breathed a sigh of relief — which turned into a hiss of pain as a burning lance reminded her of the arrow embedded in her arm.

"Tempus' tits." She tore off one of her gloves with her teeth to bite down on before closing her ungloved hand around the arrow shaft. With a hissed stream of curse words, she snapped off the length of it, making it much more manageable. The glove barely did anything to muffle the sounds she made, but at this point, she was beyond caring.

A fresh bout of sweat broke across her forehead as she forced herself to her feet, tumbling free of the bushes. She held her injured arm in close by her side and took a few, unsteady steps before shaking her head, trying to clear the fog of pain.

Lottie headed off around the building as fast as she could, keeping

18

close to the shadows clinging to the wall, ears peeled for the sounds of approaching guards. Shouts and the same, resounding bells ricocheted around the stone walls, muddling everything into a cacophony.

She crept around the side of the last guard tower, peering around until she located the mass of guards responsible for the sound. The noise made her eyes water, metal crashing about and half of them thinking their shout would be heard over the rest.

Taking advantage of the maelstrom, Lottie skirted along the edge of the torch light just as a group of guards broke off and hurried down the way she'd come.

Breathing through the pain, Lottie clutched her arm close and hurried as fast as she could from the guard barracks and out into the city of Claymore. Even when she slipped into the crowds of people, she didn't stop moving, keeping herself as small as she could. She pulled her hood down over her eyes, keeping her hair hidden. Bright green hair was definitely cause to notice someone, even in a crowd.

Time slipped as she made her way through the city, her attention narrowing entirely to just her two feet, pounding on the pavement, and the warm sticky blood coursing out of her arm. When she finally crossed through the eastern gates, the stars had fully appeared above. She ducked out before any of the guards stationed along the wall could stop her, slipping into the shadows. Thankfully for her, from their relaxed state, she figured that they hadn't yet heard news of the thief.

"Emmett," she breathed, stepping out of the night and into the lantern-lit stables, pushing her hood back. She locked eyes with the overly handsome stable hand that turned her way, arm outstretched toward a horse, frozen mid-air. He was wearing a well-worn shirt rolled up to his elbows, bearing strong forearms. Lottie let out a soft sigh and swayed on the spot. Forearms were her weakness.

Possibly, too, it was the loss of blood, but who's to say.

The air was thick with the odor of horses and fresh hay, filling her senses. Emmett's eyes went wide as Lottie stumbled forward. "Lottie?"

"I need a horse."

"You need a lot more than that," he said, closing the distance between them in a blink. She flinched away as he touched her arm. His gaze narrowed, burning into her. Gods, it had been years since she'd seen him, and he still had the ability to turn her insides to soup. "Lottie, what in the nine hells did you get yourself messed up in now?"

"Horse, Em."

He shook his head. "Bandages. And water."

Emmett hesitated as he noticed her sway on her feet. He gently took her by her good arm and steered her further inside, setting her down on a bench covered partly in hay. The movement caused Lottie's attention to snag on the tiniest details of him she thought she had forgotten — from the curve of his throat to the mole on his collarbone and the golden hue of his hair much like the hay that layered the stalls around her.

He disappeared further into the stables before coming out with a box of supplies. He poked at her arm and sleeve, examining what little he could see of the broken arrow shaft and wound. "I'm going to have to cut this away. And the shirt under."

"Oh gods," groaned Lottie. "I *just* mended this jacket from last time."

"What happened last time?"

Lottie let out a breath and shook her head. "Do it."

He sliced at her sleeve with a small blade he plucked from his back pocket, carefully avoiding the wound in her arm. Lottie hissed in pain as dried blood that had glued the material of her jacket to her skin pulled, stars flashing behind her eyes. She peered at the wound, sliced deep and clean in between the whorls of bark that made up her skin, oozing dark red blood and almost-clear sap around the still embedded arrow shaft.

"Bite down." She blinked, Emmett holding something in front of her. Somehow, he had gotten hold of one of her gloves without her noticing. She started to protest, but he raised an eyebrow at her. "If you don't mind, I'd rather not have you screaming your head off, even with how far out of town we are. Now bite."

"I only let you talk to me like that when we were in bed," she murmured, feeling a wave of nausea and dizziness wash over her. Emmett's eyes softened slightly, which sent guilt spiking through her. That's probably what she liked best about him — his eyes.

The only unfortunate thing was that Emmett's sister had had those same eyes. And her hair had been equally as soft under Lottie's fingers.

She blinked away the bundle of memories that were threatening to pop into her mind and gave him a best approximation of a flirty glare. "Don't look at me like that, it's bad enough I even need your help."

She opened her mouth for the glove.

Emmett crouched down next to her and inspected the wound as a fresh wave of sweat erupted along Lottie's skin, the anticipation of new pain coursing through her. Emmett glanced up through his long eyelashes, the sight distracting her for a split second before he reached and pulled the broken arrow shaft free.

The world exploded into lights as she made sounds that no being should ever make, the sound muffled by her glove. She could hear Emmett apologizing from somewhere far away as a wave of heat washed down her arm anew.

She was lucky that he knew so much about wounds, having taken care of countless animals throughout his time in this job. He had also, in the last weeks they had been together years ago, begun dabbling in potion making. The local alchemist and potion maker in Claymore had been more than happy to have him apprentice under them. Instead of going anywhere with the skill he learned, he had remained at the stable, becoming well-known around the city and in the villages surrounding Claymore for his skills in healing horses with his poultices and potions.

A splash of liquid and a new burn sharpened her senses as she flinched away from a cloth that Emmett was scraping along her arm. He held her firmly and wiped, a slightly pained expression on his face as she fought against him and the pain senselessly.

Lottie's world blinked in and out as Emmett continued to work on her arm, the warm, cozy stable around her flickering with her consciousness. By the time she regained a semblance of self, she was looking down at a neatly sutured wound before it was hidden by a swath of clean cloth.

A light, citrusy medicinal scent cut through the haze of warm animals and the woody hay. "Whas'that?" she asked, groggy. At some point her glove had tumbled free of her mouth and was now laying on the bench next to her in a crumpled ball. She could make out vague teeth marks in the leather.

"Potion," answered Emmett, securing the bandage tightly. "One of my latest. Madame Agatha was rather proud of the healing properties of this batch, not only for use on my horses."

"I'm so grateful," she said playfully, rolling her head to one side. The pain subsided to a low, deep thrum in her muscle and bone. "The great master potion maker, Emmett Cavalry."

"I don't really need your signature Lottie sarcasm right now," he said, getting to his feet. "So. Now that I've stitched up your arm, are you going to tell me what happened to you?"

"Some silly mishap with the city guard."

"Are they currently looking for you?"

"Hence why I need a horse," she said, her voice wavering weakly. She cleared her throat and tried to sit up straighter to appear as though she had her life together and wasn't on the edge of consciousness.

He sighed and walked over to a low table along the far wall and returned with a beaten-up old tankard filled with water. He pushed it into her hands and glared at her until she took a sip.

A gentle snuffling noise came from above her, signaling the arrival of a large nose as it began to quest through Lottie's hair. She reached up with her good arm and felt the warmth of a horse's head, sniffing her interestedly. Horses, she found, were the only kind of creature that paid particularly special attention to her biological make-up. Perhaps there was something about her scent that confused them, as though they thought she was a plant, but couldn't find anything edible on her.

She had yet to have one of them try and take a bite out of her, thankfully. At least they were smart enough to realize she was a person, despite being made up of bark and smelling like fresh leaves.

"Hello," she said, patting it as it blew out a soft burst of air into her face. She took a moment to steady herself, sipping slowly at the water as it refueled her and helped her fully awaken, before she put the mug down and began to push herself to standing.

"Lottie." Emmett was there suddenly as she swayed, blinking away a fresh bout of stars. "Where are you going?"

"I have to," she answered, standing up straighter and tossing a mussed braid over her shoulder. Gods, she must be a *mess*. "Thanks for the quick med stop, but —"

"It's been a few hours, Lottie," he answered, frowning. "I don't think any guards are coming out this far to search for you, if they haven't already. And besides, I can't in good conscience let you get on one of my horses like this. Stay the night."

"You really know how to charm a girl, don't you?" *A few hours?* Gods, she should have been long gone by now. "Despite your lovely attention, I am perfectly fine."

"Sure, of course, having almost bled out from a bone deep wound, you're *perfectly fine*." He sighed heavily and shook his head as she moved toward the exit. "There really is nothing I can do to make you stay, is there? What if —"

"Don't," she hissed, closing her eyes to stop herself from seeing his soft expression, the wanting there. She breathed deeply, steadying herself, before she pasted a smile on her face. "It's best to leave in the dead of the night anyway, as you know."

Emmett sighed, long and weary. Lottie adjusted the bag across her chest to avoid looking at him and flashed her best Lottie grin. "Do you mind handing me my sleeve?"

"What do you want with a sleeve?" He bent and plucked it from the floor, brushing a bit of hay from it. The material was rather stiff with blood. She was going to have to wash it well.

"I love this jacket," she answered before turning her eyes to the horses occupying the stables around them. "Please, Emmett."

He sighed. "You know I can't say no to you."

She smiled at him, trying to ignore the way her head swam as she stepped to the horse that had nuzzled her hair. Riding a horse probably wasn't the best idea right then, but she was known for her bad ideas.

Lottie hoisted herself up into the saddle one handed before pulling her hood over her head, covering her green hair once again.

"Until next time, stable boy."

"Until the next catastrophe, little thief."

4

IT IS A HORSE

Kir – 36 Days Before

Kir's head swam with familiar exhilaration as she walked home after her set, the lantern-lit cobblestone streets empty of people. She sang the last few bars of 'The Song of Adelina,' a love ballad that had had half the bar crooning along with her, under her breath.

"Round the sea, winding clearly

A song came to his ear so truly

The song of Adelina."

Contentment and a sense of rightness settled into Kir's chest as she slowly shed Kir-the-Bard and walked herself back into Kir-the-Person. These few solitary moments at the end of the night, when the streets of Arrowmount were silent, were a perfect balm to her day.

As she turned down her street, her family home appearing at the end of it, she ran a hand through her thick hair and drew it back atop her head, baring the back of her neck to the cold night air. The sweat that had accumulated there during her performance cooled instantly, sending goosebumps down her spine.

Light from a lantern flickered in a couple of the main floor windows as she approached home, their house the only one still lit from within along the stretch of dark stone buildings.

Her father, as always, had left the main lantern lit on the table, the flame a soft greeting. The house was quiet as she pushed open the heavy wooden front door except for a gentle *sshhck-sshhck-sshhck* sound that came from the workroom to the left.

Their father had built the room for the whole family once he realized that he wasn't the only one who enjoyed to tinker in his off hours. Kir's brothers and her didn't share the same passion for iron and steel as their father did, but whatever their passion was, their father accommodated for it.

Five tables sat in a mismatched pattern throughout the room, leaving just enough space to pass around the perimeter if need be. Cabinets adorned the sides of the room that were stocked with everything from scrap pieces of metal and wood, to oils and paints, and even a few spare strings for Kir's lute. Three of the tables were overladen with things — unfinished projects, discarded bits of material — waiting for someone to pick them up again.

"Hiya."

Kir walked in, setting her lute case down by the door with a soft thud. Kharutto, her eldest brother, sat hunched over his worktable in the middle, shards of wood scattered around him like leaves. He had a tiny chisel and blade in his large, dark blue hands as he worked. Kir smiled as Khar flicked a bit hair out his face. Her giant of a brother, who stood at seven feet tall and towered over the entire family, curled into the smallest ball whenever he worked.

It was endearing to see him with his sleeves rolled up, a pair of thin spectacles on the edge of his nose, focused entirely on whatever delicate project he had in hand. He got this little crease between his eyebrows and his tongue curled around one of his large tusks, jaw jutting out more severely than usual. If one didn't know him, they might think that he was terrifying to behold — he took mostly after their fully orc father with his blue coloring and fuller jaw, where Kir and her other brother Morgam had lighter grey skin and more of their mother's graceful elven features — but Kir knew Khar was entirely soft right down to his core.

Khar blinked at her through his spectacles as though adjusting his eyes to a bright light, jaw relaxing. He flicked his head once more, moving the bit of annoying fringe out of his eyes. He'd had his once long hair cut only a few months ago to a much shorter style, since it was easier to handle in the smithy all day. The top part, though, was getting longer, and had started to hang in front of his eyes as he worked. "Kir. How's the day?"

"Day's long over, Khar," she answered, settling into the seat across from him. "Set was good, though."

"Oh." Khar glanced around him, realizing, she assumed, how dark it had become. He rolled his tongue around his mouth with a look of mild surprise as though he couldn't quite believe time had slipped away from him yet again. "I should've been there. I always like catching your sets, if I can. I didn't —"

"Notice," she finished for him, smiling. She never really minded when her family missed her sets. They had been there for her when she was growing up and learning to play and were probably more than tired of hearing her through the walls. "You never do notice, Khar. Didn't Morg tell you to breathe?"

"He might've," he answered with a soft shrug, bending back down to carefully chisel an infinitesimal piece of wood from the chunk in his hand before peering at it, considering. Kir could already see him slipping back into the work. "I should probably stop, shouldn't I," he muttered.

Kir chuckled before reaching over and plucking the piece from his hands. "What is this going to be?"

"Not sure," he answered, uncurling from his hunched form. He stretched back with a soft groan. Both of his hands were curled inward, as though he was having trouble letting go of the tools he had laid down.

After a moment, though, he massaged them into place, stretching them out. Khar stood, letting both of his arms reach up, fingers brushing the ceiling. His back cracked audibly from the base of his spine up to his neck. "Oh, that felt good."

"One day, you won't be able to undo the kink in your spine if you keep sitting like that," said Kir, admonishing. "It's bad enough that Dad has you doing the detail work at the smithy, and then you come home and continue to hunch over your table."

Khar raised an eyebrow at her. "I could say the same to you. How many hours do you spend hunched over that basin of water at work, then over your lute?"

She shifted almost involuntarily, mirroring her brother's straightened posture. It was second nature for their family to curl down to make themselves slightly smaller in a world that was made for shorter, regular sized beings. Sure, goliaths like Corwek did often have the same struggles, but most folks fit comfortably.

Their house was one of the only indoor spaces Kir's family could stand fully upright in, because their father had built it long before any of them were born, especially for him and their mother. At six and a half feet tall himself, he knew very well how often he had to hunch to fit. And their mother, too, had stood just over six feet tall.

"We'll all be as hunched as grandfather is one day," said Morgam, their middle brother, as he walked in. He ruffled Kir's hair as he passed, dislodging it from her bun in a spray of tangles. She lunged off her chair to tackle him but only managed to elbow him sturdily in the side as he stepped around the worktables with a laugh. "Did you bring down the bar, Kiri?"

Kir rolled her eyes at the nickname before settling back into her seat. "Kind of. It was good."

"Always is." Morgam leaned against Khar's back, bending over his older brother to peer at his work in progress. Morgam ran a hand through the top half of his shoulder length black hair and secured it with a thin leather cord. Both of his grey hands were speckled with various shades of dried paint from whatever new masterpiece he had been working on. "Is that... a horse?"

Khar considered his project. "Might be. What were you painting?"

Morgam straightened and frowned at the corner where his latest canvas sat leaning against one of the chairs, turned at an angle that none of them could actually see what was painted there. "Not sure."

"A horse," said Kir, noding. Morgam snorted and raised his hand in a rude gesture.

"Dad and Nudge are both snoring up a storm, so mind not tripping over him as you go upstairs," said Morgam.

"Is Dad lying in the hallway *again*?" Khar joked. Nudge, their greathound, had a knack for taking up the entire hallway if he fell asleep.

Khar flashed an amused grin at Kir as she snorted. He picked up the small chunk of wood he had been slowly whittling and appraised it. If they weren't careful, Khar would work through the night and most of the next day before he realized he was even a bit tired.

"Seriously, Khar, put that down." Morgam shook his head, plucking the half-made wooden-whatever out of Khar's hands, followed by his tools. "You know, sometimes I feel as though I am the oldest sibling with how much I take care of the two of you."

Kir wrinkled her nose. "Me? What do I have to do with anything?"

"Did you consume anything other than ale today?" He looked at her pointedly. "Dinner's sitting on the table, and there's lunch waiting for tomorrow in the cold box."

"I didn't forget to eat *all day,*" she said with a grumble. Thanks to Morgam leaving breakfast out on the table for her, she had eaten that — but she wasn't going to give him the satisfaction.

As she followed her brothers from the room, Kir finally felt a soft tiredness settle into her bones. It was the sort of tiredness that came with a long day of being on her feet but softened by the quiet company of her brothers. The three of them stepped over their snoring dog sprawled in the middle of the hallway on the second floor with practiced ease, Kir bending to scratch Nudge between his ears. Khar and Morgam bid her goodnight in their own way — Khar with the slightest touch on her shoulder, Morgam with a wink — and left her to climb up the last stretch to her attic bedroom.

The bedroom had once been her mother's studio, specially built by their father to overlook Arrowmount around them. Along the outside wall there were a series of three large windows, larger than probably was wise in a seaside town that often had nasty winter storms, but Kir had never minded much if a bit of salty air spilled into her room.

Her mother had been an avid painter like Morgam when she was alive. She had preferred to keep her work up here where the air and light came in through the windows the brightest. When Kir first moved up to this room, the light comforted her. It was like her mother was still there, in the motes of sunlight trailing across her vision in the morning.

A soft snuffling sound rose up behind her from the floor below, followed by the gentle thundering of Nudge ascending the stairs after her. The greathound was incredibly large to most people, usually coming up to hips and stomachs when he loped around Arrowmount after their father. Gnomish and dwarfish folk usually avoided him – not because he was scary, but because it was well known that he would, given the opportunity, attack folks with kisses if their faces were anywhere near his.

"Nudge," called Kir softly, undoing her shirt by a few buttons and sliding her boots off her feet before tossing them into the corner.

Nudge moseyed over and collapsed against her as she laid down in bed, his heavy warm body flopping happily onto hers. He yawned before laying his head on her chest, letting out a sleepy sigh right into her face.

"Ah, thanks bud. Exactly what I need."

5

THE DODECAHEDRON

Lottie – 44 Days Before

Lottie traveled further than she should have through the night. She tried to keep her head up and ears sharp for any noise other than the methodical clopping of her horse, but the exhaustion kept pulling her chin down to her chest. She could have passed countless guards roaming through the forest, looking for her, and she never would have heard them.

She reached the outskirts of a farm before she started to slide right off the horse, unable to hold on any longer. She crumpled into a pile with a soft groan and fell into unconsciousness without moving an inch.

What felt like mere minutes later, Lottie awoke to her horse's nose investigating her hair and bright late-morning sunshine.

"Good morning to you too," she murmured to the horse, brushing away its nose.

After rifling through her bag to confirm that she had not packed any rations the day before or an extra shirt, Lottie pulled out the artifact, warmth melting comfortingly through her gloved hands. Her stomach growled, but she ignored it, staring instead at the artifact. At least this part of her job didn't go upside down. She had gotten out with the artifact.

Maybe this will be enough to sway the Guild, she thought to herself. Even though the job had gone seriously sideways at the end, she had completed the one task they had hired her for: to steal the artifact being stored at the top of the western guard tower in Claymore. Surely that had to count for something.

She knew, too, that the job had been her test to see if she had what it took to be officially indoctrinated into the ranks of the Guild — something that she had longed and worked for for over ten years. Alros, her contact with the Guild, had been her go between, and had given her so little information about the artifact Lottie's curiosity had taken over before she even considered the job.

It hadn't taken her long to fall in love with the idea of the wares she stole, back when she first started thieving. She would try to find out whatever information she could about the objects she stole, occasionally delaying handing off the finds to whatever client she had. Sometimes, she'd come upon an artifact that had not only an extensive history attached, but a story that she stored in her mind to replay over for herself in the days after she handed off the piece.

It gave her a tiny little bit of joy to know that she had become part of that piece's history, even if no one else would know other than her. After living a life so impermanent, moving from town to town throughout the empire and leaving very little behind, it felt rather gratifying to know the weight and history of a piece that she had altered the life of.

The ancient artifact in her hand looked less impressive in the daylight, whatever glow that had emanated from it in the darkness of the guard tower all but invisible now. It pulsed heat into her fingers, a comfort in the chilled early autumnal air.

She tilted it this way and that, inspecting every inch. She couldn't quite tell what was creating the light, whether there was a core inside that lit it from within like a heart, or if it simply exuded the light itself.

The surface of the dodecahedron was a softly etched and pitted molten bronze, uneven beneath her fingertips. It took a moment of her closing her eyes and feeling along the surface, letting her instincts of opening locks and discovering hidden secrets within small spaces take over, before she realized she was feeling tiny script.

She narrowed her eyes, trying to decipher what was written there. The surface was too worn to recognize any of the script, let alone what language it was written in.

I bet Berold would love this, she thought, picturing the aged scholar she'd met after unearthing a large pile of lost art beneath a cavern of falsified gold and silver coins outside the Kingdom of Zidien years ago. Berold was a particular scholar who lived atop a rather intriguing tower that sometimes grew and shrank depending on its master's mood. He was a curator of ancient art for many museums and royalty in Zidien, but loved researching and learning about antiquities over all else. She could imagine how his wizened face would split into an intrigued smile before he adjusted his glasses higher on his nose to take a closer look.

The thrill of finding out stories about the objects she found coursed through her, momentarily overwhelming anything else.

In the back of her head, she imagined her sister's voice, haunting her as always. *"Lottie, you seriously need to get your priorities straight."*

"Oh, dear sister, they are as straight as I am," she breathed out, dropping the artifact back into the safety of her bag. Thankfully, no one was around right then except for the horse to hear her talking to herself.

"It's like you want *to get killed."*

"I do not. This is living, Ceci."

"Mhmm. Sure. Because almost becoming an entire city guard's pin-cushion is living."

Lottie pushed her sister's voice out of her imagination and forced herself to her feet. If she wanted to keep her shot at entering the Guild's ranks, she was going to have to hand over the artifact without discovering anything about it, and she was going to have to be fine with that.

She was out of a home, yet again. Though the tiny, leaky hovel that she had been staying in for the past few months was far from good, it had been a roof over her head.

Seban's nagging, horrible voice pushed into her mind from the night before, the betrayal fully setting in. What had she done to deserve that? She and Seban had been colleagues — she had thought they were *friends* — for years now. Not once had he ever shown signs of disliking her or blaming her for his brother's death.

Ilmater's mercy, there was no way she was getting back into Claymore now. A few of the guards had seen her without her hood up when she fell, she was sure of that — and, with her bright green hair and her multicolored, whorled bark for skin, she was fairly recognizable.

The horse began to nuzzle the top of her head again, bringing Lottie back into herself.

"Come on girl," she said, standing shakily and putting both hands on the horse to give her pats. Slowly, her mind churned together a plan. There was only one place she could go right then, and even that was risky. Alros had told her about a Guild hideout just off the path to Shadyside, though he hadn't given her specifics. She would have to try and see if anyone would let her in.

6

HIDING PLACES

Lottie – 43 Days Before

The stretch of endless fields toward Shadyside numbed Lottie as the day passed and night fell. If she hadn't already been in love with mountains and being by the ocean, this journey would have solidified that fact unerringly.

It was just endless *nothing*.

That night she happened across a farm with a line of washing out, hanging fresh and dry in the chill wind. Lottie glanced around the yard to find it quiet and empty, no lights flickering in the windows of the farmhouse nearby. She slid off her horse and darted to the line, pulling the thickest shirt down. It was, happily, slightly overlarge as she drew it on, careful of her injured arm, running back to her horse. That, with her one-armed jacket, she was marginally warmer as a chilled autumnal night fell around her.

If she continued on this trail toward Shadyside, she might be able to find the secret Guild hideout. *It's not as though there's much out here to hide it with*, she thought to herself, glaring straight ahead. If only Alros had told her more about it.

Alros, despite him not wanting to reveal, as he called it, 'sensitive Guild information the Boss wants kept secret,' had looked rather proud of himself when he was hinting about the hideout. Alros had a knack for constantly referring back to the Boss whenever she asked him questions about the Guild – it was always "oh, the Boss has final say," and "the Boss prefers if no information is shared of the Guild," or "the Boss has rules for this kind of thing, don't mess it up, Lottie."

The Boss of the Guild had become almost legend-like to Lottie. She had never met them, and honestly didn't even know their name. She wasn't entirely sure if Alros knew the Boss' name, even if he was a part of the Guild. They simply went by "the Boss."

She should never have brought Seban on. It had been her one shot to get into the Guild's good graces, why did she think that she should bring anyone with her?

You thought Seban was your friend, she reminded herself as the horse plodded on. *Lifelong partner in crime, wasn't that what you called him once?*

She should've known better. So what that she had seen him grow from a measly, spotty teenager to an angry, wiry adult alongside their band of thieves? So what that they had both lived through that night that had not only torn Lottie away from Ceci, but killed his brother?

We were all to blame that night for how badly things went. Not just me.

A cloud of gloom settled around Lottie as she hunched over the horse. She couldn't help but poke through her memories of the jobs she had done with Seban, trying to parse out the answer, garnering nothing but annoyance. The only person who could answer why Seban turned on her would be Seban himself.

Ceci's face appeared in her imagination, marked with dust. *"How could you do this to us, Lottie?"*

Lottie closed her eyes and swallowed. The memory of smoke and ash, a sickly-sweet taste of burning wood and books and life, filled her senses. "I did it for us. I did all of it for us."

"I'm leaving. Don't you dare follow me."

Lottie had hired one of her few contacts left to tail Ceci out of the city to ensure she arrived safe, wherever she was going. They had eventually brought back news that Ceci had settled in a small seaside town called Arrowmount.

Ceci had never wanted anything to do with Lottie's life of thieving. She had tried to keep Lottie off the streets, tried to work hard enough at the menial jobs that left her worn and exhausted at the end of the day — but nothing was going to stop Lottie. Lottie drew her sister into the life bit by bit, because Lottie couldn't help herself. She wanted Ceci to see how good they could have it.

Then it all burned down.

Arrowmount, in Lottie's mind, was this quaint town where everyone had smiles on their faces and it was always sunny. She was sure that that wasn't possible, but in her imagination, that's where her sister was. Sunny, wonderful Arrowmount.

To increase her already dower mood, the darkening sky decided it was time to rip open. Lottie sighed heavily and threw her hood up to cover her head as the downpour soaked her clean to the bone.

"Hold!"

Lottie peered through the sheets of rain. A figure stood, holding up a hand, right in the middle of the road. She yanked on the horse's reins and narrowly avoided squashing whoever they were. "Watch it!"

The hooded figure reached up and grabbed hold of her knee.

"Piss off," she said, kicking out. Her foot caught awkwardly in the stirrup and sent her sliding off the horse, careening into the figure. They grunted in surprise as they managed to keep Lottie from falling fully into the mud below.

They pushed back their hood, revealing a familiar face marred with a scar that sliced cleanly across his left eye down to his nose. Lottie had always known Alros with that scar, though he had never told her the story of how he got it. He gazed at her with eyes that resembled pools of ink, shining from a dark, frowning face.

"Oh, Alros, thank the gods —"

"I've come to head you off," he answered, his tone clipped and tight. "Have to, after you pulled a stunt like that."

Lottie blinked at him. "It wasn't —"

"I don't want excuses, and neither does the Boss," Alros interrupted, holding up a hand to forestall her. "Were you followed?"

"I —" Lottie's hand drifted to her bag preemptively, ready to take the artifact out and stop him in his tracks.

"You don't know, do you?" Alros let out an angry sound. Lottie had never seen him this riled up. "Are you really that thick that you think coming out this way, heading toward one of the Guild's places, was a brilliant idea after fucking up so hard that the entire city's guard is on your tail? You have to *think* Lottie!

"I've been running around trying to clean up your mess, not knowing if you had gone underground in Claymore or been caught by the guard, trying to smooth feathers. Do you know how that is, trying to explain why the thief that you brought in as a possible initiate fucked up a job so badly that —"

Lottie's face flamed as he berated her, irritating her more than anything else she had endured in the past few days. She took a step forward and glared at him with every ounce of fury she had, shoving her finger into his face, cutting him off.

"I have been betrayed, shot at on a roof, fallen from said roof, run through an entire city while bleeding, and rode night and day to get here. I don't need your petty ass yelling at me now."

Alros pointed viciously at the horse. "Get back on your horse and turn around. You're not welcome."

"I'm here to —"

"I don't know what you mean by *here*. If you haven't noticed, you are exactly nowhere." Alros seethed, looking entirely unlike the suave, charming self he usually was. "I know what you're trying to find, but you're not getting in, Lottie. You're not part of the Guild. And honestly, you never were going to be, either. The Boss was just humoring you, after years of you badgering us to let you in."

Weary, bone deep exhaustion shuddered through her, cutting the rage down to a simmering annoyance. "Be reasonable, Alros."

"This *is* me being reasonable. I'm telling you the truth, aren't I? It's better than anyone else would do. If the Boss knew that you were trying to get into one of our places after what you did, I —"

"For what *Seban* did," she snapped.

"— swear, it's not just your neck on the line. I'm happy that the Boss never wanted you in the first place," Alros ploughed on, ignoring her interruption. "You're just a liability. You can't even do one, simple job right. A simple job that we had to *make up* a client for. There was no client. It was simply something the Boss wanted, and now I will have to deal with the disappointment, once again cleaning up your mess."

Lottie straightened her spine, despite the pain and exhaustion radiating through her. The weight of the artifact settled against her hip as she adjusted the grip on her bag.

The Guild never wanted her.

She pushed the churning unknown at the fracturing of her entire focus for the past ten years down, anchoring it into pure and unbridled rage. She made two decisions then, staring down yet another person to leave a bad taste in her mouth.

One, there was no way she was handing over the artifact. This man and his organization didn't deserve the win after treating her like this.

Two, if she ever saw Alros again, she was going to punch him in the face. She was trying really, really hard not to right then, but she figured she should retain at least a shred of her dignity. He wasn't worth her energy.

"Right. Well, thanks for your time," she said, nodding once to him and turning back to her horse.

Alros fell silent. When Lottie turned in the saddle to look back at him, she found him gaping at her, bewildered.

"What did you expect exactly? Me to break down and cry? To beg for forgiveness?" Lottie chuckled dryly, shaking her head at him. "Please. I know when I'm not wanted."

Alros sputtered slightly, his mouth opening and closing as he tried to hold his thoughts together. She could practically see them falling out of his ears. "And — where — if we need, to — where will —"

"Arrowmount," she said, the word leaking out of her before she could stop it. "I think I could do with a little vacation in a seaside town, after all of this. Will I be hearing from you?"

"I — well —"

Lottie didn't wait for a fully worded response.

Scalding hot nausea at the loss of her entire structure of life washed over her as she headed back over the same, flat ground, her horse plodding wearily beneath her. Lottie's shoulders wilted as she threw her head back, her hood slipping off, and closed her eyes against the rain.

For ten years, she'd been working toward one single goal. Gods, she'd been thinking about the Guild as a dream since she met Seban and his friends — well before Ceci had left her behind.

Arrowmount. Why did she say Arrowmount? She could have said literally anywhere else. Hutton, Mosfell. Anything besides Arrowmount.

Being at the beach in the fall sounds perfectly depressing, she thought bitterly. *That's an apt place to be when your life has just fallen apart.*

Lottie corrected course with a sigh and headed south-east toward the sea. Toward Arrowmount and Ceci, the sister who had left her behind a decade ago.

7

POTATO CAKES

Kir – 35 Days Before

Kir woke with a large wet nose shoved in the crook of her neck. She cringed away from Nudge, laughing. Half aware of her surroundings, she tumbled from her bed and sat up on the floor. He *wuuf*ed at her in greeting as though he hadn't done anything wrong, thumping his tail against the wall happily.

"Yes, good morning to you too," she said, rolling her shoulders around to try and rid herself of the cold feeling against her skin. He continued to whack his tail against the wall, looking at her with soft, sappy eyes, until she caved and scratched him around his floppy grey ears. He closed his eyes and a toothy smile spread across his muzzle, his tongue lolling out to the side.

Kir gazed out her wall of windows at the dull, early morning light bathing Arrowmount. She tried and failed to suppress a yawn, rubbing the bridge of her nose. Nudge stretched on her bed, tail coiling up behind him as he sprawled his front legs forward on Kir's blankets, toes extending. Without much ceremony, he loped of her bed and toward her closed door. Nudge cocked his head at her expectantly.

"Not everyone wakes up at the crack of dawn," she murmured to him, shuffling to the door. Honestly, how did their family end up with a dog that existed on an opposite sleep schedule? "Dad won't even be up yet."

Nudge *wuufed* at her quietly as he left as though saying, *not if I have anything to say about it.*

Kir tried to fall back to sleep, but now that she had been up and moving, her brain started to stumble forward, thinking about her day. She let out a groan and pushed herself up, rubbing her face hard, before she stumbled after Nudge down the stairs.

She was going to need a *really* large coffee. Maybe two.

Nudge pawed at her father Noghorn's door as she passed. With a silent turn of the knob, Kir pushed it open to let him in. Her father, out of all of their family, was the only one who had to wake early, to his great chagrin, because he started his day at the smithy long before most of them made their way out of bed. He would be up soon anyway, and what better way to wake up than a cold dog nose to the face?

Sure enough, as Kir descended into the kitchen, she heard a disgruntled voice from above her, exclaiming at Nudge, followed by the soft *thunk* of feet as her father got out of bed.

She smiled sleepily, turning to slip out the front door and head off to May's Cafe. It was routine now to grab the large metal carafe of coffee for her family. May sourced the coffee beans down from the Manid Empire specially, and when she brewed them, she did something that elevated the coffee to practically god-like. No matter how many times Kir had watched her brew the beans, she still couldn't figure out what May did to make it taste so *good.*

The nutty, deliciously fragrant coffee wafted out of the carafe in Kir's arms as she walked back home with it a while later, her mouth watering.

She returned to find her father standing over the stove, something sizzling pleasantly in a pan, releasing a deliciously salty scent into the air. He had on his usual simple brown trousers, worn and burned in places from mishaps at the smithy, and a well-made cream shirt rolled a few times up his forearms. Like Khar, he had his hair cut relatively short to keep out of his face as he worked.

"Ah, Kiri, you're awake early."

"Nudge," she said in way of explanation, placing the carafe onto a nearby counter before fishing a few mugs out of a cupboard. They clanked in hand, each a slightly different size and shape, handmade from one of Morgam's earliest attempts at pottery before he became enamored with painting.

"Silly dog. It's nice to see you up this early, though. And you're just in time," he said, turning back to the stove and transferring the contents onto an incredibly large plate, where there was already a pile of bread and cheese waiting. Perfectly glistening potato cakes, bacon, and sunny-side-up eggs joined them, their scent instantly making Kir's mouth water. "Breakfast is served."

The potato cakes were some of her father's specialty. Even though he made them often, they were some of Kir's favorites. It helped, she supposed, that they were bathed in butter.

Sometimes the local farmers from around Arrowmount that came to the market set aside a sack of potatoes just for them, they went through so many. More than Corwek did at the bar, and that was saying something.

She poured from the carafe for her father and slid his favorite mug, which was particularly misshapen, across to him. Morgam had accidentally grabbed it too tightly before it was fired and left perfect finger holds embedded in it. Her father liked it too much to allow Morgam to scrap it completely. Then, Kir grabbed the sugar and milk from the cold box to add to her own coffee.

"Are you working on anything good at the smithy today?" Kir dug a few plates out of the cupboard and made a point of slamming the door shut, the sound a hard snap in the kitchen. From years of having her brothers or father wake her in the same way, the sound of the cabinet doors shooting straight up to the bedrooms like a crack in the earth was a great wake-up call.

"There was an order of a couple new axes, but nothing exciting," he answered, shoveling food onto a plate for himself. "I miss the days when adventurers would come in and have weapons commissioned from me — they always had the neatest of requests. Once, I had to get a local wizard to help me imbue a spell to loosen one's bowels onto a short sword."

Kir snorted at the thought. She, though not a fighter or adventurer of any kind, would never want to be on the other end of an enchanted weapon.

"Do you remember when you made your first axe at the forge?" Her father spoke around a fluffy potato cake before swallowing. "You were so tiny; I was sure that you wouldn't be able to lift the hammer. But you did it, all by yourself. I was so proud."

Kir smiled, remembering the days she spent with him in the smithy. At the time, all three siblings worked alongside their dad, allowed to do the safer chores around the heat and various metals. It had been one of the best days she could remember, actually being allowed to make a blade of her own. The axe, though not very well made, still hung with her brothers' first weapons at the smithy on display.

"I remember wanting it to be much better and bigger than I ended up making," said Kir with a soft laugh, listening to the sounds of her brothers moving above. She sipped her coffee, the steam and perfectly nutty scent of the brew wafting over her, waking her up better than anything else could.

"Ah, if only you kept at it. Then you'd have far outmatched your brother."

"Hey," said Khar himself, walking into the kitchen, rubbing sleep out of his eyes. He snatched one of the bigger mugs from the counter before Morgam could, coming in behind, and took a long gulp. "I, at least, was the one of all three of us who decided to help you out at the smithy, even though my passion lies in wood, and not metal, despite how often you have me doing detail work on the blades."

"Yes, yes," their father chuckled, waving a large dark blue hand at them. "All my children are equally talented in different ways *blah-blah-blah* and whatever else I'm supposed to say as a wonderful father."

Morgam lunged for the table and immediately snatched up a potato cake, shoving it into his mouth and speaking around it. "The best, really. No one else makes potato cakes like you."

8

THE MOON FESTIVAL

Kir – 35 Days Before

Kir walked through Arrowmount a little while later, heading toward the town center with an old crate under her arm. She often picked up fresh produce for the bar on her way into work, stocking the back for Corwek.

She passed by Neema and Della, two married elderly gnomes who Kir had known her entire life. They were bent toward each other by the bakery stall, harried expressions on their faces.

The fresh scent of baking bread wrapped itself around Kir, momentarily dazzling her with its comforting scent. Gable, the baker, had a knack for finding the perfect way to draw people toward their stall. Sometimes it was their cinnamon buns, or their freshly baked miniature cakes. Most often, though, it was loaves of fresh bread, made with locally milled flower from the Whellan farm outside of Arrowmount.

I'll have to pick up a few loaves, she thought. *Gods, that smells divine.*

"Kirandir, goodness me," said a gentle voice from behind her. Kir turned on her heel. It took her a second to peer down by her thighs where

48

the two gnomes were standing, staring up at her. "You walk so fast, dear, our little legs cannot keep up. Oh, how serendipitous to have you here!"

"Della, darling," said Neema, grasping her partner's arm, "it's like you conjured her out of thin air. The perfect solution!"

Kir blinked down at the two of them as they talked between one another. Both Della and Neema gave her the impression of puffed-up birds of song whenever she saw them, from their layers of colorful clothes to keep out the chill and their puffs of white hair atop their heads.

"Can I, uh, help you two ladies?"

"You would not believe what has gone on today," said Della, putting both hands up in the air, exasperated. "We have been dealing with the most stress as we're pulling together this year's festival —"

"It's fast approaching after all," added Neema, adjusting a small basket on her shoulder. "Every year, Servune's moon travels across the sky at the same rate, and yet every year, we seem to be bamboozled by time passing and are always in a rush to gather everything for the Moon Festival. And you know very well, Della dear, that you take on too much."

"Yes, well." Della sighed dramatically. "This morning we woke to news that the previous Entertainment Committee chair is no longer going to be participating — something about their family being incredibly gravely ill off in Zidien, and they have to go take care of them indefinitely."

"Tragic!"

"Oh," contributed Kir.

Della nodded. "We have been left totally adrift! The most important committee, chair-less! All without them having done a *lick* of work — I cannot believe that Gral managed to slip under our radar for so long. All those meetings, and never once did they say that they weren't keeping up. Or any warning at all that they were about to up and leave us high and dry just before the festival starts!"

Kir cleared her throat. "Uh, yeah. Awful."

Della clapped her hands together and looked back up at Kir. "We got to brainstorming, trying to fix this absolutely abhorrent issue before it got out to the other committees and caused an absolute catastrophe around town. I mean, imagine! A Moon Festival with no proper entertainment!"

"A travesty," added Neema. "We're about a month out, and there is positively *nothing* lined up."

Kir thought that talking about this in such an open area without dropping their voices at all was probably not a good idea if they wanted to keep this quiet, but she couldn't find the right time to interrupt them.

"A *travesty*," repeated Della with emphasis. "But then, oh! You walked by like a beacon of purest light, and I was struck with the most brilliant idea I have ever had. Ever!"

Kir's stomach gave a soft lurch, seeing where this was going. "Um —"

"And I said, that's an absolutely wonderful idea," said Neema.

"Of course, I said it to her before I came running after you," said Della reasonably. "Had to run it by my best judge."

Neema grinned. "Our very own beloved local bard, the Entertainment Committee chair!"

"Of course, it would be up to you love," said Della very quickly, patting Kir's knee as Kir's brain began to short circuit. Her? Take over the entire Entertainment Committee, with no prior experience? There was no way.

Kir suppressed a shudder at the thought of having that much responsibility, of organizing that many people.

You can't leave them high and dry, though, said a little voice in the back of her head.

She sucked in a breath. "Is it really only a month away?"

"I know, the way time flies," said Neema, putting both her hands up in front of her as though she didn't know what to say. "We really are down to our last possibility, Kirandir."

"It is up to you," added Della, glancing at her wife. "You *would* be saving the town a great deal of strife, though."

"And us, my goodness," said Neema. "I'm sure your fantastic musical expertise would be an incredible asset."

"Uh —" Kir tried to run through any possibility of how she could get out of this, but the way that the two elderly ladies were looking at her was making it incredibly hard to say no.

"And of course, because you would be ever so gracious doing this on relatively short notice," continued Della, steamrolling on. "You would be the last spot in the festival, on closing night, for your troubles. I know it's the most coveted spot, so why not give it to our very own Kirandir? How does that sound? Shall we pen you into the spot? Entertainment Committee chair?"

"I —" Kir swallowed. She'd known these two ladies her entire life, growing up here in Arrowmount. They had done so much for the town over the years, and were often the backbone of events, especially the Moon Festival. Della herself ran it.

Kir let out a half groan, half sigh, already nodding. "Yeah, sure. I'll help."

"Fantastic!" Della clapped excitedly, beaming up at Kir with a glow in her face that was so warm and motherly that Kir couldn't help but smile back, despite the panic clawing up her throat.

Neema and Della danced around in a jig, their boots clacking on the cobblestones. Della waved a few townsfolk off as they moved to step closer, expressions of intrigue on their faces. Everyone in Arrowmount knew that the elderly gnomes were always up to something, so it would be only a matter of minutes before someone around them who had overheard spread the news. *Great.*

"Oh, Kir darling, this is going to be absolutely wonderful," said Neema, grasping Kir's hand with her two smaller ones. "You have no idea how grateful we are."

"So grateful," said Della. "And if you need anything at all, please feel free to reach out. No matter how busy we are, you know we'll make the time to help."

"Right."

"Now, Neema love, we should really let Kirandir get back to her morning shopping. As must we!"

"Goodness, yes. I have half a mind to badger Gable for their bread recipe, it smells *divine.*"

The two gnomes waved as they left, cheerily bouncing into the town center and disappearing amidst the market stalls, leaving Kir feeling breathless. Kir looked down at the still empty crate in her hands, and a list that Nova had written out for her the previous night. She'd almost entirely forgotten about it.

Her? The Entertainment Committee chair, having to deal with and organize a large group of people? She was best behind her lute, not the one organizing folks with the instruments.

Gods, what had she gotten herself into?

Kir spent the majority of her day trying to do her job, but her body and mind were battling with her to turn into a statue.

It was not as though she *hated* change. Sure, she disliked when her usual day-to-day routine was thrown into a wrench by something new — especially when she didn't know exactly how something was going to change her schedule. That's why she kept her routine so similar, and for years, she'd never varied unless forced to by something outside of her control.

But she wished she disliked it less.

Usually, against her will, change pushed Kir into a nearly statuesque state, to the point where even speaking became difficult. She wished that she could pick up and go with the flow, but when she decided to do things, it was always after weeks or even months of thinking it over, gradually dropping herself into the idea.

"Kir, you okay?"

Corwek walked by with a few bowls in hand, steam wafting from them. Kir blinked at him, the scent of his specialty soup wrapping around her senses and bringing her slightly more into her body again.

"Yeah, just." Kir shook her head slightly, as though to clear it of cobwebs. "Having a hard time. D-doing things."

Corwek frowned slightly, eyeing her. "Have you eaten today?"

She thought back to her morning, the coffee and the lovely breakfast that her father had made. She remembered definitely drinking the coffee — she never missed out on her coffee — but she couldn't recall actually eating anything. "Coffee."

"Ah, Kir, you know coffee isn't a food! It's not a meal!"

"Yes, well." Corwek knew very well that food wasn't the fix to problems like this. She'd told him many times.

"Stay put, I'll be back."

Corwek sped out into the bar to deliver the bowls of soup to customers before he returned, grabbing an empty bowl as he came back in. Kir watched, feeling as though she was on the edge of tears, as he broke a nob off of a fresh loaf of bread, spooned in a healthy heaping of soup to the bowl, and passed the gathered bits to Kir. "Take a minute, eat this."

"I —"

"Even if it doesn't help," he added, exasperated from having had this same conversation a few times over the years, "at least you won't pass out from not eating. How you haven't already from the amount of caffeine you consume is beyond me. *Go.* No wait —" he reached over and sliced off a few chunks of cheese from a brick nearby and laid them on the bowl in her hands. "Now go."

"Thanks."

Kir managed to spoon a few spoonful's of the warm, comforting meal into her mouth, watching the patrons in the bar. Most of them had bowls of the same soup in front of them, steam curling around their faces as they dunked chunks of bread into the rich broth.

A dusty black catfolk, a regular Kir sometimes caught glimpses of from the back, was curled over their bowl of soup as though they were inhaling it without a spoon. Their ears were relaxed down over their head, eyes nearly closed in pleasure. Another patron entered the bar then, dressed in a thick woven jacket lined with leather that looked as though it was about fifty years old. The elderly man stood up, towering over most of the patrons with his dark blue skin and horns. Chervil, the old lighthouse keeper, sauntered over to the bar, waving at a few of the other patrons before settling onto a stool. He smiled kindly at Briar, who was pouring ale for another patron.

Kir's attention hooked onto other patrons briefly, the whole time her body slowly relaxing bit by bit. Kir pushed the thoughts of the committee out of her head as best she could, replacing them with her observations. It didn't always work, replacing thoughts with the simple calmness of life, but when it did, Kir was incredibly grateful.

Soon enough, she moved to grab the knob of bread only to find her hands grasping at nothing, surprised to see that her lunch had vanished.

"Better?" Corwek asked as she walked into the back, tossing her bowl into her water basin to wash.

"Slightly, yes." Kir cracked her neck before plunging her hands into the water. She did feel steadier, physically. She now also felt slightly sleepy, which was helping her brain not focus on the upcoming change in her life. That had to count for something.

"Good. Good." Corwek nodded with a self-satisfied smile on his face. He clapped her on the back amiably as he went back to his station.

Washing dishes, though menial and usually enough to let her shut off her brain, was not enough today. She needed to do something different. To move, to get out, to dive into her music — anything but stand there, scrubbing.

"Just get through the day," she said to herself under her breath, shaking her head. It'll be done soon enough.

9

GOLDEN STROKES OF LIGHT

Lottie – 35 Days Before

L ottie arrived in Arrowmount about a week later, worn through and sufficiently tired of being on horseback.

She had stopped at a farm along the way to barter for food and had lived on increasingly stale bread and dried meat, something that she very much did not like to consume on a regular basis. At that point, she would do anything for a proper meal. And a soft bed — gods, a *bed*. What a wonderful idea.

A chill, salty wind whipped around Lottie and tossed the colorful branches outside of the town around her, sending a rivulet of goosebumps down Lottie's spine as leaves every shade of orange, red, and gold launched danced in the air around her. She patted her horse's neck, murmuring, taking a moment to breathe in the salty air. She couldn't see the ocean from where she was, but if she focused hard enough, she could hear the roaring waves between the rustling leaves. It had been far too long since she had seen the sea.

Lottie nodded to the stable master as she handed the horse's reins off to him and turned toward the two guards stationed at the town entrance. Large, salt-stained stone walls rose up over them, stretching off around the perimeter of Arrowmount, wrapping the stone and wood buildings tucked inside in a protective barrier. Some of the cities and towns that Lottie had traveled to had imposing walls built to keep others out, but this was the first town that felt as though the walls were wrapped around the town like a hug.

"Evening," called one of the guards as she walked up.

"Good evening, gentlemen."

"You're coming in rather late."

Lottie slid her hood back and gave the tall, exceptionally handsome guard a flirty smile, letting her eyes run up his perfectly tailored uniform. Seriously, who on the pantheon allowed men like this to walk around freely?

He chuckled at her appraisal, and, gods be damned, if it wasn't already too dark to see properly by Lottie would swear that he was blushing. The guard tucked a stray bit of his shoulder-length hair behind his ear, dropping his gaze down before looking back up at her, his dark blue eyes slightly sharper. Hadn't they been grey when she walked up? Lottie must have been mistaken.

"Been traveling a while," she said. "I'm here to see my sister."

"Oh yeah? Who's your sister?"

"Cecily Little."

"You're related to the woman who runs the magic goods stall?" The other guard appraised her before nodding. "Ah, yeah I see the resemblance."

Lottie held back a laugh. The only resemblance between her and her sister was their green hair and skin the color and mottled pattern of tree bark. In the increasing darkness, though, she wasn't sure if they could see her skin properly.

"Well, head on through," said the handsome guard. "If you happen to see Cecily before the end of the night, tell her that Zanve says he'll stop by right after I'm done here."

Lottie nodded thoughtfully at this Zanve and wondered briefly who he might be to her sister, before she walked between the gates of Arrowmount.

Pools of yellow and white light lit the dark cobblestone streets, lanterns both fueled naturally or through arcane means hung outside dark buildings. The town was mostly empty of people this late, letting Lottie walk in peace, trailing along until she picked up the distant sound of music.

The further she walked down the main road, the clearer the music became. Above her, the slightest ruffle of small flags along many lengths of string caught her attention, their colors almost indistinguishable in the darkness. She narrowed her eyes, trailing the strings as best she could, marking where they tied around various balconies and window ledges and plant pots, lining the skies above the cobblestones.

How charming.

Lottie walked by a number of dark-windowed buildings that had no signage on the front. She nearly missed the closed post office but made a mental note to return there in the morning to ensure that any messages from Alros and the Guild were passed on to her.

Letting out a long sigh, Lottie clenched her fists around the strap of her bag. She had the artifact, and it probably wouldn't be long before the Guild came seeking it out. She would have to think about what she wanted to do with it further, but for now, she needed to find a place to rest.

Lottie followed the music, drawn to a well-lit road that had a mix of differently sized buildings along both sides, stretching up toward the night sky. She peered into a set of lit windows along her right side, catching sight of a well-stocked bookstore with two figures by the desk. A dark-haired human leaned toward a pale-haired elf as they talked, smiles on both of their faces.

Further down, she peeked beneath an awning entirely covered in plants to see an equally plant-covered cafe, still open at this late hour. A woman with luxurious curled honey hair and long pointed ears manned the counter, deep in conversation with a tall, lanky being, pairs of spectacles on both their noses as they discussed a paper spread out between them. The giantkin leaned over steaming mugs and a plate of cookies and nodded sagely at the woman, their long, soft flopping ears shifting with the movement.

Though Lottie would probably find delicious food and comfort inside, she was on the hunt for noise and ale, so she continued on.

She found her way toward the music, the quick beat catching inside her bones and waking her up in a way she hadn't felt in days. Warm, welcoming light leaked out through a skinny window and a partially open door, calling her in.

She ducked into a place, which was tucked inside a skinny space between two other buildings. A thin rickety wooden sign above read THE OLD'N NARROW.

Warm, joyous atmosphere washed over her. The distinct scent of ale, mead, and buttery food hung on the air as her ears sang to the raucous chatter and music. The bar was lit by a multitude of candles and lanterns that cast the interior in a golden shine, infusing the dark wooden furniture and walls with a richness that instantly calmed Lottie. She stood up a bit straighter to peer over folks, eyes catching on a few people who looked her way, and spied a path to the bar.

Lottie wound around the tables with ease, letting her hips swerve through the gathered patrons as she kept one hand on her bag, ensuring it didn't bounce into anyone. She perched on one of the bar stools and motioned to the barmaid before gazing around the cramped building, narrowing in on the source of music in the corner.

Her breath caught, eyes locking onto the bard bent lovingly over her lute. Long black hair, shaved on one side, tumbled in thick waves down over one of her shoulders, casting part of her angular face in shadow as she played. She wore a simple white button shirt that had been rolled back to her elbows, revealing strong, muscled forearms that rippled as she strummed.

Good gods, she's so attractive, Lottie thought abstractly as the half-orc woman looked up and over the crowd, a smirk playing on her lips, pearly white tusks glinting against her slate-grey skin. The bard sat up a little straighter, flicked her hair out of her face, and began to sing.

Lottie's heart gave a hard, sharp pang. All she could do was watch as the bard weaved music like a spell around the bar. Maybe it was the golden glow, or the comforting sound of chatter blanketing Lottie, but Lottie could've sworn it was magic.

For a shining moment, Lottie imagined walking up to the bard and taking the place of the instrument, being caressed in the same way, being held that lovingly.

It took her a solid thirty seconds before she pulled herself out of the reverie, clearing her throat and blinking hard, realizing that the barmaid was back, a knowing smile on her face as she leaned onto the bar. She slid Lottie's tankard of ale across the surface with a wink.

"Can I get you something to eat?"

"Whatever is delicious and easy," Lottie answered, before thinking of the tough dried meat she'd had on her journey and adding, "Without meat, if you have it."

"You've got it."

Lottie took a long drag of her ale, filling her senses with the delicious beverage. It settled on her tongue with a slightly bitter fruity taste and hit her stomach pleasantly.

Partway into her second one, the alcohol began to paint the bar in soft, blurred golden strokes of light.

What a perfect night, she thought, leaning onto one elbow and gazing at the bard in the corner.

The barmaid brought over a plate with a thick chunk of bread and a bowl of steaming vegetable stew, which Lottie dug into in moments. She lost herself in the thick, spiced broth. Potatoes melted on her tongue like butter, warming her inside and out. The bread, too, was perfectly fresh, and was the exact right amount of crunchy on the outside and fluffy soft on the inside. It sopped up the rich stew broth perfectly.

Once the bowl was empty, Lottie leaned back and started to undo her long braids, rubbing feeling back into her head.

The bard in the corner kicked into an energetic tune, now on her feet, and towered above the rest of the crowd as she sang. The whole bar started to stomp along with her as she strummed so fast and hard on her lute Lottie was sure the strings would break. The bard tossed her hair, nearly hitting the low ceiling beams, and grinned out at the crowd. Her energy was absolutely intoxicating.

Lottie leapt up before she could stop herself. She let the crowd of people guide her toward the bard, easily side stepping to keep herself moving along with them, her hips swaying to the beat.

She found herself dancing with a black-haired elf who had an aggressively handsome face, his ears speckled in jewels and rings. His body pressed in close to hers, the two of them moving as one. She forgot about the wound in her arm, as the music carried her through the night, the beat hammering into her bones.

10

STRANGERS AND FAMILY

Lottie – 35 Days Before

The bar began to empty once the bard had finished playing and disappeared into the back, the late hour calling most folks home to their beds. Lottie sat back in her spot in front of her now empty tankard. She watched the bar around her, completely and utterly comforted by the atmosphere. It felt as though she had been steeped in the glow of the place.

The bard returned from the back room after a few minutes and settled into one of the tables near where she had played. She waved at the barmaid who was currently scrubbing at the bar top.

"Do you mind bringing that over to Kir there?" The barmaid slid two full tankards that had been resting to the side over to Lottie. "And here's a fresh one for you. I have an absolute barrel full of glasses to clean, and…" the barmaid appraised Lottie carefully then gave her a knowing look. "Well."

"Ah, I haven't been subtle, have I?" Lottie chuckled and took the tankards in hand. She slid a few coins across the bar to cover the bard's drink on top of her own. "What's your name, by the way?"

"Briar, dear. There's no need, Kir works here."

"It's on me either way. I'm Lottie Luck."

Briar pocketed the coin with a warm smile. "Pleasure."

Lottie straightened and flicked her hair out of her face before she made her way to the back of the skinny, narrow room, and slid the drink over to the bard. Kir had her head in her hands, strong grey fingers digging into her hairline much the same way Lottie's own had massaged her scalp free of her braids.

"Drink up," said Lottie, sliding into the chair across from Kir. "It's on me."

Kir flinched upright, frowning at Lottie. Her mouth worked a few times before she croaked out, "Who're you?"

"Lottie Luck." Lottie extended her hand toward Kir with a demure smile. "I simply had to come over and commend you on your performance. Truly, I have never seen someone play the way you do. And I've been around many places in this empire, so you can take it from me."

Kir's frown deepened as she peered at Lottie's outstretched fingers as though they were entirely foreign to her. There was a long beat of silence as they both sat there, Lottie feeling more awkward as the moment stretched uncomfortably, before the bard lurched into movement. She wrapped her large hand around Lottie's, enveloping her fingers with warm, calloused ones. Again, there was hesitation, almost as if Kir just wanted to let go, before she shook once and dropped Lottie's hand. "Uh, thank you?"

It sounded more like a question than a proper thanks, but Lottie let it slide. She played with the edge of her drink, leaning in toward Kir with every flirty bone in her body, feeling empowered by the glow of the bar. "Where did you learn to play like that?"

"I, uh, taught myself." Kir cleared her throat and drank from her own tankard heavily, tossing it back in a few gulps before she set it down between them, the sound dull and empty. Her eyes landed anywhere but on Lottie, skating around the bar. Both her hands flexed and tensed into fists on the tabletop.

Lottie was about to open her mouth again as Kir pushed herself up from the table, knocking her knee into it, which threw her empty tankard askew, and cleared her throat.

She hesitated, still not looking at Lottie, before darting away.

"Great," said Lottie, gazing after her as the bard sped off to the back of the bar and didn't return. A sense of bittersweet dejection settled into her chest. She sighed heavily and drank her ale before grabbing Kir's empty tankard and bringing it back up to Briar.

The barmaid stood at the bar, one eyebrow cocked, as she dried a glass with a well-worn towel. "Don't mind our Kirandir," she said kindly, placing the glass down and leaning in conspiratorially. "She doesn't take well to strangers."

"Ah, so there wasn't something on my face, then."

Lottie stood there for a moment, wondering where in the hells she went wrong in all her lives that such a gorgeous, talented bard would be so uninterested in her.

A different shape moved into her vision, one much lither and wirier.

"Did I hear that right, before?" said the black-haired elf, leaning over the bar toward her with a warm, alluring smile. He moved his head slightly to the side, letting his curtain of hair slide over and reveal one of his bejeweled ears. "Lottie Luck, is it?"

"It is," said Lottie, feeling her face relax into a matching smile. "Should

I just call you Dancer from the way you moved before, or is there something else I can call you?"

The elf chuckled; the sound warm in the back of his throat. "I like Dancer."

"Aeric, stop flirting with our patrons and help me clean," snapped Briar playfully, coming around and flicking her towel at him. He shot to the side with a sly laugh, shooting Lottie a wink.

Lottie laughed, and got up, deciding to try and find a place to sleep for the night. She slid on her one-armed jacket and slung her bag back over her chest, the comforting weight of the artifact inside settling against her hip.

She barely got to the door, however, when someone pushed it open from the outside. A vaguely familiar shape stepped in, yellow-grey eyes landing on Lottie with a jolt of recognition. It took her a half second to place the man as Zanve, the town guard, before he grimaced at her apologetically. *His eyes* are *changing*, she thought, as they shifted fully to yellow in the warm bar light.

Lottie stopped in her tracks and found the half-formed smile slipping off her face faster than Kir had exited the bar as another person stepped in from behind him. "Huh, you were telling the truth."

A face that had barely changed in the past ten years, right down to the whorls of bark and the small scar by her lip from when she'd tripped over Lottie's toys as a child, frowned.

She was still branch-thin, too. Barely there. The complete antithesis to Lottie's soft, round body that demanded to be noticed. Her hair was longer, the warm summer-green tendrils drifting down to her lower back in loose curls. She'd had the left side shaved, which was new. But the expression on her face was one that Lottie knew well.

Her sister's face had been twisted into that pained expression countless times when she came home from work, having dealt with another miserable day. Seeing it turned on her, now, sent a spike right to Lottie's heart.

She should've expected that look, though. Some things never change. Especially disappointment in your little sister.

Ceci.

Lottie felt every ounce of her bravado shrink inside herself, recoiling back a step, and suddenly she was a teenager, watching her sister walk away from her covered in ash.

"What in all the gods' names are you doing here, Lottie?"

PART TWO

Dreams and Reality

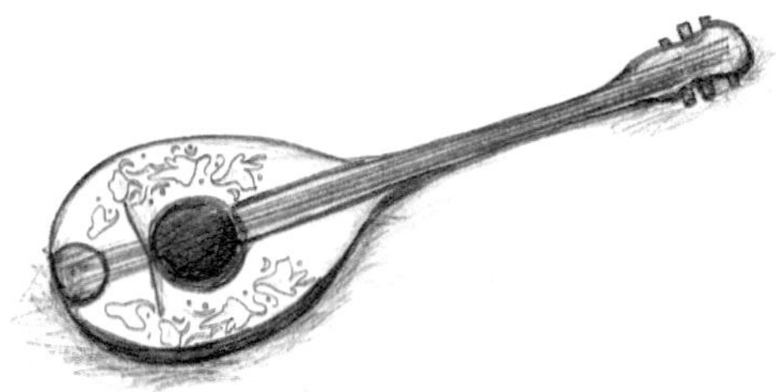

11

A Nudge in the Right Direction

Kir – 35 Days Before

The memory of rhythmic pounding reverberated through Kir's chest as she walked home from the bar in crisp darkness, stars winking above her. When everyone around her felt the music, their bodies carrying the beat out into the room, their voices calling out the words along with her — *that* was everything Kir loved about performing.

She couldn't stop thinking about the green-haired woman.

Lottie. Lottie Luck.

Gods, she was gorgeous.

In the midst of dancing, Lottie had leaned over and grabbed a tankard from a random table and drank it in full, tipping her head back, Kir's attention had snagged on her. In her memory, Kir traced the woman's neck as a bead of ale ran down her throat before her gaze burned down the woman's curves, traveling over her ample hips and absolutely *incredible* thighs.

Kir forgot how to breathe, the cold night air doing nothing to cool her face.

Who *was* that woman? Kir had never once been distracted from a set by someone, no matter how gorgeous they were.

Kir had dragged her attention back to her lute and the crowd with difficulty after that, barely able to start up another song to keep the crowd dancing. The beautiful, curvaceous woman twirled in her mind, dancing to the beat thundering through the bar.

The cobblestones clicked under Kir's boots as she shook her head slightly, feeling as though she was coming off of the effects of a spell. She scraped her loose hair into a bun atop her head, hoping that the icy air on her neck would help cool this feeling rushing through her.

After all that, Lottie had come over to her. Come to *talk* to her, with a smile so bright it looked as though she was lit from within.

And of course, because Kir was having a hard time formulating sentences that weren't lyrics or backed by the sound of her lute because of the anxiety that had been roiling through her all day, she had run away.

If one person does that to you, just imagine what running the Entertainment Committee is going to do, said a nasty voice in her head, cutting through the rhythmic joy coursing through her.

Kir tripped on a cobblestone and sucked in a sharp, painful breath, barely catching herself.

Is this something I can even do?

Kir hadn't paid much attention to how the Moon Festival was actually run every year. Like the majority of Arrowmount, she enjoyed the festival when it arrived — playing the games, eating incredible food from vendors, and watching the entertainment.

For most of her life, Kir had placed the performers of the Moon Festival on the level of kings and queens, in awe of their bravery and talent. That awe had never faded as she grew older, even as she came to realize they were just people like her. To audition, to put yourself out there like that, that was something Kir wished she could do. But, whenever the time came around to audition, she'd always been too busy helping her father at the smithy, she'd been too scared, or she created some other excuse to avoid it.

The bravest thing Kir ever did was walk into the Old'n Narrow to ask to work for them, after being encouraged by townsfolk who'd heard her playing on the beach or in secluded parts of the town to try. Briar and Nova had looked slightly confused at Kir's offer to work in exchange for her to be able to play as their bard, but they agreed wholeheartedly.

She'd put auditioning for the festival out of her mind long ago. Now, she was going to be the one *running* the committee, not simply auditioning to be part of the entertainment.

Gods, this is too much.

She had no idea how to run a committee. What would that even entail? How on earth was she going to handle it?

Kir blinked at her surroundings, realizing that she had come to a stop in the middle of a dark street, nothing but a distant flickering lantern light to keep her company as her insides twisted with renewed anxiety. What felt like a rope tightened in her chest, pulling her taut, making it entirely too difficult to breathe.

Breathe, Kir, she told herself, closing her eyes and trying to find the space in her lungs to inhale. Her chest began to shake with greater intensity, heart pounding in her ears.

She took an ambling step forward, the effort to move increasing with every heartbeat. Her lute case strapped to her back shifted with the movement — Kir brought it to her chest and squeezed it tight. She tried to envision the energy of the night again, feel the rhythmic stomping of feet in her imagination, but it was gone.

Too many emotions, she thought absently. *Feeling too many things.*

Kir kept her lute case pressed against her as she forced her feet forward again, her legs unsteady as they tried to carry her home.

The workroom glowed familiarly from a singular work light as Kir finally stumbled over the threshold. A soft *ssschk-ssschk* sounded from inside, but Kir didn't stop to see if Khar had made any progress on the project he had been working on. Instead, she stumbled upstairs, taking a slightly unsteady step over Nudge's sleeping form in the hallway, and collapsed onto her bed. Kir stared at the dark wooden beams that ran the length of her ceiling as uncontrollable shivers expanded from the rope in her chest out into her limbs.

Easy, Kir, she thought desperately trying to control her breathing. She strained to hear the sounds of her family and house around her, looking for any bit of comfort. Kir strained her hearing out, trying not to focus on the sound of her erratic heartbeat, until she could hear her father a floor below, snoring.

She forced herself to breathe slowly, in the rhythm of his snores. But it wasn't working.

Why isn't it working?

Thud-thud-thudthud. Kir turned toward her door at the sound of paws on her stairs, announcing Nudge before he padded in. He sniffed at her hand that hung from her bed, letting out a low whine of concern, before he hopped up next to her. He huffed noisily as he stretched and settled his head on her chest.

She forced out a long sigh, tapping Nudge's head with one finger continuously. The weight of his head was comforting and solid.

Nudge let out a low groan, the rumble shuddering through Kir's chest, counteracting her panic. The greathound knew, somehow, exactly how to help her. It took her the better part of an hour to come down fully, but with Nudge's head heavy on her, she managed to finally relax.

"Thanks, Nudge," she said quietly, turning her tapping finger into a soft caress on his snoozing head. He grunted happily in his sleep.

We don't deserve dogs, she thought, finally able to close her eyes.

12

MASKS AND USELESS WARES

Lottie – 35 Days Before

Nothing could have prepared Lottie for seeing her sister again. It's so strange and completely *wrong* how time can turn people into strangers in seconds but be completely unable to erase some sense of intimacy, no matter how long it had been.

Briar eyed Ceci as she reached the bar before unearthing a fresh drink from behind the counter. Ceci reached for the glass of completely clear liquid and drank it back with one smooth swallow. Briar refilled the glass without comment before sliding a tankard over to Lottie.

"Gods, Ceci," said Lottie, a little impressed and surprised. Ceci hadn't ever drunk anything other than wine when they lived together. "I would have never pinned you for a hard liquor person."

"When your little sister that you thought was dead suddenly comes into town, you'll take anything."

"You thought I was dead?"

"Well, what else was I supposed to think when I don't hear from you in a decade?"

Lottie blinked at her, mouth slightly ajar, as Ceci took the refilled glass and sat on a bar stool, not once looking at Lottie. *She thought I was dead? After she was the one who walked away?*

Lottie scoffed, taking a generous gulp of her ale before setting it on the counter a little harder than she should have. "Says the one who left and told me not to speak to her again."

Ceci closed her eyes and sighed, entire body stiff as a board.

Lottie traced the rim of her tankard with a finger, trying to steady the unease roiling through her body. Each of her nerves stood on end, prepped to flee or fight or simply get up on the bar and start screaming, she wasn't sure which.

"So." Lottie cleared her throat and forced one of her choice, sharp smiles onto her face, turning fully toward her sister. "I hear you're still running a market stall."

"I am," responded Ceci as she took a sip of her drink, staring at the wall behind the bar, lined with bottles and empty tankards.

"Cute." Lottie leaned onto the bar with one arm. "Tell me, how's life here by the sea? It's been such a long time, dear sister. How wonderful is your life now, without me in it?"

"Not here, Lottie," Ceci snapped, turning a fraction toward Lottie, her eyes flicking to Briar who was a little way down chatting to one of the remaining patrons.

"Whatever could you mean?" said Lottie, feeling as though her entire body was sharpened into a blade. She tossed back the rest of her ale in one and smacked her lips. "Dear sister, am I a *burden* to you? A problem that you would rather not discuss out in public?"

"I am not going into this with you."

"Oh, I think you are."

Ceci turned away, putting up both hands. "If you want to talk, I'm happy to talk. But we're not going into this line of conversation while there are others around us."

Lottie cast a glance around the nearly empty bar. There were maybe two people in the bar other than them and Briar at the moment, who was pointedly not looking at them.

"Let me get this right. You don't want to make a scene, is that it? No, no no, how can I be so silly — you don't want *me* to make a scene, do you."

Ceci pierced her with a hard, cold stare, sending shards into Lottie's already bruised and battered heart. "Why are you here, Lottie?"

"I came to visit."

"Why now? Why after ten years?"

"Why not now?" Lottie lifted a single eyebrow, challenging. "Can't I want to visit my sister? Besides, Arrowmount is the perfect seaside town. You know how much I love the sea."

"I really wish we could just have a civil conversation for once."

Lottie cackled, the sound mocking and cold. "For once? *For once?* Ceci, you walked away from me in the burning wreckage of our home. *You* walked. I was there, every —"

"You burned everything that I had — that *we* had — to the ground, and you know it. Do not throw that back at me."

The two of them sat for a collection of heartbeats, staring daggers at each other, before Lottie reached over and took her sister's half-drunk glass and finished it. The liquor burned all the way down, searing into her soul.

"Fine, we can be civil," said Lottie. "We can have a totally *normal* conversation. I needed a place to stay for a bit. A job went bad. Arrowmount was top of the list."

"A job."

"You know how it goes," said Lottie, waving a hand dismissively, not wanting to get into the semantics right then. The liquor and ale sat uneasily in her stomach as she shifted on the barstool. "I had a chance with the Guild, my accomplice blew it. Seban — you remember him right? The slightly creepy one with mind magic? He totally threw me under the carriage. That shot's gone, so I figured I should probably hide for a bit. What better place to bury my face in the sand than by the sea?"

The Guild doesn't want you. They never wanted you.

Lottie ignored the thought and focused on her sister.

"Ah," said Ceci, smiling a cold, tight lipped smile. "What was the job for?"

Lottie hesitated. "What?"

"What did you steal this time? How big did you go?" Ceci reached over the bar and took the bottle of clear liquor and filled her glass back up, hand shaking. More sloshed out the sides than into the glass, but she didn't seem to care. "I can't believe you're still doing this, still pursuing this life. I thought, maybe, just maybe, that you would have had a conscience after burning our life to the ground. That perhaps you would think, 'huh, you know, maybe I shouldn't continue down this path where the only thing I will ever be good enough for is a jail cell.'"

"It wasn't my fault that they —"

"Still blaming everyone else but yourself? This job for the Guild you mentioned — it was the *accomplice's* fault? Seban? You had nothing to do with this going ass over tea kettle?"

Lottie ground her teeth together. "It was for some kind of ancient artifact. A buyer wanted it and the Guild thought I could grab it. That's enough for me. Seban set the entire city guard on me, and I had to run."

"You're working for the Guild now?"

"No," Lottie answered, the single word laced in malice and regret.

Ceci's eyes traveled over Lottie, taking her in. Her eyes snagged on the ripped, one armed jacket sitting on Lottie's chair, the bag touching Lottie's leg, and the ruined and road-worn clothing Lottie wore.

"Your job is entirely too dangerous," said Ceci admonishingly.

"Oh really? I hadn't noticed." Lottie smiled, making sure it dripped with venom. "I do love becoming a pincushion for guards. It makes for an enjoyable lifestyle."

"You're being ridiculous. This — this world you live in. All of it. I told you over and over when you were a child. You should never have gotten mixed up in all of that."

Lottie bristled. "Oh? And what do you do, Ceci? *Still* running a market stall, pawning useless wares rather than actually valuable ones? Sounds like you've changed your life so much since you left me behind. You know how good we were together, thief and seller, finding wares that were actually worth something —"

Ceci stood abruptly, every inch of her seething. She reached into her pocket and threw down coins onto the counter with a clatter, so loud that Briar and the patron down the bar flinched toward them. As though she could physically feel the gazes turning to them, Ceci straightened and wiped her angry expression blank, sliding one of her perfected masks on. She looked down at Lottie over her nose. "I'm going home. Goodnight."

"Wait," said Lottie, standing up and following her to the door. "Listen, Ceci, I —"

Lottie stepped from the Old'n Narrow after her as Ceci stormed off. Lottie stood in the middle of the dark cobblestones outside of the Old'n Narrow, watching Ceci leave, feeling as though her life was steps away from being upended once more.

Ceci didn't look back.

Watching her sister walk away from her again, Lottie never felt so sober in her life.

"Fuck," she said softly to the darkness. A chilled autumnal breeze wrapped itself around Lottie, sending shivers straight down her spine.

Why, Lottie, she thought to herself. *Why do you always find yourself watching her walk away?*

"Hey," said a soft voice behind her. She turned to find Aeric standing there, pulling on a coat, door to the Old'n Narrow closing behind him. He was illuminated by the moon and a nearby flickering lantern, handing her her bag and jacket that she'd forgotten inside. "Everything okay?"

"Yeah," she said with a forced laugh, trying desperately to tamp every awful emotion roiling in her down deep inside. She bundled her things close to her chest. She did not want to cry in front of this complete stranger. "Thanks."

"No problem at all."

"Do you know of a good place to spend the night?"

Aeric softened, looking at her with a gentle lace of concern as his eyes skated over her features. "Why don't you come with me, you don't seem like you should be alone right now."

"Oh?" She tilted her head up slightly, gazing down at him over her nose with a sultry smile that she had to rip up from the depths of her soul to pull onto her face. Her core felt raw, like a gaping wound, and if she didn't fill it with something in the next ten minutes, she was going to fully shatter on the overly charming cobblestone street around her.

He could be a good solution. She appraised him anew, running her eyes across his face and down his body. His casually confident stance, his long sheet of black hair, the gently concerned expression on his face, and the angles of his cheekbones that were almost sharp enough to cut if she touched them — everything about him was exactly the kind of distraction she needed.

"Aeric, you truly could be the best solution right now."

His mouth opened in slight surprise, then, as though trying to stop himself from laughing, he crinkled his nose in an absolutely adorable way. "Oh honey, you're not my type."

"Ah. Right. Okay."

"No — ah, gods, I'm — I'm gay."

"Oh, oh shit, I'm sorry." Lottie took a shaky step back and stumbled on a cobble, before letting out a high-pitched laugh. "I really shouldn't just throw myself at strangers, should I?"

"No worries at all, it happens a lot. Come on," he said, extending his arm as he winked at her. "Let's get you somewhere warm."

To her absolute horror, she burst into tears.

13

A LETTER TO BEROLD

Lottie – 34 Days Before

Bright sunlight streamed into the room directly into Lottie's eyes, waking her. She squinted and turned away from it, peering around the room with a frown. It took her slightly too long to realize where she was, pulling together the events of the night before.

As though she had been run over by a carriage going full speed, she felt the guilt and the hangover in one. Ceci's face swam in her mind's eye, making her headache double. *That was quite possibly the worst way that our reunion could have gone*, she thought, letting her head fall back onto the pillow.

A soft snore sounded beside her, reminding her that she was not alone. Lottie sat upright slowly, taking in the sleeping elf next to her. Even in slumber, he was entirely too attractive. His hair was an ink spill against the pillow, framing his sleep-softened face.

He had been so lovely last night, too, from what she could remember through the haze of her hangover. Chatting amiably with her, giving her water, talking about nothing important when she made it clear she did

83

not want to discuss her sister. And he had even let her sleep in his bed, after all that.

Lottie spilled clumsily out of bed and headed toward the bathroom and the waiting wash basin, running her hands through her hair to tame the birds nest it had become through the night. With quick, practiced efficiency, she braided it back into her two braids, feeling slightly more alive.

Once reconnected with her bag, she peered back over at Aeric, still sound asleep in bed. *I should probably just leave,* she mused, trying to push the memory of him taking care of her from her mind. She bit her lip and padded back toward him, digging around in her bag until she found a small scrap of parchment and left a small *thank you* note next to him.

Lottie made her way out of Aeric's place and into the bright autumnal sunshine, pulling her bag up onto her good shoulder. Surprisingly, her injured shoulder didn't ache as much as she expected — in fact, it felt nearly back to normal, thanks to Emmett's ministrations. She wasn't sure if she would need to change the bandages, but it probably wouldn't hurt picking up some fresh ones, just in case.

And, *gods*, she needed a few changes of clothes. The farmer's shirt she stole was lovely and keeping her nice and warm, but she couldn't wear it every day she was here. From the looks of it, her pants, too, still coated in road dust, needed a desperate wash.

The weight of the artifact settled against her hip, reminding her of its presence.

She glanced around the street in front of her, noting the throngs of people milling about. Revealing an ancient artifact that glowed and oozed magic in the middle of a crowded street probably wasn't the best idea, so she simply ran a thumb over the surface a few times, feeling the dulled script there.

I should send a letter to Berold, just to see. Perhaps he knows what's written on here.

With a bit of searching, she found her way to the post office and asked for a bit of parchment, some charcoal, and a pen to write a letter with, before exiting out onto the street and finding a secluded spot to do so. She took a moment to describe the dodecahedron and what little she knew about it, and asked if he knew of an artifact such as this. She then set a spare bit of parchment on one of the twelve sides of the artifact before taking a soft rubbing of what was etched there with the bit of charcoal. It captured an outline of the surface's pattern, including the dulled script. Though illegible to her, perhaps Berold would find something familiar in it.

She rolled both the rubbing and the letter up into a scroll and went back into the post office. Once it was sealed and set to be sent with the day's mail, she asked for any letters addressed to Lottie Luck to be delivered to the Old'n Narrow on Fetterly Place.

Then she set off into Arrowmount.

By day, the town looked entirely different. The decorative fluttering flags lined above the streets tossed around joyfully in the chilly autumn wind, their multicolored facades faded from the summer sun. She turned down another street at random and found a bunch of townsfolk in the process of taking down a length of entirely sun-bleached ones. Lottie wondered briefly if they took down the flags for the winter season, or if they kept replacing the older ones with new ones as their colors faded, no matter the time of year. She couldn't imagine the winter storms along the seaside were good for the delicate decorations.

She spent the next little bit finding her way through the town, acquiring a fresh bundle of bandages from a lovely dwarf manning a minuscule hole-in-the-wall medicine shop, and a few worn, used bits of clothing that would help keep her warm in the cooling temperatures. The wares ate at the remainder of coin she had, but she wasn't planning on truly needing much else while she was here.

Unless, of course, she needed to find somewhere other than her sister's place to sleep, then the coin would quickly become a problem. But that wasn't something she was going to ponder — she had to try, at least.

When she found herself back on Fetterly Place for a third time, she stopped in at the plant-covered restaurant called May's Cafe and picked up a couple of hot coffees and asked her way to the market stalls to see Ceci.

May as well show up with something in hand, soften the blow of my arrival, she thought. It was a good way to start an apology.

The market stalls appeared a little way down the street, a cluster of wooden and metal structures of all different styles grouped strategically along the large, open central square, surrounded by buildings. Some had colorful cloth hangings to protect from the sun, others with nothing but a table of wares in front of them, and one had a spectacular plant display growing over a latticework of wood above the stall keeper. Each stall held all kinds of wares, from small trinkets to vegetables and fresh bread.

She spotted a noticeboard in the town center as she passed through, posted all over with bits of messages, some advertising sales and wares now available, and others with odd jobs people were seeking to hire for. The old notice from King Zoren announcing the hunt for the notorious assassin the Shade from last year hung weather-beaten and barely legible. She'd seen a notice that announced the death of the Shade back in Claymore earlier that year, but here, there didn't seem to be one pinned.

It didn't take long for Lottie to spot Ceci's stall as she turned from the board, scanning the area. She caught the sign "MAGIC GOODS" at the top, painted jauntily by hand on a slab of reclaimed wood. The memory of a previous sign, painted by two pairs of hands instead of one, that read "THE MAGIC GOODS OF THE LITTLE SISTERS," surfaced in Lottie's mind before she could shove it down into the depths of her consciousness.

Tiny arcane baubles lined the stall's canopy along the inside above Ceci's head. The stall's surface was covered in a smorgasbord of trinkets — from decorative bric-a-brac to handmade items and statuesque art pieces down to what appeared to be beautiful stones and odd things she'd found were all laid out neatly.

Lottie caught a glimpse of her sister before she saw Lottie. Ceci smiled at a customer as they stopped to chat, her face lighting up in a way that Lottie hadn't seen since they lived back in Alieweth as children. She even stood straighter as she occupied the space behind her stall.

As she talked, Ceci's delicate, branch-like hands moved animatedly, drawing Lottie's attention to the soft, burnt-orange knitted fingerless gloves she wore. They matched a thin headband running around her ears, contrasting her green hair. Steam rose from a large plate next to her with an incredibly gooey pastry that was stabbed through with a fork.

Ceci smiled after the customer as they left her stall with a wave, before she began to scan the market. Lottie's heart snapped in two as the open, kind expression shuttered itself the moment Ceci noticed her. The smile on Ceci's face faded into an expressionless, closed-off line. Her posture shifted into one akin to a soldier putting on armor as Lottie walked up. She crossed her arms over her chest and lifted an eyebrow at her sister.

"Morning," Lottie said carefully, extending one of the coffees to her. "I figured that you might want something hot to stay warm."

Ceci let out the tiniest sigh before reaching for the drink, wrapping her fingers around it as though they were seeking warmth. They probably were, even with her fingerless gloves. Lottie remembered the long winter nights when her sister's fingers and toes would turn to ice, the dainty limbs seeking out any little bit of warmth they could.

"Where is the pastry from?" said Lottie after an awkward beat of silence, hunting for something to say.

"Gable's, over there," said Ceci softly, pointing to a baked goods stall tucked in next to some of the fresh produce. Lottie tried to sneak a peek at the baker, but too many people stood in the way. "They like to treat us stall owners to something warm and tasty occasionally."

The two looked away from one another as another customer came up, talking to Ceci about one of the pieces on her table. Ceci, without fail, managed to slip back into her charming self and sold the piece with barely a hassle, before turning back to her sister.

Ceci sniffed and took a tentative sip of the coffee, the softest glimmer appearing in her eyes. "May's?"

"I hope you still like cinnamon in your coffee."

Ceci glanced at her briefly. "I do. This is good."

Lottie swallowed and tried not to let the warm feeling of approval settle over her shoulders. It was just coffee, after all. "I wanted to clear the air."

"Mm?"

"You know, since I am going to be around for a bit," said Lottie peering down at her fingernails. "I want to apologize for the scene I caused last night."

"It would be nice if you had been more civil," said Ceci. She pulled some of her pastry apart, revealing a melted stream of buttery cinnamon through the middle of it, and popped it into her mouth.

Lottie turned partially away, hugging her injured arm to her chest unconsciously, a chill breeze slicing through the stalls. "Do you know any good place to stay? Something not overly pricey, since I don't have any way of making money while I'm here, and don't really have a lot on me at the moment."

"Don't be silly," said Ceci, ducking behind her stall for a moment, pulling out a few more wares and placing them on her counter. "You can stay at mine."

"Yeah? I thought maybe after last night, you..." Lottie let the end of the sentence hang.

"What would it look like to leave you staying at some inn when I have a perfectly good apartment?"

Ah, of course Ceci would be concerned about the way it would appear to others if she left her sister, who'd arrived out of nowhere after a decade, to stay in an inn. "Well, thanks."

"However," said Ceci, turning to her. "I do not want any of your work coming home with you. In fact, while you're here, you're not going to do that job at all."

"Yes, sure," said Lottie automatically, trying not to think about the artifact in her bag or the letter she had just sent off. Hopefully, if the Guild wanted anything to do with her after this, they wouldn't come calling in person. Letters could be hidden. A person, much less so.

"And I don't want to be cleaning up after you, either," Ceci continued, picking apart another piece of her pastry meticulously, not eating it. "You did have a tendency to leave things trailing behind you."

"Right," said Lottie quickly. "Of course."

Ceci hesitated for a moment, looking wary, a small crease appearing between her eyebrows. "Okay."

"Okay."

14
MAGIC GOODS

Kir – 34 Days Before

I should've brought Nudge with me, thought Kir, peering down at Della who barely made it up to Kir's kneecaps, scrambling to keep up even as Kir slowed to half her normal speed. Nudge loved the elderly gnomes — he especially loved that they often carried food in their giant bags, which he would shove his whole face into at any opportunity — but both Della and Neema did not enjoy the greathound, seeing as he was taller than them.

But today, like most days, Nudge had accompanied her father to the smithy. So Kir was stuck with Della at her side, where she'd been since Kir arrived in the market to pick up fresh bread and vegetables for the bar. Kir wasn't entirely sure what reason Della had for following her around this morning, but as so far, it seemed motivated entirely by her need to tell Kir the inner workings of the Moon Festival volunteers' drama.

"...and you must know that all the volunteers have to do not only the work for their separate committee but also help with just general festival work, which is proving to be rather annoying to get anyone to want to help." Della huffed impatiently. "Don't even get me started on how Eiris gets going about their partner's piano when any of us actually want to get work done!"

Kir stopped at the vegetable stall and nodded to Pakon, a young copper-skinned goliath manning the stall positively bursting with fresh produce. Kir held out her crate that had only a few bits inside and a list that Briar and Corwek had given her. Pakon gave Kir a knowing smile as they began to fill the crate, eyes shooting toward Della.

"And — oh, those are lovely muskmelons, Pakon, goodness — we still are waiting to hear anything about the Games Committee's plans for their changes to the beach layout, which worries me," Della continued, peering at the array of vegetables in front of her. "But, then again, they always worry me. They do pull things together at the end."

"Mmm," said Kir without much emotion before nodding as Pakon held up a couple apples with an eyebrow raised. They weren't on the list for the day, but Corwek often made a killer crumbly apple dessert if the feeling swayed him.

"Ah, Kirandir darling, I must leave you, I have to do my own shopping," said Della, reaching up and patting Kir on the thigh. "Let me know if you need anything!"

Kir peered down, but Della was already bustling off into the throng of the market with nothing but a backward wave. The multitude of maroon knitted clothes draped over her billowed out like wings as she greeted another stall owner.

"She's roped you into helping with the festival?"

Kir turned back to Pakon and accepted the now mostly full crate, hefting it to rest on her hip. "Yeah, you could say that."

"When there's a will, Della will find a way," they said, waving Kir off with the goods. "Briar came by earlier with the weekly deposit, so no charge."

Kir headed toward Gable's stall that had an array of freshly baked breads and pastries, her eyes traveling over the crowd of people around her. She waited in line behind an older man with salt-and-pepper hair bundled in layers of tweed and his partner, an elegant elf with the longest ears Kir had ever seen, as they debated over their weekly bread purchase. From her height, Kir couldn't see much, as her view was mostly obscured by the stall canopies, so she entertained herself by peering at those who passed by.

The couple smiled up at her as they left the stall, a bag of fresh pastries and two long sticks of bread in hand, the man's round spectacles winking in the thin autumn sunshine. Gable smiled at Kir softly as she stepped up, their kind eyes crinkling at the corners as they always did.

A chill wind sliced through the market stalls and tossed Gable's short, auburn hair awry, turning their cheeks slightly pink. They tucked a stray bit behind their long, pointed ear, before reaching for Kir's partially filled crate. Their fingers were protected from the chilly morning air in thick handmade fingerless gloves, and a thick new scarf was wrapped twice around their neck, cozy as a blanket.

"Same as always?"

Kir nodded and glanced at her list, noticing a small note Corwek had added at the bottom in his spiky writing. "And any hard ends you have left from yesterday, Corwek has a new dessert he's trying."

Gable's eyes lit up before loading Kir's crate with a few choice pieces of baked goods. They dug around behind their stall for a moment before withdrawing a cloth bag of discarded ends and day-old bread, sliding it in as well. "Oh, I'll definitely have to swing by later, I love what he does with sugar."

Kir chuckled and shifted the crate back on her hip. As she stepped away from Gable's stall, her eyes caught on a flash of summer green. Kir scanned the crowded market, wondering what it had been.

Kir ducked around the awning of Gable's stall and spotted Cecily Little, the owner of the Magic Goods stall, talking to Della as the gnome gestured brightly. Some folds of the tiny old lady's clothing fell into her neck, and she adjusted them with a huff, sliding her capacious bag higher up on her shoulder. Cecily nodded amiably at something Della said, taking a gentle sip from a large mug.

That must've been the green, she thought, peering at Cecily's hair. Slightly confused at herself for focusing in so fiercely on such a trivial detail, Kir started to turn away before her eyes fell on another figure that shifted into view.

Oh.

Lottie Luck. Or rather... Lottie *Little*? That was her sister's last name.

Lottie stood off to the side of Cecily's stall, looking between Cecily and Della with a slightly wary expression on her face.

Kir absently shifted closer, pretending to peer at the stalls around so she could see Lottie more clearly. As far as Kir knew, Cecily had lived here for about a decade, and in all that time she hadn't had any familial visitors.

I wonder where she's been, she thought, eyeing Lottie.

The closer she approached, the clearer Kir could hear the tail end of their conversation.

"...It just occurred to me," said Cecily, tilting her head to peer at Lottie. The movement brought both sister's faces into view. Kir tracked the similarities of both of their faces, from the matching soft planes of their noses to the high rounded cheek bones, and the mirrored dip between their eyebrows as they looked at one another with surprising animosity. "Since my sister is going to be staying in town for a while on a break from her work, she'd be perfect to help you! She was just wondering what to fill her time with."

Kir glanced at Lottie's face in time to see a flicker of incredulous annoyance before the woman schooled her features into neat indifference. Della, on the other hand, looked as happy as a four-year-old who had been presented with a chocolate birthday cake bigger than their whole body. She clapped excitedly, her rosy cheeks glowing. "Oh! How wonderful!"

"I'm sure that she would be *more than happy*," said Cecily, eyeing her sister pointedly, "to help with anything you need."

"Lottie, darling, that would absolutely wonderful," said Della, clapping her hands together. "I have the absolute perfect place to put you. It's like the gods themselves sent you here, truly. I'll have to introduce you to — Oh, where did she go —"

Shit.

15

CO-CHAIRS

Kir – 34 Days Before

S *hit shit shit.*

Kir tried to slide away unnoticed back into the crowd in the market, but it was rather difficult to hide when you were the height of most of the stall overhangs.

"Ah! Kirandir, wonderful." Della's strong, age-spotted hand grabbed hold of Kir's free one and steered her toward Cecily and her sister. Trying not to show her intense discomfort, Kir hoped the smile on her face was actually a smile and not the grimace she was feeling.

Cecily hid her expression behind a sip of her coffee as Lottie straightened, locking eyes with Kir.

Gods, she's so pretty. Who let women be this pretty? Kir blinked, taking in the soft whorls of bark detailing Lottie's cheeks and the light dancing in her eyes as her expression softened. Delicate tendrils of her summer-green hair danced in the soft breeze around her face, having escaped from the two long braids it was bound in.

"Kir, this is my sister, Charlotte Li —"

"Lottie Luck, of course," interrupted Lottie, sticking out her hand. Kir managed to not drop the crate of shopping on her hip and blinked at the extended hand. She remembered absently what it had felt like to hold from the bar. It was delicate yet strong, and —

Right. She actually needed to *shake* Lottie's hand.

"I remember. You're the woman from the bar," said Kir, her mouth saying the most obvious thing she could have.

Kir quickly enveloped Lottie's fingers in hers, immediately noticing a number of rough calluses along Lottie's skin. They weren't the same as the ones along Kir's hands, from playing an instrument for one's entire life, but something similar — perhaps they were craftsmen hands, specialization hands like Morgam or Khar —

Kir, seriously, get a grip. They're just hands. *And you might want to let go.*

Lottie smiled and lifted one eyebrow. "Yes, I am. It's nice to see you again, Kir."

She was still holding Lottie's hand. *Oh, Icharr's tits —*

Kir dropped it and took a half-step back, clearing her throat. Lottie settled into the side of her sister's stall and crossed both arms, gazing at Kir with a soft smirk playing on her lips.

"Right, uh, yes I wanted to, um —" Kir cleared her throat again as Lottie's eyes skated across her face. "I, uh."

Della saved Kir from saying anything further by cutting in, both physically and verbally as she stepped between them and put her hand on Kir's thigh once again, drawing her attention. "Kir, Lottie here has volunteered to be your co-chair! Isn't that fantastic?"

Lottie froze, looking down at the elderly gnome in confusion.

"What?"

"Well, you need help, don't you, Kir?" Della beamed. "There is barely a month left until the Moon Festival, after all. And you Lottie, are here to help, so why not pair the two of you together? Kir may be an incredibly capable woman, but it never hurts to have an extra mind and opinion by your side, especially when it comes to the arts."

As though the concept was entirely foreign to her, Lottie glanced at her sister before mouthing *co-chair?* Cecily attempted to hide a bemused smile behind her coffee mug.

Della tapped Kir amiably on the thigh before sighing happily.

"Well, ladies, I must be off," she said, waving at them, stepping away from Cecily's stall. "Neema is waiting for me and my still-to-be-done shopping."

Kir, Lottie, and Cecily watched as Della puttered off into the market again, waving to a few of the vendors, who immediately started to do whatever she called after them.

"Co-chairs," said Lottie under her breath. "Right."

"Sorry," said Kir, without really knowing what she was apologizing for. Della? Kir's awkwardness? Lottie being roped into it all? Everything above?

Lottie shrugged and shot a murderous glance at her sister before turning to Kir with a charming smile. The hasty shift in her expression unsettled Kir. "Well, what does that entail, exactly?"

"Uh," said Kir, as she tried to parse an actual sentence together, blinking more than she should be. "I-I don't know. Tonight?"

"What about tonight?"

"Let's meet. At the bar." Kir cleared her throat and let out a sigh. "By then I'll know what, uh, all of this," she gestured vaguely with her free hand, "should entail." At this rate, she didn't think it was likely she would know, but maybe by then she could get her mouth to function properly.

"Okay." Lottie nodded. "The bar. After your set, I presume."

"Yes."

Kir could have sworn that Cecily had just choked back a laugh in her throat as she took a hurried sip of her coffee. The three of them stood together for a moment, silence falling between them like a brick.

"Right. I — I have —" and she jostled the crate on her hip slightly before she nodded again and headed off toward the bar, cheeks burning.

Lottie called after her, her voice warm and clear over the din of marketgoers. "See you, Kir."

Kir hefted the crate up higher on her hip as she shouldered open the back door of the Old'n Narrow, releasing a torrent of sound. Corwek sang at the top of his lungs as he stood over the sizzling cook top, his boisterous mostly in tune voice greeting Kir as she lifted the crate for him to see, before moving to the storage unit and cold box on the opposite wall.

Partnered with Lottie Luck.

Kir dug out handfuls of potatoes and slid them into a nearly empty bucket. Partnered with someone she had just met, didn't know anything about, and who was so incredibly beautiful it was already a problem being around her. How was Kir going to get anything done if the only words that came out of her were half-formed sentences?

You have to get over that, she scolded herself. *No one likes to be stared at like they're a museum piece. She's a person, treat her like one.*

Kir's mind churned back to the fact that she was definitely, no-going-back, locked into this position. A position of leadership. Entertainment Committee Chair. *Co-*chair, she corrected herself.

Her purchased vegetables found their way into the buckets and boxes on the storage shelf, filling up any missing produce, as Kir's brain whirred with senseless noise, trying to land on something more than her internal monologue of panic.

16

A NAME IN ARCANE LIGHTS

Lottie – 34 Days Before

Lottie found her way to the Old'n Narrow as the first few stars appeared in the sky, walking with her shoulders up by her ears and jacket-less arm close to her side to keep the chilled evening air away. She was going to have to mend her jacket soon.

Tonight, music spilled out in waves of warmth, calling deep into her bones. As she stepped through the doors, the bar hummed with a softer energy than the night before. This time, no one was dancing, but the mood was light and happy.

She smiled at Briar who filled tankards behind the bar and winked over at Aeric who served drinks to patrons at their tables. He lifted his eyebrows briefly at her before winking.

Briar leaned over the bar and set a tankard down, full of delicious golden liquid. "Ale?"

Lottie grinned her thanks before turning her attention to Kir playing in the corner. Her music tonight was intricate and evocative, drawing Lottie in even more that the heart pumping beat the night before.

"*...Round the sea, winding clearly*

A song came to his ear so truly

The song of Adelina."

Gods, this woman can play, she thought to herself, watching Kir's fingers pluck at the strings on her lute. Lottie leaned on the bar and frowned slightly, trying to conflate the magnetic woman playing in front of her with the awkward, standoffish person she had talked to earlier.

Much later, once Kir had stopped playing and the bar began to empty out, Lottie moved to an empty table with two tankards of ale to wait for Kir. Kir vanished into the back with her lute and returned, oddly, with a box full of blank parchment. Lottie was rather glad to see Kir's wild, thick black hair still unbound and around her shoulders.

Kir hesitated slightly before putting the box down on the table, her throat moving as she swallowed. She carefully slid the crate closer to Lottie. "I thought... for notes."

Lottie nodded, glancing up at her. "Are you going to sit?"

"Right." Kir cleared her throat and sat, scratching at the short-cropped side of her hair a few times. Kir caught her eye, before looking instead to the box of parchment, then the table, then down to her lap. This woman was so unlike the easy, confident performer that Lottie had been in awe of all night it almost didn't make sense. Almost. Lottie knew a fair bit about how people could slide into a performance or a hidden part of themselves easier than breathing.

Kir moved then, scraping her hair up into a familiar bun, erasing the last bit of the musician. Lottie made a sound in the back of her throat without meaning to.

Kir's stone-grey eyes snapped up to hers. "What?"

"I really like your hair down," said Lottie without thinking. She bit her tongue to stop rectifying it, and instead smiled at Kir, hoping that would ease the weird, awkward tension between them.

Kir's eyes locked on Lottie, gaze intensifying, as though she was seeing through into her soul. Lottie shifted on the wooden chair beneath her, slightly uncomfortable being stared at so intently. Kir's eyes, a slightly darker shade of grey than her skin, shimmered with something Lottie couldn't name.

Kir sat back, still gazing at her. She put her hands out on the table and stretched out her fingers before tensing them into fists. Every inch of her was taught like a string on her lute, like sitting at this table with Lottie was the last thing she wanted to be doing.

To break the tension building, Lottie leaned forward. "Now it's my turn to ask. What? Is there something on my face?"

Kir's cheeks darkened slightly before she coughed, blinking rapidly. "Uh, no. Not at all, sorry." She sniffed and reached into the box for a spare bit of parchment.

"Alright, well." Lottie raised her eyebrows at Kir before letting it go. *Maybe she's just nervous.* "Let's start. What exactly does the Entertainment Committee do, then?"

"Plan what entertainers will be at the festival, when they perform, and where they go."

"Do we... host auditions?"

"Yes."

"So... we'll be planning the flow of the performances, putting performers where they will be best during the day, helping them during the festival?" Lottie took a deep breath as Kir nodded and started running through the possibilities of planning in her head. Kir's face flickered with unease as she ran a hand across her face, staring at the empty page.

Lottie softened her face into a conspiratorial smile. "Can I confess something to you?"

"Uh, sure?"

"I don't even know what this festival is for."

"You don't have a Moon Festival where you live?"

Seeing as Lottie hadn't properly lived somewhere for longer than a couple years at a time, and even when she did, she was most often out hunting for artifacts, so taking stock of local festivals was the least of her worries.

"I suppose there might have been, but." She shrugged lightly. "I don't really even know what gods they worshiped there, other than the usual big ones like Iluinn."

"The Moon Festival honors the change of seasons," started Kir. Lottie noticed a soft crease appear between her eyebrows, as though thinking something over. The more she talked, too, Kir's shoulders relaxed. "I think at one point it had something to do with the goddess Servune directly, since the moon is her child in the myths, right?"

"Right, yes, I remember my sister reading me some of those."

"The Moon Festival happens at the end of the transition of the moon across the sky, as it changes into the Hunter Moon. Once I think it was a big religious thing, but Arrowmount is now — I don't know —" Kir shrugged and motioned around as though that encompassed her point totally. "Less traditional. People care more about the food and the activities set up, something to last us into the colder months."

"Mm, okay." Lottie began to trace her finger around the lip of her tankard, letting a demure smile leak onto her face. "What about you, Kir? What do you like best about the festival?"

"I enjoy the music."

A laugh came from behind them as Aeric approached, sliding his arms into his jacket. "That's an understatement, Kir," he said, placing a hand on Kir's shoulder. "If you merely enjoyed the music, we wouldn't be where we are today, would we?"

Kir rolled her eyes.

"Has Kir told you how she wants to be a star yet, Lottie?" Aeric glanced over at Lottie, his eyes alight with pleasure. "Our Kir wants to see her name in arcane lights."

"Oh, does she now?" Lottie smiled, matching Aeric's flirty energy and leaning on the table, resting her chin on her knuckles. She let her eyes travel across Kir's face and lifted an eyebrow. "Do tell."

"There's really nothing to tell," said Kir, looking distinctly uncomfortable.

Aeric snorted and patted Kir on the shoulder. "Sure, sure. Anyways, Kir, Lottie, I'm off — goodnight, ladies."

He waved back at Briar and Nova who were behind the bar, cleaning out mugs, before heading out the front door.

Lottie shook her head and turned back to Kir. "You want to be... famous, then?"

"Um, no, not... not that." Kir grimaced and shifted on her chair. "I... I have always wanted to be more."

"You're pretty great, from what I've seen. Exceptionally talented."

Kir's cheeks darkened as she dropped her gaze to her hands. "Yes, well. I want to maybe — I don't know, it's silly."

"I don't think having a dream is silly at all."

The bard cleared her throat. "I'd like to bring my music to people for more than just nightly entertainment. I want to create stories, to share them with as many people I can."

"I like that idea," said Lottie. She appraised Kir anew, from her sharp grey eyes to her slightly wary expression, down to the softly calloused hands resting on the table. "Really. I mean, you're probably going to have a bit of a hard time here in a tiny seaside town, but..."

Surprisingly, Kir chuckled. "Well, dreams are dreams for a reason. One day, maybe I'll get out of here and see more of the empire. Anyways."

Kir leaned closer over the table as she pulled the crate to her, peering inside. She brought with her the soft scent of lemony soap and something distinctly warm that made Lottie want to curl up in her lap. Lottie caught herself leaning in and quickly sat back, taking a hasty gulp of her ale.

Get a grip, Lottie, she thought, feeling incredibly ridiculous. *Kir is a practical stranger, rein it in.*

"We should start with the basics."

"Basics it is. Let's make a list of to-dos." Lottie sat up a little straighter as Kir unearthed a pen from the crate. Without hesitating, Lottie reached for it, wanting to do something with her hands.

As they sat there, slowly mulling over what their tasks would be, Lottie learned a bit more about what to expect from this festival. The Moon Festival ran annually over four days, which was a surprisingly long time to Lottie. *That is going to be a lot of space to fill,* she thought.

"There are always a bunch of different kinds of performances," explained Kir, absently rubbing the shaved side of her head. "Some that have to be set up outside, some inside. Storytellers and musicians don't really need much other than space and their voices — but the puppet and magic shows might need specific things. And dancers as well."

"Ooookay," said Lottie slowly, marking a few columns on the parchment in front of her, labeling INSIDE and OUTSIDE across the left, and DAY and NIGHT across the top. "We need people to fill both inside and out, day and night. Storytellers — daytime?"

"Daytime mostly," answered Kir, tilting her head back and forth, considering. "Some work best for children's entertainment, some move throughout the town, and some will set up in one spot to draw listeners in. Then there's always one or two to fill the spaces at night, before and after the musical arrangements."

"Before and after?"

"Before to set the mood, after to bring the energy down and wind out the night."

"Ah, got it." Lottie made notes in quick, neat writing that sprinted across the page in front of her. "And did you say — puppets?"

"They're some of the more intricate acts, but always worth seeing. I guess we'll see what kind of acts come through, but hopefully we can advertise for any and all."

Lottie was vaguely interested. "Are there a lot of people who are repeat entertainers?"

"We do see repeats, yes. Regulars, fan favorites." Kir took a slow draw of ale. "But sometimes new folks come in and audition. Changes it up year to year."

"Do we need to book performances for the entire time? All four days, all day and night?"

Kir shook her head. "No, but enough to keep folks interested. We'll have to schedule them in, but there are usually breaks where people can decide to look at the other aspects of the festival, if they haven't yet. But what people usually all come out for is the closing spot."

"That'll be a big spot to fill."

"I'm the closing act."

Lottie blinked up at her. *Just like that?*

"Not — not that I'm picking for myself," said Kir, cringing slightly. "Della and — it was part of the deal. For my trouble."

"That's fantastic, Kir. And an even better chance to garner attention if you want to one day leave and test out other crowds, no?"

Kir snorted. "It's compensation for taking over with such short notice, nothing else."

"I'm serious, Kir." Lottie leaned toward her and carefully touched Kir's hand. The heat of Kir's skin radiated through Lottie's fingers. "You're very good at what you do, and I've only seen you play twice. I'm not surprised that they want you to close out the festival."

She wrote Kir's name in the end slot on her list with a flourish as the bard herself blushed furiously across the table.

Lottie was a little surprised to see how frazzled Kir became the more they discussed about the festival. She rubbed her hands over her face so often that her fingers kept tugging her bun loose. The fifth time she redid it, Lottie couldn't help but melt inside, watching her nimble fingers twist up in the same practiced way.

As the bar around them emptied of its last patron, Lottie took their few notes and stacked them on top of one another. Her eyes itched with tiredness. "I can't look at any of this anymore."

"I should head out," Kir said, grabbing the parchment and placing it into the box. "It's late. Sorry about having the meeting at this time."

"I don't mind, I'm a creature of the night anyway." Lottie wiggled her eyebrows to punctuate her point and stood, too. She let her eyes travel up Kir's chest to her face, smiling a sultry, suggestive smile. Old habits die hard, apparently.

Kir furrowed her brow before she took a step back, lifting the box in her arms almost like a shield. "Um. See you."

"Right." Lottie let out a soft sigh. Well, she had to try. It seemed as though Kir simply wasn't interested in her. "Goodnight, Kir."

17

BY THE TINIEST SLICES

Kir – 34 Days Before

The kitchen glowed with soft lantern light as Kir walked in the front door to their house. Her father was sitting at the table, halfway through the local newspaper, ARROWMOUNT TODAY.

"Kiri!" He stood and immediately enveloped her in a hug, the paper crinkling noisily between them. One of his tusks dug into the side of her face as he squeezed her tight.

When he let her go, she set her lute case down in its usual spot by the workroom door. Nudge lifted himself up off the floor with a happy huff, walking over to demand pets. "What're you still doing up, Dad?"

"What do you..." her father glanced toward the dark window and let out a sound of surprise. "That's why I'm so tired — your brother had me in the workroom when we got home from the smithy, showing me something to do with a new pitting technique that he figured out with a wood chisel, but to use on very thin sheets of metal. Next thing —"

"You were both starving, and it was four hours later?" Kir smiled

108

before moving toward the leftovers sitting on the counter. Cold stew greeted her, but she took a spoonful all the same as she heated up the pan. It was her father's best recipe. Delicious, perfectly seasoned meat practically melted on her tongue.

"It was more like six this time. Then I decided to pick up the paper I had intended on reading with breakfast, and here we are." Her father settled back into his chair in the kitchen, Nudge following suit by settling around his feet with a low groan. He wasn't used to staying up this late, and whenever that happened, Nudge made sure everyone knew how displeased he was. Her father bent over and gave Nudge a scratch between the ears, chuckling. "Khar has some incredibly nimble hands. I'm constantly surprised by him."

"Has he figured out what he's making out of that piece of wood yet?"

"Nope," answered Khar himself as he padded into the kitchen from the workroom. "But we'll find out sooner or later, I suppose."

Kir smiled at her older brother as the stew on the stove began to heat through. "What's this new technique you've discovered?"

"It started with a specific angle that I needed," he explained, holding up both hands to demonstrate. "Everything has to be done by the tiniest of slices, almost the width of a hair. Incredibly time consuming, when done the usual way. But I've discovered, if I lean the piece at a specific angle, the wood peels away in sheets so thin that you can almost see through them. Exactly what I need. Then I tried it on a piece of metal at the smithy today, and it works beautifully for minuscule detail work."

"Interesting," answered Kir, raising her eyebrows at their father, who shrugged in response. Neither of them really knew much about wood-working, but it was great when Khar became so animated talking about it that both of his hands moved at once.

"How was work, Kiri?" asked her father. "Did you get any further with that committee thing?"

"Work was fine, as always." Kir frowned at her father but wasn't surprised that he'd already heard about her taking over the Entertainment Committee. News traveled fast in a small town. She fished a wooden spoon out of a container nearby and stirred once. "Della assigned me a co-chair."

"Oh?"

"Yeah. She's okay, I think," said Kir, conjuring up the image of Lottie in her head. "Her sister is Cecily, you know —"

"Hmm, her sister?" Khar leaned on the back of a chair, eyebrows knitting together. He and Cecily had known each other for quite some time, nearly as long as Cecily had been living in Arrowmount. Kir was fairly sure that they had dated a while back, too.

Kir nodded and turned toward her stew, watching as tiny bubbles were beginning to form. "I don't really know what to expect of her, but hopefully she'll help."

Khar cleared his throat behind her. "Is she... pretty?"

"Yeah." Kir thought back to Lottie dancing with Aeric the first night she saw her, and the way the sunshine in her soul seemed to cast a real-life glow on the others around her. It wasn't really that Lottie was pretty — because gods, she was — but it was more along the lines that Lottie might possibly be the most interesting person to look at. "She's not like Cecily at all. Cecily's very thin and delicate, but Lottie's all curves — and she's strong, too. She's got this life to her, and —"

She turned back to the kitchen, where Morgam had appeared, covered in paint, standing frozen in the middle of the floor with his mouth slightly open. Khar looked as though he was trying to hold back a laugh, and her dad glanced at both her brothers, a significant look on his face.

She blinked at them. "What?"

"It sounds like you might like this girl, Kiri," said her father happily, his eyes glittering in the flickering lantern light.

"I've never heard you say so many words in one go before," said Morgam, teasing. "Except maybe when you were chewing our ears off about your lute and the music you were playing. You must *really* like her."

Kir snorted, waving her stew spoon at them. "I only just met her."

"Yeah, but you think she's *pretty,*" said Morgam with a suggestive wiggle of his eyebrows. "Full of *life.*"

Khar laughed. "You absolutely have a crush on this girl."

"She's definitely got to be something out of this world," said Morgam, sliding into a kitchen chair and leaning over the table. "I mean, who do we know has ever caught Kir's eye?"

Their father chuckled amiably, leaning back and crossing his arms over his chest to appraise Kir's face. "She's got to be an absolute stunner, that's for sure."

"Seriously? You're all on this page right now? I literally just met her. I don't even know what she's like. Her and Aeric seem to get along, though."

"Aeric?" Khar sucked in a bit of breath through his teeth. "Ah. She's already been corrupted by him, that's a point off in her favor."

Morgam coughed. "What's wrong with Aeric?"

"You know what Aeric does," said Khar with a wave of his hand.

Kir pointed the spoon at him sharply, causing a bit of stew to fall to the floor. Nudge lapped it up quickly. "Khar, you know those are all rumors, and that's it. He's wonderful. Lottie... she has the same way of holding herself when talking to someone that he does," said Kir, trying to explain. "Confidence."

"Flirty, outgoing," said Morgam. "Gotchya."

"This is all beside the point," said Kir, brandishing her spoon at them all. "I don't like her like that."

"Yes, you do-o," sing-songed Khar as he pushed away from the table, giving her a smug grin. "I look forward to meeting her."

"She must be wonderful," reiterated Morgam, following Khar into the workroom. "Seriously. I might just come down to the bar one of these nights to catch a look at her."

Kir rolled her eyes at her brothers as they ducked from the room.

"Kiri, when you do realize that you like this girl, make sure you bring her home so we can all meet her, okay?" Her father winked at her.

She shot him a look.

"Alright, alright, what do I know." He put up both hands in surrender and stood. Nudge got up from the floor with particular vigor, realizing that his person was finally heading up to bed. "When I first met your mother, I was a bumbling mess. Couldn't string two words together, let alone a full sentence! She must have thought I was the rudest person alive, just standing there having nothing to say while everyone around us kept up conversation."

"Ugh, not this again," complained Kir amiably, turning off the heat from the stove and grabbing a bowl.

"But, thankfully, she was beautiful enough and smart enough to know why I was having such a hard time opening my mouth around her, and broke through to my insides, turning them all warm and mushy. And before I knew it, I couldn't stop talking." Her father smiled fondly as Kir set her bowl down on the table, taking a seat in the chair her father had just vacated. "Your mother. When she knew what she wanted, she would go for it, no matter what. I thankfully landed in that category, though gods know what her reasoning was."

Kir snorted lightly, amused despite the number of times she'd heard this same diatribe.

"She really was everything." He leaned over and kissed the top of her head before heading toward the stairs, Nudge following in close behind. "Goodnight, Kiri."

Kir sat in front of her stew for a moment, staring through the steam spiraling around her in the dark kitchen. Lottie was beautiful, sure, but that didn't mean Kir *liked* her like that. Maybe it was just because Lottie was new. She did have trouble, sometimes, talking to new people.

Lottie makes your brain stop functioning, which is not your normal reaction to new people, said that traitorous little voice in the back of her mind.

Kir clenched her spoon tight and dug into dinner, trying all the while to shove the image of Lottie's smile from her mind.

18

KNOCK OVER A DRAGON

Lottie – 33 Days Before

Lottie woke for the second time in a row in a strange room. A dark, tiny space came into focus through dusty, unused air. Packed shelving sat ominously tilted toward the bed all around her, as though she was lying in a cave of trinkets. She frowned at the objects around her, illuminated by the slightest bit of light leaking through sealed shutters partially hidden by an array of things at the foot of her bed.

It was more of a closet than a room. The bed itself sat tucked into the shelving, dangerously pushing against a variety of bins hiding even more trinkets, as though it had been an afterthought. Lottie sat up, her head brushing against a piece of decor that was built out of what looked entirely like string and clay beads and peered around the space as best she could.

A thin stream of light leaked between the shelving, slicing a bright line across the bundle of blankets at the foot of Lottie's bed. With careful maneuvering, Lottie managed to shift a few bits on the shelves out of the way to let more light in as she revealed a small window.

Lottie had sat up much too late after she had come home from the Old'n Narrow sewing the arm back on her jacket, trying her best to line up seams to ensure that it didn't look as though an arrow had shot her. Which, unfortunately, proved to be rather trickier than she anticipated.

Lottie found her jacket in a lump on the floor and peered at her sewing job. It wasn't perfect, but it would do. She took pride in the little skills she had picked up over the years of being on her own, but this one — sewing and restoring pieces of her clothing so that she wouldn't have to keep paying other people to do it or continuously buying new pieces — this one made her heart warm in a way she couldn't quite place.

Now awake, she took a moment to finally unwind the bandage around her arm and inspect the wound there. She braced for pain that never arrived as she lifted the cloth away. The whorls of dark, green-brown bark that made up her skin were completely knitted back together. There was only the slightest raised scar where the arrowhead had sliced into her, tracing an uneven line where stitches held her skin together. Other than that, there was hardly any sign of a wound at all.

"Emmett, you're a genius," she whispered, padding into the kitchen to find a knife to cut away the now useless stitches. She hunted in the tiny space for a second before sliding one free of a drawer. Whatever that potion Emmett made was had sped up her healing to an almost unimaginable speed. A soft pang of guilt rang through her gut as she slid a knife tip under the first string and removed it with only the slightest of stings. He could've simply stitched her up and sent her on her way rather than use one of his better creations on her.

I should go back one day and properly apologize, she thought, slicing through the next.

Lottie set the knife down after finishing the rest and peered around her sister's apartment. Last night, most of Ceci's place had been cloaked in darkness, the only pool of light from the two tiny arcane lamps set up in Ceci's and Lottie's rooms. This morning, she got a good look at the space, suddenly awash with a deep nostalgia.

The apartment itself was tiny, set out of the way up a set of stairs in a building off a side street that Lottie couldn't remember the name of. Somehow, Ceci had lucked out with a corner unit, and had windows on two sides of the place, lending a lovely natural light to the swaths of life inside.

Every inch of the place had Ceci written all over it. From the slouchy green couch and matching armchair to the aged wooden cabinets, the well-loved table set to the crockery that lined shelves around the tiny kitchen, it was all Ceci. On every surface and shelf and in every corner, Ceci had nestled some kind of unique piece that might have a place at her stall but was probably something that she had fallen in love with and couldn't let go of. There was also a wooden basket of overflowing half-knitted goods and balls of wool tucked beside the cushy armchair.

The walls were painted a soft yellow and green, colors that were brought up again and again throughout the various art pieces and mirrors on the walls, and in the multitude of plants that had found their way into the mismatched plant pots throughout the place. If Ceci took out all the plants she would probably have much more livable space to move around in, but Lottie knew that her sister would never even dream of it.

Ceci had always insisted on gathering one or two plants and little pieces to make their space feel warm and lived in, even when they didn't know how long they would be there for. Now that she'd been here for a decade, it made sense that Ceci's collecting habit would explode out into the space around her.

To Lottie, having this many things was a hindrance. With a life like hers, owning more than you could carry often meant things were left behind. She missed living in spaces that held this much life.

Pushing these thoughts out of her mind, her eyes traveled back toward the kitchen. Left on the counter, right in the middle, was a mug full of black coffee. She lifted the mug carefully in her hands, noting how cold it was. Lottie didn't mind though. As she took a sip, she closed her eyes, tasting the perfect amount of sugar in the silky black liquid, so strong that it could probably knock over a dragon.

She hadn't realized how much she'd missed Ceci's coffee.

Lottie took her time drinking the coffee before heading back into her room to dress. She carefully redid her braids, smoothing back the bits that had fallen out through the night, and picked up her bag on her way out.

She didn't have a real aim today, other than to enjoy the town. Perhaps she would head off down to the beach, and possibly head to the Old'n Narrow, to check and see if anyone was in.

As she hopped down the last few stairs and stepped off into the crisp day, she felt the weight of the artifact settle against her hip inside her bag. She peeked in, watching the glow of the dodecahedron for a moment.

What would the Guild do if they knew I had this? They'd have to know by now that it was stolen, wouldn't they? Will they come after me?

She swallowed. Without a doubt, they'd come after her. She had what they wanted. If there was anything she'd learned in all her years in this business, it was that you did not cross the Guild. You didn't know when you'd wake up with a knife to your throat.

A nearby animal snuffed, startling her from her thoughts. She turned to find a soft, snoozing dog leaning out of a window that was covered in ivy and vines. He allowed her to pat him between the ears, his fur ruffling up pleasantly under her ministrations and soft cooing, before she headed off toward the bar.

Nova was behind the bar when she entered, the lone person there. The scent of rich, cooking stew wafted toward her, making her empty stomach rumble.

"Morning," she said.

"Ah, miss Lottie Luck," said Nova, smiling at her. "You, my dear, have a knack for knowing where you need to be, don't you?"

"Needed or wanted?" Lottie winked. Nova bent behind the bar and withdrew a small, sealed scroll. Lottie's stomach did a flip.

"Both, of course. The courier was in this morning."

"Why, thank you." Lottie pushed a smile onto her face, taking it. *Berold or the Guild*?

"Shall I save you a seat at the bar for tonight?"

Lottie winced at Nova's knowing look. "I'm pretty sure all of you are going to start thinking I'm obsessed with the bar."

"The bar, sure." Nova smiled.

Lottie pocketed the scroll and left, heading off toward the beach. She found a spot in the middle of the cold, damp sand, looking out toward the waves. With a steadying breath, she withdrew the scroll and sighed. It was tiny, much smaller than she would expect from the scholar — Berold had a knack for writing very lengthy, intricate letters in the past — which only meant one thing. She unfurled the scroll to find Alros' familiar, short and clipped writing.

L —

Boss knows.

Those two words alone sent a sinking stone into Lottie's gut.

CONTACT INFORMED US BEFORE THE NEWS LEAKED THAT IT WAS GONE. I ASSUME YOU HAVE A REASON FOR NOT HANDING IT OFF LAST WE SPOKE. IT WOULD GO A LONG WAY IN SMOOTHING RUFFLED FEATHERS ON OUR END.

I am up north on business and expect an answer as to when you wish to meet when I return to Claymore within three weeks.

- A

Lottie snorted at Alros' audacity. *Would go a long way in smoothing ruffled feathers — expect an answer —* who did he think he was? The Boss himself? Alros had made it very clear that the Guild didn't want anything to do with her and was just using her for her skills, so why would she cooperate now?

She dug around in her bag and withdrew the artifact. The soft, glowing warmth of its magic coursed into her skin, a strange comfort in the chilled sea air. Her curiosity burned once again, wanting to know its story. It was going to be difficult to do anything with it now that the Guild knew she had it. If she didn't hand it off, they were probably going to come hunting.

The smart choice would be to leave Arrowmount, now that Alros knew where she was. But if she did that, the Guild would come here looking for her, and once again Lottie would have brought danger to her sister's doorstep.

You are committed to the festival, said a small voice in her head. *If you leave now, you'll leave Kir alone to struggle against that tight deadline.*

She could handle it on her own, Lottie tried to tell herself. Kir was a capable person. There were other people who could help, weren't there?

The image of Kir fixing her bun for the fifth time from the night before rose in her mind, overwhelmed and at her wits end.

Della did say it was an emergency kind of role, said that pesky voice. *You said yes.*

Lottie sighed. It was only a month. One month until the start of the festival. If Alros had written from Claymore before heading north, there was a little more than two weeks left on his expected deadline. Then, depending on how fast he decided to come hunting, it would take him about that same time to come here, give or take a few days in between.

Lottie didn't doubt for a moment that it would be Alros himself hunting her down, either. She was his responsibility, after all, as her contact with the Guild. It was his fault she was known by them in the first place.

There was about a month for Lottie to figure out what she was going to do about the artifact. A month, then Alros would come knocking.

Right around the start of the Moon Festival. That's when she should be leaving, either with or without the artifact.

Berold still has yet to answer, she thought, running a thumb over the surface of the artifact absently. Perhaps with his letter, she would know whether it was worth pursuing the knowledge this artifact could bring.

Pursuing that knowledge lit something in her soul as she sat on the beach. The idea of taking this piece to Berold, to help him study it and find out what mysteries were etched into its surface, felt like a path had opened up for her to take after this festival business was over with. And after that, who knew what would happen. But this was something.

She stared out at the ocean, breathing in the salty cool air, thinking about the possibilities that could come with this little ancient artifact. If only she could figure out how to keep it out of the Guild's grasp.

19
BEAST OF LONELINESS
Lottie – 28 Days Before

Lottie woke to a rainy, miserable morning. Far-off ocean waves rocked against the shore with a ferocious roar as the wind ripped between the buildings around her. She peered out through the tiny window in her room, watching the storm for a beat, before deciding, rather firmly, that a day like today was best spent inside curled up with a book and a blanket.

There had been an odd tension between her and Ceci for the last few days. They barely saw one another, and when they did, it was as though they were walking on glass. Ceci was gone in the morning when Lottie woke up, and by the time Lottie came home from the Old'n Narrow at night, Ceci was usually tucked in bed fast asleep.

Lottie didn't really know how to open up a conversation with her sister to try and diffuse the weird energy around the two of them — she didn't know if she really wanted to, either.

After poking around Ceci's kitchen for food and coffee, Lottie settled herself on her sister's cushy emerald green couch and picked a book at random from Ceci's small collection shelved beneath a small table nearby and began to read.

Lottie was careful not to leave a single mark on the book as she read, carefully opening it and turning the pages, since she knew that her sister never liked when she bent books, marring their surfaces. Ceci was precious about books, which Lottie never understood, since reading books was their purpose. When a book had signs of being read, it was as though someone had left marks of life behind.

She got so caught up in the book that she ended up on the couch long after she had originally planned to go out. Footsteps sounded on the stairs amidst the sound of rainfall a number of hours later, startling Lottie out of her book as the last few chapters came up, a soft misting of tears in her eyes.

Ceci opened the door and looked vaguely shocked to see her sister on her couch. "Oh."

"I got caught up in this book," Lottie said quickly, holding it up as evidence. Ceci's eyes narrowed. "Don't worry, I was careful with the spine."

Her sister slid out of a soaked cape and popped it on a hidden coat rack that was tucked behind a particularly leafy plant. Lottie watched her sister for a moment as Ceci moved to the kitchen, wringing out her hair in the basin they washed their dishes in. Her usually brilliant and luxurious green hair was limp and stringy around her face as she stood up, flicking her hands with a grimace of distaste on her face.

Ceci disappeared into her room for a few long minutes, which gave Lottie an opportunity to dive back into the book. She polished off the last few chapters in quick succession, becoming caught up in the beautiful prose and the sweeping climax of both the story and the romance.

It was utterly perfect. Lottie laid her head back and sighed, pressing the book into her chest.

"Good read?"

"Exceptional." Lottie turned her head on the couch to see her sister hovering, dressed in dry clothes with her hair piled on top of her head in a sad, sopping bun.

Ceci eyed Lottie's cold mug of coffee resting on the coffee table. "Make sure to clean that up when you're done it."

Lottie let out a sigh and shot her sister a look.

Ceci stalked off into her room once more before she returned with a different book in hand, one marked partway in with a thin slice of parchment that poked out the top. Lottie moved off the couch and stood, stretching up to the ceiling, her body cracking and popping in relief from being curled up for hours, lost in another world.

Wrapping herself in a thick knitted blanket, Ceci dropped into the adjacent armchair, huddling down in the layers for warmth. She looked rather wrung out.

"Are you okay, Ceci?"

"Would you be if you had just spent the day out in the market getting rained on?" Ceci opened her book. "Are you going out?"

"I plan to, yes."

Ceci nodded slowly, shooting her sister one last glance. "Well, enjoy, whatever you're doing."

Lottie walked out of her sister's apartment a while later hoping to head off to the bar to find that warm, golden glow. She popped in and out of shops at random as she made her way toward the Old'n Narrow, trying to avoid the rain. No matter what she did, though, she was soaked through by the time she arrived.

Kir wasn't playing as she walked in, which was gently disappointing.

Lottie would have loved to see that beautiful woman in the corner, serenading the crowd. Instead, the bar was filled with the noise of people talking and laughing, stock full of folks searching out a hearty dinner and a respite from the weather.

Lottie smiled absently, remembering being seated around a table much like this back in Pralon when she'd found a group of like-minded people. The city called them thieves, but they had been so much more than that. They had their own little family and would often find themselves around a table in a noisy bar like this one, exchanging stories.

They hadn't quite been the Guild, the nine of them, but they were close to it in Lottie's mind. They would do anything to protect each other — or so Lottie believed. That had been when she met Seban and his brother, Loth, and had found herself swept up in the world of sneakery. She owed her life and her skills to that group.

A soft ache thudded through Lottie's chest as she scanned the room, settling herself down on a bar stool, letting the conversations wash over her in a wave of noise.

Friends. She knew now that she should never have trusted them to actually be friends. Especially in a world where money ruled all.

"Lottie Luck," said a warm voice. She smiled at Aeric as he leaned against the bar and sat down on the stool next to her, settling his knee against hers. "What brings you here on this awfully rainy evening?"

"Perhaps I'm here to see if there are any other people around who might give me a bit of company for the night." She winked as she turned toward Briar. The barmaid slid a tankard toward her, continuing to talk to other patrons.

"No sister to join you?"

"No, Ceci isn't one to partake in... well I wouldn't know what she partakes in, truth be told. But I know she would rather not be spending the evening with me."

"Hmm." Aeric leaned forward a little more and searched her face for a moment. "I think there is much more to that story, isn't there?"

"Ah, it's rather boring," she said with a soft smile.

"I could go for a boring story, if you have the time later," said Aeric.

"What, you don't have some hot date waiting for you?"

"I haven't had a hot date in years," Aeric snorted. "Well, there were a few dates, but I don't know if I could really call them *hot,*" he conceded. "Besides, being with someone without putting on a show to try achieve an excitable end is much better."

She smiled at the notion of not needing to put on a show. It had been so long since she had spent time with someone who didn't expect something of her.

Aeric stood, adjusting his shirt and nodding to Briar, who slid a couple tankards across the bar to him, motioning to a table in the corner. "When I'm done here, I'll have Corwek cook us up some food to go. What do you say?"

"Darling, that idea sounds like the best thing I've heard all day."

Lottie perched atop Aeric's kitchen counter hours later, a glass of cool water in hand soothing the gentle fog of ale she was seeing through from a night of dancing to Kir's music.

Aeric busied himself with a few dishes left in his sink from earlier in the day, washing them methodically and placing them on a drying rack that hung over the sink. His kitchen was built in a tiny square, the sink trapped between two counters with barely any space for anyone else to occupy the kitchen. He kept brushing up against her knees.

His apartment was fairly dark, with only a couple arcane lights situated around that he mostly kept off. He lit a number of candles when they arrived and only one arcane light above the kitchen, encompassing them in a soft cocoon of light.

"Have you ever fallen in love with someone?" It was like her alcohol-lined tongue was speaking all on its own.

He sighed and shook his head, grabbing a nearby towel to dry his hands. "There have been moments that I thought maybe, but it was really just obsession or infatuation."

"There has to be someone," said Lottie, poking him with her toe. "You're incredibly attractive, there's no one around here who's tried to get to know you?"

Aeric wiggled his eyebrows at her. "You among them."

"Aeric."

"Well," he said with a resigned sigh, "There's this one person."

"There always is."

"He's muscly and tall, and gods is he good with his hands. Not just in the way you're thinking —" he said quickly as she cackled, "he's an artist. But I don't think anything will ever come of it."

"No?"

"He's... he's someone," he said with a long-suffering sigh. "And he made it quite clear that people can never find out about us."

"Well, I'm not people, so don't worry about that." Lottie shook her head, astonished at the unfairness of it all. From the way that Aeric's eyes lit up when he talked about this man, whoever he was, this wasn't just a simple date.

"What about you, Lottie? Ever fall in love, or are you as sad as I am?"

"That's a definite no on the love part." She lifted her water in the air as though addressing a crowd. "I've come to believe that romantic love doesn't truly exist. All those people out there who claim to be in love? It's just a farce they've made up to make us single people sad about our single-dom."

Aeric laughed and leaned against the opposite counter. "You might be right."

"'Course I am. Besides, if love is truly real, then nothing good can ever come of it," she said. "But there's something intoxicating about the unknown of it, I guess."

"I toast to that," said Aeric, picking up his own drink and lifting it in her direction. "You and I, we're cut from the same cloth. We think alike, we like the same drinks, and we recognize the beast of loneliness in one another."

"I'm not *lonely*, I am simply alone."

"Lottie, that's quite possibly the loneliest thing anyone can ever say." Aeric shook his head slowly. "We have to fix that. From here on, we're friends, okay?"

She chuckled, the sound getting caught in her throat. "Gods, I'll have to write this day down in my diary. The day I've finally made a friend."

"What, you don't have friends back where you live? You must have had some where you've gotten together and gossiped about work over coffee on a random morning, at least."

Lottie sputtered out a laugh, thinking of how absurd the image of her and Seban seated around a cafe table was. They'd belonged in dingy bars with liquor between them.

"Friends aren't exactly the easiest to come by in my line of work," she said. She adjusted herself on the counter, trying to keep her face playful and not betray the ache spreading through her chest. "When you think you have them, they can turn around in an instant and decide they like you better beneath them. Which is why I work best alone."

"Goodness me," said Aeric. "Lottie, what *do* you do for work? It sounds rather cutthroat."

"You could say that," she answered. "I'm a curator of goods. A treasure hunter."

He frowned playfully at her. "So, you're a thief?"

"Why is it whenever I explain what I do people automatically jump to that conclusion? I simply..." she waved her hand in front of her, searching for the words, "liberate objects from their homes to find better ones."

"Maybe it's because people who are thieves tend to paint over their titles a bit to make them look better." Aeric took a slow sip of his drink, his eyes sparkling at her. "I like it. It suits you. Lottie Luck, thief extraordinaire."

Lottie snorted out a laugh, her heart warming at his easy acceptance of what she did. "That's what I'll call myself when people ask about what I do from now on."

"It does explain why you don't have many friends. But you must have some sort of organization that you run out of, no?"

"I was trying to become part of one," she said, sighing. "It's why I'm here. Things went a little bit sideways, and well — I needed to find a place to lie low for a bit."

"And it's nice to see your sister again, I bet," he said. "Come, let's move somewhere more comfortable than my minuscule kitchen, and you can tell me all about your brilliantly exciting life."

Lottie snorted and hopped off the counter, following him from the tiny space. "What, isn't living in a beautiful little seaside town exciting?"

"More like enough to put you to sleep," said Aeric, groaning in response. "Please, regale me with the most exciting bits of your life. You must have tons of stories."

She settled onto his couch, sinking into the cushions. "It comes with the job. What would you like to hear first — the time I found a stash of magical artifacts in the depths of the Blackshell, or when I raided a library that ended up being a front for jewels down near the Manid Empire?"

Aeric gasped as he settled on the couch next to her, tucking a leg up under himself. "All of it and more."

PART THREE

The Grandmother Trees

20

ALE AND PLANNING

Kir – 26 Days Before

Kir stared into the middle distance, hands submerged in the cooling soapy water of her basin. There had been a lull in the day's traffic, so no dishes waited at the bottom for her to clean. She should have been taking this time to replace the water, gathering fresh from the well outside, and reheating it with the small stove set up beneath the basin. Instead, though, Kir was thinking about her lute.

These daydreams were fairly common. She'd often spend her time thinking about songs and how she played the previous night, working through ways where she could keep improving her craft. Today however, her mind wandered to the past few evenings. Something about them felt different, her music filling the bar in a rather magical way, for lack of a better word.

In her mind, she studied the instrument as her fingers strummed, her voice humming low in her chest. Her lute was the same as it always had been. The bar also hadn't changed and the songs that Kir played were pulled from her regular repertoire.

Kir blinked slowly, shifting the scene from last night in her mind. Lottie's dancing form came into view. Kir's mind snagged on the image, and for a moment, imaginary Kir let her eyes trail over every curve of Lottie's body — from her ample thighs to her gorgeous tummy that moved sensuously as Lottie danced. Even though she herself couldn't dance to save her life, what Kir wouldn't do to be out there alongside Lottie, touching her, feeling the way she moved.

Ah.

Right. Maybe *that's* why her evenings had been so magical lately.

Kir blinked herself back into the bar, peering down at the water in the basin below her. It had turned slightly brown from the morning's washing, which instantly disgusted her. She grabbed a few buckets to transfer the old water out and fresh water in as she continued to puzzle through her thoughts.

It didn't quite make sense to Kir why this past week hadn't affected her the way she expected it to. Usually, changes to the normalcy of her life set her off balance for weeks. She'd wake up exhausted from being barely able to fall asleep, anxiety coursing through her day and night.

But this week, with Lottie...

It had been easier than playing one of her favorite songs. Lottie's presence seemed to erase any worries she had about the festival coming so soon. Even in the dead of night, after a couple tankards of ale and dancing along to Kir's music, Lottie was alert and happy to be there. *"I am a creature of the night,"* Lottie's voice floated through Kir's imagination from their first committee meeting. Lottie was proving to be a woman of her word.

Though Kir herself still hadn't found a way to completely unlock her tongue around Lottie yet, she did pride herself on not completely running away at the slightest bit of teasing from the other bar members or Lottie's amiable chatter night after night. And, every day, it was becoming easier. Like second nature, having her there. Though, Kir also didn't quite know what to do when Lottie turned her flirtatiousness on her. It reminded her so much of Aeric's joking that Kir wasn't entirely sure if it was a joke coming from Lottie or not. It was very rare that someone directed that kind of energy toward *her*.

Kir cranked the well in the back alley, fresh water gushing into the buckets she'd placed around it. She stood for a moment, letting the cool outside air take the edge off of the sweat that had been gathering along her brow. The chilly air was the perfect balm, carrying with it the tiniest bit of salt from the sea.

Tonight, she and Lottie were going to plan out their next steps and make advertisements for the auditions, which were going to be held in ten days from now. Both Lottie and Kir figured that having the auditions then would allow folks to ready something for an audition and also allow them to prepare for the festival in the remaining few weeks after.

Nova and Briar had been kind enough to offer up the bar when they overheard the two of them trying to think of a good place to host the auditions. Kir hoped the bar would have enough space for the performers; minstrels, bards, and most puppeteering acts wouldn't need much more room, but the space was going to be fairly cramped if any dancers came through.

Heaving the buckets up by their handles, Kir made her way back inside. She listened to the soft *ticktickhisss* of the stove below the basin and Corwek singing to himself in the corner as he prepared the evening's soup, pouring fresh water into her basin.

Would it be better to host the auditions all in one day, drawing every-

thing out? That way they would only inconvenience the bar for a day, but then both her and Lottie might end up exhausted, not to mention the performers. Perhaps the best thing to do would be host the auditions over two separate days, or perhaps three.

I should ask Lottie.

Kir hurried out from the backroom after her set, bringing with her their crate of parchment. Lottie was already stationed at their regular table, alit by a lantern mounted on the wall, two tankards of ale waiting. A smile spread across Kir's face as she took in Lottie's profile, glowing softly in the orange light. Simmering anticipation shuddered through her and Kir almost ran into a nearby table in her haste to join her.

Lottie beamed up at her as Kir slid into her chair. "Fantastic set," she said, her eyes glimmering in the soft lantern light around them.

Kir's face heated and she cleared her throat, trying to ignore the way Lottie's attention made her whole chest warm pleasantly.

"Thanks," she said.

"It's been a while since I heard 'The Witch and the Whale' — I forget how much that gets everyone up on their feet." Lottie beamed before reaching into their crate full of parchment and drawing out their notes.

"It really does." Kir took a long drag of her ale, letting the rich, slightly bitter liquid warm her all the way down. "So. Auditions."

"Auditions," Lottie agreed, nodding and folding her hands together, ready for whatever the night brought them.

Good gods, Kir thought as she mimed reading over the top paper of their notes from the night previous, her eyes not focusing, overly aware of Lottie's presence. *This crush is the very last thing that I need right now. This is entirely debilitating.*

A crush.

Maigsir's tits — is that what this is?

Kir chanced a glance at Lottie over the sheet of parchment in her hands and felt her chest constrict. That was confirmation enough.

Lottie's lips quirked into a smile before she looked up between her eyelashes, noticing Kir watching her. "Kir?"

Kir blinked at Lottie over the paper a few times before putting it down, running a hand over her face.

Lottie's flirty expression faded into slight concern. "Are you okay?"

"Yeah, I just can't seem to get out of my head today." Surprising herself, Kir laughed, shaking her head.

"Gods, don't I know that feeling," said Lottie, smiling kindly at Kir. Kir marveled at the little lines that formed next to her eyes as she did. *Gods*, she was so pretty. Lottie quirked an eyebrow and brought Kir back into the moment. "What did we decide on last night?"

"Ten days out, advertisements to Della as soon as we can."

"Right, then we set up shop here for the auditions — and we have to then source locations in Arrowmount for people to perform?"

Kir nodded. "There are a number of regular spots, we will have to make sure they are still available this year. We should start doing that as soon as we can."

For the most part, the popular locations in town became stages for the performances — from the town center to the sandy beach down by the lighthouse. Even Lord Wymarc, the Lord of Arrowmount, offered the grounds of his manor house to host a few choice acts. And, of course, many establishments opened their doors, including the Old'n Narrow. The main stage would be set up down by the beach, alongside most of the games, activities, and incredible amounts of food for townsfolk to enjoy.

Lottie tapped her lips with a pen. "We'll have to talk to Della to see if she can put us in touch with whoever is in charge of booking spaces, maybe cross-compare to the food folks, just so we can work with the spaces around."

"Yes, yeah." Kir blinked at Lottie, wonderingly. "And we have to find where last year's stage supplies are stored. Gods, there's a lot."

Lottie let out a low murmur of agreement, leaning back to look at her notes. "I'm sure once we get the performers lined up, we will see how everything falls into line. Planning is always best done when you have all the information you can at once."

They sat in relative silence for a few moments as Lottie made a couple notes on the sheet of parchment in front of her. A tiny little crease appeared on her brow in her focus. Trying *not* to stare, Kir's eyes wandered to the scant few remaining patrons around the Old'n Narrow. Briar and Nova were talking behind the bar, both going through the first motions of closing up, Aeric already gone home. Corwek, too, was moving around in the back, cleaning his space.

"I was thinking," said Lottie, tapping the parchment in front of her with the pen absently, "When we do the auditions, we should ask each performer where they prefer being, outside or inside. Maybe that way they can actually be in a place they want to be, rather than us trying to place them somewhere. I think it could help streamline things on our end."

"That's... that's a good idea."

"Thank you, I am a fairly good planner." Lottie winked at Kir, almost causing Kir to choke on her next sip of ale. "Let's start on these signs, that way I can have them off to Della tomorrow."

They worked for an hour more, pulling together a number of pieces of parchment that advertised the auditions. Lottie had a knack for steady, striking letters, so Kir took over the detail work, creating a bit of a frame around the parchment. Morgam had taught Kir to draw a bit before he dove headlong into his love of painting years ago.

"One task down," said Lottie, stretching her hand after they had accumulated a substantial pile. Nova and Briar were closing the bar slowly around them, the final patron having gone off home to sleep.

"We just have to do it all in twenty-six more days. Or rather, twenty-five now."

Lottie leaned back, a confident smile spreading across her lips. "I have faith in us. We'll get it done. No problem at all."

21

POCKETS OF WHIMSY

Lottie – 25 Days Before

Lottie waited for Aeric to join her outside Ceci's apartment the following morning after receiving a quickly scrawled note delivered by a small child who'd run up, practically grinning with glee, and took off again into the town after handing it off. The note asked if Lottie wished to spend the day together. *Since you and I are newly friends, after all,* Aeric had signed it, which had made Lottie laugh.

The stairs around her were littered with plant pots, vines and flowers curling up and around the stone stairs and the iron rail. One particular plant that Lottie recognized as a creeper was making its way up the stone wall of Ceci's building, wrapping it in a web of green.

Lottie breathed in deeply through her nose, letting the scent of plants and magic fill her senses. Most of the other plant life around Arrowmount was dying off, but Lottie knew the scent of Ceci's druidic magic more deeply than any other from the years she'd been swaddled in it. It was a natural, earthy scent, tinged with the slightest hint of a flower that Lottie hadn't ever been able to pinpoint. The plants were flourishing despite the autumnal weather.

She tilted her head up toward the sky and relished the surprisingly warm autumnal sunshine that was making its way through a break in the cloud cover.

"Miss Luck, my oh my," Aeric's voice drifted over to her, followed by the sound of boots clacking sharply on the cobblestones. "Who let you be this beautiful in the sun?"

Lottie smiled demurely at him and did a dramatic bow. "Ah, what can I say. The sun makes me happy. I am part tree, anyway, so that probably has something to do with it."

Aeric offered her his arm. "I am going to treat you to lunch today, my little sapling."

Lottie sputtered out a laugh as she laced her arm through his. "Luinn's mercy, that actually is a first. No one has ever called me a sapling before."

"Well, good thing I'm a genius then."

"Did you send a little child to hand me that note?"

"There are always a few kids around who will do an errand for you if you pay them a small coin or two," he said. "Della has a few at her beck and call. She calls them her errand runners. I co-opted one to do a quick side run for me."

Lottie beamed, her cheeks heating through with genuine joy. She couldn't remember the last time that she'd felt so comfortable with someone, especially someone she didn't want anything from and didn't want anything from her.

It's too good to be true, said the traitorous little voice in the back of Lottie's head. *Everyone who you think is a friend always turns around and hurts you, so why trust this one more than anyone else?*

She tried to ignore the way her heart dropped at the thought, forcing her smile to stay on her face. If something was too good to be true, then why not bask in the good for a little while, at least? Besides, Aeric hadn't done anything to prove that he was going to hurt her. Yet.

"Where to, Dancer?"

"May's? I'm craving some of her coffee."

"Oh, yes to coffee," said Lottie, stifling a yawn.

"Long night?"

"We closed down the bar with Nova and Briar." Even after making her way home, Lottie had stayed up staring at her ceiling, mapping out the next twenty odd days in her head. She worked best with a plan, one that she could work through many times over, learning it until it lived in her brain effortlessly.

Though this wasn't a typical job, treating it as one was helping her ignore the looming threat of the Guild and the artifact still tucked away inside her bag that she had yet to deal with.

And, surprising herself, she wanted to do a good job here in Arrowmount.

That probably has to do with Kir, breathed that same little voice, which she ignored. Today wasn't a day she was going to get stuck in her head — today was about spending with Aeric.

Her friend.

The two of them headed toward Fetterly Place, through Arrowmount's cobblestone streets, and ducked under the plant-covered awning over May's Cafe. May served them delicious, steaming mugs of coffee, and after one look at Lottie and the bags under her eyes, slid a plate of steaming, shining buns onto their table.

Lottie smiled at the amount of greenery throughout the cafe — Ceci probably loved this place. May had a shelf that ran all around the perimeter of the room, flourishing with innumerable plants. They filled the small space with a soft, fresh smell that mingled with the richer, heavier scent of cooking food and brewing coffee.

"So, tell me about the committee you and Kir are running," said Aeric after taking a long sip of his coffee. "I know a bit from seeing the two of you every night in the bar, but I have to know — how did you manage to get pulled into that?"

Lottie shrugged softly in response, wrapping both of her hands around her mug. It seeped warmth into her fingers much like the artifact hidden away in her bag, a magic all of its own. "I was volunteered by my sister to take part. Or rather, she and Della did, but I don't blame that little old gnome. She's too cute to blame. How could I say no to her?"

Aeric nodded knowingly. "I think Kir got roped into her position in a similar way."

"Oh?"

Aeric chewed on his words for a moment, looking slightly amused. "Kirandir is not the kind of person to go out of their way to volunteer for much, unless it's quiet and quick. Any day of the week she'll help you out if you ask — you don't even have to most of the time when she sees you need it. She has a knack for knowing you're in need, like she can read it in your eyes. But when it comes to being in charge of things? No way."

Lottie took one of the buns that May had brought over but didn't bring it to her mouth quite yet. It was pillow-soft under her fingers.

"Would you say that Kir is a person who... oh I don't know. Is she usually...?"

"Reserved?"

"Yes, and no," said Lottie with a soft laugh, trying to find the right words to describe Kir. "I mean — it feels like whenever I'm around she wants to be on the other side of the room until we settle in. I have never had that kind of effect on anyone other than my sister, but at least Kir relaxes into it. Ceci just always wants to leave."

"Kir is a pretty quiet person," answered Aeric, before reconsidering. "Well, quiet, but also not? You often have to let her come to you. Let her have space to say what she wants, when she wants to. New people and Kir don't mix, because they often don't give her time."

"Hmm." Lottie took a contemplative bite of the bun in her hand. It burst with sweetness, a warm berry jam oozing in the middle. The outside was coated in a sweet honey glaze, and for a moment, Lottie couldn't do anything but chew with her eyes closed. It was absolutely *divine.*

After she gathered herself, she continued. "I figured that she needed a bit of time to get used to me. I am, after all, a lot."

"You are perfectly just enough, Lottie Luck."

Lottie laughed, letting the compliment roll off her.

Aeric narrowed his eyes and waved a half-eaten bun at her, a bit of jam threatening to drop out onto the table. "Seriously. Don't just shake your head at me. Anyone who tells you otherwise, send them directly to me."

Heat rose in her cheeks and she had to look away. Sometimes, sincere compliments were a touch too much to handle. She took a sip of her coffee and tried to change the subject. "Tell me a bit about her."

"Kir?"

"Yeah."

Aeric eyed her carefully, before breaking out in a mysterious smile. "No, I don't think I will. If you want to get to know Kir, you'll have to unlock her on your own. I think you'll be able to pretty easily."

"What does that mean?"

"It's a hunch I have." Aeric wiggled his eyebrows at her and took a large bite of a bun, speaking around it. "All I'll tell you is that Kir is probably the best person I know."

"Oh?"

"She comes from a great family, her brothers are the best, and her father is the blacksmith over near the town center. If she likes you, you're in for life. But if you hurt her, I and many others will come after you, I will warn you."

"Okay," answered Lottie, nodding. "Good to know."

They fell into easy conversation as May ventured over, bringing with her another plate of what looked like fried dough twists dusted in sugar. Lottie discovered a decadent caramel middle as she took a bite that paired perfectly with the dusting of cinnamon sugar on the outside.

"May, my goodness," Lottie breathed as she refilled her mug. "What do you put in these? Pure magic?"

May chuckled, looking pleased. She leaned a small, gleaming metal carafe against the table as she tilted her head thoughtfully. "I've been experimenting this month, trying to see how many desserts I can stuff with various things. Pockets of whimsy, if you will."

"I will eat anything you decide to put in front of me," Lottie answered, plucking another twist from the plate. "I trust you with my life, after these."

"I'm glad they're going over well." May winked at her conspiratorially. "If you come by a little later, I'll give you an apple and cheese pastry I've been trying to perfect."

Lottie watched as May went around her cafe with a couple watering cans, stepping up onto a nearby chair or table periodically to reach the plants sitting up high near the ceiling. As she moved around her cafe, the plants yearned after her. Flowers bloomed out toward her like she was the sun, vines and leaves swaying her way as though drawn by an intangible breeze.

If I had abilities like that, I'm sure the Guild would never be an issue again. Especially Alros.

"I know, eh?" Aeric said softly, his eyes following Lottie's. "Magic."

"Do you know any magic?"

Aeric sighed. "I wish. I tried, as a kid, because as an elf, I figured I should be able to learn *something*. But nothing ever came naturally. If you want to see some really cool magic, head over to A Second Story and ask Arileas for a demonstration."

"Oh?"

"Yeah, he's got some neat tricks up his sleeve. Wizard, I think. He can do these amazing illusions — once, I saw him create a perfect miniature version of their cat."

Lottie's heart lurched in her chest. *Magic.* Illusions. Perhaps that was the key to keeping the artifact. What if she had one created that was an exact replica — and she kept the original?

Aeric didn't seem to notice her momentary lack of response. "How about you, little sapling? Any magic in your bones?"

"Not a drop," she said with a soft laugh, tucking the idea away to ponder later. "I'm much better with my knives and sneaking. There is supposed to be something in my blood to make it easier to do magic, as it is for my sister — she's a druid, if you didn't know — but for me? Nothing."

"I've heard a rumor that earth elementals have a knack for walking over any surface with ease, no matter what it is," commented Aeric. "Maybe that's why you find it so easy to be such a wondrous... collector."

Lottie laughed. "That's nothing but a rumor, though I wish it was true. I do have a pair of gloves that make climbing easier, but I'm not immune to falling off a roof or two. If I had any proper magic, that would be the first thing I'd fix."

"Ouch." Aeric cringed. "You really must have a lot of luck stocked up somewhere to get out of situations like that. It's as though you're living in an adventure novel. Maybe that's your magic."

"If only."

She shook her head at him and took another sip of her coffee. Luck, if she ever had any of it, was a fickle thing. That was why she picked it for her last name, because you never knew what kind of luck to expect in her line of work, and sometimes you had to make your own.

22

POSTERS AND MAGIC

Lottie – 24 Days Before

The thought of magic clung to Lottie through the rest of the day and into the night, spinning around and around in her mind. It was a perfect idea: why not have someone magically replicate the artifact for her so she could fool Alros? It wasn't as though Alros had ever seen the artifact himself, of that she was sure.

When he had originally given her the job, he described something only vaguely similar to what she had actually found. *"You'll be grabbing a smaller piece,"* he'd said. *"Something easy to stow away and carry around. It's ancient, something from back around the Centurion, we think. Whatever little reports we could find of it say that it's also bronze or gold, depending on the source."*

Lottie sat on Ceci's couch and inspected the artifact. It *was* bronze, she would give Alros that. The dodecahedron continued to glow, unbothered, in her hand, warming her through.

"Well, I'm not entirely sure what you're for, but at least you'll keep my hands warm in the winter," she said to it. "And if I was to ever need a fancy looking paperweight, you'll do in a pinch. Perhaps someone in this town *can* replicate you."

Lottie stored it in her bag with half a mind to head right to A Second Story to meet the magical Arileas, before she eyed the pile of signs that Kir and she had created the night before from Ceci's counter.

Right.

With one last swig of cold coffee, popping the mug into the washing rack, Lottie grabbed them and headed out into Arrowmount on the hunt for Della.

After asking around, she found the gnome muttering to herself over some shining, perfectly red apples in the town center. The grocer lifted his eyebrows at Lottie as she approached, an amused smile playing on his lips.

"Hello, Della," said Lottie, announcing her presence.

"Oh! Lottie dear, how lovely to see you. Have you seen Pakon's apples? I can personally attest that they taste absolutely divine. I simply cannot decide how many to get!"

Lottie eyed the apples. "I don't know much about baking, but if you get a few more than usual, you might be able to bake them into something tasty."

"You, my dear, are a veritable genius." Della's eyes shone. "Pakon, package me up a dozen of the best ones. I'm going to make some of my late mother's apple pie — it's quite positively the best you'll ever taste. I'll bring you some for your trouble."

Pakon chuckled under his breath and grabbed the apples for Della as she turned toward Lottie.

"Now, Lottie dear, to what do I owe the pleasure?"

"I wanted to hand these off to you," said Lottie, handing Della the stack of advertisements. "We've decided to host auditions in nine days from now, at the bar."

"Ah yes!" Della exclaimed, her eyes brightening. She grabbed the stack and leafed through the first few. "I will make sure these are sent out to the neighboring farms and villages right away and have some of my errand runners go around Arrowmount to hang them up and pass them out. I'm so glad the both of you are doing so well together."

"I rather think we are," said Lottie, a soft smile spreading across her face, unbidden and a little surprising. She usually controlled her expressions fairly well.

Della practically glowed up at her. "It's so good for Kirandir, having more friends. I pride myself in knowing the goings on with the folks of Arrowmount as best I can, and I've often wondered why Kir is so solitary."

"She —"

"I know she has her family, and her lovely brothers — have you met them yet? Well when you do, you'll see — but I have often wondered, you know, because she is a *bard*. Don't bards have more charisma and charm? I know everyone is different and that's probably a stereotype, but I don't know. She's just so quiet."

Lottie, who had now spent a bit of time around Kir, agreed and disagreed. Kir deserved all kinds of people around her, yes, but she had her group of people that she'd curated to her liking. There was Aeric, Corwek, Nova, and Briar at the bar for one, and she had brothers and her father as well.

"I hope I can be a friend to her. If anything, we're good co-chairs, so far."

"I'm so glad. I had a good feeling about you, and I'm usually perfectly correct when it comes to my good feelings." Della turned back to Pakon, who was holding the bag of apples ready, and beamed. "I'll be back with a pie, Pakon."

"I look forward to it," said the grocer with a soft sigh. He and Lottie watched Della toddle off along the cobblestones in silence. Lottie turned a knowing smile to Pakon, who chuckled and shook his head.

Weak autumnal sunshine broke through a thin layer of cloud above as Lottie headed back to Fetterly Place, her boots clacking importantly on the cobblestones. The air today was a bit warmer than it had been for the past few days. She smiled at the townsfolk that passed by, recognizing a few of them from her nights spent at the Old'n Narrow.

Lottie removed her jacket and rolled up her sleeves, reveling in the unseasonably warm autumnal day. The breeze smelled faintly of baked goods, which she could only assume was from May's down the street.

A Second Story appeared in front of her, the façade a lively, fresh yellow, doors thrown wide open to reveal a wonderfully cozy interior. A few patrons perused the shelves quietly. The walls inside were painted a warm, dark green that went perfectly with the honey-toned wood shelves and countless plants that bloomed from nooks and crannies.

May must've helped them out, Lottie thought, brushing a particularly leafy vine with her finger. It bounced back cheerfully.

At the moment, she couldn't see either the white-haired elf or his partner around, so she decided to get a lay of the bookshop. Because, after all, what better thing to do when in a place of books than to browse?

At the back in a cheerily decorated room with low shelving, a little dragonkin girl and her mother were hunting through some children's books. As she came around the romance corner, eyeing a few beautifully filigreed book spines, she heard a soft clearing of her throat behind her.

"Hello," said a white-haired elf, dressed in the softest looking blue knit sweater Lottie had ever seen. He'd drawn his hair back in a messy bun threaded through with what looked like dried wildflowers. "Welcome to A Second Story."

"Hi," she said, straightening from where she'd crouched to look at a lower shelf. "Are you Arileas?"

"The very one. Can I help you find anything?"

"I was actually here to see if you could help me with something magical," said Lottie before casting her eyes around. "It's a bit... of a secret matter."

"Ah, alright." The elf looked slightly surprised but smiled nonetheless before gesturing to a corner of the shop. "Follow me, uh —"

"Lottie Luck."

He smiled a softly questioning smile. "Luck?"

Lottie chuckled. "You, Arileas, are the first one to question me on that. My family name is Little, yes, but I prefer Lottie Luck. Rolls off the tongue a fair bit better than 'Charlotte Little,' wouldn't you say?"

"Lottie Luck sounds like a name pulled straight out of the pages of a novel." He tilted his head to the side amiably. "Well, Lottie, it's a pleasure. Follow me back here, we don't usually have any folks in this space at this time of day."

He led her to a side room that was filled with seating and the occasional table, but was, as he predicted, empty of other patrons. There were more book filled shelves in here, too, extending into the space from the rest of the shop.

"This is lovely," she commented, looking up at the baubles of arcane lights strung around the perimeter of the room. "Are those from Ceci?"

Arileas chuckled. "Yes, my partner got those when we first moved in here. This used to be our bedroom, actually. But, since most of our patrons enjoy reading with a snack or drink in hand from May's down the way, we figured we should offer up space for that, since we now sleep up in the apartment above the shop."

They sat at a table and Arileas eyed her with a pleased, intrigued smile.

"I heard that you're rather skilled with magic," started Lottie, "that you'd be the one to come to if you needed help."

"Well I don't know if that's exactly true," said Arileas, blushing slightly. "I do offer my help occasionally, though. What is it I can help you with?"

"I happened to come across an artifact in my travels — part of my job, you see — and I accidentally angered a group of folks by doing so," said Lottie, embellishing her story slightly. "So much so that they're interested in taking it back from me. I was wondering, possibly, if there was something magical I could find to maybe fool them into thinking that they got their way?"

Arileas touched his chin thoughtfully. "I am not exactly a master in mind magic, truthfully. Not that I've ever tried. I find it rather... invasive, that branch of magic, without the consent of the person's mind you are poking into."

"Oh, myself as well, I've had dealings before." Lottie made a face, thinking of Seban. "I wasn't really angling that way — I thought, perhaps, illusion, or something along those lines, to recreate the artifact?"

"Hmm. Do you mind if I see the artifact in question, if you have it with you?"

Lottie plucked it from her bag and held it up for him to see. His eyes glittered with interest as he leaned forward, not touching the piece, eyes tracing the dodecahedron. For a beat, Lottie felt overwhelmingly protective of the piece and had to fight herself from drawing it back from him. "Would it be possible to make a copy so that they think they actually had it themselves?"

"Unfortunately, magical copies are not quite as corporeal or physical as you are describing." Arileas gestured delicately with one hand on the table, weaving a small pattern in the air. Seemingly out of nothing, an exact copy of the artifact appeared and rotated in the air above his hand, intangible, a perfect image. "As far as I know, to create something lasting can only go so far with magic. You can, of course, befuddle their minds or charm them into believing they have indeed taken what you are trying to keep, however, that too will fade. Memory magic can be fickle, but occasionally it does work. Unfortunately, again, I do not have the expertise to do such magic."

Lottie wrinkled her nose, the bloom of hope in her chest wilting. She sighed and pocketed the artifact once again. "I never thought of that. The physicality of the object. Thank you for your time, though."

"Of course. I am always happy to help, with magical or bookish needs." Arileas and Lottie stood, Arileas keeping the illusion in hand. He looked at it curiously. "Do you know what this artifact is?"

"I know very little," she answered. "Something from the Centurion, possibly."

He made an interested sound in the back of his throat. "I have never seen anything like it, it is rather fascinating. I unfortunately do not have much expertise in the artifact or ancient history department, but goodness this piece is quite intriguing. Thank you for sharing it with me."

Lottie smiled at him kindly as he dropped the illusion and led her back out into the store. "I might have to come back and browse your wonderful book section some more, this place is absolutely lovely."

"Of course, any time! If you are ever looking for a particular book, I can help you find it." Arileas moved to the front counter as a small, brown cat jumped up onto it, searching for attention. He began to scratch the cat under the chin as Lottie moved to leave. "Ah, Lottie? It's just a thought — but, if you want to trick someone into thinking they have something physical, then there is a logical next step."

"Oh?" She eyed him curiously.

"You give them something they believe is what they're looking for. Something physical. Unless of course, they've seen what it is you're holding onto."

"They haven't," she said softly, realization clicking into place. If she had someone physically *make* a passible replica of the piece, could that work? "Is there anyone in this town known for their craftsmanship or metal working?"

Arileas started to smile. "Well, we have a particularly wonderful blacksmith just off the town center. Noghorn Dulra is the proprietor's name, who works with his son Kharutto. Forgive me, but this town often has news travel like wildfire — I believe you're working with Noghorn's daughter, Kirandir, for the upcoming Moon Festival, are you not?"

23
LORD WYMARC'S MANOR
Kir – 24 Days Before

Kir couldn't get Lottie out of her head. Every time she did anything, Lottie's face was there in her mind's eye, distracting her. Washing dishes? Kir was lost in her mind, thinking about the night before, watching Lottie dance all over again. If she was walking around the market stall, getting supplies for the bar, Kir was looking over her shoulder to see if a flash of green would appear, followed by Lottie's smile.

Having a crush was incredibly inconvenient.

Somehow, both her and Lottie had come to an unspoken agreement to meet nightly, regardless if they had Entertainment Committee bits to go over. And now that they were waiting to begin auditions, there really hadn't been much for them to discuss.

It became second nature to look up from her lute and see that beautiful woman there, lost to the music.

Kir would be halfway to a beaming smile whenever she spotted her in the crowd. Each time, Kir had to remind herself that she barely knew Lottie — she was simply getting caught up in the mystery of her.

And how beautiful she was. And —

Gods.

Several days in a row, Kir found herself leaving work mid-day to attend to a number of odds and ends for the Committee — meetings with folks who were in charge with booking the spaces around Arrowmount for the festival, and those who were helping her track down any equipment they would need for the performances — and occasionally to help Della with whatever she needed. It was the first time in years that Kir missed work, and the guilt of it roiled in her stomach every time she came into the bar late or had to hand off her duties to Aeric and leave early.

Each time, too, she'd have a similar conversation with Nova and Briar, who she kept apologizing to. Both of them just chuckled to themselves, waving her off, not bothered at all.

"But my work —"

"We're putting Aeric to use for once," Nova would say, motioning to the back. "He could do with some actual hard work."

Aeric, too, would have a similar reaction each time. If she came into work late, she'd find him disheveled and dripping in the back, his sleeves rolled up above his elbows and his hair bound back at the nape of his neck with a thin cord that looked as though it was taken from one of the potato sacks that Kir herself had brought in the day before. She'd never seen him so sweaty.

"Kiri, thank the gods you're here, you are saving me from living eternally with wrinkly fingers," he'd say, reaching for a towel, relief washing across his features. "I don't know how you do this for as long as you do, every single day, and still play your lute every night. My poor hands!"

Twenty-four days before the festival began, Kir had an appointment set up with Lord Wymarc to discuss the ins and outs of what they could use his property for. She exited the bar just before noon, heading up Fetterly Place and nearly ran headlong into Lottie as she exited the bookstore.

Lottie smiled up at her with the softest, prettiest smile "Oh, hello!"

"Hi."

"Where are you off to today, so early? Is something wrong?" Her eyes flickered with concern.

"I have that meeting with Lord Wymarc in a few minutes."

"Oh, right," she said, before wincing. "I would come with you, but I have a few errands to run. Do you mind?"

"That's okay, I think I have everything covered." Kir shrugged, trying not to notice the disappointment rolling through her. From the few times she'd seen or spoken to him, she knew that Lord Wymarc was a fairly kind man.

It's just another person to speak to, she told herself. *You've done this a few times already with other people in Arrowmount, with and without Lottie to help you. One person, no matter their station in life, is simply another person — nothing more or less.*

"If you need me for anything, I'm sure you can track down one of Della's errand runners. They seem to be around more these days, eh?"

Kir chuckled. She herself had been one when she was eight years old around this same time of year. "It's easier than sending letters around town if you need help with things. And Della always paid well."

"You were an errand runner?" Lottie's nose crinkled as she smiled, pleased.

"I was, and I was quite good at it, I'll have you know. Helps when you have longer legs than the others."

Lottie laughed. "Alright, well I won't keep you. I'll come find you after."

The Lord's manor had been built in a lovely part of Arrowmount that overlooked the forest that blanketed the outside of town. His manor had been built high enough on a particularly hilly part of the landscape that the outer walls of Arrowmount did not block the view. Lord Wymarc himself had been lord for nearly a decade now, living alone within the sizeable house.

Kir walked through the high walls surrounding the place, nodding to a guard stationed out front. She walked up the path that led through the perfectly manicured gardens and stretches of grass, winding up toward the manor.

A neatly dressed man in a deep purple uniform walked up, smiling at her vacantly. Gods, even his shoes shone so perfectly Kir could nearly see her reflection in them. "Hello, may I help you?"

"I have an appointment with Lord Wymarc," she answered, fighting the urge to straighten her large, knitted sweater that was currently sitting unevenly on her collar. "I'm Kirandir Dulra."

"Oh, yes of course. Come right on in."

The man led her through the wide front door and into a much smaller entranceway than she was expecting. Happily, though, she did not have to duck or hunch to fit inside, as the ceilings were lofty and everything was still, to normal-sized folk standards, spacious. She followed the perfectly purple-dressed man down a carpeted hallway that was bedecked in gently patterned warm, creamy wallpaper, her footfalls muffled.

"Please wait in here, if you do not mind. I —"

"No need, Reihmir, I am already here." Lord Wymarc's gentle, warm voice came from behind Kir, and both her and the man — Reihmir — turned. "Hello, Kirandir, it is a pleasure to speak with you."

Kir extended her hand and shook Wymarc's firmly, clearing her throat. Lord Wymarc was a little bit older, with kind eyes that had smile lines permanently etched around them. His hair was a thick, waving mass atop his head, speckled with grey. Unlike his man, Reihmir, Lord Wymarc was dressed much like those out on the streets of Arrowmount — if only in slightly better-quality clothing.

"Thank you for meeting with me."

"Of course!" Wymarc gestured for her to enter a rather plush room which Kir could only assume was created entirely to sit in with guests. The couches were a rich maroon, the elegantly curved legs a deep, shining wood.

Aside from a few of these and a longer, low couch-type chair that looked slightly uncomfortable to sit on, there was only one small decorative table. The walls had large landscape paintings occupying each of the walls beside one, which hosted a large window that was practically a painting all on its own, with gorgeous leafy trees and part of the garden in view.

Wymarc seated himself on a chair and gestured again for Kir to sit opposite him. "So, I believe you were asking to meet regarding my property and the upcoming festival, yes?"

"I was, yes."

"I've been wondering if anyone was going to come around to ask this year," he said, chuckling amiably. "But I understand that this year you've been given this job with rather short notice. Usually it was Gral, I believe, who came to see me."

Kir nodded. "It's only been a few weeks, sir."

"Goodness me. Well, from what I hear from my staff and other folks around town who frequent your bar, they are quite looking forward to seeing what kind of entertainment you pull together. I, for one, know it's going to be a fantastic festival."

Kir tried not to blush as the compliment set her off balance. "Thank you, sir."

"I believe previously, Gral requested the use of my front property, the lawn that runs between the manor and the gate, bringing in his own tables and chairs and the like." He drummed his fingers on the armrest of his chair.

"We have our own equipment, yes," said Kir. "We would love to be able to set up a small stage as we did last year, and whichever of the acts you prefer will be stationed here."

"That *I* prefer! Oh, Kirandir, you don't know what you've done." His eyes shimmered like stars with an almost childlike glee. "I absolutely must have a puppet show, if possible. And magic! As a non-magic user myself, I simply cannot get enough. If you need the space for any musicians and dancers as well, feel free. I adore the Moon Festival and cannot wait to see what you have lined up."

"Our auditions are only a few days away," said Kir, smiling. "We'll know soon, and I'll let you know which ones we can set up here on your property."

"Wonderful. I'll put you in contact with Reihmir for any bits and set up you need on the property — any other volunteers that you have helping you set up, you all have access to whatever you need from me."

"I appreciate it, sir."

"Please, it is my honor to host such talent here. Anything you need, I am at your disposal." He rose, shaking Kir's hand again. "Did you know, my parents used to bring me to Arrowmount as a boy, purely because they knew that this little seaside town had one of the best festivals on this side of the empire?"

"Oh?"

"Perhaps that's when I fell in love with the town," he said softly, almost to himself, as he walked her out. "There is a charm to this place."

"You're right about that, sir," said Reihmir, who appeared at his side.

Kir was led out to the gates by Wymarc himself, the man nodding to servants who passed and the guards standing outside his gates. Everyone that Kir saw had a genuinely kind smile for him as they passed.

She set off toward the bar once again, feeling rather light on her feet. Perhaps the nervousness about talking with new people — or even people she knew but not well, like Lord Wymarc — was simply the apprehension of being received in a negative way. When dealing with someone as outwardly kind and amiable as Lord Wymarc, it made the day a shade brighter.

Another task off the list.

24
THIN AS PARCHMENT
Lottie – 24 Days Before

Lottie made her way toward the town center, as Arileas had described, and followed the sounds of hammering and the distinct scent of metal as she turned off a side street. She picked up her pace as the blacksmith's came into view. Her ears rang with repetitive clanging of someone working metal, but as she approached, no one was out front.

"Hello?" she called between clangs, peering around. Within the shadow of the mostly open smithy, a dark blue-grey skinned man, hefting an incredibly large hammer in the air glanced at her briefly before doing a double take and grimacing apologetically before he brought the hammer down on a long piece of red-hot metal in his hand again, the sound banging through Lottie's skull. She clasped her hands over her ears as he kept hammering, every so often twisting the metal in his hand to check his work.

"Just one moment!" he yelled to her between clangs.

Lottie watched the way that his incredibly large arms rippled with strain, taken aback. He was stripped down to a thin sleeveless undershirt that clung to him with sweat, heat radiating from the glowing furnace a few feet away from him. He was young, his hair a pitch black much like Kir's, although his was cropped closer to his head.

This must be Kharutto, her brother, she thought. *The attractiveness must run in the family.*

As Lottie glanced around, wondering if Kir's father was in as well, Kharutto finished with whatever he was doing to the piece of metal and plunged it into a basin of water, the resulting hiss procuring a cloud of steam around him.

"Hello," said Kharutto, leaving the metal in the water and moving toward her, wiping his hands on his shirt and trousers. They left behind blackened scuffs, dirtying the already well-worn material. "How can I help you?"

"I'm on the hunt for an expert with detail work," she said, extending her hand.

"Well, you came to the right place. I'm Kharutto Dulra," he answered, his face breaking into an incredibly handsome smile. "You can call me Khar, though. Hardly anyone calls me by my full name anymore."

"Pleasure. I'm Lottie Luck."

"I thought you might be. You look a fair bit like Ceci."

Lottie hesitated. He called her Ceci. Not a single person Lottie had met yet in Arrowmount had called her sister by that name.

Interesting.

Khar leaned against a front table, bending slightly down closer to her level. Gods, she thought Kir was tall. This man towered over her. "What kind of detail work are you looking for? Do you have a blade that needs refining?"

Lottie glanced over her shoulder, checking to see if anyone was in hearing distance. "It's a bit... different. I'm actually hoping you can help me craft something of a replica."

"A replica... of what, exactly?"

"I came across this artifact on my last job," she said, reaching into her bag and pulling the dodecahedron out. "It unfortunately garnered the attention of a few people, and I was hoping to create something to... try and trick them into believing they have the real thing."

Khar's eyes sparkled with amusement. "How intriguing. May I see it?"

She handed him the artifact after hesitating for a moment. Again, that protective pull was at the center of her heart, wanting to hide the artifact away, as though this man would steal it from her and never give it back. *Ridiculous,* she thought. *Come on, Lottie.*

"How intricate," he murmured, holding it very gently by the tips of his fingers as he rotated it around. "Come back with me to my office, for lack of a better word. I need to take a closer look."

She followed him into a space that was absolutely exploding with metal. Bits of curled, shining slices dotted the floor; half-finished and finished blades hung on the wall with tags on them, the script on it tight and leaning to the right, denoting who they were for. Along the wall as she walked in there were three crudely made axes were mounted in full view, as though whomever hung them was incredibly proud of each one. Lottie peered a little closer, noticing a small tag on the bottom-most one that read "Kirandir" in looping, unsteady writing.

Khar made his way to a small worktable in the back that had been propped up on a few haphazard crates and one spare chunk of metal so thick that Lottie knew it must weigh a ton, raising the surface to his level. As he sat on his stool, Lottie smiled, knowing that someone had taken into account the possible back pain from bending over a much smaller table for hours on end.

Khar slid on a pair of delicate spectacles and grabbed a spare lantern, lighting it with a quick snap of some matches so he could inspect the artifact more clearly. "This is a really interesting piece. Is there... something written on the surface?"

"Yes, though I have no idea what it could be. I don't even know what language it is," she said, joining him at the table.

"And you're seeking to create a replica of this."

"Is it possible?"

"Well, I don't know exactly how the magic works, since that's entirely out of my wheelhouse."

"Oh, I don't think I'll need the magic part," she said quickly. "The people who are after it haven't actually seen the piece. I don't think they need to have something imbued with magic — as long as it's physical and convincingly passable as an artifact, I think I can fool them into thinking they have the real thing."

He glanced up at her with an all-too-knowing flicker in his eyes. Slowly, he nodded, sliding his thumb over the surface. "I think I have some bronze I can form into plates like this. We may also be able to give it a core to add weight to it. As for the detail, how much of an *exact* replica would you like?"

"I leave that up to you," she answered. The writing, if that's what it was, was incredibly intricate work. "I know it's going to be quite detailed."

"Are you sure they've never seen the piece?"

"Well," she chewed her bottom lip, thinking. "I'm fairly certain they haven't, other than what's been described in old records and research texts. My contact, from the sounds of it, didn't know what it looked like exactly, which leads me to believe there weren't any drawings of it in their possession. But I'd at least like to make it passably recognizable as something old, at least."

Khar reached into the mess around his workstation and withdrew a small sheet of shining, silver metal, so thin that Lottie thought it could rival parchment. He dug around further, brushing aside a large number of the metallic flakes to reveal a small surface to place the artifact on, and then withdrew a number of fine tools from the mess.

"Hmm, alright," he said, eyeing the piece. "Let's try something."

He began to punch patterns in the sheet of metal, testing their sizes, before he would shake his head minutely and grab something else, trying to find the right match. Eventually, he mapped out a whole line of the garbled script before sitting up again to look at her.

"It is doable, I think," he said. "Though it's still a bit too large to pass as that script there. I think I can find a tool small enough to achieve."

"Truly?" Lottie's heart lurched and she laughed, relieved. "Iluinn's disgraced teapot, that's the best thing I've heard all day."

Khar spluttered out a laugh, his eyes crinkling. "That's the first time I've heard that saying."

"Sometimes you hear something once and it sticks better than glue," she answered, thinking back to the Madame of the orphanage her and Ceci grew up in and her creative swears. "Are you going to take this on?"

"Most of my work takes me a number of weeks of monotonous hammering and grinding and sharpening. The detail work is my favorite bit — it reminds me of working with wood, though metal will never compare to wood. So yes, I'll take it on." He smiled at her, crossing his arms over his expansive chest. "I'll see how quickly the physical piece comes together in the next few days, and I'll let you know about the detail work."

"Fantastic."

Khar took out a few pieces of paper and sketched out the dimensions of the piece, his handwriting cramped and matching the writing on the labels around the small room. He took a little more time taking a much more careful rubbing of the piece than she had when writing her letter to Berold — he captured the exact likeness of the script almost perfectly. Each side got a separate piece of parchment as he went, occasionally making notes to himself on the side. Then, he handed her back the artifact.

"You don't..."

"Not at the moment, no," he said, frowning slightly at his drawing and notes. "Perhaps to double check when I'm done or if I come across something particularly tricky, but. This will be enough, I think. The body will be the easiest bit, the metal. Once the details come in, then we're going to have some fun."

"Thank you, Khar, this means a lot."

Khar eyed her, a slightly concerned expression washing over his face. "You're in a rather dangerous job, yeah?"

"It can be."

"I remember Ceci telling me about you once, a long time ago." He rubbed the back of his neck, looking somewhere to her right, not quite making eye contact.

"You know, I haven't heard anyone else call her that. 'Ceci.'"

His hand froze, and his eyes flashed to hers. A dark color rose in his cheeks. "Ah, you caught that, did you? Your sister and I used to be fairly close, when she first moved here."

"Close?"

"Yes."

Close enough to tell him about me, she thought as she sized him up. He was incredibly handsome, she couldn't fault her sister on that. *To tell him about what I do.*

"Does Ceci know about this? Does my little sister?" He motioned with his chin to the artifact in her fingers.

"No, neither of them. I had hoped to keep it a secret, but it turns out that I can't really do everything by myself."

He chuckled at that and relaxed slightly, his arm dropping down to his side. "Alright, good to know. Secret it is."

"Thank you."

"Of course, Lottie."

Lottie left the smithy feeling as though Khar knew more than he was letting on about her. And that he had opinions, though she couldn't really say what they were.

As she flagged down someone nearby to ask for the directions to the Lord's manor, she turned her mind to the artifact settled back inside her bag. She'd found a solution, thanks to Arileas and Khar both. Something she may be able to fool the Guild with.

"Lottie!"

She turned toward her name, seeing Aeric walk up from the market at the town center. "Hiya, Dancer."

"What brings you out this way?"

"I'm off to meet Kir at the Lord's manor," she answered, leaving Khar and the smithy out of things. "To what do I owe the pleasure?"

"A courier came in a little earlier today with a letter for you, I've been hoping I'd run into you to pass it off." He dug into his pockets and unearthed a thick, sealed scroll. "Whoever it is had a lot to say."

"I'm sure he did," she breathed, taking it in hand with a swoop of her heart. *Berold had written back.*

Aeric eyed her curiously. "Well, I'm off, Corwek sent me on an emergency grocery mission to track down some of Pakon's cabbages — see you at the Narrow later?"

"Always."

Lottie stepped off toward a slightly empty part of the street and slid her thumb under the seal of the scroll, unfurling Berold's letter.

MISS LUCK,

IT IS A PLEASURE TO HEAR FROM YOU AFTER ALL THIS TIME. I HOPE YOU ARE KEEPING WELL AND HAVEN'T FALLEN INTO ANYTHING OVERLY DANGEROUS, DOING WHAT YOU DO.

WHAT AN INTRIGUING LITTLE ARTIFACT YOU'VE COME ACROSS — I WOULD LOVE TO SEE IT IN PERSON, AS THAT IS ALWAYS THE BEST WAY FOR ME TO STUDY ANY ARTIFACTS THAT COME THROUGH MY OFFICE. I DO ALSO KNOW THAT IT'S SOMETIMES DIFFICULT FOR YOU TO BRING ME OBJECTS PHYSICALLY, SO I WILL DO MY BEST WITH WHAT YOU SO GENEROUSLY GAVE ME. FROM THE ESSENCE OF THE ETCHING, I CAN FAIRLY CONFIDENTLY GLEAM THAT THE PIECE IN YOUR POSSESSION IS IN FACT FROM <u>BEFORE</u> THE CENTURION.

I'LL SAVE THE LONG SPIEL FOR IF (WHEN?) WE ARE TO MEET IN PERSON, AND NOT CONVERSING OVER PEN AND PARCHMENT. HOWEVER, I'M SURE THIS BIT OF INFORMATION IS AS INTERESTING TO YOU AS IT IS TO ME, SO I WILL SHARE IT TO TIDE US BOTH OVER. PIECES FROM BEFORE THE CENTURION ARE INCREDIBLY RARE — IN FACT, SO RARE, THAT THEY ARE BELIEVED TO BE MOSTLY LEGEND AT THIS POINT IN HOUR REALM'S HISTORY. YES, NOT ONLY THE EMPIRE, BUT THE ENTIRE <u>REALM</u>, MISS LUCK. THE LANGUAGE ETCHED IS, I BELIEVE, ONE USED BACK WHEN THE GODS WALKED THE EARTH AND WERE TREATED LIKE ROYALTY. <u>BEFORE</u> THEY DECIDED TO TURN OUR MATERIAL REALM INTO A WASTELAND FOR THEIR PETTY BATTLES — OR SO US SCHOLARS SAY. IT IS BELIEVED THAT THE GODS HAD THEIR OWN LANGUAGE, ONE THAT WAS WRITTEN IN TOMES LONG LOST AND ETCHED INTO ARTIFACTS TO IMBUE

THE PIECES WITH POWER — AGAIN, ACCORDING TO US SCHOLARS' STUDIES.

SO YES, WHAT YOU ARE ASSUMING IS CORRECT. I BELIEVE YOU HAVE A TRUE GODLY ARTIFACT IN HAND. WHAT IT DOES, THOUGH, I CANNOT SAY. I WOULD LOVE THE OPPORTUNITY TO STUDY THE PIECE, IF YOU ARE INTERESTED TO FIND OUT MORE ABOUT IT.

I MUST BE HONEST WITH YOU, MISS LUCK. IF WORD EVER GOT OUT ABOUT THE PIECE'S EXISTENCE, YOU'D BE RECEIVING OFFERS FROM AROUND THE REALM TO SET YOU UP FOR LIFE. NOT EVEN TO HAVE THE PIECE IN THEIR COLLECTION, BUT SIMPLY TO STUDY IT AND LEARN FROM YOU, MISS LUCK. LEARN WITH YOU, IN FACT. HOW WORD ABOUT THE PIECE'S TRUE IDENTITY HASN'T GOTTEN OUT BEFORE NOW IS BEYOND ME. WHOEVER HAD IT MUST NOT HAVE KNOWN WHAT KIND OF TREASURE THEY HAD IN THEIR POS-SESSION.

THANK YOU FOR SHARING THIS WITH ME, AND I SINCERELY HOPE WE TALK MORE IN THE FUTURE. I OFFER MY SERVICES IN WHATEVER RESEARCH AND TESTING IS NEEDED.

- PROFESSOR BEROLD, CENTURION RESEARCH WARD.

Lottie let out a long, heavy sigh, feeling slightly unmoored. A *godly* artifact? She almost couldn't believe the glorified finger warmer tucked in her bag could be such a powerful thing — but, then again, the size of an object most often didn't denote how deadly or powerful it could be.

I have to make this fake artifact plan work, she thought, swallowing hard. *It* has *to work. If I don't have this, I have nothing left.*

Lottie reeled at the thought. Without the artifact, she'd be stripped entirely bare. Nothing would be left for her — her hope that the Guild wanted her was long gone, which had been the only thing she'd worked for over the past ten years.

Taking a slightly unsteady breath, Lottie gripped the letter tight in her hands. Right.

"Let's make this work," she said to herself quietly, before stashing the letter in her bag and heading off toward Kir and the Lord's manor.

25

THE GRANDMOTHER TREES

Kir – 25 Days Before

Kir saw Lottie at a distance, her face set into a contemplative frown, before Lottie saw her. As she did, Lottie's face slid into a happy expression, though Kir wasn't entirely sure if it was real, or if it was a mask she'd slid into place.

Kir fell into step beside Lottie as she turned around, heading back the way she came. "Lord Wymarc is a go."

"Fantastic," said Lottie, gripping the strap of her bag tight.

"How did your errands go?"

"A little better than expected," she answered, her eyes focusing on Kir for a brief moment before darting away.

They fell into silence, Kir pondering what could be on Lottie's mind. The sounds of Arrowmount at mid-day swirled around them. Distantly,

173

the sounds of clanging built up in the air from her father's smithy.

"If you had to do anything else for work or pleasure other than your bardic gig at the Old'n Narrow, what would you do?"

"Uh." Kir blinked, surprised at Lottie's sudden chattiness. "I don't know. Why?"

"It's just a hypothetical." Lottie shrugged, eyes twinkling in the weak autumnal sunshine. "I'm trying to get to know you more, Kirandir Dulra. Isn't that what friends do?"

"As long as I get to ask some questions as well."

Lottie peered up at Kir. "Alright. You can ask me anything you want to."

Kir nodded slowly, thinking.

"But," Lottie continued, "you have to answer my question first."

"If I didn't have my job now, I would be helping my father at the smithy."

"That's rather kind of you."

"My brothers and I helped him as kids a lot, but now it's mostly just Khar who does. My turn."

"Hold on —" Lottie laughed, shaking her head. "I was going to say, that that's rather kind of you, but it's not really an answer as to what you would want to do. What would you *want* to do?"

Kir snorted. "I think you're forgetting that the only thing I *want* to do is play music."

"Fine, fine. You're an incredibly kind person. If you didn't do music, you'd be helping out your family — *fine*, that's a perfectly acceptable answer." Lottie peered sideways at Kir with an odd expression on her face. Kir couldn't quite place it — her mask had descended over her expression once again, like she was trying to force the playfulness there. "Your turn."

"What do you do for work?"

"I'm..." Lottie hesitated, eyebrows twitching together. "I'm a collector of sorts."

A collector.

Kir eyed her, taking her in. Lottie was wearing worn leather gloves paired with her equally loved jacket that looked as though it had been recently repaired along one arm, well-used boots and thick, sturdy trousers. Everything seemed, though worn, to be made well enough to last. She could picture a few knives hidden in the folds of the jacket, or perhaps in the tops of Lottie's boots.

She looks like a character from an action novel, said a voice in the back of Kir's mind. *Like a thief.*

"Collector of what, exactly?"

Lottie shook her head before shooting Kir a sly, sideways glance. They stepped down a side street, moving aside to let a pitch-black catfolk pushing a small wheelbarrow of rock pass.

"You don't necessarily want to know."

Kir eyed her playfully. "I thought friends shared things. Got to know one another."

"Hmm." Lottie flicked a few strands of hair that had come free of her braids out of her face. "Alright. I'm a collector of artifacts and special treasures. I travel the empire hunting precious, one of a kind, powerful things that other people might want. Some people would consider me a thief."

A character right out of a novel.

"I prefer the term collector, if I'm being entirely honest," she continued. "But my sister would disagree." Lottie lifted her chin as though in defiance, her expression suddenly replaced with a much harder, sharper one.

Kir nodded thoughtfully. "Alright. Is that why you're here, in Arrow-mount? A job?"

"It's my turn to ask a question, Kirandir."

"Right, sorry."

"What is your favorite place in Arrowmount?"

Kir hesitated. "My... favorite part?"

"Yes. Somewhere you love to go. Not the bar, since we've already been there."

Kir thought fast, trying to think of a place that wasn't her bedroom with her mother's windows or the stage sitting in the corner of the Old'n Narrow. "Why do you want to know?"

"You're my friend, Kir. I want to know these things about you," continued Lottie. "For example, when I'm overwhelmed, all I want to do is dive into a good book."

"A book?" What did that have to do with a favorite place?

"I don't really have a place to run back to in my line of work. So I find it in the fictional worlds between pages."

That sounded so incredibly lonely to Kir for a moment she couldn't formulate a proper sentence. Lottie, misreading the blank look on Kir's face, reached out and took Kir's hand.

"I didn't mean to upset you —"

"No, no I'm fine, I —" Kir cleared her throat, marveling over the warmth of Lottie's palm against hers, the way their fingers laced together perfectly. "That's... that's so lonely."

"It can be," breathed Lottie.

Kir's mind whirled, thinking of the places in town that she had gone to every day, each of them more mundane than the next. Then she remembered one of the places that she used to love as a kid, one that — she realized with a soft pang — she hadn't visited in a number of years.

"There's this spot, a little outside of town," answered Kir. "It's quiet, and you can watch the sea. I know it's not *in* Arrowmount, but..."

"I'd love to see it sometime. Alright, now your turn."

Kir repeated her question from before.

Lottie breathed out; the sound shaky. "I'm not here to steal anything, if that's what you're thinking. My last job went sideways, and I had to go into hiding for a while. Reevaluate a few things. What better place to hide than somewhere where your estranged sister lives, by the sea?"

Estranged? That would make sense, she figured, since most had been surprised that Cecily Little had a sister at all. But this was the first she was hearing of it. Drama like that was the bread and butter of a town like theirs. If it wasn't being spoken of, then no one even had an inkling as to Ceci and Lottie's relationship.

Kir worried her bottom lip as they walked, periodically looking at Lottie's face. It had shuttered closed, wiped almost entirely blank.

Kir wanted nothing more than to reach out and hold Lottie, to let her know that she didn't have to be so closed off. But that was something Kir herself didn't know how to do, so she simply kept on walking.

When they reached the bar, Kir turned to Lottie. "May I ask you one more before you ask me something?"

Lottie nodded her expression wary. "Alright."

"Whatever happened with Cecily — was that because of your work?"

"Yes."

"Your *collecting* work." Kir watched Lottie, gauging her reaction.

"Yes." The tiniest smile started to crack through Lottie's mask.

"Will you tell me about that, if I ask more? About your life?"

Lottie sighed, peering around at the buildings and shoppers around them as they passed slowly through Arrowmount. "Perhaps. It's not your turn to ask a question, though." Lottie cleared her throat. "Before we go to the bar for the night — can you show me your favorite place?"

Kir chuckled softly and nodded. Absently, she tapped the back of Lottie's hand with a finger twice for luck. Why, she wasn't entirely sure.

Kir led Lottie off into the chilly afternoon, the two of them falling into step with one another, hands falling apart naturally as they walked. In the distance, weak autumnal sun shone on the water like glittering silver, winking on the waves. It framed the lighthouse that sat at the end of Fetterly Place like a piece of art.

The further they walked from the bar, the more nervous Kir became, though she couldn't quite pinpoint why. She found herself biting the skin on her lip, worrying at it over and over.

Her mouth started moving before she could stop it. "It's a bit odd."

"What is?"

"Uh — um — you know —" Kir gestured at the two of them as though that could encompass her meaning. Kir had become comfortable with the idea of Lottie in the bar, seated at their usual table with a tankard in hand, surrounded by the chatter of the patrons. It had just occurred to her how odd it was to see Lottie in the sunshine.

"You mean us being outside of the bar?"

Kir tripped over a loose cobble that she didn't catch as she turned to look down at Lottie. "Yes. How did you know?"

"I'm beginning to understand you a bit more," answered Lottie. "Or at least try to. Is that alright?"

"I don't mind, no." Kir swallowed, chewing on her words. In fact, she rather liked Lottie trying to understand her.

"Good."

They fell into a comforting quiet, walking close together. Every time Lottie's knuckles brushed her own, Kir's stomach fluttered as though she had butterflies trapped within her. Their silence wasn't the usual awkward one that Kir anticipated with others — it was the kind of quiet that Kir found at night, listening to her family settle around her; the kind of quiet that came at the end of a song, or a drawn-out sigh. Every moment was perfectly balanced, and there was no need to break it.

They passed in view of the lighthouse, rounding off to the right and continuing down the stretch of sand.

Kir watched from the corner of her eye as Lottie's shoulders relaxed bit by bit as they neared the sandy shores of the beach. Lottie stood a little bit taller, too, as the soft moving waves lapped at the shore. Kir became more curious and entranced by her by the minute.

Sharp sea mist greeted them the closer they got to the water, slowly drenching them head to toe.

Quietly, Lottie asked, "Where to?"

Kir pointed off toward a small outcropping of trees and rock that sat down by the sea. They turned to walk parallel to the shore and continued on for a while, passing the small outcropping of the ruins of Eldar's Wall that extended up into the hills around Arrowmount.

Before long, Kir found herself approaching the same spot she and her mom used to sit when she was a small child. She reached out and pulled aside a low hanging branch to let Lottie head up first.

The ancient trees still stood sentinel over the spot, their long, stretching branches reaching down toward the surface of the water. Once, Kir's mom had worried about them falling into the water. But they remained, stoic and protective over the small space.

Their branches waved to Kir as she passed beneath them, helping Lottie up the rocky path a few feet. There, at the top, was a large, perfectly flat stone that offered a perfect vantage point to look out over the ocean, framed by the two ancient trees.

A blissful contentment crossed over Lottie's features. "I always forget how much I love the ocean. It's been so long."

"When was the last time you saw the sea?"

Lottie smiled softly and leaned back on her hands. "I used to live in a coastal town outside of the Kingdom of Alieweth. "My sister and I would constantly find excuses to go down to the water whenever we could. When we moved to Pralon, we'd dream about it every day. Maybe it was because I thought that if I returned to the seaside, even if it wasn't my childhood home, something in me would not be able to leave again," she said quietly. "Which is incredibly terrifying, when you live the life I do."

"But now you're here."

"Now I'm here."

Kir nudged her shoulder amiably. "Will you leave, now that you've seen the sea again?"

Lottie's lips quirked into a smile. "Unfortunately, I do have to. Probably after the Moon Festival, once that's all wrapped up. I have a... loose end I need to attend to."

Trying to ignore the pang echoing through her chest, Kir nodded. *Lottie is going to leave.*

"How on earth did you find this spot?" Lottie breathed after a stretch of silence interrupted only by the rhythmic rushing of waves. "It is... absolutely wonderful."

"My mom used to bring me here," answered Kir, her voice low. She smiled at the two trees, nearly stripped bare of their autumnal foliage. Whatever few leaves left clung on by nothing more than spite, their brittle husks rattling in the misty sea breeze. "Sometimes my brothers came too, but it was mostly me. Mom wanted to show us all the places in Arrowmount that she loved the most — this spot was a favorite because of the two trees down there."

"They kind of look like two old ladies hunched over together, laughing."

"That — yes, that's exactly why." Kir chuckled. It really was like Lottie lived in her head. "My mom called them the Grandmother Trees. In summer, their branches are so heavy with leaves that they often skate in the water, getting caught up in the waves. But they remain standing, year after year."

"What was she like? Your mom."

"Pure sunshine," said Kir, leaning back on her hands, the rock beneath her palms icy and damp. "She could find the best parts of people, places, moments, anything. I don't really remember her, exactly, what she looked like or anything — but I remember the happiness that she had inside."

"How did she die, if you don't mind me asking?"

"Illness of some kind, I'm not entirely too sure, I was too young. We knew it was coming and were well prepared." Kir cleared her throat. It had been a long time since she had spoken this much about herself. Though she sang long nights at the bar, this conversation had already turned her throat raw. "Some people are so vocal in their grief. Often because it's a violent, unprecedented loss, and in that, grief is unbearable. But we were prepared, and she kept telling us that if we were sad when she was gone, to also try and balance it with happy memories of her. Because what is life without being remembered in the brightest of ways?"

"I think I would've really liked her."

"She would have liked you too." Kir smiled, warmth spreading through her chest. "She also would probably be telling me to get back to work because we might catch a cold sitting here drenched in sea spray."

But, Kir added in her mind, *there is nowhere else I would rather be than right here with you.*

Lottie sat up straighter, tucking one of her legs up to rest her chin. She looked so small right then — entirely different from the bright, brilliant Lottie Luck that spun on the dance floor to Kir's music. Kir could see the sorrow and loneliness cracking the mask that Lottie tried to keep on. What had happened so long ago that had distanced her and her sister?

"Your mom would probably be right," said Lottie, her lips quirking in the tiniest smile. "But I don't want to go back just yet. How about you ask me one more question before we rejoin reality?"

"Any question?"

Lottie gazed at Kir thoughtfully, as though knowing where Kir's thoughts had gone. She hesitated for a moment before finally saying, "Yes."

"What happened between you and Ceci?"

26

LOTTIE'S STORY

Kir – 24 Days Before

Lottie started slowly, drawing the words out. "The gist of it is that some of the people I worked with got us wrapped in something awful, with other terrible people, and they came after our families in retaliation. Ceci and I lost everything, and she had had enough."

Lottie's shoulders curled in as she talked, becoming smaller on the cold rock, as though shielding herself from further pain.

"I'm sure she's glad you're here now," said Kir, extending a hand to Lottie as Lottie had done earlier for her. "I know I would be, if my sister came back into my life."

Lottie opened her mouth slightly as though to say something, but instead hesitated and looked down at Kir's offered hand. She slid her fingers into Kir's gently, holding on.

"I never thought about it that way." Lottie cleared her throat and paused for a moment longer, a small crease forming between her eyebrows. The Grandmother Trees rustled, a few more dried leaves breaking free and dancing to the water below. "Ceci and I've lived on our own most of our lives. We were shipped off to an orphanage really young, but the second Ceci was old enough to work, we left. We moved from Alieweth down to Pralon, in a room off the back of a mill where Ceci had found work, but I was too young to properly find a job. So, I found one the wrong way."

"Doing your... collecting?" Kir raised an eyebrow.

"Yes," said Lottie, chuckling softly. She nudged Kir's thigh with her own amiably, pulling Kir's hand further into her lap and wrapping her other hand around it. "I was a small kid, and fairly nimble, so I picked up tricks that I needed to get into places I really shouldn't have been going — honestly, I was so suspicious, I kept looking over my shoulder at every turn."

Kir let out a soft laugh, picturing a tiny Lottie, running around trying to be sneaky, long summer-green hair flying behind her.

"I once tried to sneak into one of the city official's houses," continued Lottie. "Why I got the idea that it would be easy for me to do, I don't know, and of course I was caught. Not by the official, but by another group of kids, a little older than me, trying to do the same thing.

"Seban was this scraggly kid with too-long hair and a scar that ran up his arm, which instantly made me think he was the best. He told me off for trying to get through the back gate, which was too obvious a spot. His brother, Loth, came up and bet him that he was sneaky enough to get through the gate, which ended up with the three of us running full tilt away from the manor, a cook brandishing a ladle at us."

"Terrifying."

Lottie shook her head, amused. "I followed them to their hideaway and tried to steal one of their apples for my trouble. But, instead of leaving when they of course caught me, I stayed. Met some of their other friends, other kids a bit older and more experienced. They called themselves the Nine.

"I felt like I had finally found a family. Sure, I had Ceci, but to me, that wasn't the same. People say that family is the blood that runs in your veins, but when I was on those streets with them, *that* was the family I knew like the air I breathed. They understood what it meant to seek out danger, to push boundaries, to *want*.

"Over the few years we were in Pralon, as Ceci was making ends meet with a proper job, I was on the streets with the Nine. As we all got older, though, the jobs got bigger. We started going after artifacts that the older members would pawn off at markets to make more coin."

"Markets, like what we have here?"

Lottie nodded slowly. "A bit, but much bigger and definitely dirtier than what Arrowmount has. Seedier. Less safe than buying bread from Gable."

"Not really the place you want a young girl to be," Kir commented.

"It really wasn't. I roped Ceci into the job, got her to start selling the pieces that I stole, because out of all of us, she was the one with a proper appearance that could fool those buying. We started to make enough that Ceci and I found a better place to live. The little apartment was barely any bigger than before, but we each had our own rooms, and that was enough.

"Ceci and I started to do our own work on the side, making our own money that we didn't share with the others. Ceci didn't like the Nine and often refused to sell what they found, but if I was the one supplying her, then... you know. We made do. Until the others started to become obsessed with joining the Guild. We started to become more brazen.

"And then Seban came to us with a Job. Capital J Job. We thought that it would be exactly what we needed to impress the Guild enough to let us in."

Kir furrowed her brow, a burst of goosebumps rising on the back of her neck at a change in the wind. *"The* Thieves Guild?"

"You know about the Guild?"

"It's, you know." Kir waved a bit with her free hand, searching for the right term. "Infamous? There're always warnings about when you go into big cities, things that parents would tell kids. 'Watch out for the pickpockets or conmen, they're operatives of the Guild.'"

"Ah, of course," Lottie chuckled under her breath. "Well. Maybe it is a good thing parents warn you all away from the Guild. Because that job..." Lottie let out a long sigh, her eyes slipping off of Kir's again with the tiniest flinch of pain. "It cost me everything."

Kir squeezed her hand twice, much like she did when tapping her lute for luck.

"I should've known then. I should've listened to her," said Lottie, her voice wavering slightly. She sucked in a tight breath and hesitated, before clearing her throat and continuing. "Ceci told me so many times I needed to stop. I was too deep in, too close to the danger that she saw around every corner, but I saw only opportunity. I thought she was too scared. Too much of a... a close-minded person who couldn't see the dreams I had for the two of us.

"Everything went up in flames. I had been ready with Seban and his brother, waiting for a drop, but we were made. The Nine had crossed paths with an incredibly dangerous crime family — one of the biggest ones with connections further up than we could ever have imagined. None of us could see the danger until we were the mice being hunted across the city, being taken out one by one.

"By the end of it, Seban and I were the only ones left, I think. There may have been more of us, but both Seban and I never heard from them again if so. In one night, the Nine was gone. It felt like years, running through the city. But it all happened in minutes."

"Were you okay?" The idea of Lottie in pain, running for her life desperately around a city bleeding was causing a storm inside of Kir that she didn't exactly know what to do with. "Did they hurt you?"

"I was fine, physically. I tried to get home, but I ended up leading them straight to her."

"Oh," Kir breathed.

"There is nothing," Lottie said, her voice shattering, "*nothing* like running so hard that you can feel every bone in your body to get away from someone who will definitely kill you the long and hard way, and then coming up to your street, thinking you're safe, then smelling smoke.

"I remember nothing but screaming for Ceci, crawling toward the flames but not being brave enough to walk into them to see if I could find her. But Ceci, like always, found me first. She had crawled out, saving only the clothing on her back, a few minutes before I arrived home. We stood there together, watching our home burn.

"And then she turned to me and..." Lottie stopped, her voice tightening like a vice as she screwed up her face in an effort to stop crying.

Kir carefully wiped a tear that dared to leak from her beautiful eyes. Lottie leaned toward the touch.

"She was tired of living in constant fear. She said I could live whatever dangerous life I wanted, without her in it." Lottie's voice had gone flat and weak, as though she had spent everything inside of her to tell this story, and she had nothing left to get these last few sentences out. "She walked away, leaving me there. And came here."

"How did you know where she went?"

"I had one of my contacts track her for me. I wanted to make sure I knew where she was, that I knew she was okay. And since then, I hadn't seen her, until the day I walked into the bar, because she was my only choice. My only option."

Kir sighed thoughtfully, gazing out at the rippling waves. "She wasn't your only choice, was she?"

Lottie turned to Kir, frowning. "Yes, she was."

"I mean, you had to go into hiding right? You could've gone to any town or city and holed up there."

"I —" Lottie's voice stopped but her mouth continued to work, shaping words that came out haltingly. "The Guild... the last job, the one that fell apart, was for them. I thought it was my last shot to get their attention, but they never wanted me. The Guild, everything I had worked for — they never wanted me. I never had that chance I thought I was fighting tooth and nail for. My contact, Alros, told me before I decided to come here. I had nowhere else to go."

As gently as she could, Kir continued. "This isn't really any of my business, but since we are... friends," her voice nearly betrayed her, catching on the word, "I think you came here because you *wanted* to, not just because you needed to. You sound like you only needed an excuse."

"I don't know. Maybe you're right." Lottie's eyes locked onto Kir's as though she was searching for answers in their depths. "Gods, I can't believe I just told you all of that. I haven't told *anyone* that story."

"There's something special about this spot that does that to you sometimes," said Kir, smiling at the Grandmother Trees below them.

Lottie leaned into Kir's arm, her warmth permeating through Kir as though Lottie was a fire burning hot enough to incinerate the realm. "Seban is the reason the job went sideways."

Kir furrowed her brow. "Your friend? The only other one left?"

"He betrayed me. I brought him on because I thought he was loyal — or at least he was enough of a good person that he would watch my back. But instead, he sold me out. And everything crumbled with it."

A deep fury rolled through Kir, the emotions that she had been feeling through Lottie's entire story coalescing in a burning hatred for this man who dared go against Lottie.

"Asshole."

Lottie let out a shocked sputter, looking up at Kir with an awe that sent Kir's heart immediately in the other direction from hatred.

Ah, Maigsir's tits, this woman. *This woman.*

"Yeah, asshole is right." Lottie blinked around them as though taking it in properly for the first time. "Gods, how long have we been here? We should probably get going back to the bar. Though, I would much rather spend my day with you out here."

Lottie pushed herself to standing, all the while keeping her hand locked in Kir's. Kir, unable to form coherent thoughts other than *she would rather spend her day with me*, stood to help Lottie down from the rocks.

The heat coursing through Lottie's hand into Kir's was heating Kir through enough that she barely noticed the cold autumn air and icy ocean spray as they made their way back up the beach.

"You know something, Kir?" said Lottie as they stepped onto the cobbles of the Fetterly Place. "When I first met you, I thought you hated being around me."

Kir gaped at her. She didn't know what to say, the words threading themselves together in her mind in jumbles. *I could never hate you. I never hated you. Since you arrived in the bar, I've been trying to not make a total ass of myself and obviously that's absolutely failed. I'm sorry I'm so unable to put these thoughts into real words. I really don't hate you. Please don't think I hate you.*

Lottie's face slowly broke into a soft, genuine smile, watching Kir's face react. "I'm glad that I was wrong."

As Lottie walked back toward the bar, at last letting go of Kir's hand, Kir stood rooted to the spot, a blooming realization spreading like heat across her chest.

"I could never hate you," she said, probably too quiet for Lottie to hear. "I really, really like you."

Too much for my own good.

27

A SECOND STORY

Lottie – 23 Days Before

Weak autumnal sunlight met Lottie the next morning as she rolled out of bed, eyes barely open. The conversation with Kir had left her feeling as though someone had taken her apart and put her back together again slightly different. Like something broken inside of her she had long forgotten was even there had begun to heal.

I think you came here because you wanted to, not just because you needed to. You sound like you only needed an excuse.

Maybe this is your chance to make things a bit better with her.

Iluinn's mercy, Kir was probably right. Maybe she should be trying harder to fix things with Ceci, instead of avoiding her all the time. She stood up a little straighter and ran her hands over her face, feeling entirely exhausted.

Unsurprisingly, when she padded out of her room, she found the apartment empty.

A cold mug of coffee waited once again on the countertop, calling to

191

Lottie's soul. As Lottie reached for it, she noticed a small note written hastily next to it on a scrap of parchment.

L —

I FINISHED THAT BOOK YOU READ THE OTHER DAY. YOU'RE RIGHT, IT WAS QUITE GOOD.

Lottie blinked at it, entirely confused. She picked it up and turned it over, just to make sure that it was a real, tangible thing, before letting out a baffled laugh. Ceci, leaving her notes that were just... to leave a note? Tell her something?

Huh.

Lottie took the coffee in hand and sipped at it, leaning her hip against the countertop. Should Lottie do something nice for her? Perhaps, Lottie thought absently as she gently touched the note, telling her *you're right* — maybe she should buy Ceci another book that she might like.

It was an idea.

Lottie headed off through Arrowmount a little while later, after taking a moment to refresh herself and braid her hair, pulling the pieces of herself back together strand by strand. She bundled in her thick farmer's shirt and jacket and walked out into the grey world outside.

From outside of A Second Story, as she turned to look down the street, Lottie could just see the churning waves beyond the lighthouse, white caps winking hello. She ducked into the shop, shivering as the warm interior wrapped around her. The weather outside had tipped toward truly chilly today, with a mist clinging to the air like soup everywhere she went.

Lottie passed through the shop once again, smiling at details she missed before. There was a beautifully carved sign in the front desk, the honey-warm wood buffed to a glorious shine, and a small little bed in one of the front windows made for the brown tabby now laying atop it. Carefully, Lottie reached out to her, letting her sniff her fingers before scratching her gently between the ears. The cat started to purr immediately.

Lottie spent a little bit of time trying to recall the books that her sister loved when they were younger, but she could only vaguely remember the scope of sweeping romances and fairytales that she herself read. As she came around the romance corner once more, gently fingering the spine of a book that looked rather intriguing, she heard a soft clearing of her throat behind her.

"Ah, Miss Lottie Luck," said Arileas. He had his hair down today, flowing in soft waves down his back. "I didn't expect you to come back so soon."

"I'm actually on the hunt for something for my sister, but I can't for the life of me think of what she would like."

"Well, what do you like to read? Maybe she would enjoy the same thing."

Lottie suppressed a snort and turned it into a laugh. "Ah, yeah, probably not. Ceci and I don't usually share the same taste."

He chuckled and bent down, picking up the brown tabby cat that had materialized around his feet. "I take it you like romance, yes?"

Lottie peered obviously around at the section they were standing in. "How can you tell?"

"It's a knack of mine," he chuckled, eyes shining. "Is there anything you've read that your sister has also liked?"

Lottie nodded slowly and told him of the book she read a few days ago. The drama of it had drawn her in in a rather addicting way, and she just couldn't put it down. Arileas nodded thoughtfully.

His presence was incredibly calming, as she followed him around the store as he commented on various books he thought might be a good fit for what she was looking for. Lottie felt almost like herself around him, which was the strangest experience that she had ever felt around a nearly complete stranger. This man's calm, careful attitude, the warm atmosphere of the shop, and the way that the cat hadn't moved an inch from his arms completely relaxed her.

By the time they reached the front desk of the shop once more, Lottie found herself holding three books, each of them something that she felt both Ceci and her would enjoy.

"Gods, you've been wonderful," she said, putting the three volumes down on the counter. The tiny brown tabby finally leapt from Arileas' arms, settling down on the counter to nose the books carefully, before she began rubbing her cheek against the spines. "I never would have found these without your help."

He smiled at her before noticing the cat, and *tsked* in the back of his throat. "Sophie, please," he said, pushing her slightly out of the way. "Customers don't like when you rub your face against everything they own."

"It's alright," Lottie laughed, reaching out to scratch her between the ears. She leaned into Lottie's fingers. "She's such a sweet girl."

"Ah, she learns all her bad behavior from my partner," commented Arileas.

"You mean she gets her best assets from me," said a voice from slightly above them. Lottie gazed up the spiral staircase to see a dark haired, incredibly handsome man coming down, a grin on his face. "Ari, are you bad mouthing me to our customers before I've even had a chance to meet them?"

"Lottie, this is my partner, Finn," said Ari, waving a hand to the man. "Finn, this is Lottie Luck, Cecily's sister."

"Oh! What a lovely surprise! Ari was telling me about you yesterday."

Finn extended a hand and shook hers warmly before scooping up Sophie the cat from the surface of the counter. "Welcome back to our tiny little slice of bookish heaven."

"You really do have a lovely store. You have outdone yourselves."

"Ah, it's all down to Ari's work," said Finn, smiling, as he leaned in and planted a kiss on Arileas' cheek. Arileas turned slightly pink with pleasure. "Ari, love, I'm off to May's — hot or cold?"

"Hot. I'd love to try one of her new caramel creations, too. I think she's calling them pockets of whimsy?"

"Oh, I highly recommend," said Lottie emphatically, remembering the caramel filled twists she'd had with Aeric. "Those little pastries are *divine.*"

Finn winked at her. "Alright then, coming right up. It was lovely to meet you Lottie, I hope to see you around again. I have half a mind to pick your brain on what it is you do for work. Us adventurous types always have the best stories."

Finn turned toward the exit of the shop, depositing Sophie the cat on her bed by the window as he left. She meowed softly in protest, watching him leave as her tail flicked back and forth.

Lottie turned to Arileas, a question on her lips.

"Don't worry, I didn't tell him of the artifact or what you're doing with it," he said holding up a hand. "Finn and I used to be adventurers of a kind, so I told him about your rather adventurous lifestyle. He always gets excited to pick the brain of someone else like us."

Lottie chuckled, relief washing through her chest. "And now you own a bookstore?"

"I know, who would've thought." Arileas slid the books back across the counter to her as she handed him a handful of coins in exchange. "It's where we belong, though. There's something about this town. I'd be careful too, those cobblestones outside have a knack for drawing people in and never letting them go. You'll be here on a vacation one day and suddenly the next, you're buying the local bookstore with your partner."

"Well, as I have little interest in taking this place off your very capable hands, I am not worried." Lottie beamed at him. "Thank you again for your help."

"I really hope your sister likes these, and you as well if you get a chance to pick them up."

"I think I'll make a point to," answered Lottie, depositing the books into her bag. They thunked against the artifact inside, reminding her of its existence. She glanced down into her bag for a beat, briefly wondering if Khar had made any progress on their project. "I will have to make a point of coming back to your lovely store as well."

"I'll count on it."

She waved goodbye, gave Sophie the cat a little pat between her ears, and walked back outside into the mist, laden with her new purchases.

Lottie made her way up Fetterly Place after stopping at May's Cafe to pick up Ceci a coffee, heading toward the town center. Townsfolk were bundled in various amounts of layers trying to stay warm against the grey mist clinging to the air, hurrying from place to place to stay warm.

Lottie turned toward her sister's stall, weaving through the market, sucking in a breath to steady the onset of soft anxiety roiling through her. Why was she so nervous to see her sister? "Hey, Ceci."

Ceci looked up as she approached, a softly curious expression on her face. "Lottie."

"How's business faring today?"

Ceci narrowed her eyes, immediately seeing through her falsely cheery exterior. "What do you want?"

"Is it so hard to believe that I care about things my sister is doing?"

Lottie crossed her arms over her chest and mock-frowned at Ceci.

"Lottie, really."

"Fine." Lottie sighed. "I *really* came out this way to give you a gift. Or four, actually. This coffee is also for you"

"A... gift?" Ceci blinked, expression blank, taking the mug from her.

Lottie produced the three books, handing them to Ceci. "I stopped by A Second Story and picked these up, after your note this morning. I thought maybe you would like these. In exchange for letting me bunk in your closet."

"Spare room," corrected Ceci, though her heart wasn't really in it. She carefully slid the books into her hands, sorting through to inspect each of their covers in turn. "I just use it to store things."

"That's what a closet is for, Ceci."

Ceci thumbed through one of the books thoughtfully, her face relaxing into something softer than her usual expression. It wasn't quite a smile, but it was something less harsh than Lottie was accustomed to. "I haven't ever heard of these, but they don't look too bad."

"Arileas helped me pick them out. Hopefully they amount to something."

Ceci peered up at Lottie with a thoughtful expression. "Well, if Arileas was the one who picked these out, then I guess they'll be good enough to give a try."

Lottie scoffed playfully. "Excuse me? Are you saying that I have bad taste? Didn't you just read a book that I enjoyed and had a good time reading it? Telling me that I was *right?*"

"Fine, fine, yes, I concede, you did have that one good choice, Lottie." Ceci placed the books down on her stall and leaned against it with her hip, crossing her arms over her chest. "Thank you, Lottie. This... means a lot."

Lottie smiled down at her hands. "Well, you'll have to let me know how they are, because if you hate them then blame Arileas."

Ceci, to Lottie's surprise, snorted.

PART FOUR

Knitting and Possibilities

28

BREAKFAST

Kir – 18 Days Before

Kir's days passed in a blur of work, music, and nights at the bar with Lottie as time rolled forward to the first day of auditions. Kir woke earlier than usual one morning, weak dawn light leaking through her fogged-over windows.

Nudge was wrapped around her body like a hot water bottle, the room around them chilled through. Kir detached herself from him and stood, stretching her hands up to release the kinks from her spine. She drew on a large, handmade woolen sweater before crouching near the windows, drawing the sleeve of one over a pane to peer out into the misty, slightly blue-grey world beyond.

Today was the day. *Auditions.*

Though she had Lottie as co-chair, something about today felt heavy — meaningful — like Kir had to prove to herself that this leadership thing was something she was capable of doing. Something in the back of her head kept telling her that if she could handle this, if she could really pull the performances together for the festival, then perhaps she could also make it on her own as a bard outside of Arrowmount.

There wasn't a perfectly rational correlation between those two things, but her mind had latched onto it. She wasn't entirely sure when *that* had happened, when the panic and unease of being in charge of something had turned into an urge to prove herself. Kir breathed out long and slow, quieting the gentle anxiety in her chest. There were nerves, but instead of the heightened anxiety she usually felt at something new, this was manageable.

She stood up, catching the brief glimmer of sun appear reflected on the lighthouse standing sentinel over the shores of Arrowmount, and turned toward the day.

Lottie met her at the bar with an incredibly large coffee in hand, steam curling around her. The mug was nearly the size of Lottie's head.

"Morning," said Kir, lugging her lute case along next to her.

"Kir." Lottie spoke through a yawn, her eyes still puffy from sleep. "How is it possibly morning already?"

"Did you sleep okay?"

"Barely at all," said Lottie, blinking wearily. "How do people do this getting up early thing?"

"Have you had breakfast?"

"In the last year, or?"

"I'll take that as a no."

"Usually I'm not really awake enough for food."

Kir nodded knowingly and gestured at the bar. "Well, Corwek won't be in until mid-day to start cooking for the night's food, but I'm sure we can whip something up."

She unearthed a key from behind a loose board at the back of the bar and let Lottie into the back room, walking through to unlock the door at the front.

Everything inside looked odd, bathed in the brightening morning light that shone through the few windows. It felt as though the bar itself wasn't yet awake. Chairs and stools were placed up on the tables, which Nova and Briar did every night after everyone went home to wash the floors together and close up. This morning view of the bar was a paler, more drawn out version of the usually warm interior. It lacked the energy that thrummed through the place when it was open and full of patrons.

Lottie swayed sleepily by the bar, holding onto her coffee, as Kir began taking down a few of the chairs. It took very little time for Kir to clear a spot for their auditions in front of the small corner where she usually performed, pushing some of the bar's tables out of the way.

"So, about that breakfast," said Lottie from where she was now leaning almost fully onto the bar top on one elbow, fighting off sleep. Kir set her up on a chair nearby Corwek's stove to sip at her incredibly large coffee and keep her company. Slowly, whether it was the coffee or the scent of cooking butter, Lottie began to wake up.

Kir pulled out a store of bacon from the cold box and a few eggs, before quickly whipping up some of her father's potato cakes with the remainder of Corwek's potato stash.

"You can play the lute *and* cook breakfast," commented Lottie as Kir went through the motions, trying to keep everything in line and not burn anything. "A multi-talented woman. Where did you learn to cook?"

"My father and here," answered Kir, motioning at the stove with her wooden spoon as eggs and an assortment of well-seasoned veggies sputtered away in bubbling fat. "Corwek sometimes needed help when it got a bit busy, so it was helpful that my dad taught my brother's and I to cook as we grew up. This potato cake recipe is his, so if you hate it, you'll have to take it up with him."

Kir plated the breakfast and toasted a few pieces of roughly cut bread in the pan after the eggs were done, sopping up the remaining butter and spices with them. After sliding Lottie her plate, she leaned against one of Corwek's small preparation counters and started to eat her own breakfast, feeling slightly exposed as she watched Lottie dig in.

Cooking was something that her father did for her mother every day when she was alive. It was done with love, with care. Every bite mattered. That's what her father had taught all of them — Khar, Morgam, and her. To cook is to show someone how much you care for them.

"What?" asked Lottie after a moment, alerting Kir to the fact she was staring.

"Oh. Um." She swallowed and looked down at her plate, quickly popping a bit of food onto her fork. "How is it?"

Lottie nodded solemnly and chewed her eggs, contemplating, before sinking her teeth into a potato cake. Through the mouthful, she said, "Kirandir, this is quite probably the most delicious breakfast I have ever had."

"This coming from someone who basically admitted that she never eats breakfast." An incredible, unending happiness bloomed inside of Kir. She hid a grin by shoving a potato cake into her mouth.

Lottie snorted in response, spewing a few crumbs out of her mouth before swallowing her bite. "Out of all the breakfasts I *have* had, this is by far the best. It helps that I also have an incredibly beautiful woman cooking breakfast for me too. That, I can definitely say, has never happened for me before."

"Oh. Well."

"I have had one cook me dinner though. Wasn't nearly as good, but to be honest, we didn't really care about the food right then." Lottie lifted an eyebrow playfully. That cheeky little grin playing at her lips sent heat up Kir's neck, burning hot against her skin. She had no idea what to do with that. Honestly, whenever Lottie flirted with her, it was like every good part of her brain malfunctioned.

This woman.

Once their plates were clean, Lottie stood, much more awake. "I'll clean, since you cooked. That way you don't have to deal with work on your day off."

Lottie began to tidy, turning toward Kir's basin, dropping the dishes inside. She bent down to turn on the burner below it, tucking a stray strand of hair behind her ear. "Gods, how does this thing work?"

"Here." Kir stepped in and crouched by her, their fingers brushing as she turned it.

She tilted her head and gave Kir a look she couldn't quite read, and lingered there, their barely touching hands sending sparks across Kir's skin. "Thanks."

Lottie's eyes flickered down to Kir's mouth, then back up to her eyes, something shifting in them. Perhaps it was the shadows from being below the basin, or the lingering effects of a delicious breakfast, or because they were so close that Kir could see the details in each of Lottie's eyes, noticing the subtle changes in green —

Their heads were so close together all one of them had to do was shift.

I could kiss her right now.

The thought sent Kir to her feet in a panic, nearly bowling Lottie over. "I'll, uh, I'll grab the last few things."

What was that, Kirandir? the voice inside her head raged. *Maigsir's tits, you could have just kissed her!*

Kir sucked in a breath and turned from her, her cheeks burning. She stepped out into the main bar and took in a deep breath. Gods, she'd wanted to kiss her so badly — why hadn't she?

"You okay?" Lottie had followed her, stepping through the doorway and coming in close to Kir. She peered at Kir, a knot of concern between her eyebrows.

"Yeah, sorry." Kir motioned at her head. "Brain."

"Silly brain, you have to let our Kirandir free every so often." Lottie reached up and gently touched the small crease between Kir's eyebrows, her fingertip as soft as a flower. It sent shivers down through Kir, and for a moment, all Kir could see was Lottie. Her green eyes locked onto Kir's, bright and searching.

Kiss her.

Before she could do anything, though, Lottie stepped away with a soft smile on her face, before she slipped into to the backroom.

Kir dropped her head back and closed her eyes as her heart gave a great pang of affection. Everything about this woman was just —

This was going to ruin her.

29

A LITTLE LUCK

Lottie – 18 Days Before

A few minutes before they were scheduled to start their day of auditions, both Kir and Lottie sat waiting inside the bar. A number of voices chattered beyond the front door, announcing the crowd of folks waiting their turn.

Lottie, though, wasn't concentrating on anything around her, even though she was shuffling a number of papers in her hands, trying to look busy.

Gods, she had to get a grip on whatever was happening inside her chest every time she looked at Kir. Something had shifted since Kir had shown her the Grandmother Trees. The way her mood lifted when Kir was near, and the way her thoughts strayed to Kir, no matter what she was doing. She kept replaying the scene after breakfast, when her heart was seconds away from taking over her body and kissing Kir senseless.

Iluinn's disgraced teapot, this is too much. For all the pantheon's sake, Lottie, get a grip on yourself.

Lottie shook her head slightly, forcing herself to pay attention to what was happening in front of her, pushing the image of Kir's eyes darkening slightly as Lottie touched her face, featherlight, the soft opening of Kir's lips —

Voices outside. Performers waiting to come in.

Right.

As per Lottie's suggestion, they had made a sign-up sheet detailing that the performers were to write their name in the order in which they came. They were then to wait outside until they were called in to perform, so Lottie and Kir wouldn't have the bar crawling with people, overwhelming both those auditioning and themselves.

At the bottom of the paper they had noted that anyone who arrived after the page was full should come back the next day, so they wouldn't wait around all day for nothing.

Kir's face had gone blank, her eyes staring off into nothingness, as her fingers twiddled a pen back and forth. The crease had reappeared between her eyebrows and Lottie had to resist the urge to kiss it away.

She straightened her back and cleared her throat gently, drawing Kir's attention back into the room.

"Ready?"

Kir nodded and put down the pen, turning toward the door. She tapped the table in front of them twice with a finger, steel grey eyes coming back into focus. "Yes."

"What was that?" Lottie asked, pointing to Kir's hand.

"What was what?"

Lottie, settled back on one hip to gaze up at Kir, realizing how close together they were. Gods, Kir was tall. "The two taps. I've seen you do it a few times."

"Oh. Um. I picked it up from my mom — it's silly, really."

"I bet it's not."

Kir chuckled under her breath. "It's for luck. Two taps."

"A little luck," breathed Lottie, her voice catching slightly as her heart squeezed tight. The sight of the soft, slightly embarrassed smile on Kir's face was enough to send her to her knees. "Huh."

"Huh what?"

"Nothing at all."

Fuck.

Fuck.

Kir smiled, eyebrows pinching together in slight confusion, before turning toward the doors of the bar, away from Lottie. Lottie let her eyes fall closed.

Feelings that Lottie thought she would never feel surged through her. It took everything in her to not sit down on the floor and start crying — or laughing or stand up on the table and start to scream her feelings out into the room around her — she wasn't entirely sure which.

Shut it away, shut it down, she thought to herself. Deal with whatever this is later. Not right now.

Using whatever tiny bit of willpower she had left, Lottie swallowed down the knot of emotions tightening in her chest. With a nod to herself, she tossed a braid over her shoulder and straightened her spine.

A little luck.

Kir turned, hand outstretched toward the door. "Let's get this started, shall we?"

"Let's."

The auditions kicked off, taking hold of Lottie's attention and pulling it along into the afternoon. There were puppeteers, magic users, bards and minstrels, dancers, and a couple storytellers that absolutely captivated Lottie.

One of her favorites from the morning was the Montarali Family, who were a puppeteering troupe that came with their own stage. Instead of auditioning in the bar, they had Lottie and Kir come out to them, having set up their puppet theatre outside the bar.

Passersby and other performers waiting to audition joined the audience as the Montarali's began a quick yet absolutely riveting show with beautifully painted puppets. After, the two heads of the family walked into the bar to give Kir and Lottie their information, detailing a bit more about their act. Ainsley and Edwin were the main puppeteers; however, they also employed two apprentices named Lyndal and Tierri, who specialized in what they called roaming puppetry.

"Roaming puppetry is best described as something akin to what storytellers do," Ainsley had explained as the blank looks on both Kir and Lottie's faces. "Lyndal and Tierri have their puppets do the storytelling. It's rather fun, and we've had great success with their act in a few of the neighboring villages, and even as far as Pralon."

Lottie stood, trying to feel slightly more awake after a particularly mesmerizing illusionist finished their act. They had quite literally spun stories around the room, casting them into a world of starry galaxies and cosmos. Coming back to the reality of the bar was almost as though she was waking up from a realistic, perfect dream.

"Iluinn's mercy, I need to move," she moaned, stretching her arms up to the ceiling. "We've been at this so long."

Kir glanced at her before choking on a sip of water.

"Oh gods, Kir, are you okay?"

"Yes, entirely, completely." Kir was a deep scarlet as she turned from Lottie, coughing heavily. "Totally okay."

Lottie watched Kir out of the corner of her eye as she loosened her neck again, noting how Kir's eyes tracked down her body, her entire face red from suppressing a cough. *Well.*

Kir took a moment, turning away from Lottie, before she cleared her throat one last time. "You ready for the next set?"

Lottie sat back down in her chair, trying not to grin. "Bring them in."

The rest of the day passed in a bit of a blur, filled with various music acts and storylines that stuck in Lottie's head in threads and lost limericks. Kir had remained fairly stoic and calm the whole day, exuding an air of professionalism as she passed the occasional comment and praise to the performers, impressing Lottie over and over.

Once the last of the performers had left the bar — a sibling dance duo named Tresrel and Jael — Lottie let herself finally stand and stretch out properly. The dancers had been a fantastic final act. They had arrived with no minstrel or bard to accompany them, to which Lottie and Kir exchanged a curious glance. However, as Tresrel began to move, she started to cast spells with her body. Both she and Jael created the music they needed as they danced.

It was absolutely breathtaking.

Kir busied herself at their table, collecting all the bits of parchment they had accumulated over the countless performers had come through. All around them, the bar lanterns had been lit, casting the entire scene in the familiar soft golden glow.

"I can't believe we have to do this all over again tomorrow," groaned Lottie, closing her eyes. "There are so many people in this town that want to be part of this. Did you see the line we had still around midday?"

"It was smart to have sign-up sheets," said Kir as she put the stack of parchment into their committee box.

"Having to sit around for hours to be told to come back the next day is disheartening," said Lottie. "The idea to call in Corwek and make everyone some food was genius, by the way. Both I and my stomach thank you for that."

"I like being called a genius idea," said Corwek as he moseyed out from the back room, wiping his hands on his trusty towel.

Lottie pushed herself up from her chair with a groan. "Let's get this place back into order before Nova and Briar come in."

Corwek nodded in response, helping the two of them put the bar back into some kind of shape before Nova herself walked in the door, bringing with her a burst of cool autumn wind.

"Good evening folks!" She said, unwinding a long burgundy scarf she had wrapped around herself. She gave both Lottie and Kir a smile and a satisfied nod as she scanned the bar. "Like it never happened. I knew I could trust you two."

Lottie looked sideways at Kir as Nova bustled around, getting the bar ready for the evening's patrons. "What say you to some celebratory ale?"

"Absolutely."

30

STEEL GREY EYES

Lottie – 16 Days Before

Instead of running the auditions for two days as they had planned, Lottie and Kir had to add an extra third day due to the sheer demand of performers. The next two days went by with their own little surprises and excitement as Lottie and Kir grew their list of performers. On the second day, someone had come in with what they advertised was a dance performance but ended up being much more death defying. Kir had to rush out to find the local cleric to help when the performer had accidentally swallowed a sword the wrong way.

The third day, when a few magical acts came in, Corwek's soup exploded in a showery hot rain when a small child had attempted to make a few of the tables around the bar hover for their act. Corwek had been rather impressed at the child's skill to explode things and had sent the boy home with a few tankards full of salvageable soup for his family.

Kir's eyes sparkled as she waved the child out. Lottie laughed in ripples,

213

bent over in her chair. It was the kind of laughter that turned into uncontrollable wheezes and tears that streamed down her face, and she couldn't stop it.

When she thought she finally got a handle on it, she accidentally glanced up at Kir, who was trying not to laugh, and the two of them burst into fresh laughter all over again.

Corwek, who was still standing in the middle of the bar, surveyed the two of them shaking his head. He had a soft smile on his face, as though he knew something the two of them didn't.

"Cor-wek," wheezed Lottie, "You have — s-soup —" she pointed at the top of his head where bits of vegetables and meat had stuck in a mess of broth, occasionally slipping down and plopping unceremoniously onto his shoulder. Kir snorted and had to lean against their table to keep herself standing.

The next performer came in and frowned, shocked, taking in Corwek covered in soup and Kir and Lottie hardly able to breathe. Corwek started to clean the mess with a mop, shooting significant looks at Lottie and Kir as they tried to pull themselves together. Lottie put a hand to her chest as hiccups forced themselves out, tears streaming hot down her face.

She hadn't laughed like this in a really long time. They continued on, feeling slightly giddy throughout the rest of the day.

Once they had finally returned the Old'n Narrow to its usual state on the last day of auditions, both Kir and Lottie turned to their table in the corner, their trusty box of parchment in hand.

Lottie smiled at Briar as she slid two full tankards across their table to them, who winked in return. "For the two heroes of the day. I can't believe you two are through all of that hubbub. I passed by at mid-day to check on how things were going, and there was still a line up!"

"Arrowmount, it turns out, has an incredibly talented population," said Lottie, taking a long drag of ale and leaning back. "And an adequately funny one, too, if we take into account the few mishaps."

Briar chuckled. "Let me know if you two ladies need anything else."

Kir grabbed a stack of parchment from their box and withdrew their notes from the past three days of performances. "Right. So. What do we want to tackle first?"

The bar, right then, was exactly how Lottie liked it. A soft hum coursed through the air, rather than the usual nightly cacophony that built during the busiest hours.

Not long after they both had drained their tankards of ale, Lottie and Kir had a finalized list of who they wanted to perform throughout the festival. Though there had been an enormous number of auditions to parse through, the two of them agreed quickly on a few acts that stood out amongst the rest. Aside from those, they were able to weed through the rest of the performers and decide on who was going to fill out the last few spots of the schedule.

What took slightly longer was deciding who was going to perform when, and where.

Lottie twirled her pen around her fingers, analyzing the list of possible locations and times in front of her, frowning at the number of blank spots.

"You're in the last spot, that much is settled." Lottie smiled at Kir, finger brushing her full name at the bottom of the page where she'd penned it weeks ago. "Do you know what you want do to sing?"

"I've been tossing some ideas around," said Kir slowly, running a thumb along the side of her tankard. "It's always a good idea to play the popular songs, but I've been wondering about sprinkling in some of my own work?"

"Your work?" Lottie leaned forward, intrigued. She tracked Kir's face and marveled as color rose in her cheeks.

Kir dropped her eyes down before looking up between her eyelashes, eyes sparkling in the lantern light. "I've been working on my own music my whole life, though recently it's actually gotten good enough that I think I could share it."

"That's fantastic," said Lottie, her heart warming. "I think you'll do amazingly, Kir."

"You're just saying that."

"No, I'm sincerely sure that you will." Lottie reached out and grasped Kir's hand that held her tankard. "You should test out more of your own material on the bar some night, see how it goes. To see how you want to gauge your show."

"You're wonderful, you know that?"

The intensity with which Kir looked at her sent shivers down her spine, and all of a sudden Lottie felt as though she was back in the depths of her childhood with a crush on the next-door neighbor girl that she grew up playing with. Gods, it had been literal decades since she'd thought of her.

She swallowed. The ball of emotion from the first day of auditions was back with a vengeance. It threatened to spool out right there on the table between them. Slowly, Lottie began to brush her thumb across the back of Kir's knuckles.

Lottie, what is happening? Are you really developing a crush on this woman?

No, she thought firmly. *This is only happening because of the light in the bar, and how it makes Kir's eyes glitter in a certain way, and that Kir herself is incredibly beautiful, and I'm super tired after three long days —*
Ah. Why am I even trying?

Even the cynical voice inside of Lottie's head wasn't enough to talk herself out of these feelings.

She *liked* Kir. This was more than just a crush.

"Where did you go?" asked Kir softly. A gentle, warm knuckle settled under Lottie's chin and drew her eyes back up, sending her heart into a tailspin. Kir's eyes traced her face with so much intensity Lottie could feel it on her skin.

"I'm right here," answered Lottie with a sly lift of her eyebrow, panic coursing in from behind. *Oh, oh gods, oh —*

Kir closed the space between them marginally. The two of their faces were about a hand's length away from one another now, close enough that Lottie could see the moment when Kir's eyes began to darken, that same expression she had on her face three days ago spreading across her features like ink.

"It's... it's as though you have these masks," said Kir haltingly, trying to put her words together. "You put them on to hide."

Lottie swallowed and pulled back. She smiled at Kir then, forcing a smile that was entirely too sharp for this moment onto her face because she found herself entirely unable to do anything else. "Whatever could you mean?"

"Just like that," said Kir, continuing in a soft, low voice. She hadn't leaned back, her knuckle still holding Lottie's chin up, the heat of her finger burning into Lottie's core, amplifying everything inside of her. "You slipped away behind that smile. Before, you were just you."

The way Kir spoke, so plainly and matter-of-factly, didn't undercut the way her words went right to Lottie's heart. For an excruciating heartbeat, Lottie felt the back of her eyes burn. She locked eyes with Kir and, slightly horrified at herself, felt her mask slip aside a little bit. Kir's eyes registered the exact moment that it slipped, her gaze sharpening.

It was too much. Being seen was too much.

Lottie pushed herself up from the table. "I should go."

She turned from Kir, much more sharply than she ever intended, trying to ignore the pain in her own chest. Feelings were not things that she had for others. She could not be falling for this woman — *love* wasn't something that she even believed in.

What in the nine hells is going on?

How was this person who was tucked away in this little seaside town able to break through her armor so easily?

She didn't get two steps out of the bar before Kir came out too, catching the door before it closed.

"Lottie?"

"Hi."

"Are... where are you going? Did I say something wrong?"

"No, no, you're — you're good." Lottie breathed out a short laugh. "I don't know. I was just..."

"Stuck in your mind?"

"Yeah, you could say that."

Kir took a tentative step forward, closing the space between them again. Lottie had to crane her neck slightly to keep her eyes locked on Kir's. "Are you sure you're okay?"

"Yes, I'm... I'm fine. I think I just needed some air," said Lottie, dropping her gaze slightly only to be assaulted with the excellent view of Kir's collarbone, slightly unbuttoned shirt, and swell of her chest. She swallowed before looking back up slowly, finding Kir's gaze burning into hers.

I'm terrified of what being here is doing to me, and yet I can't seem to turn away.

Everything about this moment should be sending Lottie running down the cobblestone streets. She had gotten started, the fear bubbling up too hot and scalding, but —

Kir had come after her.

No one had ever run after *her* before.

Kir's eyes traced Lottie's face, snagging on her lips, before Kir's own parted ever so slightly. As though perceiving it through a different body and hers at the same time, Lottie watched as Kir's hand reached for hers, pulling her closer. A heat started to burn through Lottie's gut, want and fear and apprehension building to a crescendo.

She's going to kiss me.

And oh, oh gods, every fucking one of them, do I want her to.

The door to the Old'n Narrow opened, the heavy *clunk* causing the two of them to jump apart. Aeric stuck his head out, a curious look on his face. He eyed the two of them, narrowing his eyes.

"Are you two coming in to finish your ale, or are you going to leave Briar a mess to clean up?"

"Right." Kir cleared her throat and ducked inside after shooting Lottie a sideways glance that Lottie, entirely too frazzled, couldn't read. Lottie stood in her wake, feeling entirely too hot and cold all at once. Aeric raised his eyebrows at Lottie, a cheeky smile blooming across his face.

Gods.

31
SOMETHING MORE
Kir – 14 Days Before

A few days after the auditions, Kir found herself being dragged down Fetterly Street by Lottie who had a fierce grasp on her hand once again. Every time Kir found Lottie's hand in hers, she would lose herself for a moment. Her body yearned closer to Lottie's almost unconsciously, as though it knew, without a doubt, that this woman was exactly where she needed to be.

"We really don't need to go, Lottie," said Kir, slightly exasperated and equally as amused with Lottie, skipping to keep up without tripping on any loose cobblestones. "We would get more work done back at the bar."

"This is a *mandatory* meeting, Kirandir. For all of the festival volunteers." Lottie shot a look over her shoulder, lifting an eyebrow in challenge. "Besides. I want to meet some of the other people that are helping, since you and I have been holed up in the bar all alone."

A fresh bout of butterflies started up in her stomach. Kir, wanting to keep Lottie's attention a little more, leaned away from her and let her weight settle into her arm. Lottie immediately careened backward as Kir unsteadied her, drawing Lottie back into her embrace. Both of them let out a surprised gasp as Lottie turned in the circle of Kir's arms to meet her gaze.

Kir, for the first time, let her hands settle on Lottie's waist, keeping her steady.

There was a beat in which Kir saw a pure expression she couldn't quite read cross Lottie's face before Kir watched Lottie's expression flicker, falling back into a soft cheeky smile. Lottie took a step away, letting Kir's hands slide off her, creating distance between them. "Come on."

Ever since the moment outside the bar, when she had decided she was going to kiss Lottie before Aeric had so rudely interrupted them, Kir found it more and more difficult to stay still in Lottie's presence. Everything that the two of them did sent shivers up Kir's spine, even if it was simply sitting in the bar juggling the performers around a schedule, trying to find the perfect fit. Their energy together pulled back and forth, tension growing in glances and occasional touches.

And Kir had no idea what to do with it all.

She wanted to do *something,* but what? She had never really been this close with someone before, never wanted someone like this.

She ached to take Lottie's hand and draw her along toward something more. Find a moment like the one outside the bar where Kir could, instead of hesitating, fold Lottie into her arms and kiss her.

You don't know if Lottie wants the same, said a soft voice in her head. *And she's leaving at the end of the festival. Just be friends.*

And yet.

Every morning, her first thought was of Lottie, and how excited she was to see her that day.

Like clockwork, they kept seeing each other every day, too. Kir would sometimes run into Lottie out in the market, a smile on her face and a coffee in hand for Cecily, and it would brighten her whole morning. When she saw her at the bar talking amiably to Nova or Briar or Aeric, whoever was drawing her up a drink, Kir became even more excited to get out of the back and play. To see Lottie dance again. After she played, Lottie would stay, and the rest of the night could be theirs.

Even if the two of them were just friends, Kir didn't think she could handle watching Lottie walk away. She wanted to see Lottie every damn day for the rest of her life, if she could.

But that's not possible.

"So, this meeting," said Lottie, drawing Kir out of her thoughts. They finally fell into step with one another, heading toward the town center, a few fingers still intertwined as though they had forgotten they were touching in the first place. Kir felt that connection like the thrum of her lute strings. "Do you know what's going to happen during it?"

"Not a clue," Kir answered. "I've never been to a meeting in my life, unless you count my family's meetings. But those are unofficial and usually happen over a bowl of my dad's stew."

"Will I get to meet your family?"

"Do you want to meet them?" Kir blinked down at Lottie, a little shocked. "I never knew that."

"Well, I have already met Khar —"

Kir tripped on a cobblestone. "What?"

"I had to go to the smithy one day for one of my errands. He's rather lovely. I've been back a few times since, too. He's working on a project for me. But I do want to meet your other brother and father, too. You speak so highly of them."

"I'm sure they would love to meet you, too." Kir cleared her throat and made mental note to ask her about the project a little later. Why hadn't Khar said anything about meeting her?

They found their way to the meeting, arriving at a building marked on the outside by a jaunty yellow flag. The building had been built in between other structure like an afterthought, like many that ran along Abercorn Avenue. This part of Arrowmount was one of the older neighborhoods of the town, distinguished by tighter spaces and smaller buildings. Kir's neck started to ache preemptively. She hoped there were chairs inside so she wouldn't have to spend the whole time standing like a question mark.

Upon walking into the building, Lottie stepped slightly away from Kir to peer at a sign pointing them through, dropping their clasped fingers.

The hallway they walked through to get to the main room was so tight that both of Kir's shoulders brushed along either wall. She held in a breath and straightened up in an attempt to stop feeling as though she was so closed-in on both sides, but instead of helping, she smacked her head into the ceiling. Lottie turned at the sound, nearly elbowing Kir in the stomach.

"Small buildings," Kir said, rubbing her head, "really don't like me."

Lottie bit her lower lip, eyes sparkling with laughter. "Apparently."

"Welcome!" Neema bustled over, appearing at the end of the hallway. She was wearing layers of woolen garments so voluminous she looked like a warm, cozy snowball. "Come on in, we're just about to get started. I'm so glad you two could make it, and I'm sure Della will be overjoyed."

They followed Neema as she ushered them up a set of stairs — both of them had to duck, Kir nearly bending in double, to ascend without hitting their heads — to a second floor where it opened up right away into a fairly large room, almost four times the size of the hallway downstairs, with slightly higher ceilings.

Lottie lead her toward a couple empty chairs next to Cecily. It took a moment for Kir to remember that Cecily regularly volunteered for the Moon Festival, though she wasn't on any specific committee. Cecily glanced up at Lottie with a slightly detached expression. Kir could see the exact same moment where both sisters slid their masks into place, identical smiles of pleasant apathy settling into place.

Kir eyed the two sisters. They were almost perfect alternative versions of each other. Lottie, full of life as she took up space with her personality and her bod, thighs pressing into Kir's with a comforting warmth. Cecily was branch thin and held knotted up tight, a neutral smile on her face.

Lottie leaned into Kir, pressing their arms together, away from her sister. Whether she was doing that consciously or unconsciously, Kir didn't know. Cecily pulled out a bundle of knitted material and two needles from her bag, gazing forward as her hands started to work.

A sharp *raprap* called Kir's attention to the front, where Della was gathering up a bundle of parchment and trying to all the papers into a nice pile. The low murmur of conversation circling the room settled as everyone gave Della their attention.

Without consciously thinking about it, Kir shifted her hand over toward Lottie's again. Lottie, feeling the touch, lifted a pinky finger and linked it with hers, all the while gazing forward. The contact made Kir's heart swell and ache at once.

I am making this so much harder on myself.

32

KNITTING NEEDLES

Kir – 14 Days Before

Della beamed around at them.

"Well, hello hello! Welcome to both the first and last Total Committee Meeting." The room laughed as Della smiled kindly at them all. "As many of you know, we don't often have meetings with the whole lot of us in one place, because many of our specific jobs don't overlap during the Moon Festival itself. But I always say, what's a festival with volunteers without having at least one time where we can all come together and chat?"

"'Ere 'ere!" called someone from the other side of the room, eliciting a few more chuckles.

"So. We're here to discuss everything that we need to, to make sure that we are all on the same page as the Festival draws near. We are also here to fill anyone in on any problems that might have arisen over the past few days — and we are also here to lend a hand to anyone who needs it in the

225

last few days before we truly kick off the Festival."

Kir readjusted herself on her chair and leant back a bit. She glanced at Lottie out of the corner of her eye. Lottie was engrossed. She had this open expression on her face, as though she was trying to map every bit of what Della said. Kir slid her eyes over to Cecily to see if she was having the same reaction.

Instead, Cecily watched Della with the gently vacant air of someone trying to seem like they were paying attention but was actually far off in their own brain. Her hands worked tirelessly at the piece, her knitting needles tapping together gently. Kir studied her for a moment, unbothered, and noticed the gentlest of twitches between her eyebrows, as though she was trying to think through a complex situation. Lottie had gotten that same twitch when they were working through the schedule, just the night before.

Lottie leaned over to her for a moment, hissing something under her breath that Kir didn't catch. Kir watched as Cecily's face sharpened back to the present with a soft countenance of surprise that switched almost immediately into one of hidden, deep pain as Lottie leaned in close. Kir tracked the flicker of guilt pass over the elder sister's features before a mask slid expertly into place as she hissed a short answer to Lottie.

That must be where Lottie learned it from, thought Kir, turning to Della, who was still talking up a storm.

"Are you listening?" a voice murmured. Kir jumped slightly, realizing that Lottie was looking at her out of the corner of her eye. "Or are you just spending this meeting staring at me?"

"You are really lovely to look at," whispered Kir back, leaning in closer to Lottie's ear so that no one else would hear. Lottie's cheeks flushed with color, and she bit her lip, turning her focus back to the front. Her pinky curled tighter around Kir's.

The meeting passed on without much incident as Della had each of the committees give progress reports, which Kir was happy that Lottie took over without hesitation. Lottie was more than happy to stand up in her place, detailing plans and their newly established schedule they sent out to the performers the previous night.

"And what about you, Kirandir dear?" asked Della suddenly. The crowd of onlookers switched their attention to her, sending prickles of unease down Kir's spine. "Do you have your own set list planned out yet? Are we allowed to know anything about it? You know how exciting the last show of the Festival is, everyone is just bursting to hear it!"

Kir swallowed and shifted on her seat, trying to ignore the way that her tongue felt too heavy for her mouth. "Uh, I'm still thinking it through."

"It's going to be great," piped up Lottie then, smiling at Kir with a brilliant grin before casting that light on everyone else in the room. "We all know how fantastic Kir is, so her performance won't be an exception. In fact, it's going to be better than anything you all have seen from her yet."

Kir felt her cheeks heat as everyone in the room murmured their assent.

"Too right you are," said Della, clapping her hands together happily. "I cannot wait. Can't we get a little hint at your plans, Kir, or are you going to make us wait?"

"You'll have to just wait to hear," said Lottie, sparing Kir the response.

Della shook her head amiably, reminding Kir of a pleased mother goose witnessing her young growing up and doing wonderful things. What none of them in that room knew, though, was that Kir hadn't spent much time planning out her set.

Instead, her nights had been spent with Lottie, and other than occasionally wondering about a song she could sing for the bar, she hadn't put much thought past her preliminary plans.

Della moved onto a new part of the meeting as Lottie settled back into her seat once again. The soft heat from her side pressed into Kir's with a gentle familiarity.

"Do you have a set planned?" whispered Lottie, leaning over so just Kir could hear. Kir glanced up and noticed Cecily watching them, a slight crinkle appearing between her brows. Ceci's gaze flicked down to their entwined pinkies before shooting back up, catching Kir momentarily watching her.

"Uhm, sort of?" Kir whispered back to Lottie, focusing back on her, Lottie's side profile leaning in close as she kept her eyes and most of her attention on Della. "I haven't really had time recently to give it good thought."

"That's probably my fault, isn't it? We've been seeing so much of each other after your sets, I didn't even think." Lottie shook her head and peered sideways up at Kir through her eyelashes. "I'm a distraction."

Kir snorted and tried to cover it into a cough. "You're a good distraction."

"Well that nearly brings us to a close," said Della from the front, rubbing her hands together and looking over all of them. "One last thing — we need someone to help with a few of the decorations, as our lovely friend Fayri is unfortunately out with a family emergency and cannot help their co-chair wrap up the bits and bobs needed."

Della scanned the crowd before her eyes fell onto the corner where Kir, Lottie, and Cecily were sitting. "How about you, Ceci dear?"

"I might be able to," she answered, sounding a bit as though she very much could not take on more at the moment. "However, I really... I don't know if I could give them the right about of effort they need to be exactly right."

Della nodded understandingly. "I understand completely, you already do so much for us."

"But my sister might be able to take it on," said Cecily quickly. Kir caught Lottie's eyes fall closed in exasperation for a moment. "Then, at least, if I can devote some time to helping, she'll be right on hand. And you know how much I love helping out when I can."

"Of course! That sounds lovely. Lottie dear, we will kit you up with the supplies for the decorations before you leave. As for the rest of you, meeting adjourned! I wish you all a fantastic Moon Festival, and if you need any help, you know where to find me."

Lottie stood along with everyone else and turned a glare on her sister. "It always surprises me, though I don't know why it should, that you have the ability to charm and get your way with everything, Ceci."

Cecily gave her sister a softly superior smirk. "Best go pick up the supplies then, *Lottie dear.*"

As Lottie rolled her eyes and walked away, Kir watched Cecily's face slip into a slightly worried expression. She started to bundle away her knitting, sliding it into her bag after spearing it with both her needles.

"Are you alright?" Kir asked quietly, taking a step closer to her.

"Oh, yes, quite fine," said Cecily quickly, giving Kir a soft smile that matched the smiles she gave customers at her stall. "I'm — I'm happy that Lottie is finding a little bit of a place here, at least while she's around. Is she doing alright, with you and the Committee?"

"She's wonderful," answered Kir. "Has she not said anything to you about the work we've done?"

Cecily's kind expression slipped as she bit her lip and looked down and to the side nearer somewhere near Kir's shoulder. "We don't really talk all that much. We're not on the same schedule."

"Ah," said Kir, nodding slightly. "Well then yes, she's doing great. I really enjoy having her as a partner."

"I'm glad."

Kir let her eyes trail along Cecily's face as she watched Lottie, who was currently being instructed carefully by Della and another volunteer.

"She really does love you a lot, you know," said Kir softly to Cecily. Cecily flinched slightly in surprise, as though she had forgotten Kir was there. "She speaks very highly of you."

"Does she? That's nice to hear," said Cecily with a soft voice. After a beat, she shifted back into her market stall smile. "Kirandir, it was lovely seeing you here. And, if Lottie ever... does anything, feel free to come and talk to me, okay? She has a history of broken hearts trailing behind her."

Kir blinked after Cecily as she walked away, wondering what that could possibly mean.

33

AN ASTRONOMICALLY DISGRACED TEAPOT

Lottie - 14 Days Before

Lottie walked back to Ceci's apartment with her arms full of crafting supplies weighing her down. By the time she got home, she felt as though her hair was a great show of how exasperated she was — tendrils flew everywhere around her face, entirely evading her earlier attempts to tame it into braids. She could even feel a clump that had escaped tickling the back of her neck.

It had taken Della and Eiris, the volunteer who needed the decorations made, an extra thirty minutes to make sure that Lottie knew what she was doing when it came to her crafting — so long, in fact, that Kir had left to the bar to prepare for her set and the rest of the volunteers had vanished.

Once inside Ceci's, Lottie swore under her breath and kicked off her shoes. A bunch of the crafting bits tumbled free, clattering to the floor. She walked over to Ceci's tiny table nestled against one wall to deposit the crafting material onto before bending to pick up the fallen bits, cursing gently.

"You alright?"

Lottie looked up in surprise at Ceci's voice. She was curled up on the couch, eyeing her from a nest of blankets, two knitting needles and a ball of yarn in hand.

"Yeah, just dropped some bits."

Ceci nodded and peered at the table once before turning back to the knitting in her lap. Lottie could almost hear her sister's brain whirring about the mess that was about to be left behind.

Lottie organized her workstation as best she could, sliding her bag off her shoulder and onto the floor beneath it. A few of the kitchen chairs around the table overflowed with used a few of the kitchen chairs to help store some of the things so she could easily access it when she needed.

Ceci eventually got up to put on a small music player, which cast a soft ambiance to the room that immediately relaxed Lottie's shoulders.

"I haven't heard this since we were kids," said Lottie cautiously.

"It's one of my favorites," answered Ceci, shifting on her chair before peering at the project in her hands. She took a moment to readjust the yarn, poking at a few of the stitches on her needles.

"I found a record of it in an old shop here, one day," continued Ceci. "I think it was on my birthday, a few years ago."

"Oh." Lottie's voice felt so tiny, then, realizing with a painful jolt how many of Ceci's birthdays she'd missed. "Did... do you do anything special for your birthday?"

"This and that," answered Ceci, looking up briefly. "A couple of my friends here have tried to make me more social over the years."

There was a few more minutes of silence mixed with the record of gentle music, casting the two of them into deep memories.

"What about you?"

Again, Lottie was startled to hear her sister's cautious voice from the couch. "Oh. Um. I don't... I don't really celebrate," she answered, trying not to think of the years, one after another, that she had dreaded her birthday as it approached. She'd throw herself into whatever distraction would work, whether that was alcohol or a stranger's arms. The next morning she'd wake with her head hammering out a painful tattoo, but her birthday would have passed, and she wouldn't have to think about getting another year older without her sister at her side.

"Oh."

The two of them fell into silence once again as Lottie turned her attention to her task at hand. It was proving to be a lot harder than she had previously figured, watching Della and Eiris help her through the motions of putting the things together.

The task reminded Lottie of the little flags that ran over the streets of Arrowmount, but on a smaller scale — each of the handmade leaves had to be tacked along a handwoven bit of twine to create a garland. There were about twenty leaves allotted for each length of the twine, and countless lengths of twine to go through. It had looked simple enough, but the materials were proving to be tricky to pull together. The leaves simply *refused* to stay fused to the twine.

"Come on," she muttered under her breath after a while, feeling slightly distressed, as her now completely sticky fingers caught on a bit of a leaf that shouldn't have been glued together and everything slid sideways. "No! Ugh, come *on you godsforsaken thing.*"

"Lottie?"

Ceci materialized beside her elbow, arms crossed over her chest, looking warily at the crafting going on around Lottie.

"Sorry, Ceci, I didn't mean to bother you, I —"

"You're not bothering me." Ceci peered around at the mess, a small crease appearing between her eyebrows as she contemplated it all. "Do you want help?"

"Oh, no, that's fine. I — I think Kir might pop over to help —" That was a lie, and she knew it. Kir was playing at the Old'n Narrow tonight.

"About that — what is going on between the two of you?"

Lottie blinked up at her sister. Her cheeks started to heat up against her will. "Uhm, what do you mean?"

"I noticed that you and she had some interesting energy at the meeting." Ceci bent to move a basket of unused twine off of the chair next to her before sitting down carefully. "She could barely keep her eyes off of you. There was also the way *you* stepped in for her."

"I mean, she's my friend." Lottie slid a plain smile on her face, hoping it was enough to hide the burning heat that was threatening to surface in her cheeks. "Isn't that what people do for friends?"

"I'm pretty sure friends don't hold pinkies and share secret whispers." Ceci raised an eyebrow at her, a smirk playing at her lips. "And the way that you two look at each other — honestly, if I was blind, I still would have seen something."

Shit. Lottie sputtered out a forced laugh.

"So, what's going on between you two?"

Lottie bit her lip. She had been planning on bombarding Aeric with a bottle of mead at some point to discuss her feelings, but at the moment, it was almost nice to have Ceci here. "I..."

"You don't have to answer," Ceci said quickly, sitting up a little bit straighter. "I didn't mean to pry."

"It's fine, really." Lottie breathed in deep. "It's been so strange. I don't know what it is with her — I can't seem to get her out of my head. Every waking moment, I'm thinking about her. Or something to do with her, like the Committee, which just turns into me thinking about her again. And when I see her, I have to refrain from jumping out of my skin to get close to her. I… I don't know."

Ceci started laughing. Lottie marveled briefly in the sound, having not heard it since she'd been small. "You don't know? What do you mean you don't know?"

"I don't know what to do with all of these feelings, it's like they're eating me up from the inside. I want to be with her all the time. I…"

"Lottie." Ceci leaned forward and tentatively touched Lottie's hand. "You like her. You *like* her. *Love* her, from the sounds of it."

Lottie felt slightly nauseous and lightheaded. "Love isn't real."

"What in all the nine hells do you mean love isn't real?" Ceci snorted. "Lottie, seriously. Think like a functioning adult for once."

"Love just hurts people," Lottie said softly, gazing up at her sister slowly. "It's a burden. Nothing good ever comes of it."

"*Nothing*… Lottie. Love is not a burden. Yes, it can be incredibly painful, but it is also the best feeling that you can ever experience." Ceci eyed Lottie before she turned fully toward her. "What is it that you feel when you're around her?"

"Peace," Lottie said without thinking. She felt her face heat up.

"Like the world has stopped hurting, for a little bit?"

Lottie let out a defeated sigh and closed her eyes. "Yeah, exactly that."

"Do you want to kiss her? To be with her?"

A strangled sound escaped Lottie's throat. "What?"

"Do you want to kiss her?" Ceci repeated. She lifted a pragmatic eyebrow, turning back to the craft in her hands. "It's a simple question."

Lottie opened her mouth like a fish, unable to make a sound. *Gods yes.* One hundred times over. Every moment that she was with Kir, she wanted to. When Kir smiled. When Kir got that little look of confused concentration on her face as they were trying to sort out a particular sticky bit of the schedule. When she played and sang at the bar.

"I knew it."

"I..."

"It's okay to feel this way, Lottie," Ceci said quietly, continuing to work on the length of twine in her hand. "In fact, it's very normal to feel."

Lottie picked at the bits of paper leaf stuck to her fingers, letting the remnants fall to the tabletop. Ceci, without prompting, reached over and started to pull things toward her, watching what Lottie was doing so she could help.

"Thank you, Ceci," Lottie breathed.

They slowly fell into a rhythm of quiet crafting as the soft, lilting music filled the room softly behind them.

"Do you remember the first time we got our hands on some glue?" asked Ceci a while later, pulling Lottie gently out of her focus. She looked up and chuckled, her hands pausing for a moment.

"Wasn't it with when we tried to put together our first market stall?"

"Yeah, exactly that."

"I don't remember — did it have a sign?"

"It did, though it ended up being covered by anything we could glue onto it," answered Ceci. Lottie marveled at the soft smile crossing her sisters face and the way that it softened everything about her. It was rare to see, this true smile. "But we didn't really care."

"And we didn't sell anything, either."

"That's because you got your hand —"

"Stuck," finished Lottie, laughing, the hazy childhood memory slowly surfacing of the two of them during the brief time they had lived in a House for Lost Children. "Then, didn't the Matron have to cut our sign into pieces just to free it? And even then —"

"You had to walk around for a week with a piece of wood fused to your hand until the Matron could contact a magic user to help remove it."

"That glue must've had some kind of god-like strength stuff infused into it," said Lottie, chuckling.

"I think we used something they were using to reface the floors."

"At least we figured out what we were doing after that."

Ceci rubbed her fingers together, beading a bit of the sticky glue off her skin in tiny balls of gunk. "I guess you could say that."

Lottie looked up at her sister through her eyelashes and swallowed. She broached another memory, and soon the two of them were quietly remembering as they continued to craft well into the night. After a couple hours, Ceci sighed and put down her finished length of twine, pushing herself to standing. She yawned wide and stretched.

"I think I'm going to go to bed, this is later than I've stayed up in a long time."

"Thank you for helping me."

Ceci hesitated before she laid a warm, soft hand on Lottie's shoulder. "Lottie, I know I'm not really the person to be telling you what you should or shouldn't be doing with your life, but... think about what you are going to do after this committee thing is over. Where you're going to go. If it's anything other than spending the foreseeable future with that woman, you're going to break her heart."

Lottie blinked after her sister as she vanished into her bedroom.

Love.

Lottie had never expected to fall for someone. Ever. All she had in her "foreseeable future" was tucked inside her bag and oozed ancient magic.

Now — Gods, she had no idea.

And she was falling for someone. Actually *falling for her.*

Falling for someone who was too good for her. Kir had her talent, the way that she read people, the easy gentle way she simply knew how to get through to Lottie. She'd opened Lottie up more in weeks than anyone had ever done in Lottie's entire life.

And gods did she want to kiss her. So fucking badly.

Iluinn's astronomically disgraced teapot, I need to get a grip.

Lottie dropped her head into her hands, letting out a soft groan.

34

POSSIBILITIES AND INSPIRATION

Kir – 12 Days Before

Kir trailed her hands through the warm, sudsy water, barely paying attention to what she was doing. Her brain had taken her fully away from the bar as a lull hit, Corwek's light whistling as he cooked slowly in the corner adding to the scenes flowing through her mind.

Onstage, lit with an arcane spotlight aglow around her, Kir glanced up from her lute into the crowd, which was usually clouded in shadow in her fantasy to see clearly. This time, one face stared back. Beautifully soft, gentle whorls of bark accenting her cheeks as she smiled, tendrils of summer-green hair falling into her face out of one of her braids.

Lottie Luck.

In her mind, Kir's hands danced across her lute, playing better than she ever had. Songs danced from her fingertips, every note played exactly the way she wanted. And when she started to sing, her voice was exactly the right quality that she wished she could hit every night.

"Is that a song you're going to play for the festival?"

Kir jumped, her hands splashing slightly in the water. Aeric had appeared next to her, two plates in hand.

"What?"

"You were humming under your breath." Aeric winked as he dropped the dishes into the water basin. "It was quite lovely. I don't recognize it, though."

Kir chuckled and shook her head. "I wasn't paying attention."

"Maybe it's your brain working for you, getting you ready for the festival performance."

"I haven't really thought about what I want to play at the festival show. I know," she said, noting his look of shock, "I just haven't... had it on my mind. Been busy with other things."

Aeric's face split into a knowing smile. "It's been replaced by one Lottie Luck, hasn't it?"

Her cheeks heated. "I meant the Entertainment Committee."

"Oh, I'm well aware how busy the two of you are, being all cute in your little corner of the bar every night." Aeric leaned against her water basin and crossed his arms. "But really — you haven't thought about your set at all? Even when you go to your little mind palace as you work?"

She grimaced. "I haven't."

Aeric frowned thoughtfully for a moment then burst into movement, clapping his hands and standing up straight. "I have the perfect solution. Since it's slow, you take the day to go find that inspiration. See where it takes you."

"Agreed. We'll have Aeric wash the dishes in your absence," said Corwek, chuckling from by his stove.

Aeric's glee froze and shattered on his face. "That's not what —"

"I can't leave," Kir said, gaping at the two of them. "I've already left multiple times this month."

Both Aeric and Corwek shrugged as Nova walked into the back room. Nova wiped a tankard dry with a towel. "Do you need the day, Kir?"

"She's going to go off and find inspiration," said Aeric for her, all but pushing Kir out of the back room.

"I —"

"That sounds like a grand idea," said Nova with a smile. "Our favorite musician does need some time to herself, to refuel that wonderful well. Besides, when was the last time you had a day off to yourself, to actually do whatever you wanted? All the times you've left these past few weeks have been for other reasons, and you've always come back within an hour or two. Take the day."

"But —" Kir stared at the three of them as they ushered her out the back door, pushing her lute case firmly into her hands. "Really?"

"Really. We can make do without you for one evening, Kir." Nova waved her off.

So, without much other choice, Kir turned and began to walk away from the bar, winding through the back alley out to Fetterly Place.

Inspiration. It had been so long since she had found any scrap of it, with her brain busy with Lottie and the committee. Whatever she played at the bar came from her usual arsenal.

She had originally planned for her show to include something new, but as she was only fourteen days away from the start of the Moon Festival, there was hardly any time left. If she was going to write anything new, now was the time.

She thought about going home, locking herself into the workroom or her bedroom and seeing if anything happened to bloom in her mind, but something in her bones told her it wasn't the right place to be.

Kir hesitated, coming to a stop in the middle of Fetterly Place as a few townsfolk bustled by her, wrapped in warm scarves and thick layers against the chill autumnal wind.

Her gaze traveled toward the lighthouse that sat framed by the grey ocean at the end of Fetterly Place, the sound of the waves imperceptible over the wind and chatter of townsfolk around her. Seabirds above called sharply, hovering mid-air as they banked against the currents of air. Without meaning to, Kir started to walk toward the water.

Her feet took her toward the Grandmother Trees, running along the damp, cold sand. Sea spray bit at her neck and face, but instead of drawing her shoulders up against it, Kir turned toward it, closing her eyes, letting the wind tease her hair free.

By the time she was settled behind the Grandmother Trees, Kir was soaked through. The ladies' hulking forms blocked some of the weather, but it was definitely not the best place for her lute. As she settled onto the rock, though, Kir withdrew it from its case anyway. Cold seeped up from the rock through her trousers, sending shivers up her spine.

She let her fingers pluck at her lute without real direction, testing chords here and there as her mind wandered. She thought of Lottie for a long while, as she had been for the past few weeks non-stop. Her fingers began to pluck through a familiar love ballad she regularly played at the Old'n Narrow.

Since Lottie first walked into the bar and entranced her with her beautiful smile, Kir's life hadn't been the same. Her routine had been upended by the addition of the Committee, sure, but what had changed entirely was her mind and heart. Kir couldn't honestly say the last time she had been so consumed by someone like this.

The busyness of the Committee had kept Kir from really ruminating about it until now, but as she sat there plucking at her lute, she was rather astonished with herself. Change wasn't something that Kir found easy, but with Lottie, the change wasn't... bad. In fact, she rather liked how much it had made her life seem a little bit more alive.

I wish I could keep this feeling going, she thought briefly, her fingers changing tune once again, plucking out random chords to try and find a melody hidden within them. *Keep my life feeling vibrant and alive.*

They were nearly upon the start of the Moon Festival, and Kir was still okay. In fact, she was more than okay — she had handled the auditions better than she could have imagined, and actually had fun during them, rather than dreading the constant churn of meeting new people and having to converse with them.

You did say that if you could handle this whole committee thing, you'd be able to handle taking on your dreams.

Kir closed her eyes, her fingers momentarily stalling on her lute strings. She had thought that. The chance to prove that she could handle this much responsibility, could handle the ins and outs of planning the Festival. At this point, she and Lottie had very little left to do except for wait until they could start setting up the stages and actually start the festival with the rest of Arrowmount. They had accomplished so much work together that even Della was surprised they were ahead of the game, having only had a month to pull things together.

She'd done it. They'd done it, together, her and Lottie.

Perhaps my dreams are a lot closer than they once were, she thought to herself. Her usual fantasy of singing on a big stage flashed across her mind, the arcane circle of light aglow around her. That dream had gone as far as it could here in Arrowmount. The final performance at the end of the Moon Festival didn't really feel that large to Kir, either. Not now, not that she's been used to performing each night. Sure, it would be the biggest crowd she'd performed to before, but... the dream digging it's heels into Kir's mind knew that one day soon, she'd be playing to even bigger crowds.

Chase your dream, love, said a soft voice in her mind that she didn't quite recognize anymore.

Kir closed her eyes, trying to place it. She cast her memories back to a summer long, long ago, when she was a fraction of her size now, sitting on these same rocks next to her mom. A beautifully elegant face turned to look at her, smiling. In the memory or vision — she wasn't entirely sure which — her mother reached out to adjust Kir's hair, tucking it behind her ear. The touch was so soft, so loving, that Kir's tiny little chest swelled with love and warmth. Everything, even grown Kir drenched in sea mist, felt perfectly dry and protected.

Do whatever you can to find that passion, that happiness, I know is in your heart, my Kiri. Chase that dream.

Kir opened her eyes, coming back to the view of the Grandmothers with a smile on her face.

The concept of leaving, of finding her way through the empire and making something of her dream, wasn't terrifying anymore. It also felt less like a dream now and more like a path opening in front of her, real and close at hand.

She sighed, turning her attention to her fingers poised on the strings of her lute.

Leaving could bring about many possibilities she never even knew existed. She definitely didn't want to spend the rest of her life washing dishes just to play to a half-listening crowd at the end of the night, even though she had enjoyed it enough.

Maybe, just maybe, she could find a life that was outside of what she was used to. And maybe that life would be pretty great.

The song at her fingertips began to swell around her, new and fresh, thinking about the possibilities out there. Words hovered on her lips, and, protected by the Grandmothers, she began to sing.

"East-ward down I live, near the waves glimmerin' gold,
Singing for my people, the stories and tales of old..."

35

GAUZY YELLOW CURTAINS

Lottie – 12 Days Before

Lottie headed off into Arrowmount with her arms laden with her finished decorations and whatever leftover material there was a couple days later, following directions Della had given her to Eiris' place. She'd taken the time to make sure that all of the decorations had dried properly, that all of the leaves were staying adhered to the twine like they were supposed to, and that they were carefully bundled to transport to Eiris.

She found her way to a tiny apartment, tucked in one of the oldest parts of Arrowmount, where the buildings crouched tightly together, and the doorways were slightly mismatched and small.

"Oh, Lottie!" A voice called as she approached. She peered around the decorations in hand to see Eiris themself hurrying out of their apartment toward her. "I thought that was you, I could see you from my windows."

They motioned up to the top floor, where the buildings peered out into not only this cramped alley but the street behind.

"Here are the decorations, done and ready," said Lottie. "Would you like me to bring them up for you?"

"That would be perfect, thank you ever so much. We're all the way at the top."

Lottie followed Eiris up into their apartment, the sides of her arms grazing either side of the stairwell.

"I'm so sorry it's tight," said Eiris, the tiny human speeding up no problem. "You wouldn't imagine the trouble trying to bring furniture up here."

"Oh, that must have been a hassle and a half," said Lottie.

"We had to hire a wizard from the town over to come and help us lift some of the heavier bits, like my partner's piano, through the windows. It was a whole thing." They finally reached the top landing, Eiris pushing open their door. Inside, surprisingly, wasn't overly cramped, despite the space being quite small.

Lottie supposed it must have been the use of windows on nearly every wall possible. The light up here, on the top floor, was exceptional.

"You can put them wherever," said Eiris, motioning toward their small yet wonderfully cozy living room. They had put up gauzy yellow curtains, which cast the entire space in a lovely warm glow.

Lottie placed the decorations on a nearby armchair and stood, eyeing the aforementioned piano in the corner. She cast her mind back, thinking over the list of musically inclined folks who had come out for the auditions, trying to remember if anyone had played the piano. "Did your partner audition for the Festival?"

"Oh, no," Eiris laughed, shaking their head. "They're not overly musically inclined, they simply enjoy playing whenever they can. I love to hear it, but they've never thought about sharing that music with others. Plus, we'd probably have to have a wizard come and magic the piano out for us again, it would be a whole ordeal."

"Ah, yeah, it's not a very portable instrument, is it?"

Eiris chuckled. "Not in the least. But I can say, we are looking forward to seeing what you and that lovely Kirandir have cooked up. The music is always my favorite part."

Eiris waved Lottie out of their place and back out into the cramped courtyard a few minutes later. Lottie reached for the strap of her bag usually sitting across her chest and found nothing. She frowned down at herself, before calling up to Eiris who was still on the stairs.

"Ah, I wouldn't have left my bag up there, have I?"

Eiris hurried up to check, only to run down a few moments later shaking their head. "Nope, no bag! I don't believe you were wearing one when you came in."

"Ah, alright, must have left it at home then."

Lottie frowned at herself, making a mental note to check when she got home. It was incredibly rare that she forgot her bag, especially now with the artifact sitting inside.

I was probably too preoccupied with getting the decorations ready, she told herself as she continued through Arrowmount, heading toward the blacksmiths. She'd planned to stop by anyway and check in on Khar's progress with the replica of her artifact.

Today, as she approached, the smithy was emitting a loud, continuous scraping noise that grated. Every person she passed had a displeased expression on their faces as they walked by, some even going as far as covering their ears.

She approached, wincing, and waved to Khar, who was in the process of holding what seemed to be a large, blunt axe head against a spinning wheel. His leg pumped a pedal, which appeared to keep it spinning. Every other time he held the iron to it, he changed the angle of his hold, sending out sparks down toward the floor.

The scraping noise wasn't, as Lottie surmised, the axe head being ground to a sharp point — it was the wheel itself.

"Hiya," Khar yelled over the sound. "You might want to block your ears for a second."

She complied, trying to deaden the sound, watching him work. Finally, he stepped back from the wheel once the iron in his hand had a thin band of smooth, shining metal at one end.

"Your wheel sounds like it needs oil," she commented, her ears ringing.

"I hardly notice it anymore, but yes, something's gone a little sideways inside her." He frowned at it as it slowly ground to a stop. "What can I help you with today, Miss Luck?"

"I came to check on my replica."

"Ah, of course. Come on back."

Khar's workstation looked much the same as always as she followed him into the office, except this time it was covered in various bits of bronze and other metals, hammered thin. Khar brushed his hands across the surface, sending a few of them to the floor, but at the same time revealing the beginnings of a twelve-sided artifact.

"This is what I've got so far," he said, holding it up. Lottie plucked it from his hand, immediately surprised at the weight of it.

"That's not far off," she said, bobbing her arm a few times to feel the true heft of it. "Actually, I think that's rather exact. And the shape — the actual size of it — Khar, you did all of this just from your notes?"

"After a few tries, of course. Nothing is worth trying if it doesn't take a little bit of experimenting first." He wiggled his eyebrows at her. "But yes. That's what we're going with. From here, I work on the shape, and actually start doing the detail work. Shouldn't be overly difficult now."

"Just time consuming."

"Incredibly so." Instead of being daunted by the task, Khar looked fairly excited for it. "I've been testing some of the markings out, seeing how they hold up in the metal, how deep I have to go, how small the tool needs to be. I had to actually file down my smallest chisel to a point the size of a needle to get it right."

Lottie let out a low whistle as he held up a sheet of perforated bronze, the markings starting out large, some poking right through the sheet, before they became increasingly smaller down hear his fingers. At the bottom, Lottie could've sworn he'd taken them right from the surface of the artifact.

"This is going to work," she said quietly, almost a whisper. "Khar, that's it."

"Well, I still have to figure out how to age it, and actually work on the etchings." He put the sheet of metal down. "But as of right now, I've figured out how to keep the metal from bending or becoming overly pliable once the detailing is done. Bronze is a rather interesting metal to work with. Though it can be a bit brittle, it's strong, and it keeps hold of the details we want."

"Do you know how long it will take you to get the specifics done?"

"Well, once I get going, I may be able to have it done in a few days. But as I work on it, I want to make sure that I'm being precise and careful. So give me... a week? Perhaps a little bit more?"

Lottie nodded, relief flooding through her chest. At this rate, it would be done well before the Festival and any potential arrival of Alros, if he decided to come hunting.

36
DON'T MIND THE PLANTS
Lottie – 8 Days Before

Lottie hurried home to Ceci's apartment, the starry sky above her unmarred by clouds, with a scroll tucked between her fingers. Briar had handed her a scroll as she left, addressed to her in Alros' cramped writing. She kept wanting to slide the scroll away, out of sight, but she'd forgotten her bag again, and though she had pockets, she was nervous about the scroll falling out of them as she walked.

The unease and panic mingled in her gut with the joy of the evening, making her feel slightly nauseous. She'd noticed Kir's eyes on her more than was probably proper throughout the set. *Like she was singing to you,* said a tiny voice in her head, one brought on by ale and good music.

Gods, Kir was so good at what she did. It was as though the whole bar attuned to her music when she played — she drew in the energy and almost became a different person as she played. She became a more amplified version of herself.

Lottie would have sworn Kir had magic from the way her music sang through Lottie's soul. She bit her lip as she recalled the way Kir's eyes had connected with hers as she played the last song. Something in their depths burned, and Lottie wasn't entirely sure how to handle it.

You're leaving soon, said a traitorous voice in the back of her head, dampening her mood before she could push the thought away. *You literally are holding a scroll from someone who could ruin everything, and probably will.*

She needed to get home, to where there was enough light, to read it. As she reached Ceci's place, Lottie had mounted the stairs two at a time and carefully opened the door.

Lottie poked her head into the apartment, making sure to make as little sound as possible to not disturb Ceci's sleep. She slipped her shoes off and tiptoed toward her room through the dark, only to jump back in surprise as a figure stood up from the couch.

With Lottie's bag in hand.

Lottie absently patted her side, even though she knew very well that her bag wasn't currently strapped around her chest.

"Hi, Ceci," said Lottie carefully as her sister's still, blank expression became slightly clearer in the dark apartment. There was a light on in Ceci's room, as though she had just been about to go to bed.

"What's this?"

"My bag. You've seen that before; I bring it everywhere." *Usually.*

Ceci made a sound in the back of her throat and her mask cracked, showing the bubbling, simmering anger beneath. She reached into Lottie's bag and withdrew the artifact, light seeping through her fingers. "Not your bag. This."

"Ah. Well that's the artifact I was sent to get."

"Artifact."

"You remember, the job... before this."

"You didn't tell me you'd brought a stolen artifact into my home," said

Ceci, her voice a dangerous calm. "In fact, if I remember correctly, you told me that job went sideways. So what is this doing here?"

"It did." Lottie took a careful step forward, her hands lifting up as though she was warding off a wild animal. "I was chased out of the city by guards and decided to come here because I had nowhere else to go."

"And the Guild doesn't care that you have their artifact? Or are you on some kind of secret mission for them to — to —" Ceci shook in her anger.

Lottie winced. "I've decided to go my own way, Ceci. They know I have it, and —"

"*What?*"

"No no — ah —" Lottie kicked herself internally. Why did she have to forget her bag? She and Ceci had been doing better since the crafting night. They were no longer tiptoeing around each other. And now — "Alros knows, he sent me a letter a while back, but it's okay I have a plan, I want to find out about this artifact myself. Ceci, it's from before the Centurion — it's incredibly rare, and —"

"You — you —" Ceci let out a sharp laugh that sent shivers up Lottie's spine. "You received a *letter*? Delivered where? Here?"

Lottie bit her lip. "I —"

"Oh good, so you gave the *Guild* my *address*? Once again, you're bringing your idiotic and dangerous work into my *home?*"

Oh, oh no.

"No, not your place, I would never — I wasn't —"

"Thinking? That's not surprising," said Ceci, her rage and anger seething over as she gestured wildly with the artifact in one hand and Lottie's bag in the other. "You really haven't changed at all, have you? Here you go again, bringing this life into mine, without an ounce of care toward what I have to go through. Don't you understand, Lottie, what you do when you do this?"

"It's not my fault that the job —"

"IT'S NOT ABOUT THE JOB!" Ceci raged. "This is about you blatantly putting people's lives in danger. The Guild is *dangerous*, Lottie. Especially when you decide to wrong them, don't you realize? We lost everything once already. *Everything*, because of you and your fucking stupidity."

Lottie felt as though she had run headlong into a wall. "That wasn't the Guild —"

"You and your little crew of people, going about committing crimes, thinking that you were entirely untouchable," continued Ceci, stampeding over anything Lottie tried to say. She had never seen her sister like this, completely out of control of her own emotions as her face raged with uncaged emotion. "You — you — everything I did was to protect you, and you went around and just threw it all back in my face like it was nothing. Like I was nothing."

"Ceci, I —"

"No. *No*. You don't get to try and talk yourself out of this one." Ceci shoved the artifact and Lottie's bag bodily into her chest, sending Lottie stumbling back. "I came here to Arrowmount to get away from what you had done to us. To try and forget. To remake myself, to restart my life. And you know what, Lottie? I had been doing a pretty good job of that until you came waltzing in, claiming that you just needed a place to stay for a while, that I was your only choice."

"Please, let me explain, it's not what you think. Alros —"

"Do you ever think of anyone other than yourself?" Ceci's voice went dangerously quiet again. "Or is your brain too busy with *Lottie Luck* to see past your own damn nose?"

Lottie flinched back as though Ceci had slapped her. She wished that her sister had. Then, at least, she could have felt less pain.

Ceci took a shaking breath and pointed at the door. "Get out. Take your stuff and leave. You cannot come back into my life, pretending like you want to fix this or whatever you're trying to do, all the while with that thing in my house."

"Ceci, please." Lottie didn't know what else to say. She sucked in a tight breath, tears burning at the back of her eyes. The crumpled scroll crinkled under her fingers as she held her things to her chest like a shield.

You weren't my only choice — you were my first. I wanted to come here, even though I didn't know it. I missed you, I wanted to fix things, I —

"Get. Out."

Lottie pulled her jacket tight around her as the darkest hours of the night clung to the sky above her. Her breath spiraled from her in bursts of fog, as the aching, icy air dug deep into her bones.

Even the stars dulled above her, half covered by wispy clouds. Most of the town was entirely bathed in darkness, and only the occasional lantern flickered dully against it. The brightest spot was the rotating arcane light from the lighthouse in the distance calling ships home. Lottie walked in shadow, hearing nothing but the steady tap of her boots.

Lottie contemplated going back to the Old'n Narrow, but it was too late for it to be open anymore. Or, rather, it was too early at this point in the day. She thought of Kir, then realized she didn't know where Kir lived. Somehow that had slipped their conversations over the past few weeks.

Aeric was probably sleeping in his comfortable bed, blissfully unaware of how cold it was outside. *I don't want to bother him*, she thought, feeling like a loose thread as she wandered the cobblestones. Ceci, too, probably had fallen asleep the second Lottie walked out the door, comfortably happy once again that Lottie was gone.

No one is awake, waiting for me, anywhere.

The thought jarred her. It was a desperately lonely thought, knowing that no one right then in the entire world was waiting somewhere for her. She came to a stop in the middle of a random street, and sucked in a sharp breath, feeling as though the darkness around her was trying to suffocate her.

She clutched her bag closer to her, feeling the weight of the artifact resting inside, the catalyst to all of this. For one, desperate moment, she wanted to take it out and throw it deep into the ocean and completely forget about its existence. She wanted nothing more than to run as fast as she could out of this town and to lose herself somewhere else in the empire, forget about who she was, and start over.

Who needs this, she thought, bringing the artifact out of her bag and holding it up to her face. The warmth oozed through her fingers, a soft glow emanating all around her. *Who cares what this thing can do? Who needs stories and mysteries?*

A deep ache thudded through Lottie's chest as she remembered the scene from earlier, of Kir and her lute, weaving stories through song. Kir's eyes had flashed to hers, pinning her to the spot.

Before Lottie had met Kir, she would have run in the other direction if anyone had looked at her like that. But now that she knew Kir, and had spent time with her, all she wanted to do was find her and wrap herself around the bard and never let go.

Gods, I'm falling in love with this woman, aren't I?
The thought burned through her like acid.

Lottie didn't fall for people. People fell for her. She had spent the majority of her life making sure that people liked her, worked hard to keep them wanting more. But she kept her distance, she never got attached.

Lottie sobbed, the sound choked and painful. The darkness around her swallowed it.

She turned onto Fetterly Place, thinking of heading toward the beach to find solace in the waves. Instead, one of the buildings down the street glowed invitingly, drawing her closer.

A figure moved around inside of May's Cafe, visible through the window that was framed by countless plants. The effect was quite magical, almost like something out of a novel, where the vignette was perfectly poised, illuminating the cafe perfectly.

Lottie walked up, wondering what May was doing up at such an hour, just as May herself glanced up and noticed her standing outside.

"Cecily?" May opened the door and let the light spill out over Lottie, confusion written all over her face. "Oh, no, sorry. Gosh, you two look alike in the dark."

"Are you open?" asked Lottie, her voice achingly tired.

"I was just about to open up. You can come on in."

Lottie stepped over the threshold, suppressing a shiver as the temperature changed drastically. The plants around the walls were waving slightly, as though there had just been a warm breeze cast through the space.

"What can I get you?" asked May, drawing Lottie in with a warm smile and a slightly extended hand. As May walked behind the counter, she swatted away a bit of vine that was steadily growing toward her. "Don't mind the plants, they always get excited when I come in in the morning."

Lottie let out a soft huff of air as she smiled tiredly at May. "I'll take whatever you've got."

May nodded and studied Lottie's face before clapping her hands together and turning toward her coffee maker. "Coffee it is then."

"Do you always open this early?" Lottie settled onto a stool and leaned against the counter, the weight of exhaustion pulling her down.

May chuckled. "Yes, always. There are many of us in Arrowmount who enjoy a bit of company in the early hours of the morning when everything is closed up tight."

She slid over a plate with a delicious looking pastry on it and busied herself behind the bar as the slow, healing smell of coffee filled the space around them. Moments later, Lottie had a warm mug nestled in her hands, the fragrant steam wafting over her in a balm of goodness.

May flitted around her cafe as the sky beyond the cafe windows brightened to a milky grey. She occasionally reached up to touch a plant as it wove through the air to her, pushing it back into place along the shelf. Eventually she started up her grill and began to cook, releasing intoxicating scents of warming butter and sugar into the air.

She propped open the front door of the cafe, just a little bit. Seeing Lottie watching her with a raised eyebrow, she smiled and said, "it's to entice the boys down the street at A Second Story, and whoever else passes by. The moment they smell breakfast, people come running."

Moments later, she was right. An incredibly sleepy dwarf came walking into the cafe, heavy purple bags under their eyes, their hair and beard still scrunched from sleep. They found their way half-aware to May's counter and ordered one of her largest coffees before settling themself into a table nearby and proceeded to drink the whole thing in minutes.

Eventually Lottie moved to a table and watched the slow, early morning life circle around her. Arileas walked in a while later, a dark blue scarf wrapped around his neck multiple times. He winked at May, who had two coffees ready at hand with a bag of pastries fished out of her counter, before swooping out again, the ends of his scarf trailing behind him.

A tall, lanky giantkin settled into a nearby table after a while, nodding once to May as they walked in. They trailed their eyes around the cafe for a moment, taking in the greenery and the other morning patrons, before settling on Lottie in the corner. They smiled softly at her and pulled out a novel, beginning to read.

If I only had a novel with me, thought Lottie, dropping her eyes to her bag.

With a soft pang, Lottie glanced down at her bag and remembered the scroll she'd shoved inside as she sped from Ceci's. A fresh wave of anxiety washed over her as she pulled it out and slid her thumb under the seal.

No answer.

Why am I not surprised? You're making me come to you, aren't you?

I hope to find you amenable when I arrive in Arrow-mount.

- A

Lottie swallowed and breathed out long, staring at the note. She was on the edge of feeling, but couldn't manage to pull anything other than exhaustion together.

Right. So Alros was coming to Arrowmount. He was well on his way by now, surely — at most, Lottie had a week of respite left. Then she'd see if her plan would actually work.

Lottie fell into a kind of trance as she sat in the cafe, surrounded by a soft, ever present sound of cooking food and the sputtering coffee machine. She came back to herself with her head cradled in one hand, the other still wrapped around a long cold mug of coffee.

Weirdly enough, Lottie felt more rested than she had in a long time. She didn't know whether to attribute it to the small nap she must have had — how else did she explain the lapsed time? — or May's coffee, but either way, she was relieved.

May's cafe door swung open as she began to think about standing up, and a familiar figure stepped in, ducking to avoid the vines. Lottie straightened ever so slightly in her seat as Kir's eyes flashed toward her immediately.

"Lottie?"

"Morning," she answered, giving Kir a soft smile.

"What are you doing here so early?"

"I could ask you the same thing."

Kir chuckled. "I sometimes grab coffee for my family in the morning."

Lottie stretched out a kink in her back from sitting in the same position for too long, yawning long and wide. Kir tried to hide her own behind a hand.

"Neither of us are morning people, are we?" Lottie stood and picked up her nearly empty mug to bring back to May.

Kir glanced back at her, turning her all-seeing eyes on her once again. Lottie fought the urge to plaster on a fake smile, to slide a mask into place — she knew that Kir would see through it anyway.

Kir frowned. "Lottie, are you okay?"

"No," said Lottie quietly.

Kir's expression melted into concern slightly before she turned toward May. "Same as always, May. Plus, a round of your best pastries." May nodded before starting to dig through her counter of baked goods.

"I want to hear about all of this," Kir said earnestly to Lottie, "if you want to talk about it."

"Maybe," said Lottie. "Don't you have to get back to your family, though?"

A small smile flickered across Kir's face. "Are you doing anything right now?”

“Nothing more than sitting in a cafe.”

“Good. You’re coming home with me.”

Part Five

The Moon Festival

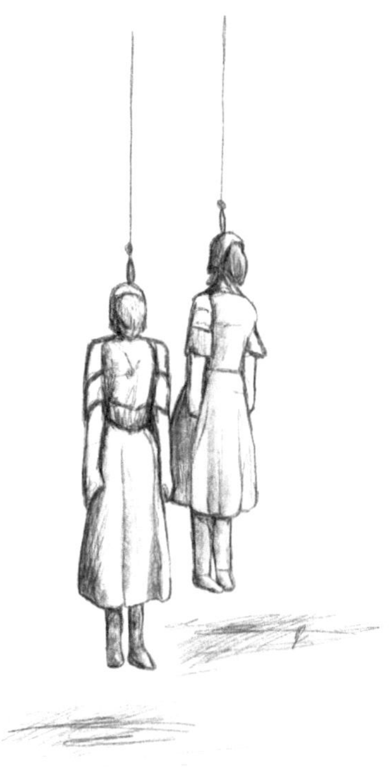

37

AN ENIGMA AROUND TOWN

Lottie – 7 Days Before

Kir led Lottie out of the cafe, cradling an incredibly large carafe of coffee. Even from behind her, Lottie could smell the intoxicating scent of coffee wafting from it. Kir hesitated in the doorway, inhaling long and deep.

"You make a lovely door," said Lottie, adjusting the two bags of pastries in her hands. Kir lurched forward and shot Lottie a sheepish smile.

"Sorry."

Lottie fell into step beside her. "Tell me about your family."

"You're going to meet them in a few minutes."

"I got zero sleep last night, my blood is half coffee, and I would love to know about your family beforehand so I don't look completely lost," said Lottie, chuckling. "Please."

"Well, you've met Khar already. He's the oldest and helps my dad at the smithy most days. Morgam is my second brother, and he comes and goes. If you can't find him, he's probably off somewhere painting."

"Painting?" How curious. Hadn't Aeric said something about dating an artist?

"Dad says we get our creativity from our mother, but I don't think he realizes that being a blacksmith is also an art of its own."

"I've seen his and Khar's work," said Lottie, remembering the intricate blades throughout the Dulra smithy. "Those blades really are like works of art."

It was only as Kir walked up to her front door that Lottie's heartbeat began to hammer through her chest. She was actually going to meet Kir's family, all together. Sure, she'd met and had many conversations with Khar, but that had been in a professional capacity. This was her *home*.

A knot of anxiety strung itself around her middle as Kir hesitated for a moment, hand on the door handle. Before she could open the door, though, it slipped out of her grasp from the inside and Khar stood there, smiling at them sleepily. His hair was plastered up on the side of his head from sleep.

"Coffee!"

"Let me in," Kir said, rolling her eyes and pushing aside her brother. "We'll all get coffee in a second. Besides, I want you to meet —"

"You're Lottie!" Another person, who Lottie assumed was Morgam, stood in the middle of the kitchen in a faded pair of soft linen trousers and an overlarge t-shirt spotted with paint, staring at her with his mouth hanging in a goofy smile. He shot a glance toward Kir and stepped forward to relieve Lottie of the food.

"I am," answered Lottie, smiling at him. "It's a pleasure to meet you."

"That's Morgam, as he so kindly introduced himself," said Kir quickly as Morgam put the food down onto the table. Lottie joined Kir as she began to pull mugs from the cabinet, filling them with coffee as Kir slid them toward her.

Khar blinked into motion when Lottie handed him a mug. Tendrils of steam rose from each of their cups and released the wondrous, rich scent of coffee into the air as they all settled in around the table.

Kir shut the cabinet door with a distinct snap, startling Lottie. Almost instantly, a gentle *tick-tick-tick* of what sounded like nails on the floor above became audible. She glanced at Khar, Morgam, and Kir to see if any would react, but all of them kept on as though this was entirely normal. She shrugged softly and started to place the pastries on a few of the large plates that Kir brought out. Both of Kir's brothers were glancing between Lottie and Kir with intrigued expressions that only became more animated as the caffeine woke them up.

Lottie tried to keep a smile from spreading across her face at their amusement. Before any of them could start conversation, though, something large and furry came tumbling into the kitchen from the stairs.

"Nudge, careful!" Kir lunged for the massive greathound as he was about to jump up onto Lottie, his enormous body straining in her arms. "We do not jump on new people, you know this, you silly dog."

Lottie gasped and immediately put her coffee down, turning toward the dog. "Oh my goodness, who is this beautiful boy?"

"Lottie, this is Nudge," said Kir, resting her hand on the dog's haunches to make him sit patiently. "Nudge, this is Lottie. Be nice to her."

"Oh, you're a good boy, aren't you?" Lottie got right up to him and gave him a round of vigorous scratches around his face, eliciting the happiest of panting smiles from Nudge.

"Careful, or you'll have a new shadow who won't leave you alone," said Khar, chuckling, nursing his coffee. "What do we owe this pleasure of you gracing our doorstep this early, Lottie?"

"I happened to come across Kir at May's," she answered, giving Nudge a kiss on his long nose before turning back to the table. The greathound lowered his head onto her lap and gazed up at her with big, round eyes until she continued to scratch him between his ears. "She invited me to join you all for breakfast, if you don't mind me crashing."

"How nice of you, Kir," said Morgam. "I've been eager to meet you, Lottie, since Kir first mentioned you. You're a bit of an enigma around town."

"Oh, am I?"

"Especially since you're Cecily's baby sister," he said, raising an eyebrow at Khar. "What brought you to Arrowmount? It's quite the talk of the town, the way you've come in when no one really even knew you existed."

"I thought it was high time I came to see the sea," said Lottie smoothly. "What are the lovely people of Arrowmount saying?"

"You're a hit with Della and the council," said Khar, eyeing Lottie over his coffee mug. "And you're quite beautiful, so I can't imagine why folks wouldn't notice you. Even a friend of mine, Zanve, remembers you from when you passed him at the front gates."

Lottie flushed with the compliment. "You'll have to tell him I remember him quite well, too. He's the one with the color changing eyes, right?"

"Yes," said Khar, blinking in surprise. "No one really notices that."

"It's, as you know, in my business to see the little details."

Morgam blinked between them, his mouth slightly open. "As you know? Khar, have you met Lottie before?"

"I have him doing a little project for me," said Lottie, taking a sip of her coffee. "A girl can never be without too many daggers."

A set of footsteps sounded on the floor above, announcing the arrival of another person into the Dulra kitchen. Nudge got up from the floor, excited all over again as someone Lottie could only assume was Kir's father entered the room. The dog's entire body moved with the force of his tail and his happiness.

"Oh!" Kir's father hesitated as he bent to pet Nudge, his eyes falling on her. "Hello!"

"Hi," said Lottie, casting one of her brilliant smiles on Kir's father and extending a hand. "I'm Lottie."

"Of course you are," he said, beaming as he clasped a warm, worn hand around hers. "Welcome to our home! I'm Noghorn, father of this establishment. I — well, you are meeting all of us in quite a state, aren't you?"

Lottie's eyes crinkled in a genuine smile as she cleared her throat and glanced between Kir's brothers and him, who were all wearing various kinds of sleepwear.

"I wouldn't have it any other way," she said. "It makes me feel like I'm almost part of the family."

Noghorn smiled happily before glancing at Kir. "Well, you know —"

"Dad, coffee?" Kir interrupted, handing him the remaining mug. He moved toward the table and took it in hand as Khar stood, offering him his chair.

"Oh, no don't, I can move," said Lottie, realizing there were only enough chairs for the four of them and making to stand.

"Don't worry about it, we've got more."

Khar walked off toward the workshop and returned with one of the stools from in there, setting himself at the edge of the table, now towering above everyone as he sat.

"So, Lottie," started her father, reaching over to grab a pastry. "Tell us about yourself. Do you have anyone special back home?"

Lottie let out a surprised laugh. "No, no sir, I do not."

"How interesting," he answered, shooting Kir an incredibly obvious wink.

Lottie had to suppress another laugh as Kir's face colored.

"But you must have interesting stories, no?" Noghorn took a bite from one of the pastries, a bit of jam catching at the side of his lip. "Where about are you from?"

"I was born up north, in a little village outside of Alieweth," she answered, "but I've been everywhere since. It's an effect of my trade, all the travel."

"What do you do for work?"

"I'm a curator of goods," she answered smoothly. "I travel all over the realm for it and have been in some sticky spots. In fact —" Lottie bent and retrieved one of the few daggers she kept on her from her boot, "I understand you're an expert in blades."

Rather than flinching back from the naked blade, Noghorn leaned toward it, as did Khar.

"Oh, now that's a lovely little piece. May I?" Her father took the blade in hand carefully, deftly turning it to inspect every angle. "What a fantastic bit of craftsmanship."

"I picked it up in Feycross a few years back," said Lottie, settling into her chair, Nudge leaning his head on her lap. He was drooling a little bit, staring up at her with big sappy eyes. "It's definitely come in handy."

Noghorn let out a low whistle, testing the sharpness. "I wouldn't want to find this at my throat. It's honed incredibly well. And look — Khar — at that dimpling along the bottom, in the metal. Almost like it's mimicking waves in the water."

Khar peered down, eyeing the blade. His eyebrows rose, impressed. "That's incredible craftsmanship. Just for the details alone."

Lottie settled in her chair and sipped at her coffee for a moment, letting the two men discuss her blade. She glanced up at Kir only to find her already watching her, a gently relieved expression on her face. Kir's smile spread as Lottie winked at her.

Lottie's heart thudded once, painfully. *Think about what you are going to do after this committee thing is over.* Ceci's words from what felt like forever ago passed through her mind. *If it's anything other than spending the foreseeable future with that woman, you're going to break her heart.*

The awareness of the artifact seemed to double in size as it sat next to her in her bag, accompanied by Alros' letter. Her heart sank.

She'd brought all of this on herself. Alros was coming to Arrowmount, bringing the danger of the Guild to her not only her sister's doorstep but to the doorstep of all these lovely people she'd met here. Everyone who'd taken her in, helped her, given her what she needed as she tried to pull her life together. Aeric, Nova, Briar, Corwek, Della, Khar — and Kir.

Gods. No matter how much Lottie herself wanted to leap across this table and kiss that woman senseless, curl up in her lap and feel Kir's arms around her, Lottie knew that she couldn't do this to Kir.

She was going to leave at the end of the festival, her artifact in hand. Whatever she had to do, she was keeping this artifact. It was her ticket to finding a new path in life, she could feel it — she had an opportunity with Berold in Zidien, to research it and see where that took her.

And Kir... no. It was best to be friends and nothing more. That way, Lottie wouldn't hurt her any more than she had to.

Lottie dropped her gaze and tried to pretend she was listening to whatever Noghorn was saying about her blade. She pushed a smile onto her face and nodded along, watching the shimmer of dimples in the dagger flash in the sunshine leaking in from the front windows.

38

MASTERPIECES

Kir – 7 Days Before

Kir relaxed as they sat around her kitchen table, finishing off the round of pastries and coffee. The morning trickled forward, and eventually her family started to head off in separate directions. Morgam murmured something about an idea for a painting, and their father headed off toward the back of the house where he had been, recently, trying to set up a garden. Khar stayed around and helped Kir and Lottie tidy the kitchen, putting away plates and swiping away any errant crumbs as Nudge handled the ones on the floor.

Kir turned to her brother as he reached down to scratch Nudge between the ears. "When are you heading to the smithy?"

"In a bit, I need to grab a few things from the workroom." He glanced at Lottie.

"How is the piece coming, Khar?" Lottie asked, taking her bag from the floor.

"It's coming," he answered, glancing at Lottie. "I... um..."

"It's okay," said Lottie, her voice tired and heavy. "I should've told Kir

272

about this a long time ago anyway."

Kir frowned at the two of them until Lottie withdrew a glowing, twelve-sided... something from her bag. Kir couldn't really put a name to it as Lottie held it out, contemplating it as though it was nothing more than an oddly shaped apple.

"This is what my last job was for," said Lottie. "I kept it from those who hired me, and now I have them chasing my tail."

"What is it?"

"Some kind of ancient artifact, I have no idea what it's for or what it does," answered Lottie. "I have the opportunity to find out, though. I have a contact in Zidien who studies ancient relics like this, mainly from around the Centurion, who has agreed to help me figure out what it is."

Kir hesitated, pulling her thoughts together. She blinked at Lottie. "Why?"

"I don't have anything other than what you see on me and what's in this bag to my name," said Lottie, closing her eyes and shaking her head. "This, *this* could be the ticket to a new path. It started more as a curiosity as to what it could be and what it could do but... I once wanted to get in with the Guild, as you know, but they didn't want me. So, I need to find another direction."

Khar whistled low.

"And now that I have this —" Lottie dug around in her bag and withdrew a rather crumpled piece of paper, "— letter telling me they know I have it and they're coming after it, I need that replica to work."

Kir slowly started to nod, piecing things together slowly. "Replica."

"It's what we've been working on," said Khar, scratching the back of his neck. "It won't be exact, of course, but —"

"It's going to be close enough," said Lottie firmly. "I'm banking on the man who sent me this letter not knowing what the artifact actually looks like or feels like to be fooled by it."

Khar scratched the back of his neck. "When is he coming?"

"A week," she answered, peering at Kir briefly. "Lines up with the Festival almost comically perfect."

Khar nodded. "I best be off then. I'll have the replica finished before then, I promise."

"Thank you, Khar."

Kir and Lottie watched as Khar gathered a few things from the workroom and left.

"So, this... man you got a letter from," said Kir softly. "He's coming here?"

"He knows I'm in Arrowmount," she answered. "I should've left the moment the Guild figured out I had the artifact, staying here just —" Lottie squeezed her eyes shut and slid the artifact back into her bag, letting out a long rattling sigh.

Kir moved without hesitating and wrapped both of her arms around Lottie. Lottie was stiff under her touch for a moment, then, as though something snapped, she melted into Kir's embrace. She was so warm in Kir's arms and fit so perfectly into her that Kir marveled as to why they hadn't held each other before. Sure, holding hands was great — but *this*? She never wanted to let Lottie go.

"Do you want to leave? You can, you know. Nothing's... nothing's stopping you."

The entire world shifted as Kir spoke, her own heart cracking open. The last thing she wanted was for Lottie to leave, but if it was what she had to do, then she had to go. Kir wouldn't hold her back.

"I can't," said Lottie, her voice muffled by Kir's chest. "I made a promise to Della and the festival and you, and I..."

Kir chuckled sadly. Of course, the reason Lottie didn't want to leave was because she felt bad about leaving the festival high and dry so close to. "The festival can make do, Lottie. We've got everything under control, and at this point it's just waiting for it to start. Is that why you didn't leave before?"

Lottie's arms tightened around her briefly. "Part of the reason."

"Part of it?"

"I didn't want to let you down. Or leave you, actually."

Kir blinked down at the top of Lottie's head, unsure of what to say. *She doesn't want to leave me.*

"Why... why don't I show you around a bit, and we can talk in my room," said Kir, forcing her arms around Lottie to relax. Lottie took an extra beat before she too let go. Instantly Kir felt cold, uncomfortable, and wanted to bring her back. She held onto Lottie's wrist for a moment as she tried to step away, her green eyes shimmering with unshed tears as she looked up at Kir, before Kir threaded her fingers with hers.

Kir showed Lottie through the main part of the house, walking her through their small living room that was absolutely bursting with blankets and soft things. The walls had a deep, rich wood paneling halfway up the wall, and a lighter stone for the rest. It was rather tricky to see much of the stone, though, since it was covered with shelves full of trinkets and hanging art.

Lottie smiled softly as she gazed around the room. This was one of the only rooms in their house that they were able to display a lot of Khar's old work, whatever he didn't then sell or give away to folks, and Morgam's old paintings that he made back when he was a kid, just learning how to put compositions together. Kir's first lute was sitting in the corner, the instrument significantly smaller than her current one.

"Dad refuses to let Morgam change out the paintings in here," commented Kir as Lottie peered at one of the oldest pieces, one that was a kaleidoscope of colors that kind of hurt to look at. "No matter how much Morgam begs him to. His work is much better now."

"It's a time capsule," said Lottie, gazing around the space with gentle awe on her face. "I guess it's pretty normal for most families to have this kind of stuff, right?"

Kir glanced over at Lottie, a slight pang echoing through her chest. "You never...?"

"No, no place we were in ever did. Maybe when our parents were alive, but I don't remember. What we had were Ceci's plants and books." Lottie ran a finger over one of Khar's first wooden horses on a nearby shelf, the chisel marks still visible. "Nothing like this."

"I hope one day you get to experience it," said Kir, squeezing her other hand. "Have some of you on your own walls."

Kir led her upstairs, gesturing toward her brother's and her father's rooms, before landing at the base of the stairs up into her space. They peered through a small window there, facing out to the back of their house. Through it, her father was visible, dragging a rake through some fresh soil. Nudge was splayed out in a ray of weak sunshine nearby, watching him.

"Is this yours?" Lottie said, motioning up to the next floor. Kir nodded, leading her up. She gasped softly as she walked in, her eyes widening at the sight of Kir's windows. Lottie stepped away, their hands slipping apart. "That's — wow."

"This used to be my mom's studio," said Kir, standing in the middle of her room, feeling slightly awkward as Lottie peered through the windows at the view. What does one do when someone else is examining a piece of your soul? "She wanted to be up high and to see the world beyond them."

Lottie turned, an expression in her eyes that Kir couldn't quite read.

Her attention caught on the wall behind Kir, her mouth falling open. Kir turned too, as though expecting to see something new there. Instead, she was greeted with the old sight of her mother's work.

"Kir, these are masterpieces." Lottie gaped between the windows and the painted scenes on the other wall, comparing the two. The series of paintings that Kir had up on her walls were all massive canvases, each depicting a different season of Arrowmount, something new in each one.

"I know." Kir beamed at them proudly. "The view is a little bit different now, since Arrowmount has grown so much since she painted them. But I still think it looks right, doesn't it?"

"It really does."

Lottie settled onto the edge of Kir's bed, exhaustion passing over her features. Kir, wondering briefly if she should sit next to Lottie or on the floor in front of her, chose to sit in front of her so she could watch Lottie's face.

"My sister kicked me out," Lottie said quietly after a few minutes. "Because she found the artifact. That's why I was at May's this morning."

Kir furrowed her brow. "Did she not know about it?"

"No," she answered, withdrawing the artifact from her bag once again. "She specifically told me not to bring work into her home, and I broke that promise by simply breathing. I brought the danger to her once again."

She leaned over and placed it in Kir's hand. Kir's palm warmed as though she was holding a freshly brewed mug of coffee. Kir peered at the artifact for a moment, eyeing the detailed, pockmarked surface. It gave off a distinctly ancient ambiance, something older than she could possibly understand.

"You said it was from around the Centurion?"

"Berold thinks it's older," she answered. "Perhaps something godly."

Godly. It felt incredibly odd to be holding something that old. It could've been a magical paperweight or the key to the end of the realm, and she would never know.

"It cost me whatever distance I had gained with Ceci," Lottie said, her voice bitter. "I should never have gone for the job. Or if Seban hadn't —" she shook her head. "Ceci herself told me that I needed to take responsibility for the things that I've done, rather than blame everyone around me."

"She could be right," said Kir softly, pressing her knuckles into Lottie's knee amiably and placing the artifact next to Lottie's bag. "You know exactly what you've done and what you want to be doing here, don't you?"

Lottie looked at her with an expression so raw and open that for a moment, Kir couldn't breathe. Slowly, Lottie closed her eyes, breathing deep. "Yeah. It's all my fault. Everything — from the Nine to the fire to me coming here. I should have listened to Ceci from the beginning. It's always been my fault."

Suddenly, Lottie leaned forward and slipped off of Kir's bed, wrapping her arms around Kir. Kir immediately held onto her, folding her soft body into an embrace once again, as Lottie dug her face into Kir's neck.

"I'm so sorry I've done all this to you," Lottie breathed, her breath tickling Kir's skin.

"Done what?"

"Come here and brought you into my problems. You're too good for me, Kirandir."

"Too... good for me?"

"I — I meant —" Lottie retracted, sitting up slightly. She closed her eyes as though in pain. "Gods, I like you, Kir. So much. Isn't that obvious? I can't get you out of my head."

Kir felt her face relax with surprise. *She likes me. She actually* likes *me.* She opened her mouth, wanting to respond that she felt the same, but Lottie kept talking.

"But I'm leaving, Kir. I — I can't do that to you. I can't drag you further into this. I'm so sorry."

Kir cleared her throat of the lump that had appeared there. "Never apologize for that — for being you — because you... you coming here is the best thing that has ever happened to me."

She wanted to be pulled into Lottie's world and never leave. She wanted so desperately to be part of everything in Lottie's life — not just a memory left in a tiny seaside town.

Kir gently tucked a bit of Lottie's hair that had escaped her braids behind her ear, watching the way her eyes flickered as she did so. Something in Lottie's green eyes sharpened, causing Kir's breath to catch. If Lottie chose to kiss her, Kir wouldn't stop her.

But Kir wouldn't choose for her, no matter how much she wanted to.

Lottie's mouth opened slightly, an unspoken question on her lips, before she dropped her gaze and pulled back. She was still mostly sitting on Kir, but Kir felt that distance like a stab to the heart. Kir reached out and took one of her hands in hers, just to keep holding some part of her. She squeezed Lottie's fingers twice, for luck.

"So, friends?" Lottie said, her voice wavering.

Kir's heart screamed in agony. "Friends it is."

39

THE REPLICA

Lottie - 3 Days Before

Lottie shifted from foot to foot as she watched Khar work. He was hunched over his worktable in the back of the smithy, the replica in one hand and what had to be the realm's thinnest chisel in the other. Her artifact sat on the desk between them for his reference.

She couldn't help but trace his face, hunting for the similarities to his sister. For the past few days, Lottie had desperately tried to keep her and Kir in the category she herself had set. *Friends.* It was becoming increasingly difficult, so, she tried to keep herself busy as much as she could. Like right now.

Instead of sitting in the bar, chatting with Briar or Aeric waiting for Kir's set to begin later, or laying on the inn bed where she was staying at Cobb's Down-By-The-Beach, staring at the ceiling for hours, she was here. With Khar.

They had the same frown when they focused, the same piercing stare with steel grey eyes, and —

"If only you could paint a portrait, then you'd be able to make this time watching me worth it," he said absently.

"Sorry." She dropped her gaze and bit her lip, trying to find anything else to look at.

"No need to apologize." He straightened with a sigh. "It may help to speak about what's on your mind."

Her cheeks heated. "I..."

"Besides my sister. I mean with Ceci."

She blinked at him, at a loss for words.

"Despite popular opinion that people don't speak with their previous lovers, I can confidently say that Cecily and I are fairly good friends."

"I don't want to burden you with this," Lottie said quickly. "It's my own problem."

"Yes, well, sometimes when we have problems, it works a fair bit better when we share them with others to see if, oh I don't know —" Khar shrugged, "— maybe they can help you think through the problem." He rested his replica on the table next to the dodecahedron. It was a scarily good replica, minus the magical glow, and the fact it still shone like brand new bronze.

"Right." She let out a long breath. "You know about the artifact."

"Yes."

"And the Guild?"

He tilted his head to the side. "Well, Ceci did allude to something happening with a large organization in your past, so that would make sense. And you mentioned something the other day after breakfast, but..."

"Did she ever tell you why she came to Arrowmount?"

"Other than vague statements, no."

Lottie filled him in as quickly and succinctly as she could about how she'd been the reason Ceci came here, due to her never listening to her sister and following a path that led her to ruin more than once.

"And now, here I am bringing that same danger to her doorstep again," she said, her voice tightening. She cleared her throat, trying to speak around the block. "It wasn't the Guild last time, like she thought, but now it actually is. I can't... I shouldn't have done this at all."

"I think," said Khar slowly, nodding, "perhaps you should tell your sister how you feel about this. How you intend to fix the solution as well, because we both know your sister works best when there are plans in place."

Lottie took a moment to marvel in how well this man knew her sister before sighing heavily. "It's all my fault, I know. I just don't know how to tell her. I don't know how to fix things. It's been ten years, and I... I feel like this time I completely ruined it."

"Try telling her exactly how you just did. I'm sure you've talked to Kir about this, too — tell Ceci like you told us."

"But —"

"The best thing you can do for those you love is give them utmost honesty and kindness, Lottie. Don't you think your sister, someone who has never stopped loving you and thinking about you since the day she left, deserves that?"

"She does," breathed Lottie. "She deserves this life of calmness, and for nothing to break that."

"Let me just clarify something." Khar crossed his arms in front of his chest. "This Guild member coming here. How did he communicate with you?"

"Through letters. I had the courier sending them to the bar."

Khar's face flickered into a smile. "Right. Maybe start with the fact that the Guild doesn't know your sisters address, okay? It seemed to be a rather big sticking point of panic for her."

Lottie grimaced. "I never told Alros that I was coming here because of my sister. They don't know Arrowmount has a hold over me in any way. I'm going to try keep it that way. I need to keep everyone here safe."

Khar started to laugh.

"What?"

"Two things. One, it's not your responsibility to keep everyone around you safe." He picked up his tools and the replica once more. "And two, fuck I'm glad you have that mindset, because I was about to have a chat with you about my sister's safety."

Lottie couldn't help but laugh. "Thank you, Khar."

"Anytime. Now. Let's see if my experiment will work."

"Experiment?"

Khar winked at her before walking from the office, replica in hand. She followed after swiping her artifact from the table, confused. He moved to a small bucket that was tucked into a corner, emanating a sharp stench of sulfur and something entirely unnatural. Without hesitating, he dropped the replica into the liquid inside.

Lottie let out a choked gasp. "What are you doing?"

"Seeing if my experiment works." Khar picked up a set of long pincers and reached into the liquid, withdrawing a seething ball of metal. Whatever the liquid was bubbled and ate at the material, sizzling in the air. He watched it for a second, then dunked it into the basin of water usually reserved for cooling metal. Instead of eliciting steam, the water simply plunked away the sizzling noise.

"You didn't think to test this with something that isn't our only replica?"

Khar lifted his eyebrows at her and swirled the replica inside for a moment as though stirring a potion. Then, with the grace of someone revealing a prize, he withdrew the replica from the water and held it out.

She gaped at it. Whatever he'd done, whatever that liquid was, had aged the bronze perfectly. It was almost a perfect copy of the artifact — despite the aging in slightly different spots. It was hard to replicate the life of an artifact when you didn't know what it had gone through. But despite that, it was perfect.

"How?"

"I know some people who work with this sort of thing," he said, motioning to the bucket of mystery liquid. "Don't ask me what it is, because even I couldn't tell you. I experimented with a lot of pieces of bronze before this, by the way."

"Thank the gods." Lottie held it next to her artifact and started to laugh. "Khar, you've done it."

"Well, I could've done that one side a bit better, I think. That weird ancient script is a total bastard to replicate. And —"

She threw her arms around him, still holding both of the dodecahedrons. He froze in surprise before he started laughing too, patting her on the back. She let go and beamed up at him. "Thank you, Khar."

"If only we could actually enchant it," he said, inspecting the two artifacts in her hands. "Then we'd really be cooking."

"Now the real test," she said, sucking in her breath. "We have to see if this fools him."

Lottie left the smithy a little while later, both artifacts weighing her bag down, and headed toward the Old'n Narrow. She kept telling herself that she only wanted to stop by for lunch. It had nothing to do with the fact she was too nervous to go see her sister or that she wanted to see Kir.

She'll go see her sister after Ceci returned home. Not now, in the middle of the day, when she'd be surrounded by people at the market.

On her way, she focused on the transformation of Arrowmount around her. They were three days away from the start of the Moon Festival, and Arrowmount was nearly ready. All of the Festival volunteers allocated to pulling things together were putting finishing touches on the physical aspects of the Festival across the town. Many of the Committees for the Festival had been preparing the whole week, constructing platforms and stalls wherever they were needed. A number of townsfolk had come out to help with decorations for the event.

Something special had happened overnight though — now there was something in the air, as though the town itself had stepped up, straightened its back, and was ready to begin the Moon Festival celebrations.

Lottie accidentally bumped into Aeric as he busted out of A Second Story. He was wrapped in a warm, clay-colored sweater a few sizes too big for him, his sharp cheek bones slightly pink.

"Lottie!" His eyes went slightly too wide in surprise and he took a few hurried steps toward her.

"Well hello there, Dancer." Lottie narrowed her eyes suspiciously and took his arm as he swooped by her, spinning her around to walk with him. "What, by chance, were you doing in the bookstore?"

"I was just checking out some of the new stock," he said, glancing over his shoulder before taking a few hurried steps forward.

Not about to be fooled, Lottie dug her heels in and spun around in time to see Morgam, Kir's brother, exiting the shop. All he had on was his shirtsleeves and trousers, as though he had just lost the use of his perfectly warm sweater.

"New stock, hmm?"

Morgam froze in his tracks as he saw Lottie looking his way, Aeric on her arm. Aeric started to try and speak, but all he succeeded in doing was making a sound in the back of his throat that sounded like a dying seabird.

"So *this* is the artist that you mentioned," said Lottie, giving Morgam a warm smile. "I thought so. Hi Morgam, lovely to see you out and about today."

"Nice to see you too, Lottie." Morgam cringed slightly before running a hand through his long hair, dropping his gaze sheepishly. He tucked his hands into his pockets and raised his shoulders slightly to his ears.

He and Aeric squirmed in the silence stretching between them.

"Oh, enough, this is fantastic," said Lottie, breaking into laughter. "I think the two of you are very cute together."

Morgam smiled at Aeric, relief washing over his face. His eyes went soft, and Lottie was momentarily unable to form words at the warm glow of adoration written across his face. She peeked out of the corner of her eye at Aeric, only to see his panicked expression melt into one of equal adoration.

Hasn't had a hot date in years my ass, she thought, thinking back to Aeric's words in his cramped kitchen. *These two are in love with each other.*

"See you, Morg," breathed Aeric.

"You too."

Lottie and Aeric waited a few beats as they watched Morgam walk away.

"So that's what he's been doing whenever his family thinks he's painting," she commented, distinctly amused.

Aeric made a strangled noise. "Oh ha-ha. But seriously, Lottie. Please don't tell Kir, okay? We're waiting until we can find the right moment."

"It's not my business to. Though, I think it might be difficult to hide if you're going to go about wearing his clothing."

Aeric turned a slightly panicked expression at her. "I was cold!"

"And now so is he, but I'm sure he's not feeling it. He's too busy thinking about how in love he is with you."

Aeric let out a splutter as he tried to form words. "He's not — we're — he's —"

"It's fine, it'll be our little secret. You two little love birds."

"Speaking of love birds," he said, eyeing her out of the corner of his eye. "I meant to apologize for walking in — or rather, out — on you and Kir outside the bar. I will say, I'd like to formally congratulate you on finally making a move on one another. We've all been waiting."

It was Lottie's turn to sputter. "There was nothing — we didn't —"

"You *didn't?*" he asked, incredulous. "Lottie. You were literally inches away from each other, gazing into each other's eyes as though the other one was on fire. What do you *mean* you didn't? We have to go find Kirandir this moment, you have to fix this."

"Aeric, no, please —" Lottie found herself being dragged a few feet down the cobblestones, a new kind of panic spearing through her chest. "There's nothing between us, we're just friends!"

That was enough to stop Aeric in his tracks. "That's complete dragonshit, Lottie Luck. I've seen the way you two look at each other, let alone the fact you've literally been inseparable for weeks."

"The Committee..." Lottie tried weakly.

"Oh, come on. The Committee required that much nightly work? I swear to all the gods old and new this better be the best entertainment we've seen at a Moon Festival if *that* is why you were together every night after her sets."

"Ah, fuck," she breathed, tightening her grip on Aeric's arm as he steered her forward. "Was it that obvious?"

"It was," he said, amusement leaking into his voice.

"We're just friends, though."

"Just friends." Aeric shook his head. "Did Kirandir say that? If so, I'll have words with —"

"It was me," Lottie said quickly.

Aeric's head snapped toward her so fast that she thought his neck might break. "Lottie Luck, say you didn't."

"I'm leaving soon, Aeric. I can't bear putting her through that, if anything was going to happen between us." Lottie sniffed, feeling the ache swell in her chest, tears pricking at the back of her eyes. "Besides, she never said that she actually had feelings for me, so I'm the one who's going to take it the hardest."

"Now that is a purposeful misconception." At the shake of her head, he softened his voice. "She looks at you like you're the most beautiful melody she's ever heard yet can't quite master but isn't going to stop until she can figure it out."

That took Lottie's breath away.

"Are you really just going to walk away from that?"

"My... I don't..." Lottie shook her head and squeezed her eyes shut. Aeric pulled her close, wrapping her in a sweater that smelled like paint and books. She'd been doing nothing but thinking these past few days. "I thought I knew my decision. I really have gone and fucked everything up, haven't I?"

"Not quite yet. But don't go running to our Kir if you haven't figured out what you're going to do," he said, the sound rumbling in his chest as she pushed her head against it. "You owe her a clear decision. Just so you know, I vote for stay, because my life has definitely been more interesting with you in it."

Lottie's heart thrummed painfully as she took a step back, wiping the tears from her face. Could she stay?

Not if you want to follow the artifact, you know that.

The two of them walked on until they found their way down to the beach where the sand was covered in people, supplies, and half-built structures.

Lottie immediately recognized Kir's strong shoulders as she helped a few others assemble part of a structure along the length of the beach, which would be home to most of the festival happenings. As Lottie and Aeric walked up, she was gifted with a view of Kir wearing a sharp white shirt, sleeves rolled up above her elbows, forearms straining as she lifted a piece of wood.

"Lottie!" Kir set the piece down and met them halfway, a slightly lopsided smile on her face as she wiped away a sheen of sweat. "And Aeric," she added as Aeric chuckled under his breath. "I didn't think I'd see you two this morning."

"You guys have been busy."

"Yeah," Kir answered, turning to examine the work they had already accomplished, before dropping her voice so only Lottie could hear. Lottie leaned in a touch, gravitating toward her. "I'd much rather be at the bar, though. Who would've said that I missed washing dishes?"

Lottie could see the expression on Aeric's face as he watched the two of them.

"Well, we won't keep you," Lottie said quickly, taking a half step back, pulling Aeric with her.

Kir's face flickered slightly into a frown before she nodded, glancing at Aeric. She did a soft double take as recognition flashed in her eyes.

"Aeric, is that my brother's sweater?"

KNITTED GLOVES

Lottie – 3 Days Before

Lottie headed back to Ceci's apartment later, after joining Aeric at the Old'n Narrow for some food. He couldn't stop smiling, no matter what they did. Even Briar noticed as he swept around the bar, a skip in his step.

Lottie chuckled to herself as she remembered Kir back at the beach, stunned, as Aeric stumbled over his words, trying to explain why he was wearing Morgam's sweater. It lasted about three seconds before he completely fell apart and told her he was in love with her brother.

The memory of Kir's expression crumbling into soft joy made Lottie's own face to break into a smile, despite what she was about to do. She held onto that image of Kir wrapping Aeric up in a bone crushing hug, Aeric's eyes popping as he laughed, as she ascended Ceci's stairs.

The sky above her was beginning its descent toward evening. She wasn't entirely sure if Ceci would be home yet, but she may as well try before she backed out from nerves.

Lottie knocked lightly, listening for any movement on the other side of the door. After a few moments with no answer, Lottie let out a long sigh and sat down on the top stair to wait.

Sitting amidst the out-of-season flowers and plants, Lottie forgot where she was. It felt as though she had slipped through to a world entirely of her own, the sound of seabirds calling above, the distant rush of waves lulling her into calmness.

"Lottie?"

Lottie sat upright, snapping back to attention. Ceci stood at the foot of her stairs frowning up at her, pulling a knitted scarf tighter around her.

"Ceci, hi."

"What're you doing here?"

"I came to see you." Lottie stood, brushing a bit of dust off her pants. "I came to apologize."

Ceci blinked at her, her face going blank. "Oh?"

"Not just bringing the artifact into your home without you knowing — everything."

"Oh," Ceci repeated. She cleared her throat and looked down at her feet, shuffling from foot to foot.

Lottie watched her sister's shoulders rise and fall as she took a deep breath before started up the stairs, a mask of indifference on her face. Lottie took a step back from the door, giving her sister enough space to unlock the door to her apartment.

"Ceci —"

"Lottie, give me a second, okay?" Ceci walked into the apartment and slipped off her shoes and coat in one smooth movement. She reached up and pulled at her hair, releasing it from the knot atop her head. It spiraled down around her as she reached her fingers into the mess, massaging it loose.

Lottie loitered by the entrance, watching her sister move around her apartment. She unwound he massive scarf from around her neck and slung it over a hook with her jacket before heading deeper into her place, putting away her things and settling into the space.

Lottie bit the inside of her cheek to stop herself from speaking.

Finally, after what felt like an hour, Ceci settled on her couch. "Gods, it's been a day."

"Long?"

"We had to deal with most of the Festival Committee crowded around, setting up for everything." Ceci cracked her neck. "Not that I'm not excited for the Festival, it was just a lot of noise and busyness."

Lottie nodded, standing a little awkwardly in the entrance way, her boots still on.

Finally, Ceci looked at her. "I don't think you've ever actually apologized for anything in your life before."

Lottie felt the jibe as though she had been slapped. She dropped her gaze to her hands and chuckled softly. "Yeah. I know. I'm... I guess I should also apologize for that, too. Gods, Ceci. I've been the absolute worst sister, haven't I?"

"You haven't. I should be the one apologizing for how I left you ten years ago. You were so young, and I..."

Lottie blinked and met her sisters gaze, only to find her sister's eyes swimming with tears.

"You did it for yourself, never apologize for that."

"Still."

Lottie closed her eyes and swallowed. "You needed to go for me to realize how absolutely ridiculous I'd been. I should have listened to you.

I'm so, so sorry for everything I've put you through. The Nine, the fire. And coming back here and making it all come up again. I — I need to do better; I know that."

Lottie kicked off her boots and walked into the room. She sat on the edge of the coffee table.

Ceci closed her eyes. "It was hard. All of it, every day. That fear — gods it was so thick I could taste it every time you walked out the door in Pralon. And then when you came here... after I thought I'd been free of it, that fear was back."

"I know, I do. And I want to make it clear, I never once told the Guild you were here. I never gave them your address — not Alros, not anyone. No one knows I even have a sister, except for Seban, but I don't think he counts anymore. Even he doesn't know where you went. I swear, I had all my letters directed to the bar, not here."

A tear began to roll down Ceci's cheek. "Thank you for that."

"I never ever wanted to bring more danger into your home, Ceci."

"I think I understand now that, back then, you were going out and doing what you do, getting mixed up in all of that, because you were trying to find people to love you," said Ceci quietly. "Trying to find a purpose."

"I was trying to make us money, at first." Lottie shifted on the coffee table. "And I was trying to find a way to keep you out of those awful jobs you always had to take. I thought that maybe, if one day I really made it big, then we could get away from all that."

Ceci flinched, expression shattering. "That was not your responsibility."

"And you think it was yours? Simply because you were older?"

"You were just a kid."

"So were you."

"I should have loved you more openly. I was so focused on trying to keep you safe that I forgot to actually be a sister for you." Ceci sucked in a shuddering breath. "I was so scared."

"You never did anything wrong, Ceci. I promise you." Lottie reached forward and took hold of Ceci's hand. Ceci squeezed back, holding on tight. "You were the best sister I could have ever asked for. You kept us both safe for as long as you could and then I came in like a wrecking ball on our life. I'm so sorry for being the source of your fear. You deserve to feel safe."

Ceci laughed sadly, the sound wet and clogged with tears. "I was scared for you, you silly goose. All those years. My little sister was out there, living such a dangerous life because I couldn't grow my own spine to do the dangerous work for her."

"Your jobs were awful," said Lottie, astonished.

"Yes, but I can deal with awful men and menial work. I couldn't deal with not knowing if my sister was going to come home okay. And when that fire happened, I just couldn't take it anymore."

Lottie sucked in a deep breath. "I thought you hated me when you walked away."

"I didn't, Lottie. Please hear that. I could *never* hate you. You're my sister, you're my family. I..." She shook her head over and over. "Thank you for coming here."

"I had to come and make things right. Or at least start to put things together again."

"No, I mean coming to Arrowmount. If you hadn't, who knows when we would have seen each other." Ceci eyed the bag still slung over Lottie's shoulder. "If it wasn't for that godsforsaken artifact, maybe you wouldn't ever have come here in the first place. And without you coming here, I wouldn't have been able to do this."

She pulled Lottie in, hugging her fiercely.

"I love you, Lottie," she breathed. The words alone tugged free a sob of emotion from Lottie's chest.

"I love you, too."

Ceci let her sister go and wiped her tears, sitting back.

"I know it doesn't fix everything," continued Lottie, "but I had to try. Maybe that's why I first came to Arrowmount at all. I mean — I could've gone into hiding anywhere in the realm. But I think I just missed my sister."

Ceci's face broke into a genuine smile. "Maybe I shouldn't be so hard on your job choice after all."

"Eh, you're pretty warranted for that." Lottie sucked in a deep breath. "I have a plan to fix that, too."

"Oh?"

She filled her sister in about what she'd been doing in Arrowmount with Khar, the possibility with Berold, and her path forward since Alros' latest letter. She pulled the two artifacts out of her bag, handing the real one to her sister.

"The Guild is going to regret not taking you on," said Ceci, peering at the artifact with interest. "Why they haven't already recognized how good you are is beyond me. You not only managed to still grab the artifact and get out of that whole job without being caught — but you're now pulling together a plan to keep this from them for longer, just to find out more about it. That, to me, would be the sign of someone who I would want on my team, if I was them. Not working against them."

"You think I'm good?"

Ceci handed the artifact back and rose to her feet. "You're my sister, of course you're good at what you do. And since you have yet to be caught or killed, I assume that means you're pretty good at what you do."

"Hey." Lottie watched as Ceci moved into her kitchen and started to grab a variety of vegetables from a bowl nearby.

"Are you sure this plan is going to work?"

"If it doesn't..." Lottie sucked in a sharp breath. "Either way, I'll figure it out. I always do."

Ceci laughed, the sound tired and full of an emotion that Lottie couldn't quite place.

"Are you happy, Ceci? Doing what you do here?" The question escaped Lottie before she could stop herself.

"More than I ever have been. My life may be small and comfortable, but that is everything I have ever wanted. No matter how much the minutiae of daily life can sometimes build up on someone. I have the life I dreamed of as a small girl, when you and I were living back in that orphanage. It just had been missing something that I didn't really realize until recently."

"Missing...?"

"My sister. My wonderful, adventuring sister who's about to depart and find out if that really is a godly relic in her hands. And what that means for her and the realm."

Lottie's heart gave a great, painful pang.

"I just wonder if you'll have any reason to come back."

"Ceci."

"I don't mean just me," she said, raising an eyebrow as she set a chopping board down on her counter. "You don't ever... see yourself making a life here? Settling down?"

Lottie chuckled at the idea of settling down. "Maybe one day, if my job stops exciting me. I really do enjoy what I do. It takes me places, lets me see things all over."

"Ah, okay."

Lottie narrowed her eyes at her. "What."

"What?"

"You're thinking so loudly I can practically hear it."

"I just wonder," said Ceci with a sigh as she peered at Lottie, a slight sparkle in her eye. "What Kir thinks of all this."

"I don't know. The two of us are just friends, Ceci."

"Now that's a lie if I've ever heard one."

"No, seriously. We... we talked about it."

Ceci, starting to chop vegetables, shot her a look that reminded her exactly of Aeric's reaction from earlier. "You're okay with leaving her? No strings attached?"

"I can't... I couldn't start something knowing I was going to leave, Ceci."

"Alright, alright. But just know, I can see how it is tearing you up, Lottie." Ceci gestured with her knife at Lottie's face. "You try and hide it, but whenever someone mentions Kir, your eyes light up and then you hold it back, shutter it all away, as though hiding from the feelings will make anything better. In my opinion — and this is the last thing I will say on this — but don't let her go."

Lottie flinched and laughed to try and cover it up. "Like you let go of Kharutto?"

Ceci let out a surprised peal of laughter. "Oh, gods. Where did you hear of that?"

"When I met Khar at the smithy, it came up. What's the deal with you two?"

"There is no deal, and barely was one to begin with," said Ceci, putting down her knife and pulling out a pan to begin cooking on a tiny cooktop. She withdrew a jar of sauce from the cold box and started to heat it in the pan. "Gods, that was ages ago. We are much better off friends."

"And... now? Is there anyone?"

The softest blush passed over Ceci's cheeks. "There may be someone, but I don't want to curse it quite yet by talking about it."

"That's absolute dragonshit and you know it. Talking about it is the best part, it makes it feel real. Who are they?" Lottie got up from the couch and moved toward the kitchen, picking up the board with the chopped vegetables to transfer them to the pan, where the sauce was starting to steam.

Ceci's blush deepened, and the softest look of adoration melted across her face. "You know the knitting I've been doing?"

"Yes?"

"Well, Gable, you know who runs the bakery stall? — they asked me a while ago if I could help make them gloves, tighter than they were able to knit, because they have pain in their hands that keeps them from getting the right tension. I agreed, of course, and well, I've continued knitting for them, trying to find the exact right pattern that not only keeps them warm but helps ease the pain a little, and well. We got to know one another, and..." Ceci cut off, clearing her throat. "I think I'm going to ask Arileas if he knows any spells I can imbue in the yarn to help ease the discomfort. I know Gable's pain isn't something magic can fix, but I'd like to help in whatever little way I can."

"Why haven't I ever seen you with them?"

Ceci wrinkled her nose. "Not that I didn't think they wouldn't love you or anything. I just... I wanted to keep them to myself for a bit longer, you know?"

Lottie laughed. "What, scared of what I might think of them?"

"Absolutely, that's exactly it." Ceci rolled her eyes and stirred the vegetables, the kitchen filling with the noise of sizzling.

41

ICING COVERED WAFFLES

Kir – Day One

The morning of the Moon Festival dawned early. Kir woke to her whole body alight with a fiery tingling that wouldn't let her stay asleep or lay still in bed. She got up and started to pace the length of her room, waking Nudge. He let out a long sigh that turned into a low moan as he watched from her bed, his head on a swivel as she moved.

Today was the day. *The* day, when everything she and Lottie had been working toward came together.

"I know, Nudge," she breathed, trying to shake the tingles from her arms and hands. "I think I need to get out."

She scraped her hair up into a bun for the third time that morning. She wondered if she should bite the bullet and wear it down for once, eyeing herself in the mirror tucked into one corner of her room. It was splattered with old, flaking paint from when her mom had used.

Kir freed her mane of black hair and ran her fingers through it to try and style it in some kind of way. Surprisingly, down, it settled how Kir wanted it to, showing off the shaved side of her head and resting easily on her other shoulder. She blinked at herself, adjusted her sweater and the collar of the shirt underneath, before finally tying a few leather strips around her wrist, just in case.

Her entertainers knew what they had to do today. Everything was in place for them, she had triple checked the night before. With a heavy, steadying sigh, she pushed open her bedroom door and made her way down to the kitchen, holding her head high.

She hesitated as she entered, eyes falling on a plate resting in the middle of the kitchen table. A pile of waffles sat, still steaming, smothered in icing, as though it was a decadent cake. Nudge came bumbling down the stairs after her, his tail wagging.

"Happy first day of the Festival!"

She turned to see Morgam and her father standing in the kitchen, dressed for the day, both beaming at her. Morgam bent and patted Nudge on the back as he collided with their knees. The two of them sported dark circles under their eyes, as though they'd been up for hours.

"Is this for me?"

"A congrats and a show of how proud we are," said her father, walking over and enveloping her in a hug. Morgam snuck in behind and wrapped his arms around the two of them. "Khar would be here, but he had to run off to the smithy for me."

"That's alright," Kir said, feeling a well of emotion burning behind her eyes. She didn't know whether to cry, laugh, or scream from all of the pressure welling up in her body, the need to move or run or shake until she fell apart almost unbearable. "This is... thank you."

Her father handed her a fork, and the three of them tore into the stack of waffles. Though Kir could only stomach a few bites, they were absolutely delicious and entirely perfect.

"We'll catch you at the Festival, I'm sure," said Morgam, adjusting his sweater for the fourth time since she'd come downstairs. At her narrowed stare, Morgam looked slightly sheepish. "I'm meeting Aeric for the day."

Morgam had finally told them about his and Aeric's relationship a few days ago. Their father and Khar had been overjoyed — and Khar not surprised at all.

"Well, I figured there was someone," he had said with a small shrug. Morgam's eyes had gone wide. "You were always out and about, passing by the smithy when you didn't think I'd see. You never had reason to come into town that much before."

"All my children, falling in love," said their father, glancing between Kir and Morgam with a sappy grin on his face as Nudge wiggled between his knees, seeking scratches.

Kir blinked at him in surprise. "What, Khar too?"

"Well, almost of them." Her father winked at her, a knowing look in his eye. "I take it that I'm right, then?"

"Oh." Kir's cheeks flamed with heat. "Well, I... uhm."

Her father cackled, clapping her on the shoulder. "I'm happy for you Kiri, truly. You're changing so much! Taking on a leadership role, finding someone to love. Ah! I'm so proud."

I'm proud too, she thought, her cheeks still burning as her father and Morgam left her with the unfinished waffle cake that was too delicious to leave behind. *Proud of me.*

Kir rested both hands on the table in front of her, leaning against the surface. Just over a month ago, when she'd been handed this job, she'd fell into a state of panic at the thought of handling something so large. Now, thinking back, it hadn't been all that hard after all. Having so much to do, having Lottie around... all of it made her life feel more alive.

You did it, Kiri, said a soft voice in her mind. She closed her eyes, thinking of her mother. *I knew you could do it. Now go out there and chase your dreams.*

Chase her dreams. The thought was no longer terrifying or felt incredibly far away and unrealistic.

She picked up the plate of waffles and covered it with a bowl that she found in the back of a cupboard and headed off into Arrowmount, walking off toward Cecily's apartment. Lottie and her sister had made up a few days previous, so Kir knew that Lottie would be back staying with her once more.

Lottie.

Kir hesitated when she came up to the beautifully adorned, flowering stairwell, as a bolt of pain and joy rammed into her chest at the same time.

"You're too good for me."

"Gods, I like you, Kir. I can't get you out of my head."

Kir shook herself, trying to knock loose the thoughts that had plagued her since Lottie had sat on her bed confessing her feelings. Elation filled Kir every time she remembered that — only to be crushed the moment she remembered that Lottie was leaving, and nothing would ever come of their feelings.

They were only friends, despite the ache in Kir's heart.

Maigsir's tits, *why* did this all have to be so complicated?

Kir walked up the next few stairs and knocked.

Lottie answered after only a moment, looking ready for the day as though she had been up already for a few hours, like Kir.

"Oh!" Lottie took an involuntary step back and opened the door wider, a brilliant smile appearing on her face, lighting up her entire expression. "Kir!"

"I brought breakfast," said Kir in greeting, uncovering the waffles and brandishing two forks. "Morgam and Dad made this this morning and I couldn't let it sit and go to waste."

"You must be a mind reader, because I was just thinking about where to go for food. Come in, Ceci made some extra coffee this morning before she left. I'm *starving*."

The two of them stepped into the apartment, which felt immediately too intimate. It was small, but not in the way that made Kir feel as though she needed to duck to fit. Every inch was covered in some kind of green, whether it was the walls or the couch or the innumerable plants pockmarking the place.

Watching Lottie walk barefoot toward the kitchen was almost too much. Kir swallowed, trying to tamp down the urge to walk over and wrap her arms around her, lift her off her feet, and kiss her until Kir forgot who she was.

Kir joined her at the small counter as Lottie picked up a mug from a small hanging rack on the wall above the sink and filled it with coffee. Lottie unearthed a couple forks as Kir set the cake between them.

Kir sipped tentatively at the coffee Lottie handed over, finding it the perfect drinking temperature, and not bad at all. In fact — Kir took another, larger sip, filling her senses with the nutty beverage — it was almost as good as May's.

Lottie leaned in and speared a bit of waffle with her fork. She looked up at Kir through her eyelashes, sending shivers down Kir's spine, and took a bite.

"Iluinn's mercy," Lottie groaned, her eyes closing in ecstasy. "What's in these? Pure love?"

Kir laughed and sliced a bite for herself. "Probably about a pound of butter and sugar, so yes."

Somehow, standing there with Lottie on either side of her sister's kitchen, Kir was able to actually eat more of the waffles. They talked about nonsense, avoiding the topic of the Festival and the artifact, just filling the room with noise. It was exactly what she needed to calm the nerves roaring around her body.

She glanced up at Lottie between bites and everything inside Kir settled entirely.

She was going to be ruined by this woman.

"So," said Kir, clearing her throat through the thickness of icing after another bite. "What's up for today?"

"Well, we hadn't really talked about doing anything specific with the performers, right? Is there something extra we need to get done?"

"No, they all know exactly what they're doing and when to do it." Kir sipped at her coffee as Lottie finished off the last bit of the waffle cake. "I'll be around if they need me, but I wanted to make sure that you had today cleared. We are going to experience the Moon Festival like we're supposed to."

Kir closed the bowl over the empty plate before extending a hand to Lottie.

"What, like a... a date? Kir, we —"

"Not a date," said Kir, feeling a surge of anticipatory anxiety bloom through her stomach. "I want to show you what being part of the Moon Festival is really like, when you're a local of Arrowmount. Like I've experienced all my life. Like friends do."

"Friends." Lottie glanced away momentarily, biting her lip, before she smiled up at Kir once more. Kir studied her face, frowning. Another mask had slid into place, one that she couldn't quite see through. "Yeah. Yeah, that's sounds like fun. Let me get my boots."

42

MYTH AND LEGEND

Lottie – Day One

Kir seemed content with ambling around the festival to simply explore everything. Lottie's stomach kept going through a whirlwind of tension and release as she relaxed into the moment before remembering that she was on what felt like a date with Kir.

It's not a date, she kept reminding herself. *You two are just friends. Calm down.*

It didn't help that she had a nagging suspicion that she'd turn around and see Alros staring at her from within the crowd, standing out like a sore thumb amidst the happy Festival goers.

It's been slightly over a week since I got the letter, he has to be here.

Lottie turned to smile at Kir, trying to push the thought out of her head. Kir stood a touch closer than usual, causing Lottie's throat to constrict. She cleared her throat and gazed down at her booted feet, feeling as though she had bubbles floating through her insides.

"Are you alright?"

305

"Yes of course." Lottie shook a bit of hair out of her face that had come loose from her braids and peered up at Kir. For approximately the twentieth time since she had opened her sister's apartment door to reveal Kir, she marveled at the fact the woman was wearing her hair down for once. "This Festival really is something."

Arrowmount hadn't cut any corners when it came to the Moon Festival. All along the beach, various tables were set up, creating a long alleyway that doubled in on itself for festival goers to walk through, winding up into the town proper. The structure that Kir had been working on was a board displaying art and notices across it, most prominently the schedule her and Kir had created themselves for the performances.

Various games were set up along stretches of sand. Children and adults crowded around them, shouts and chatter emanating as they entertained themselves.

Kir took Lottie's hand like it was nothing, their fingers fitting together perfectly, and led her up into the town. They headed toward the town center, which had been entirely transformed. A beautifully wrapped pole of silver and russet ribbon was set up in the middle, a few children hanging onto the ends of it as they twirled around and around, laughing uproariously.

Many of the merchant stalls had been decorated for the festival as well. Ceci's was wrapped in arcane baubles alit in silvery hues wrapped intermittently with ribbon that matched the pole. More than the usual number of stalls had been squished in, too; extra stalls had been added for other stores and individuals, creating a mismatch of tight alleyways, everyone chattering excitedly.

Delicious scents of spiced, roasted meat and baking breads overwhelmed Lottie's senses bread as Kir maneuvered them through the tumult. They passed a puppet theatre set up along the outskirts of it all, sitting dark with its curtains drawn, awaiting the Montarali Family to begin their performance.

The theatre was beautifully painted with tiny scenes from myth and legend and well-known stories painted along the edges. In the weak autumnal sunshine, a shimmering gold and silver thread had been painted throughout the drawings, giving the theatre a cohesive shine that drew the eye from afar.

But for now — Lottie peered around the crowd of festival goers, looking for the two puppeteer apprentices who were supposed to be beginning a performance momentarily.

"Can you see Lyndal and Tierri?" she asked, leaning toward Kir as they stopped at the baker's stall. Lottie smiled at Gable, remembering what Ceci had said about them. They were wearing knitted gloves that matched Ceci's fingerless ones, adjusting their short-cropped hair as they sold baked goods to passersby.

"No, I haven't caught sight of them yet," said Kir, nodding to Gable. They smiled kindly at Kir and Lottie, their eyes crinkling at the sides. "Can we get a couple cinnamon buns?"

"It's a pleasure to meet you officially, Lottie," Gable said, extending a gloved hand. "Your sister has spoken at length about you."

"Ah." Lottie swallowed a tiny burst of unease at the thought of her sister talking about her.

"All good things, I assure you."

"Thank you, Gable. I've heard lovely things about you as well. I hope... I, well, I don't know if I really have the right to say this, but I hope you and her are happy."

"She finally told you about me then? Good. Good." Their face melted into such a warm, wide smile that their eyes momentarily vanished. They laughed warmly as they handed over two steaming cinnamon buns. "Free of charge to Moon Festival volunteers, of course."

Lottie winked at them before turning from the stall, allowing the next person in line to walk up.

"Ah, there they are," said Kir, pointing through the crowd to two figures who had bundles in hand. They were huddled toward one another, the honey-haired elf, Lyndal, almost bent in half to speak to Tierri's tiny dwarven form, discussing something intently.

Lottie steered Kir toward them, a smile forming on her face.

"Happy first day of the Festival," she said. "Is everything alright?"

"Oh, Lottie." Tierri looked up at her with wide, slightly worried eyes.

"Happy first day," said Lyndal, their voice melancholic. "Or it would be, if we could decide on anything."

"The thing is, I want to start the festival with 'Twydnal the Bright,'" said Tierri. "It's a crowd favorite."

"But since this is Arrowmount, I figured it would be better to perform 'The Ballad of Eldar the Bold,'" argued Lyndal.

Kir nodded thoughtfully. "'The Ballad of Eldar the Bold' is a popular one with the bards. I've heard that Jilla, Anara, and Diros want to perform that tonight."

Lyndal's face crumpled. "Oh."

"It's alright, Lyn," said Tierri, comfortingly patting their arm. "We should have known. Hey, I know — why don't we do a bit from that Servune play you showed me last month instead? I think I can still remember most of the words."

Most? Lottie glanced at Kir, slightly worried. Kir, though, shrugged. "That sounds like a fairly good choice, seeing as it is Servune's Moon Festival and all. Try that."

Lyndal perked up, unwrapping the bundle in their arms with fervor. "Tierri, that is a positively wonderful idea. Once that's done, we can do your Twyndal the Bright."

Kir and Lottie stood by as the apprentices threw the covers off their puppets and propped them up into the air, walking off to a corner of the town center, the two of them conversing.

"You're not worried about that 'maybe?'"

Kir chuckled, taking a bite of her cinnamon bun. "You'd be surprised at how quick performers can adapt. It's as easy as breathing, sometimes."

"Alright, I'll take your word for it." Lottie picked at her own pastry, pulling a perfectly fluffy and gooey piece from the side and popping it in her mouth. It was absolutely *divine*.

It wasn't long before a shout ran through the crowd, calling attention to the two puppeteers in the corner. Lyndal held their puppet at about head height, whereas Tierri had a series of long poles set up to hold her own up on the same level. Both puppets were just visible above most heads in the crowd.

Both puppets held aloft were spindly wooden figures supported by a base that was fashioned like a body and was operated by long, thin poles. Lyndal's was painted to look as though it was wearing simple clothes and had a tiny hat positioned jauntily atop its bald wooden head, and Tierri's was decorated much like a court jester, draped in astonishingly bright colors.

"Hear-hear-hear us!" called Tierri, projecting her voice clearly above the chatter. The puppet above her gestured wide with a wooden arm, drawing attention.

"Hear-hear-hear our story," said Lyndal, their voice melodic and carrying. The two of them began to move through the crowd, the puppets above them motioning and talking as the apprentices spoke, the effect as though the puppets were walking above the gathered townsfolk.

"Far cast and terribly too long ago, a wondrous story began," said

Tierri's puppet. "One that we know has been told wide and far."

"Yet, hear well, because we also know the *true* story," said Lydnal's puppet cheekily, touching their hat in a mock bow.

"Do be kind, Myth. Our listeners may be sensitive to the fact that they might all be a bunch of silly numpties."

A chorus of laughter from the surrounding children rose up. Lottie found herself smiling a soft, rather impressed smile as the apprentices entranced the crowd.

"Ah, you are right, Legend. My apologies," said Lyndal's puppet as they bowed over and over in various directions to the crowd. "We shall of course, give you an account of true events, but it is up to you to believe us if you will."

"The truest of events, believe us!"

"We tell no lies!"

"We promise to try, at least."

"Millenia ago, when gods walked the earth — before they even really considered themselves gods — they were each doing whatever they pleased. Some decided to live in luxury and languor, and others —"

"Others," piped up Legend, "were on their journeys to become great heroes."

Lyndal and Tierri passed by them separately, winding through the crowd and around the ribbon pole, followed by a series of Arrowmount's children. The puppeteer apprentices danced and gestured, entertaining all around.

Lottie took the moment that both puppeteers walked by, pulling attention, to gaze up at Kir. Kir was absolutely delighted. She laughed along with the crowd at a particularly funny part that Lottie missed, the smile that stretched across her face so wonderfully sweet that for a moment, that's all Lottie could see.

Gods, how she could ever think to be *just friends* with this woman was absolutely ludicrous.

Lyndal and Tierri continued to wind a map through the town center as their story came to a close, the two of them finding each other again at the ribbon pole, ending their performance with dual, identical bows. The crowd that had amassed erupted in cheers.

"First performance of the festival went off perfectly," said Lottie, leaning into Kir so she could hear her. Kir's expression, if at all possible, brightened even more.

43

THE MAIN STAGE

Kir – Day One

Both Lyndal and Tierri were absolutely perfect. Kir beamed at the puppets as they continued to wind their way through the crowd gathered in the town center, continuing to craft a story. Beside her, Lottie laughed and clapped along with the crowd, enjoying every minute of the performance.

We chose well, she thought to herself. Happily, she shoved the rest of her cinnamon bun into her mouth and focused on the incredibly soft, perfectly sweet pastry.

"Kir?"

She smiled down at Lottie as cheers arose around them, the apprentices wrapping their first story. Lottie's face had completely changed from the open, laughing one to something more closed off, as though she was waiting for anger or retribution.

"Is he here?"

"I... I just saw him at the edge of the crowd." She pointed off toward a side street. "I hate to interrupt our day —"

"Don't worry about it," Kir said, smiling at her reassuringly. "Everything is going to go exactly how you want. You're going to be okay."

"Right." Lottie's hands twisted along the strap of her bag.

"When you're done, we'll go and play some games." *It'll be a good way to break the tension if things go wrong or celebrate if Lottie succeeds. Which she will.*

Lottie's eyes lit up as she glanced up. "I hope you're ready to get your ass kicked, Kirandir. I saw one that involved knife throwing, and you best believe I know my way around a dagger."

She darted off through the crowd, cutting through the shoppers and the festival goers as Lyndal and Tierri kicked into *Twyndal the Bright.* Kir watched for a moment, waiting to see if she could spot whomever Lottie was going to meet up with. As she tracked Lottie's green hair through the townsfolk, she only noticed when Lottie hesitated before changing directions, as though now walking with someone. Whoever she was walking with, though, didn't stand out enough to be noticed.

"Kir?"

Kir jumped slightly, glancing down beside her. A slight half-elven girl with flowing chestnut hair and a rather flashy blue tunic had appeared, holding a mandolin tight in hand, her expression tight and grave.

"Eralie, how are you?"

"I'm —" Eralie paused and swallowed, peering around. As she turned her head, Kir noticed a dusting of glitter on her high cheekbones and along the tips of her slightly elongated ears. "I have been looking for you everywhere."

"Is everything alright?" Kir ran through the schedule in her head, recalling that Eralie was due to start her set soon down by the sea on the main stage.

Eralie's forehead went through a series of stress wrinkles and flinches as she tried to pull words together. "Yes. Well, no. Yes, everything is fine nothing's wrong but —"

"Eralie."

"Sorry, sometimes when I get nervous, I talk in circles and nothing makes sense." The girl cringed and tried to laugh, but it came out more like a squeak. Kir had to bite back a smile, recognizing herself in the girl when Kir was her age. Eralie was barely a teenager and she had already come this far — auditioning, putting herself out there.

Kir placed a careful hand on her shoulder. "Being nervous is entirely fine. Why don't we head down there together?"

Eralie nodded.

Kir steered the girl out of the town center and toward a lower part of Arrowmount where she knew was fairly empty of festival activities. She turned down a side street, the sound of the festival becoming farther and farther off.

Eralie, walking in tight, quick strides, let out an unsteady breath as the streets around her emptied out of people. Out of the corner of her eye, Kir watched as the tension leaked out of Eralie's shoulders the further they walked.

She waited a few more beats, sensing that Eralie would talk in her own time. Kir knew enough about her own anxiety and mind that when people forced her to talk, the anxiety became worse and often she couldn't get any coherent words out the more she tried.

Kir gazed off around them as they exited the town at the port, breathing in deep. The air smelled special today, as though magic itself hung in the air. The day was crisp and clear, and the sun had decided to make a proper entrance despite the clouds that had been hanging around for the past few days.

"I'm sorry, Kir," said Eralie, her voice calmer. Kir turned to her, watching the way the girl's face crinkle in on itself with preemptive sorrow.

Kir eyed her up and down, eyeing her instrument at the ready. "Everything okay?"

"I think I just needed to move," Eralie answered, taking in a steadying breath. "Gods, I'm so nervous. I don't think I'm good enough for all this."

"Why do you think that?"

Eralie sucked in a sharp breath. "Because when I start playing everyone is going to be disappointed, because they're going to be expecting music from someone professional like you, and —"

Kir burst out in surprised laughter. "Professional? I am not a professional, Eralie. I simply have done enough sets to be comfortable with performing."

"Exactly. I'm not ready."

"You won't really be ready until you actually do it," Kir answered.

"But —"

"Lottie and I wouldn't have picked you out of all those who auditioned if we didn't think you were absolutely perfect for this."

The girl closed her eyes tight, her grip on her instrument tightening until her knuckles went white.

"You're going to be *fantastic.* I know the feeling of the beginning dread, the unknown. That anticipation is good, Eralie."

"How is it good if it makes me feel sick?"

Kir chuckled, remembering when the anticipation used to make her feel that way too. "It takes a while, but it'll change. For now — trust me, okay?"

"Trust you."

"You're ready for this. I know you are."

Eralie grimaced like Kir had asked her to kiss a seabird, but she nodded all the same, straightening her spine ever so slightly.

The two of them walked toward the main stage, set up a little bit away from the water where a large stretch of sand banked out around it for people to gather and listen. Kir could smell one of her favorite treats from childhood, candy and chocolate covered apples, in the air.

As they approached, Kir flagged down one of Della's errand runners.

"Yes, miss?"

"Do you mind running off to the town center and finding someone for me to deliver a message?"

"Sure!" The kid beamed as Kir handed them a small coin.

"Find someone named Lottie — she's an earth elemental —"

"Like Miss Ceci, from the stall?"

"Exactly, she's her sister. Bright green hair. Beautiful smile. Can you find her and let her know that Kir is at the main stage attending to Committee business?"

"Kir, main stage, Committee business," the boy rattled off, thinking hard to remember. "Can do, miss!"

The boy took off running from the property, a piece of colorful ribbon trailing behind him, attached to his shoe.

Eralie stood in the sand, gazing at the stalls set up along the beach and the people milling about. She nodded a few times, as though talking to herself in her head.

"Ready?"

She straightened her back and set her jaw.

Eralie walked away from her, up to the stage, as Kir walked slowly behind. Eralie found her spot onstage as folks started to mill around, noticing the act about to begin.

Kir glanced around at the main stage, a smile breaking across her face.

It was a large structure, built with the possibility of a roof if any rain was to start. For now, the wooden slats that could be slid into place along the top frame, were left out, the sky visible beyond. All around the heavy wooden frame, there had been hung tiny baubles and ribbons, matching the decorations from elsewhere in town.

The wooden platform of the stage was set up high enough that most of the crowd across the beach would be able to see the performance from wherever they were standing. It would be fantastic for the dancers, too, when they set up here for their own performances over the next couple days.

Kir couldn't help but think of herself up there, looking out at the crowd. A small thrill of anticipation echoed through her core, that familiar emotion sending shivers up her spine.

Eralie caught her eye and lifted her mandolin, ready.

"Uh, hello," she said, her voice quiet. She tried again, pushing her voice out more. "I'm Eralie."

The crowd nearby whooped politely, a few clapping as she turned to them fully. Eralie's fingers plucked at her mandolin, feeling out chords.

"This first song is probably one that you've all heard before, so if you know it, feel free to join in." Eralie's voice became stronger the more she spoke. "That's how music is best enjoyed anyway, isn't it? Together."

She began to strum the familiar notes to an old folk song as heads nodded and more claps sounded, more people gravitating toward the stage to hear.

44

NEW TALENT

Lottie – Day One

Lottie held her breath as she followed Alros down a side street. He hadn't said anything to her as she approached him through the crowd, simply gave her a nod, and slipped away.

He had a hood up, too, obscuring him from view. A few times, Lottie actually lost sight of him in the crowd, her eyes slipping from the indistinct cloak over his shoulders off to someone else who was brightly adorned in layers of warmth for the festival. She flicked her hair out of her face, feeling a slight scrape of irritation at the back of her skull.

Finally, as they turned down a quiet alley, Lottie caught up to Alros and grabbed his arm.

"You can't even say hello?"

"I simply wished that we get somewhere quiet before we spoke," he said, looking up and down the alleyway. "Seeing as I haven't heard from you in over a month. I don't know this town, is this safe?"

Lottie held back from rolling her eyes at him with great willpower.

"Yes, Alros. You're safe here."

"I meant from being overheard," he hissed.

"It would have been better to stay in the middle of the crowd if you didn't want to be overheard," she said, holding back a sigh. "That way, no one really pays attention to you. But, no one is around, windows are all closed. Say what you have to."

"Where is it?" Alros' eyes sharpened as he peered at her. "No response for months, and yet, I find you here seemingly well and healthy. Where is the artifact? Why did you not hand it over?"

Straight to business, okay. "I didn't hand it over then because I, honestly, didn't really want to. You said it yourself once, didn't you Alros — never trust a thief."

He narrowed his eyes at her.

"But," she continued, holding up a hand to stop the diatribe she knew was about to exit his throat. "I've changed my mind."

"Figured it would be better to be in the Guild's good graces, then?" Alros chuckled, the sound off-putting. She couldn't remember the last time she heard the man chuckle, let alone laugh. "Smart girl. Why, if this goes as smoothly as it has been so far, then I wouldn't say no to talking you up to the Guild again. Maybe we can broker a deal, you and I."

The last thing I want to do is work with you, you slimy rat, she seethed internally, keeping her face neutral. "I'd like that, if it was possible."

She dipped her hand into her bag and clasped her fingers around the cold, metallic replica, feigning a slight hesitation before pulling it out. Alros' eyes latched onto it like a predator on prey.

"Wonderful," he hissed between his teeth, sending Lottie's skin crawling. How had she not noticed how awful he was before? Gods, all she wanted to do was hand this off and get as far from him as she could.

She took a step toward him, stretching out her hand. "Here it is, safe and sound."

"She's lying," said a voice that she thought she'd never hear again.

The irritating scrape at the back of her skull grew, alerting her only seconds before he stepped out behind her. She threw up walls in her mind, hoping that it was enough to keep him from her thoughts.

Seban.

"Lottie, I'm sure you remember your old contact, Seban," said Alros, his voice silky smooth. Lottie took an involuntary step back, putting more distance between the two of them as Seban stepped up, brushing by her. Shivers ran up her arms.

"You've found yourself a new job, have you?" Lottie tried to keep her expression as neutral and unsurprised as possible as she took in the two of them. Seban grinned, showing all of his teeth.

"Well, the Guild always needs *useful* people to join their ranks," said Seban slyly.

"Right, of course. Your magic is invaluable." Lottie cleared her throat and extended the artifact again. "Here, as you asked. I don't want any trouble."

Alros narrowed his eyes at her before flicking his gaze to Seban. "What did you mean, she was lying?"

"Hmmm." Seban focused on Lottie, sending a spark right through her skull. Scrambling, Lottie thought of one of the only things she could to try and keep him out of her mind. She brought up a memory of the Nine, all together, after their first big job had succeeded. She focused on Seban and his brother, Loth, laughing together.

He flinched ever so slightly, and she felt the tether between them weaken.

"She was lying," he said, stumbling slightly over his words. He shifted uncomfortably, not meeting her eye. "W-what she said before."

"About the artifact?"

Lottie's heart was in her throat.

"No," said Seban after a beat. "About wanting to work with you again."

Alros let out a cackling laugh that sounded almost eerily like a crow.

Lottie forced her face to flinch back, as though she was found out. Alros, overcome with glee, reached out and plucked the replica from her hands with spindly, thin fingers. Greedily, he inspected the surface, drinking it in.

"Oh, oh yes, the Boss will be pleased."

"So *you* were the contact," said Lottie, peering at Seban as bits of the puzzle slid into place. "The one that Alros mentioned in his first letter. You knew about the artifact going missing far sooner than news got out officially — you were going after it yourself, weren't you?"

Seban smirked. "They never wanted *you* to succeed, Lottie. That was my job, didn't you figure that out? How easy it was, pretending like you were bringing me on to prove yourself. And then you happened to go in and do all the work for me!"

"Not so lucky are we now, eh?" Alros smiled at her as he clutched the replica close to his chest.

They'd planned it all. Right to her downfall.

Lottie took a long steadying breath and looked Alros straight in the eye. It wasn't until that moment, seeing his familiar scarred face, that Lottie realized she should've made this decision long, long ago.

"I'm glad you did," she said calmly. Without needing to force it, a smile broke across her face. "If you hadn't, then I wouldn't have come here, to this absolutely wonderful town. It was a perfect vacation."

"Vacation?" said Alros, frowning.

"The beach in autumn is a special kind of getaway. Most people talk about going in the summer, but no — I recommend it now," she said, gripping her bag a little firmer, feeling the weight of the artifact nestled safely inside against her thigh. "If that's all, then?"

"Ah." Alros narrowed his eyes, suddenly suspicious. "How do I know that you're not going to follow us and try your hand at it again?"

"Alros, really? Why would I do that?"

"I don't know." Alros sniffed hard, his eyes darting around the small alleyway they were in as though searching for spies. Then he shot a glance at Seban. Seban, wincing, focused on Lottie again.

The scrape of his magic caressed the back of her skull. She frowned and pushed thoughts of never wanting to be near them again at him.

"Yeah, I think we're okay," he said to Alros, pulling himself from her mind with a soft grimace. "I'm fairly certain she'll run if she ever sees us again."

"Good, good." Alros bundled the replica up in a swath of material, tucking it away in his own bag hanging over his shoulder. "Well, it's been a pleasure as always, Lottie."

"I cannot say the same without him knowing that I'm flat out lying," she said, nodding to Seban. "I'm glad we could get this over with. Now, if you don't mind, I'm going to go enjoy the rest of this wonderful festival."

"You've changed," Alros said quietly. "You're not the Lottie Luck I saw in the rain, wounded and drenched, begging for a chance."

"People change." Lottie shrugged simply, thinking of Kir and Aeric and her sister, and all the other people she'd come to know here in Arrowmount before quickly shoving them out of her mind with a sharp glance at Seban. She couldn't feel him right then, but better to be safe than sorry. "I hope you enjoy the Moon Festival while you're here. We did put an enormous amount of work into it."

Alros narrowed his eyes at her before he slipped away. Seban followed after, shooting Lottie one last glance.

"I think Loth would be proud," said Lottie gently. She knew he would've been. The two brothers had plotted for their entire childhood to one day join the Guild together.

Seban's face clouded over with anger and pain before he opened his mouth to retort something back. Before he could get a word out, though, a small boy ran past the alley, nearly colliding with him.

"Sorry mister!"

"Watch where you're going," answered Seban sharply.

The boy flinched away from him, before he noticed Lottie. His eyes went wide. "Miss — are you Lottie?"

"I am," she answered, watching Seban melt into the crowd after Alros, vanishing, hopefully, for good.

She felt lighter than she had in weeks, smiling down at the boy.

It had worked.

"Great. I have been tasked to tell you that Kir is at the main stage for Committee business."

"Oh," said Lottie, nodding to him. "I appreciate the message."

"No problem miss!"

Lottie smiled after the boy as he took off running and followed him out of the alley. She watched as he pelted toward the ribbon pole set up in the town center, glee written all over his face. She took a moment, breathing in the scent of various baking treats and the cool sea air, basking at the edge of the revelry.

Then, thinking only of Kir, she began to wind her way through Arrowmount toward the beach.

Kir was standing beside the stage as Eralie, one of the bards that Lottie had really enjoyed during the auditions, sang to a large crowd. Much like when Kir sang at the Old'n Narrow, though, most of the crowd still went about whatever they wanted to be doing on the sand, enjoying the activities and food.

Lottie took a moment to watch Kir. Her expression was overjoyed as she watched the young minstrel play, a pride that Lottie hadn't seen before painting her features.

Lottie walked up, touching her arm. "Hey."

"Isn't Eralie fantastic?"

"I knew she would be. What made you walk all the way over here?"

"She was..." Kir waved a hand dismissively. "It doesn't matter. She is really doing it, isn't she?"

"I love how proud you are of her."

Kir beamed. "I'm thinking about asking Nova and Briar to offer her some nightly sets, so she can get more comfortable with performing."

"What about you?"

Kir's mouth opened slightly, before she hesitated. For a moment, she couldn't meet Lottie's eye. "I can give up a few spots for new talent."

Lottie smiled.

Kir, then, did a double take. "Did —"

"It worked."

Kir swooped her up in her arms, spinning her around, the two of them laughing. "I knew it would. Lottie, you're a genius!"

"I don't know if genius is the right word, or simply quick on my feet," she answered, laughing giddily. "They bought it. Every bit. But — I don't want to —" she frowned, gazing at the crowd gathered around them. "I'll tell you later, okay? Once I know they're gone from the town."

"They?"

"Alros has a new friend who can break into minds," she said simply. Kir's eyes widened. Lottie threaded her fingers through Kir's, feeling as though her heart had finally settled into place. "Later. I'll tell you it all later."

45

SPECIAL OCCASIONS

Kir – Day Four

Kir woke on the final day of the Moon Festival with more energy than she ever had before. She got out of bed and began to dress, digging around until she found one of her favorite red linen shirts that she saved for performances outside of the Old'n Narrow. They were few and far between, but she liked keeping the shirt for special occasions.

She turned to Nudge, who was splayed out on her bed, as she adjusted the neckline. He stared at her, his eyes slightly narrowed, as though he knew what she was thinking.

"Nudge, I think it's time, bud."

He let out a low whine before settling his head down on his paws, big eyes looking up at her.

"Don't give me that, I need all the support I can to tell the others. You're all I have right now." She kneeled in front of him and scratched his ears right where he liked best, until the enormous dog melted into a happy grin. He licked her face from chin to hairline, making her laugh. "I'm going to miss you."

Kir took the stairs two at a time and arrived in the kitchen just as her father was placing a plate of toast on the table. Nudge came thundering down behind her. "Morning, Dad. You're up early."

Nudge whined, settling his head down on her father's knee. The greathound's eyes flicked from Kir to her father, waiting.

"I am too excited to see your show today, Kiri, I couldn't sleep," said her father, rubbing Nudge behind the ears, who again let out a long whine. "What's gotten into you, Nudge? Did you have a bad sleep? Do you want to walk Kir out to the festival with me?"

"Actually, Dad, I have something I wanted to talk to you about." Kir stayed standing, wringing her hands in front of her, unable to stay still.

"Oh?"

"I..." She cleared her throat, feeling almost as nervous as she had back when she told her dad she was starting a job at the bar so she could play every night. Nudge's eyes found her, and he let out another whine, his eyebrows concerned. With a deep, steadying breath, she nodded and ploughed forward. "I think I'm going to leave Arrowmount."

Her father froze, a piece of toast halfway to his mouth. "Leave?"

"You know that I want to make something with my music," she continued, talking a little faster so she could get everything out before she became too nervous. "I always fantasized about big crowds, singing for people who really cared about the music. Making a name for myself."

"People love your music here, Kiri."

"I know that, I do. And I appreciate everything that Arrowmount has done for me. I just think..."

"Is this because of that Lottie girl?"

Kir let out a burst of surprised laughter. "No, not at all. I haven't even talked to her about this. I... I want to do this, Dad. For me. I want to see if I have what it takes. And I've been thinking about the whole committee thing as a test, of sorts. If I could handle that, then..."

"You can handle anything, Kiri." Her father popped the rest of his toast into his mouth and chewed thoughtfully. "I always knew that you were going to be the first of my children to leave," he said finally, swallowing. "You've had something in you from when you were little. I think your mother put it there, threading dreams in with your breakfast or something of the like."

He pushed himself up, dislodging Nudge, and placed his hands on Kir's shoulders.

"Kirandir, whatever you choose to do, I approve. You have enough talent to win them all over, no matter where you go." He smiled softly at her, deep emotion welling in his eyes. "You could've done it well before this Committee thing."

"I know, I just... it felt like I had to prove to myself I could do it."

Her father pulled her into a tight, warm hug, his large form engulfing her.

"What's going on?"

Khar and Morgam appeared behind them, coming down the stairs, dark circles under their eyes. Khar yawned wide, trying to hide it behind a hand.

"Why are you up?" Kir asked, detaching from her father.

"We're spending the day at the festival, so we can catch as much of it as possible," explained Morgam, walking over to the table and stealing the other piece of toast on their father's plate. As he chewed, he motioned at them. "What's the hug for?"

Her raised his eyebrows at Kir, motioning with a hand for her to explain.

"I'm leaving," she said with a heavy breath, making sure she spoke clearly and got all her words out before anyone interrupted her. "I'm going to try and make something of my music."

Her two brothers stared at her, dumbstruck.

"Our Kir, leaving?" Khar peered at her closely. "Are you well?"

"I am better than I've been in a long time," she answered.

Morgam pointed the almost finished toast at her. "You're standing up a little straighter than usual."

She coughed out an astonished laugh. Maybe she was. "I want to do this for me. I want... I want to give my dreams a chance."

Khar's face slowly broke into a smile. "You're going to do so well, Kir."

"You better make sure you send us letters all the time," said Morgam, coming up to her and wrapping her in a tight hug. Khar came in too, throwing his arms around both of them. "That way I can come out to wherever you are, and paint portraits of you as you take over the world."

"I'll write all the time," she answered, emotion making the back of her throat thick. "As much as I can. But I'm not leaving quite yet — I have to make sure everything is in order first."

"Of course, of course." Khar and Morgam let go, leaving her feeling both warm and slightly cold in their absence. "First, you have to go and knock everyone's socks off with your performance tonight."

Kir let out a long, steadying breath and wiped a tear that escaped and rolled down her cheek. She felt so warm and full as her brothers and father lead her out of the house, Nudge gamboling along with them. The earlier nervousness bled out of her into something familiar as they walked toward the last day of the Moon Festival: *anticipation*.

Kir spent most of the day with her family, poking around as they used to when they were children. Morgam and Khar beat her at almost every game they played, which they happily lorded over her. Their father had closed the smithy for the day, specially to allow them all to attend the Festival together.

As the sun began to dip toward the horizon, she detached herself from them as they busied themselves with a strength contest that involved a mallet and a bell, heading off toward the Old'n Narrow. Her lute waited for her, stashed in the back where she always left it, the case comforting in her hands.

The inside of the bar was quiet and empty, despite the crowds outside. Briar and Nova had closed it for a few hours so that everyone could go to the beach and watch her performance.

Kir took a moment, holding her lute, to calm and ready herself as though she was simply going to perform atop her old stool in the corner.

This is it, she thought to herself, peering at the stool, feeling a wave of nostalgia wash over her. *The first biggest performance you'll do. Only up from here, Kir.*

As she pushed open the door to the back alley, absently massaging her hands to life, her thoughts strayed to Lottie, wondering where she had gotten to.

They hadn't had much time to talk over the last few days aside from when Lottie finally divulged the details of her meeting with Seban and Alros. Zanve, one of the town guards stationed at the front, had informed her through Cecily the moment the two had left on horseback. Kir was so proud that Lottie managed to pull off the deception, even with someone who could perform mind magic there. And now Lottie was free to head off into the empire and discover more about the artifact however she wished to.

Kir had kept the secret of her wanting to leave tucked away in her mind, uncertain of how her family was going to take it. But now, with her brother's and father's enthusiastic acceptance, she allowed herself to wonder what Lottie would think.

Because, said a little voice in her mind, *if I'm leaving, and so is Lottie, then why not leave together?*

It was all Kir could think about the past few days. She wasn't going to outright ask Lottie to go with her, but if Lottie mentioned it, then...

It would be fantastic. Even if they were just friends.

At the end of my performance, she thought to herself as she made her way toward the beach through the darkening skies of Arrowmount. *When everyone is celebrating. That's when I'll tell her.*

For now, though, it was time to get ready.

She nodded to a few folks who waved excitedly at her as she walked onto the beach, the sea mist wrapping itself around her. The crowd was already fairly large, milling about the stalls that had, at the beginning of the day, been packed with food and beverages. Most of the vendors were just about to close up for the final performance, selling their last wares of the day.

A few had turned into booths full of arcane sparklers they were handing out to children and adults. The main stage was aglow with lights, the baubles that Kir had noticed the first day now shining brilliantly as they illuminated the space. Someone had strung them around the stalls as well, creating an absolutely magical space.

A few of the Moon Festival volunteers waved to her as she approached, having taken their spots by the edge of the stage.

"Are you ready, Kir?" asked a voice from behind her as she reached the structure, setting her lute case down.

Kir turned, finding a tall, white-haired elf standing with his dashing partner on his arm. Arileas beamed at her. "Oh, hi. Almost, yes."

"I had an idea," he said, gesturing with his head over to the stage. "I was listening to a performance earlier and thought perhaps we amp up the final one slightly."

Kir removed her warm jacket, bearing her thin linen shirt to the crisp autumnal air. She'd be warm in a moment, she knew, up there playing. As she extricated her lute from its case, she asked, "Oh? How's that?"

Arileas smiled, gesturing her forward on the stage. "I found a bit of magic in a spell book that will help amplify your voice so that everyone will be able to hear you clearly."

"That... that would be fantastic." Kir adjusted her lute and gazed out at the assembling crowd as the sky around them settled comfortably toward dusk. The waves rushed in and out in the background, a constant soundtrack to the chatter. "Will it really let my voice cast over all of this?"

"I promise you."

She nodded and stepped up onto the stage.

Arcane sparklers began to alight around the sandy beach as children ran around with them, tracing patterns in the darkness. Her eyes caught on her family, Khar and Morg waving excitedly from a little way back. She smiled, breathing in deep and steady, trying to keep her heart still. With a quick double tap for luck at the base of her lute, she turned toward Arileas, who'd followed her up.

"I'm ready."

Arileas lifted his hands and started to form a quick, bright symbol of magic.

"Good luck," he said with a wink, pushing the magic into her chest. A burst of warm, buzzing energy spread from their touch across her skin and up her throat.

"Thank you," she said, hearing her voice echo back at her as it was amplified out over the crowd. He rejoined Finnean at the edge of the stage as the gathered townsfolk cheered.

"Hello," she said, lifting her hand in greeting to the assembled crowd. She supposed she should say something more, but as everyone cheered around her, she wasn't entirely sure what.

Her eyes scanned those gathered that she could see, her fingers testing out the strings of her lute. The energy started to ramp up, coiling up into Kir's chest as she found the right chords, starting to play the first song of the night.

She swallowed, taking a breath and a moment to watch her hands. Her hair fell over her shoulder, casting a shadow over her face, letting her feel this moment as much as she needed to.

The roar of the crowd around her was louder than she had ever heard before, filling her up. This was better than the silence of a waiting crowd. This was the vibration of anticipation, of everyone here being here for her and this final performance.

As she finally looked up from her lute, she caught sight of Lottie, right up front. Her hair was free of her braids, and for the first time in Kir's memory, Lottie was wearing a dress — one that, in the arcane light glowing from the stage, Kir could clearly see hugged every delicious curve of her body. Lottie grinned up at her, shining so bright she rivalled the arcane lights. Kir nearly stumbled on her chords.

Nearly. Kir was a professional, after all.

"Let's get this evening started, shall we?"

Kir beamed out at the crowd, tossed her hair over her shoulder, and began to sing.

46

LUCK AND CANDY APPLES

L ottie buzzed an hour later as the crowd around her cheered. She threw her hands up, dancing and cheering along with them, the stars above glittering bright. Kir, on stage, drew a hand through her hair, beads of sweat sparkling on her collarbone and chest. Her red shirt, which Lottie thought was entirely too attractive, sat open down to Kir's breastbone.

The amount of attraction running through Lottie's body right then was unparalleled as she looked up at Kir, in absolute awe of her. How could she ever have thought for one second she was going to simply walk away from his woman? If she had to stay in Arrowmount to keep her, she was going to stay. No questions asked.

"Thank you all," Kir said, her voice magically amplified across the beach. "I hope you've had a great night! I think I have one more song in me, if you'll have me."

The town of Arrowmount erupted in cheers. Up until then, the songs that Kir had sung were well known and favorites of many there tonight.

"This one's a bit of a new one, one of my own making, so let me know how you like it." Kir eyes traced the crowd, an elated smile etched onto her face, before she found Lottie and positively beamed.

Eyes locked on Lottie, Kir started to play. The beat was quick and impulsively catchy, digging itself into Lottie's bones.

"East-ward I lived, near the waves glimmerin' gold,
Singing for my pe-ople, the stories and tales of old —
Kir's energy spiked, visibly pulsing on stage as she stamped her leg to the beat. Lottie threw her hands up and cheered along with the crowd around her, letting everything go.

"Simply put, I watched, dreaming for a life of more,
Never thinking I could travel far from the shore.
O'then came a woman of bright summer green,
Eyes lit like starlight, she encha-nted me.
She stopped and said,
You're stuck inside your life,
You have to let fear go and leave it all behind."
Lottie felt Kir's eyes on her as she turned to her again, heat and warmth and passion pouring through her music. The song continued on, rocking the crowd into raucous noise. Kir absolutely flourished on the stage, occupying every inch of it, exploding with talent.

As she rounded out the song, her eyes found Lottie's again, and for a moment, it felt like she was singing right to her and only her.

"She showed me that
There's more to life out there,
So take a little luck, and leave it all behind."
The crowd exploded as Kir strummed the last chord and bowed.

Della appeared from behind Kir's thighs as a few of her fellow festival volunteers lifted her up onto the stage. She bustled forward as Arileas hurried after her, gesturing quickly in the air to perform the same magic he'd done on Kir to amplify her voice. Arileas chuckled as Della patted him on the thigh in thanks, before he quickly reached for Kir, pulling the spell off of her.

"Well well well, what a show!" called Della, her voice booming out. "Thank you, dear Kirandir, for that absolutely fantastic end to our beloved Moon Festival."

Kir bowed to her, modest as always, before turning to where Lottie was in the crowd. Whether it was the atmosphere of the end of the festival, or the arcane lights around the stage, Lottie could've sworn that Kir's eyes were alit with fire.

Without preamble, Kir jumped off the front of the stage and side stepped a few of the other townsfolk that had managed to get up to the very front. No matter who slapped her on the back or congratulated her, Kir didn't take her eyes off of Lottie.

"Hi," Lottie said as Kir closed the distance, her beautiful face shining.

"Hi."

"That was — you are —" Lottie shook her head, at a loss for words. "Kir."

"I'm leaving," Kir said, her voice now only Lottie's to hear amidst the tumult of the crowd as Della closed out the Moon Festival behind them.

"W-what?"

"I'm leaving Arrowmount. I'm going to make a name for myself. And I want you to come with me," said Kir, her eyes alight with something more than fire now.

Lottie sucked in an unsteady breath as Kir took another step forward, the space between them evaporating.

"Yes," Lottie breathed; the sound swallowed by the crowd. Lottie leaned closer to Kir, shifting her lute out from between them so she could slide into the space it took up. "I want to go with you," she repeated, her heartrate skyrocketing. She slid her hands up Kir's chest and around her neck, bringing her closer. "I want see you doing what you do best. I want you to come with me as I figure out this artifact thing. And I — I want you, Kir."

Kir's jaw softened with a gentle smile. "You —"

"You remember when I asked you about the two taps that you do? Back when we were doing auditions?"

Kir's eyebrows furrowed. "Yes."

"I do something like that too."

Lottie threaded her fingers through Kir's hair, pulling her face down until they were a breath apart.

"I like you so damn much, Lottie Luck," Kir said, the words falling from her mouth. She laughed, the vibrations ricocheting through Lottie's fingers and chest where their bodies were pressed together. "In fact, I think I'm in love with you. Gods, no, I *know* I love you."

"Say that again."

"What do you do?" Kir said instead, her lips a hair away from Lottie's. "For luck?"

"I say, just a little luck," Lottie answered breathlessly

"A little luck," Kir said, her eyes glittering in the arcane lights. She opened her mouth again to speak, but her words were interrupted by Lottie as she couldn't wait any longer.

She pulled Kir down, claiming her mouth with hers.

Lottie melted into the kiss as Kir wrapped her arms around her, pulling her in tight. Kir's lips were soft and warm under hers, the two of them fitting perfectly together as she knew they would. Her lips opened for her as shifted, her free hand grasping Lottie's body. Kir's lute butted up against Lottie's hip, but right then, she didn't care at all.

The kiss tasted like magic and salt and the gentlest bit of caramel, which Lottie couldn't place.

This was everything she had wanted for weeks, perhaps even from the moment she had spotted the bard in the corner of the Old'n Narrow that first night she came to Arrowmount. Kir was everything, everything she ever wanted. Here, in Kir's arms, she felt entirely right.

This was the path she was supposed to take, however twisted it had been. It had led her to Kir.

Kir deepened the kiss and traced her free hand up Lottie's back, sending shivers through Lottie, until Kir's fingers were in her hair, pulling her impossibly close as though Kir couldn't get enough. Kir let out the softest groan against her lips. The vibration tickled just enough that Lottie started to laugh, pulling apart for a moment to breathe.

"What's so funny?" Kir asked, panting slightly.

"I can't believe that this is happening right now," Lottie answered, gazing up at her. "And you taste like caramel and starlight and everything that I have ever wanted."

"That would be the candy apple," said Kir, pulling Lottie to her once more, kissing her fiercely as the crowd around them exploded. Lottie didn't really care if it was due to the end of Della's speech, the end of the Moon Festival, or if they had all turned to watch the two of them kiss wrapped by magic and fire and whatever else was in the air tonight. She didn't care, because all she cared about right then was the woman holding her in her incredibly strong arms.

As they broke apart for a second time, Lottie gazed at Kir, breathless. "I love you, too."

AFTER

Lottie – A Few Weeks Later

Lottie threaded her fingers through Kir's as they walked toward the beach on their last night in Arrowmount.

They were meeting a bunch of people at the Old'n Narrow who were gathering to send them off properly. Nova and Briar had decided to close the bar down so that they could all gather to send them off.

Corwek, of course, was making his infamous stew.

"Are you going to miss the town?" Lottie asked quietly. The late evening sun dipped below the horizon, dusk taking them into a particularly chilly night as they reached the water. Lottie tucked her nose inside her scarf, trying to keep it warm as her breath billowed out in the air. Winter was coming in fast. It was best if they got on the road before any snow began to fall.

"Yes," Kir answered simply. "Are you?"

"Gods, yes." Lottie turned to face the breeze coming off the ocean, the sun just peaking one last time over the horizon before it sunk beneath the waves. "There's something about the sea and the people here."

"We'll come back," said Kir. "One day, we'll be back here for good."

Lottie smiled. "You think of us as 'we'?"

"Of course." Kir frowned at her playfully. "I am not letting you go, Lottie Luck, now that I have you."

Lottie threaded her arms into Kir's jacket, finding warmth inside as she held on tight. She looked up at Kir, letting a playful smile fall on her lips. "You have me. I am yours. And you are mine, my wonderful bard extraordinaire."

Kir's face melted into an incandescent smile as the two of them huddled closer for warmth.

"You know I'm pretty much in love with you, right?" Lottie breathed. She'd been saying it over and over for the past few weeks, since the ending of the Moon Festival. She couldn't seem to get over how wonderful it felt, saying something like that. And for it to be entirely, perfectly true.

"Pretty much?"

Lottie laughed, shaking her head. "Let me say this properly: I am *totally* and *completely* in love with you."

Kir beamed before kissing Lottie gently, leaving her lips tingling with delight and a promise of more. "Your nose is cold."

"Gah, all of me is cold." Lottie buried her face in her scarf once more.

"Funny, I think I've loved you since you danced to my song when you arrived in Arrowmount," said Kir. "Your body and smile entranced me to no end."

"Well, if you must know, it was your forearms that did it for me," Lottie teased. "There's something about forearms that I can't resist."

Kir's laugh rumbled in her chest.

"I want to stay here forever," breathed Lottie.

"I could, if you asked me to."

Lottie breathed in happily, laying her head on Kir's chest, and listened to her steady heartbeat. Though they were already clinging to each other, she squeezed tighter, wanting to be as close to Kir as possible. Kir rested her chin on Lottie's head, making a low noise of contentment in the back of her throat.

"Though," said Kir after a few minutes of amiable silence, "I do think that everyone else will be angry if we never showed up."

"I hate that you're right."

The two of them made their way up Fetterly Place as night descended upon them. The warm lantern light emanating from the Old'n Narrow called them in, the sound of the people talking and the lightest chords of music drifting out to meet them.

Kir looked at Lottie, a slight crinkle in her brow, as they opened the door.

The bar exploded in cheers as they entered, people pounding on tables and filling the bar with as much noise as they could. Tears sprung up behind Lottie's eyes as Ceci jumped up, hugging her fiercely, Gable hovering in behind with a gentle smile on their face.

Along the middle, someone had shoved all of the bar's tables together to create one long, massive surface that ran down the center of the bar.

Lottie caught a glimpse of Aeric and Morgam seated practically on top of one another on one side as they raised two pints of ale in their direction before her attention was grabbed by the soft music in the corner. Eralie was set up, mandolin on her knee, on Kir's usual stool. A content smile stretched across her face as she played, music filling the glowing bar. Kir's father, Noghorn, was there too, Nudge the dog squashed between his legs, snoozing on the floor happily. Khar moved into view and clapped Kir on the shoulder, before reaching into his pocket and pulling out a small, beautifully crafted wooden horse.

All of the performers from the festival had come too, filling the back half of the room with sound and energy. The Montarali Family puppeteers launched into an animated story along with a few of their storytellers from the festival. Their illusionist as well started to cast dancing images around them all, playing out the scenes.

Ceci drew Lottie to the table as Corwek came in from the back, bringing with him a positive cauldron of food. Everyone gathered around, passing fresh loaves of bread brought specially by Gable from hand to hand as bowls were doled out.

"How was work?" she asked Ceci as they settled in next to each other at the table, momentarily separated from Kir who'd been dragged into the corner by Khar to dance. Ceci and she had been trying over the past few weeks to be better toward each other, slowly getting reacquainted. Lottie was proud that she had her sister back, even in little stops and starts.

"It was actually kind of eventful," said Ceci, smiling genuinely. "Finnean, one of the bookstore owners, came by with a veritable treasure trove in his pockets. He had a story about how he came across them — something about defeating a fey beast in its layer — and found some rather intriguing bits. Not all of the things he took were gems, and he figured he should pass them off to me."

"Oh?"

"You know I'm no longer in the business of truly magical artifacts," said Ceci with a sideways glance at her. Instead of being scathing, like it would have once been, it came with a softly teasing smile. "But, I figured, why not take them off his hands? They don't really look like much.

There's this fairly large stone that someone might like for their garden one day."

"Huh, well. I am in the market for magical artifacts if you're ever looking to part with it," Lottie said with a wink.

Ceci snorted. "I highly doubt it's magical. If you ever come back and want to settle down somewhere, though." She motioned toward Kir, who was trying not to trip over her brother's feet. "Then I can save it for your garden."

"Ha, well, you might be saving it for a while. I think we have a lot of exploring to do first."

Gable slid themselves into the chair next to Ceci and wrapped an arm around her waist. Ceci's face bloomed with happiness, a high blush rising in her cheeks.

At one point during the night, all the bards began to perform together. Someone handed Kir a spare lute so she could join in too, freeing her from Khar's attempts to teach her to dance.

Lottie took up the mantle and danced as the music swelled, the bards singing at the top of their lungs. Ceci and Gable, Morgam and Aeric, and everyone else joined in, filling the bar with movement.

Lottie stepped into the space in front of Kir as she played, the two of them moving as one, despite the instrument between them.

Lottie let out a peal of laughter, throwing her hands up in the air. The warm, golden glow of the bar bathed them all as they danced, filling the air with joy.

Back when she was crouched in front of a glowing dodecahedron, Lottie had been lonelier than she had ever known. She never thought that she'd find a life like this.

And now, with her love singing in front of her, her sister somewhere to her right spinning in the arms of someone who treated her like a treasure, and an entire room of people who she could call friends, she was perfectly happy.

Lottie's luck had finally started to turn.

A LITTLE LUCK
Song by Kirandir Dulra

East-ward I lived, near the waves glimmerin' gold,
Singing for my pe-ople, the stories and tales of old —
Simply put, I watched, dreaming for a life of more,
Never thinking I could travel far from the shore.
O'then came a woman of bright summer green,
Eyes lit like starlight, she encha-nted me.
She stopped and said,
You're stuck inside your life,
You have to let fear go and leave it all behind.
East-ward I lived, sharing tales of old,
With my dreams tight in hand, never daring to be bold,
But with the Autumn moon in the sky over head,
I didn't see her comin', fate began to weave the thread,
Connecting her and me, now I'll never leave her side
For my love shines like the summer sun on the tide.
She stopped and said,
There's more to life out there,
So take a little luck, and leave it all behind.
She showed me that
There's more to life out there,
So take a little luck, and leave it all behind.

CHARACTERS

- **Aeric**: (pronounced: Ar-ric) Worker at the Old'n Narrow bar, elf.

- **Alros**: (pronounced: Al-Ross) Guild member, Lottie's contact.

- **Arileas Damaris**: (pronounced: Arr-ih-lee-ass Dam-Ahr-iss) Owner of the bookstore A Second Story, elf.

- **Berold**: (pronounced: Beh-roll-d) Lottie's historical professor contact in the Kingdom of Zidien, who's specialty is the Centurion.

- **Boss, the**: The runner/big boss man (gender unconfirmed) of the Guild.

- **Briar**: One of the owners of the Old'n Narrow bar, human.

- **Calian**: (pronounced: Cal-ee-an) Mysterious giantkin who seems to live around Arrowmount.

- **Cecily Little**: Magic Goods stall owner and Lottie's sister, earth elemental.

- **Chervil Tealeaf**: (pronounced: shh-er-vill) Lighthouse runner and owner, blue fiendling.

- **Corwek**: Cook at the Old'n Narrow bar, goliath.

- **Della**: An elderly gnome who lives on Fetterly Place and runs the Moon Festival committees, wife to Neema.

- **Eiris**: (pronounced: Iris) A Moon Festival volunteer.

- **Emmett Cavalry**: A stable hand from the city of Claymore

- **Eralie**: A bard that performs at the Moon Festival.

- **Fayri**: (pronounced: Fey-ree) A Moon Festival Volunteer.

- **Finnean**: (pronounced: Fin-ee-an) Owner of the bookstore A Second Story, human.

- **Gable**: Owner of the bakery stall in the market square, dating Cecily Little, elf.

- **Gral**: Previous Entertainment Committee Chair.

- **King Zoren** (Zidien): The king and sovereign ruler of the Kingdom of Zidien.

- ***Kirandir Dulra***: (pronounced: Keer-ann-deer Dull-rah) Our lovely local bard, half-orc.

- **Kharutto Dulra**: (pronounced: car-oo-toe) Kirandir's oldest brother, a wood and metal worker, half-orc.

- **Loth**: Brother of Seban, a member of the Nine.

- ***Lottie Luck***: (Aka, Charlotte Little) Our lovely thief extraordinaire, earth elemental.

- **Lord Wymarc**: The Lord of Arrowmount, human.

- **May Camire**: Owner of May's Cafe, half-elven druid.

- **Montarali Family**: The puppeteering group that performs at the Moon Festival. Members include: *Ainsley* and *Edwin*, apprentices *Lyndal* and *Tierri*.

- **Morgam Dulra**: Kirandir's middlest brother, a painter, half-orc.

- **Neema**: An elderly gnome who lives on Fetterly Place, wife to Della.

- **Noghorn Dulra**: Father of the Dulra family, and owner of the blacksmiths.

- **Nova**: One of the owners of the Old'n Narrow bar, human.

- **Nudge**: The Dulra family greathound.

- **Pakon**: (pronounced: pack-on) Owner of the grocery stall in the market square, goliath.

- **Reihmir**: (pronounced: ray-meer) A servant of the Lord of Arrowmount.

- **Seban**: (pronounced: se-bān) Member of the Nine, childhood friend of Lottie, has mind magic (also called psionic powers), human.

- **Zanve**: (pronounced: zan-vee) Arrowmount Town Guard, human.

GLOSSARY

- **Alieweth**: (pronounced: ah-lee-weth) A northern kingdom, part of the Nerian Empire.

- **Arrowmount**: A coastal town, where our story takes place.

- **Catfolk**: Feline humanoids who are covered in fur and have very cat-like features. They are mainly bipedal, however can get around very quickly on all fours. They range in many different variations and colorings.

- **Centurion**: A godly war that occurred centuries ago in the history of Ravar.

- **Claymore**: A city in the Brenem Empire.

- **Dodecahedron**: a twelve-sided object.

- **Druid**: A class of magic users that are nature based, and find their magic through the force of nature itself or natural deities.

○ *Notable druids:* May, the half-elven cafe owner, and Cecily.

• **Feycross**: A small village in the Brenem Empire. Rumoured to have a portal to the fey realm nearby, but that has yet to be confirmed.

• **Fiendling**: Humanoid beings that have fiendish blood running through their veins, which gives them their often unique colouring, horns, tails, and occasionally sharp teeth. Along with average humans, they can range from about five feet to just over six feet tall.

• **Elementals**: Humanoids that take on aspects of their elemental lineage. Most commonly there are air, fire, water, and earth elementals, but as there are many different aspects to each element, you'd be hard pressed to find many elementals who resemble one another, even if they were of the same element.

○ *Notable elementals:* Cecily Little and Lottie Luck, earth elementals.

• **Giantkin**: A broad term to refer to races of folk who loosely resemble humans, in a way, but are related to giants in a distant, second or third or tenth cousin fashion. In this work, this term is used to refer to giantfolk that occasionally have large drooping ears and wide faces with a slightly snout-like shaped nose. They're very tall, often reaching well over seven feet tall, and range from having tough, grey skin with no fur to slightly softer, more furry beings.

○ *Notable giantkin:* Calian, the mysterious being that loves books and hot cocoas and often is seen wearing a jaunty bowtie.

- **Goliaths**: A half-giant race of tall humanoids, most often with varying grey-toned skin. They range from over six feet tall to well over seven feet.

  - *Notable goliaths*: Corwek and Pakon.

- **Guild**: One of the most prestigious and notorious underground organizations that run across the empire.

- **Hutton**: A small village in the Brenem Empire.

- **Illusory magic**: A school of magic that aims, usually, to deceive the senses and minds of others. Spells include the ability to go invisible and disguise one's self. There are some more lovely spells seen cast by Arileas himself as he creates an illusion of Lottie's artifact.

- **Iluinn**: The God of Life and Endurance.

  - 'Iluinn's Mercy' is but one of many curses throughout the Brenem Empire that uses the god's name, and probably one of the more tasteful ones, to be honest. Lottie likes to create her own expletives, and employs her favorite one, Iluinn's disgraced teapot (and its variations) regularly.

- **Maigsir**: The Goddess of the Sea.

  - Maigsir's tits is one of Kir's favored curses.

- **Mosfell**: A small village in the Brenem Empire

- **Narveil**: A small town in the Nerian Empire.

- **Old'n Narrow**: The local bar in Arrowmount.

- **Pralon**: Also known as the Kingdom of Pralon, a city in the Brenem Empire.

- **Icharr**: The God of Trade and Commerce.

  - Icharr's tits is one of Lottie's favored curses.

- **Sevrune**: The Goddess of Knowledge and the Changing of Seasons. Common symbol: moon.

  - The *Moon Festival* that runs in Arrowmount celebrates the passage of Sevrune's Hunter's Moon that symbolizes the changing of seasons into the colder months.

- **Shadyside**: A small village in the Brenem Empire.

- **Spider Climb Gloves**: an intriguing magical object where a pair of regular leather gloves have been enchanted with the ability to aid the wearer in climbing as easy as, say, a spider. The spell itself imbued in the leather is Spider Climb (a spell to help a being climb with the ease of a spider).

- **Wizards**: A class of magic users who learn to do magic through a spell book and lots and lots of practice.

  - *Notable wizard*: Arileas Damaris.

ACKNOWLEDGEMENTS

Aha! Book two, here we are.

Through the writing process, it can be so tricky to know whether or not your brain is going in the proper direction and that your story isn't absolutely unintelligible. Thankfully, I've been incredibly lucky to have found many people who have given their time and knowledge to help me make this story the best it can be. My lovely beta readers, you were all absolutely invaluable to this story, and I cannot thank you enough. Mariana, Grayson, and Hannah, you three are mighty and wonderful, and I thank you one hundred times over for helping me shape this story into its best form.

To my lovely friends who have offered support and excitement from day one: Yelani, Sophie, Sofia, SJ, Hannah, Alexander, Tessa, Sarah, Kait, Luke, Ellie, Kas, Yoni, Nirmal, Tamsen, Danny, and Elliott. And specially Cass, who has been with me the longest (how is it already been over a decade?) and has always been the best cheerleader to all of my endeavors. I love you all so, so much.

To Tessa Brenan, for again, being both an incredible friend and SUPREMELY talented artist. I'm so glad that you're the one that got to bring Lottie and Kir to life — truly, every single moment with you as my cover artist has been an absolute joy and I am so incredibly lucky to have you on this journey with me. Thank you thank you thank you!!

Thank you specially to all my friends from my online life who have been excited for this book even before *A Second Story* (Arrowmount Books #1) came out into the world. I am so glad I have you all as part of my life everyday. Thank you too, to Sarah Sutton, Amy Prokopis, and Hannah Long, authors I've met through the internet that I can now happily call friends, and Holly, a bookish creator I've followed for so long that it still surprises me I can call her a friend. My lovely friends, you are all the best, and I adore you all endlessly.

And of course, thank you to Belle Manuel, my wonderful proofreader, who was incredibly thoughtful with her edits when I handed over this project and helped guide *A Little Luck* to the final form you, dear reader, hold now.

There are so many more people in my life that have added fragments to my writing life and love of books, but I think the biggest contributors have to be my parents. Thank you, Mom and Dad, for supporting my love of reading and stories from day one. I know I don't say it enough, but thank you for letting me run wild with whatever stories were burning in my head.

What a ride it's been, but I'm so glad that you, dear reader, have found your way through Lottie and Kir's story. Thank you for taking a moment to visit Arrowmount.

About the Author

J. A. Collignon (AKA: Jenna, but you can call her Jenn) is a Canadian author based out of the prairies who loves everything fantasy. Fantasy books, movies, TV shows, and TTRPG podcasts; you name it, she loves it. Most often, she can be found on her couch with a thick fantasy book in hand, listening to fantastical music playlists.

Jenn is an avid member of the bookish internet community through her Youtube channel, Tiktok, Instagram, and Twitter. Follow her to keep up to date on future book releases.

Youtube: Jenn's Bookshelf

Tiktok: @jennsbookshelf

Instagram: @authorjacollignon

Twitter: @BookshelfJenn

For a playlist to go with this book, turn your ears to: